WIND THROUGH THE FENCE

And Other Stories

By
Jonathan Maberry

JournalStone

JOURNALSTONE
YOUR LINK TO ARTISTIC TALENT

JournalStone books may be ordered through booksellers or by contacting:

JournalStone
www.journalstone.com

The views expressed in this work are solely those of the authors and do not necessarily reflect the views of the publisher, and the publisher hereby disclaims any responsibility for them.

ISBN: 978-1-945373-46-6   (sc)
ISBN: 978-1-945373-47-3   (ebook)
ISBN: 978-1-945373-48-0   (hc)

JournalStone rev. date: February 10, 2017

Library of Congress Control Number: 2016962535

Printed in the United States of America

Cover Art – photo images & Design: Rob Grom
Field © LU YAO/Shutterstock, Sky © Oriole Gin/Shutterstock, Chainlink fence © Jamesmcq24/Istock

Edited by: Sean Leonard

Dedication

This is for the other two members of the Three Guys With Beards,

Christopher Golden and James A. Moore.

Doing our podcast together is a hoot.

Being friends with you cats is marvelous.

You rock!

And, as always, for Sara Jo

Table of Contents

Introduction to Wind Through the Fence   9

Pegleg and Paddy Save the World   17
Plan 7 from Sin City   37
Red Dreams   65
Saint John   89
She's Got a Ticket to Ride   119
Spellcaster 2.0   141
T. Rhymer (with Gregory Frost)   177
The Cobbler of Oz   235
The Things That Live in Cages   265
The Vanishing Assassin   287
The Wind Through the Fence   309
Faces   323

Author Bio   351

Renaissance Man

Introduction
By
David Morrell

A few years ago, I traveled to Los Angeles to give a talk at a *Writer's Digest* conference. My author friend, Jonathan Maberry, was another guest speaker. I spent the evening with an L.A. acquaintance, and when I returned to the hotel where the conference was located, I noticed Jonathan sitting in a corner of the lobby with his laptop computer open before him. I assumed that he was looking at some social media and walked over to say hello, only to realize that he wasn't surfing the web—he was working on a new novel.

"In the hotel lobby at 10 p.m.?" I asked in surprise.

"I'm trying to make up for the time I lost traveling here," Jonathan explained. "I like the energy in the lobby. I can write just about anywhere."

Indeed.

Most authors establish a daily goal of a certain number of words (perhaps 1,000) or of pages (perhaps 5). But sometimes circumstances such as travel or an unavoidable meeting or illness prevent that goal from being achieved. Not so with Jonathan. I suspect that only bubonic plague (and maybe not even that) would stop him from achieving his daily goal, and I further suspect that it's far more than 1,000 words or 5 pages.

I've never seen a more energetic author. That energy is palpable when I speak to him or when I watch him give talks about writing at various events. Ideas fly out of him as he seems to struggle to resist hurrying away and writing them down. His energy even comes off the computer screen if you go to his website, jonathanmaberry.com, and look at the astonishing amount that he's written in a vast array of forms (adult novels, YA novels, novelizations, short stories, comic books, stage plays, magazine articles, nonfiction books) and genres (action, suspense, mysteries, horror, science fiction, westerns, dark fantasy, and humor).

This variety, which earned Jonathan numerous awards, including five Stokers from the Horror Writers Association, is paralleled by his myriad occupations before he became a full-time author: assistant janitor, bodyguard, bouncer, martial arts teacher at Temple University, graphic artist, medical-information specialist, expert martial-arts witness for the Philadelphia District Attorney, and police trainer, among others. Perhaps his diverse background explains the source for his abundant ideas and his impressively various ways of expressing them. Certainly, his martial-arts experience (he has an 8th degree black belt in Shinowara-ryu Jujutsu) is manifest in much of his work.

The Wind Through the Fence, Jonathan's newest short story collection, exemplifies his diverse creativity. The twelve titles included here range from his first short story, "Pegleg and Paddy Save the World" (a hilarious zombie tale about the true cause of the Great Chicago Fire in 1871), to his latest, *"Faces"*, a bit of dark urban fantasy written especially for this volume. Between them, he includes his first mystery, "The Vanishing Assassin" (featuring C. Auguste Dupin, Edgar Allan Poe's classic detective). "Red Dreams" provides an eerie vision of the Wild West while "Saint John" portrays a haunted avenger in a disturbing apocalypse. "The Cobbler of Oz" switches tone and introduces us to a poignant, smile-producing little creature of Oz, whose wings never grew but who has the courage to pursue her dreams. In "She's Got a Ticket to Ride," a man who rescues children from cults discovers that the teenager he's been hired to liberate has a dismayingly good reason to believe in one particular cult. The title story, "The Wind Through the Fence," is devastatingly vivid in its depiction of a future cataclysm.

While these are all short stories, Jonathan manages to fill them with so much energy that they're full to bursting with emotion and invention. Each reveals a new approach and a new surprise. You'll have difficulty picking a favorite among the imaginative abundance that you're about to enjoy.

WIND THROUGH THE FENCE

Pegleg and Paddy Save the World

Author's Note

This was my very first short story. My first novel, *Ghost Road Blues*, had just come out when Dr. Kim Paffenroth reached out and asked if I'd be interested in writing a short story for his anthology of 'historical zombie stories.' I said yes—because I always say yes—and then I had to figure out how to write a piece of short fiction. Prior to that my works had been many hundreds of nonfiction magazine articles (ranging in topics from martial arts to bartending!), as well as college textbooks, mass-market nonfiction books, greeting cards and a couple of plays. And that very long novel. Short fiction wasn't in my skill set. That said, I have always loved short stories and tend to devour them like M&M's.

So, I gave it a shot and wound up writing something that I found fun to write and which has been collected and reprinted so often that it suggests that other people find it fun, too. Yes, it's an historical zombie story…but it's also slapstick comedy.

I had fun. Hope you do, too.

PEGLEG AND PADDY SAVE THE WORLD

I know what you've heard, but Pat O'Leary's cow didn't have nothing to do with it. Not like they said in the papers. The way them reporters put it, you'd have thought the damn cow was playing with matches. I mean, sure, it started in the cowshed, but that cow was long dead by that point, and really it was Pat himself who lit it. I helped him do it. And that meteor shower some folks talked about—you see, that happened beforehand. It didn't start the fire, either, but it sure as hell *caused* it.

You have to understand what the West Side of Chicago was like back then. Pat had a nice little place on DeKoven Street—just enough land to grow some spuds and raise a few chickens. The cow was a skinny old milker, and she was of that age where her milk was too sour and her beef would probably be too tough. Pat O'Leary wanted to sell her to some drovers who were looking to lay down some jerky for a drive down to Abilene, but the missus would have none of it.

"Elsie's like one of the family!" Catherine protested. "Aunt Sophie gave her to me when she was just a heifer."

I knew Pat had to bite his tongue not to ask if Catherine meant when the cow was a heifer or when Sophie was. By that point in their marriage Pat's tongue was crisscrossed with healed-over bite marks.

Catherine finished up by saying, "Selling that cow'd be like selling Aunt Sophie herself off by the pound."

Over whiskey that night, Pat confided in me that if he could find a buyer for Sophie, he'd love to sell the old bitch. "She eats twice as much as the damn cow and don't smell half as good."

I agreed and we drank on it.

Shame the way she went. The cow, I mean. I wouldn't wish that on a three-legged dog. As for Sophie...well, I guess in a way I feel sorry for her, too. And for the rest of them that went to meet their maker that night, the ones who perished in the fire…and the ones who died before.

The fire started Sunday night, but the problem started way sooner, just past midnight on a hot Tuesday morning. That was a strange autumn. Dryer than it should have been, and with a steady wind that you'd have thought blew straight in off a desert. I never saw anything like it except the Santa Anas, but this was Illinois, not California. Father Callahan had a grand ol' time with it, saying that it was the hot breath of Hell blowing hard on all us sinners. Yeah, yeah, whatever, but we wasn't sinning any worse that year than we had the year before and the year before that. Conner O'Malley was still sneaking into the Daley's back door every Saturday night, the Kennedy twins were still stealing hogs, and Pat and I were still making cheap whiskey and selling it in premium bottles to the pubs who sold it to travelers heading west. No reason Hell should have breathed any harder that year than any other.

What was different that year was not what we sinners were doing but what those saints were up to, 'cause we had shooting stars every night for a week. The good father had something to say about that, too. It was the flaming sword of St. Michael and his lot, reminding us of why we were tossed out of Eden. That man could make a hellfire and brimstone sermon out of a field full of fuzzy bunnies, I swear to God.

On the first night there was just a handful of little ones, like Chinese fireworks way out over Lake Michigan. But the second night there was a big ball of light—Biela's Comet, the reporter from the *Tribune* called it—and it just burst apart up there and balls of fire came a'raining down everywhere.

Paddy and I were up at the still and we were trying to sort out how to make Mean-Dog Mulligan pay the six months' worth of whiskey fees he owed us. Mean-Dog was a man who earned his nickname and he was bigger than both of us put together, so when we came asking for our cash and he told us to piss off, we did. We only said anything out loud about it when we were a good six blocks from his place.

"We've got to sort him out," I told Paddy, "or everyone'll take a cue from him and then where will we be?"

Pat was feeling low. Mean-Dog had smacked him around a bit, just for show, and my poor lad was in the doldrums. His wife was pretty but she was a nag, her aunt Sophie was more terrifying than the red Indians who still haunted some of these woods, and Mean-Dog Mulligan was turning us into laughingstocks. Pat wanted to brood, and brooding over a still of fresh whiskey at least took some of the sting out. It was after our fourth cup that we saw the comet.

Now, I've seen comets before. I seen them out at sea before I lost my leg, and I seen 'em out over the plains when I was running with the Scobie gang. I know what they look like, but this one was just a bit different. It was green, for one thing. Comets don't burn green, not any I've seen or heard about. This one was a sickly green, too, the color of bad liver, and it scorched a path through the air. Most of it burned up in the sky, and that's a good thing, but one piece of it came down hard by the edge of the lake, right smack down next to Aunt Sophie's cottage.

Pat and I were sitting out in our lean-to in a stand of pines, drinking toasts in honor of Mean-Dog developing a wasting sickness, when the green thing came burning down out of the sky and smacked into the ground not fifty feet from Sophie's place. There was a sound like fifty cannons firing all at once, and the shock rolled up the hill to where we sat. Knocked both of us off our stools and tipped over the still.

"Pegleg!" Pat yelled as he landed on his ass. "The brew!"

I lunged for the barrel and caught it before it tilted too far, but a gallon of it splashed me in the face and half-drowned me. That's just a comment, not a complaint. I steadied the pot as I stood up. My clothes were soaked with whiskey, but I was too shocked to even suck my shirttails. I stood staring down the slope. Sophie's cottage still stood, but it was surrounded by towering flames. Green flames—and that wasn't the whiskey talking. There were real green flames licking at the night, catching the grass, burning the trees that edged her property line.

"That's Sophie's place," I said.

He wiped his face and squinted through the smoke. "Yeah, sure is."

"She's about to catch fire."

He belched. "If I'm lucky."

I grinned at him. It was easy to see his point. Except for Catherine there was nobody alive who could stand Aunt Sophie. She was fat and foul, and you couldn't please her if you handed her a deed to a gold mine. Not even Father Callahan liked her, and he was sort of required to by license.

We stood there and watched as the green fire crept along the garden path toward her door. "Suppose we should go down there and kind of rescue her, like," I suggested.

He bent and picked up a tin cup, dipped it in the barrel, drank a slug, and handed it to me. "I suppose."

"Catherine will be mighty upset if we let her burn."

"I expect."

We could hear her screaming then as she finally realized that Father Callahan's hellfire had come a'knocking. Considering her evil ways, she probably thought that's just what it was, and had it been, not even she could have found fault with the reasoning.

"Come on," Pat finally said, tugging on my sleeve, "I guess we'd better haul her fat ass outta there or I'll never hear the end of it from the wife."

"Be the Christian thing to do," I agreed; though, truth to tell, we didn't so much as hustle down the slope to her place as sort of saunter.

That's what saved our lives in the end, 'cause we were still only halfway down when the second piece of the comet hit. This time it hit her cottage fair and square.

It was like the fist of God—if His fist was ever green, mind—punching down from Heaven and smashing right through her roof. The whole house just flew apart, the roof blew off, the windows turned to glittery dust, and the log walls splintered into matchwood. The force of it was so strong that it just plain sucked the air out of the fire, like blowing out a candle.

Patrick started running about then, and since he has two legs and I got this peg, I followed along as best I could. Took us maybe ten minutes to get all the way down there.

By that time, Sophie Kilpatrick was deader'n a doornail.

We stopped outside the jagged edge of what had been her north wall and stared at her just lying there amid the wreckage. Her bed was smashed flat, the legs broken; the dresser and rocker were in pieces, all the crockery in fragments. In the midst of it, still wearing her white nightgown and bonnet, was Sophie, her arms and legs spread like a starfish, her mouth open like a bass, her goggling eyes staring straight up at Heaven in the most accusing sort of way.

We exchanged a look and crept inside.

"She looks dead," he said.

"Of course she's dead, Pat; a comet done just fell on her."

The fire was out but there was still a bit of green glow coming off her and we crept closer still.

"What in tarnation is that?"

"Dunno," I said. There were bits and pieces of green rock scattered around her, and they glowed like they had a light inside. Kind of pulsed in a way, like a slow heartbeat. Sophie was dusted with glowing green powder. It was on her gown and her hands and her face. A little piece of the rock pulsed inside her mouth, like she'd gasped it in as it all happened.

"What's that green stuff?"

"Must be that comet they been talking about in the papers. Biela's Comet, they been calling it."

"Why'd it fall on Sophie?"

"Well, Paddy, I don't think it *meant* to."

He grunted as he stared down at her. The green pulsing of the rock made it seem like she was breathing, and a couple of times he bent close to make sure.

"Damn," he said after he checked the third time, "I didn't think she'd ever die. Didn't think she could!"

"God kills everything," I said, quoting one of Father Callahan's cheerier observations. "Shame it didn't fall on Mean-Dog Mulligan."

"Yeah, but I thought Sophie was too damn ornery to die. Besides, I always figured the Devil'd do anything he could to keep her alive."

I looked at him. "Why's that?"

"He wouldn't want the competition. You know she ain't going to Heaven, and down in Hell…well, she'll be bossing around old Scratch and his demons before her body is even cold in the grave. Ain't nobody could be as persistently disagreeable as Aunt Sophie."

"Amen to that," I said, and sucked some whiskey out of my sleeve. Paddy noticed what I was doing and asked for a taste. I held my arm out to him. "So…what do you think we should do?"

Pat looked around. The fire was out, but the house was a ruin. "We can't leave her out here."

"We can call the constable," I suggested. "Except that we both smell like whiskey."

"I think we should take her up to the house, Peg."

I stared at him. "To the house? She weighs nigh on half a ton."

"She can't be more than three hundred-weight. Catherine will kill me if I leave her out here to get gnawed on by every creature in the woods. She always says I was too hard on Sophie, too mean to her. She sees me bringing Sophie's body home, sees how I cared enough to do that for her only living aunt, then she'll think better of me."

"Oh, man…" I complained, but Pat was adamant. Besides, when he was in his cups, Paddy complained that Catherine was not being very "wifely" lately. I think he was hoping that this would somehow charm him back onto Catherine's side of the bed. Mind you, Paddy was as drunk as a lord, so this made sense to him, and I was damn near pickled, so it more or less made sense to me, too. Father Callahan could have gotten a month's worth of hellfire sermons on the dangers of hard liquor out of the way Pat and I handled this affair. Of course, Father Callahan's dead now, so there's that.

Anyway, we wound up doing as Pat said and we near busted our guts picking up Sophie and slumping her onto a wheelbarrow. We dusted off the green stuff as best we could, but we forgot about the piece in her mouth and the action of dumping her on the 'barrow must have made that glowing green chunk slide right down her gullet. If we'd been a lot less drunk we'd have wondered about that, because on some level I was pretty sure I heard her swallow that chunk, but since she was dead and we were grunting and cursing trying to lift her, and it couldn't be real *anyway*, I didn't comment on it. All I did once she was loaded was peer at her for a second to see if that great big bosom of hers was rising and falling—which it wasn't—and then I took another suck on my sleeve.

It took nearly two hours to haul her fat ass up the hill and through the streets and down to Paddy's little place on DeKoven Street. All the time I found myself looking queer at Sophie. I hadn't liked that sound, that gulping sound, even if I wasn't sober or ballsy enough to say anything to Pat. It made me wonder, though, about that glowing green piece of comet. What the hell was that stuff, and where'd it come from? It weren't nothing normal, that's for sure.

We stood out in the street for a bit with Paddy just staring at his own front door, mopping sweat from his face, careful of the bruises from Mean-Dog. "I can't bring her in like this," he said, "it wouldn't be right."

"Let's put her in the cowshed," I suggested. "Lay her out on the straw and then we can fetch the doctor. Let him pronounce her dead all legal-like."

For some reason that sounded sensible to both of us, so that's what we did. Neither of us could bear to try and lift her again, so we tipped over the 'barrow and let her tumble out.

"Ooof!" she said.

"Excuse me," Pat said, and then we both froze.

He looked at me, and I looked at him, and we both looked at Aunt Sophie. My throat was suddenly as dry as an empty shot glass.

Paddy's face looked like he'd seen a ghost, and we were both wondering if that's what we'd just seen, in fact. We crouched over her, me still holding the arms of the 'barrow, him holding one of Sophie's wrists.

"Tell me if you feel a pulse, Paddy, my lad," I whispered.

"Not a single thump," he said.

"Then did you hear her say 'ooof' or some suchlike?"

"I'd be lying if I said I didn't."

"Lying's not always a sin," I observed.

He dropped her wrist, then looked at the pale green dust on his hands—the glow had faded—and wiped his palms on his coveralls.

"Is she dead or isn't she?" I asked.

He bent, and with great reluctance pressed his ear to her chest. He listened for a long time. "There's no ghost of a heartbeat," he said.

"Be using a different word now, will ya?"

Pat nodded. "There's no heartbeat. No breath, nothing."

"Then she's dead?"

"Aye."

"But she made a sound."

Pat straightened, then snapped his fingers. "It's the death rattle," he said. "Sure and that's it. The dead exhaling a last breath."

"She's been dead these two hours and more. What's she been waiting for?"

He thought about that. "It was the stone. The green stone—it lodged in her throat and blocked the air. We must have dislodged it when we dumped her out, and that last breath came out. Just late, is all."

I was beginning to sober up and that didn't have the ring of logic it would have had an hour ago.

We stood over her for another five minutes, but Aunt Sophie just lay there, dead as can be.

"I got to go tell Catherine," Pat said eventually. "She's going to be in a state. You'd better scram. She'll know what we've been about."

"She'll know anyway. You smell as bad as I do."

"But Sophie smells worse," he said, and that was the truth of it.

So I scampered and he went in to break his wife's heart. I wasn't halfway down the street before I heard her scream.

* * *

I didn't come back until Thursday, and as I came up the street smoking my pipe, Paddy came rushing around the side of the house. I swear he was wearing the same overalls and looked like he hadn't washed or anything. The bruises had faded to the color of a rotten eggplant, but his lip was less swollen. He grabbed me by the wrist and fair wrenched my arm out dragging me back to the shed, but before he opened the door, he stopped and looked me square in the eye.

"You got to promise me to keep a secret, Pegleg."

"I always keep your secrets," I lied, and he knew I was lying.

"No, you have to really keep this one. Swear by the baby Jesus."

Paddy was borderline religious, so asking me to swear by anything holy was a big thing for him. The only other time he'd done it was right before he showed me the whiskey still.

"Okay, Paddy, I swear by the baby Jesus and His Holy Mother, too."

He stared at me for a moment before nodding; then he turned and looked up and down the alley as if all the world was leaning out to hear whatever Patrick O'Leary had to say. All I saw was a cat sitting on a stack of building bricks, distractedly licking his bollocks. In a big whisper, Paddy said, "Something's happened to Sophie."

I blinked at him a few times. "Of course something's happened to her, you daft bugger; a comet fell on her head and killed her."

He was shaking his head before I was even finished. "No...*since* then."

That's not a great way to ease into a conversation about the dead. "What?"

He fished a key out of his pocket, which is when I noticed the shiny new chain and padlock on the cowshed door. It must have cost Pat a week's worth of whiskey sales to buy that thing.

"Did Mean-Dog pay us now?"

Pat snorted. "He'd as soon kick me as pay us a penny of what he owes."

I nodded at the chain. "You afraid someone's going to steal her body?"

He gave me the funniest look. "I'm not afraid of anybody breaking *in.*"

Which is another of those things that don't sound good when someone says it before entering a room with a dead body in it.

He unlocked the lock; then he reached down to where his shillelagh leaned against the frame. It was made from a whopping great piece of oak root, all twisted and polished, the handle wrapped with leather.

"What's going on now, Paddy?" I asked, starting to back away, and remembering a dozen other things that needed doing. Like running and hiding and getting drunk.

"I think it was that green stuff from the comet," Paddy whispered as he slowly pushed open the door. "It did something to her. Something *unnatural.*"

"Everything about Sophie was unnatural," I reminded him.

The door swung inward with a creak and the light of day shone into the cowshed. It was ten feet wide by twenty feet deep, with a wooden rail, a manger, stalls for two cows—though Paddy only owned just the one. The scrawny milk cow Catherine doted on was lying on her side in the middle of the floor.

I mean to say what was *left* of her was lying on the floor. I tried to scream, but all that came out of my whiskey-raw throat was a crooked little screech.

The cow had been torn to pieces. Blood and gobs of meat littered the floor, and there were more splashes of blood on the wall. And right there in the middle of all that muck, sitting like the queen of all damnation, was Aunt Sophie. Her fat face and throat were covered with blood. Her cotton gown was torn and streaked with cow shit and gore. Flies buzzed around her and crawled on her face.

Aunt Sophie was gnawing on what looked like half a cow liver, and when the sunlight fell across her from the open door, she raised her head and looked right at us. Her skin was as gray-pale as the maggots that wriggled through little rips in her skin, but it was her eyes that took all the starch out of my knees. They were dry and milky, but the pupils glowed an unnatural green, just like the piece of comet that had slid down her gullet.

"Oh...lordy-lordy-save a sinner!" I heard someone say in an old woman's voice, and then realized that it was I speaking.

Aunt Sophie lunged at us. All of sudden she went from sitting there like a fat dead slob eating Paddy's cow to coming at us like a charging bull. I shrieked. I'm not proud; I'll admit it.

If it hadn't been for the length of chain Paddy had wound around her waist she'd have had me, too, 'cause I could no more move from where I was frozen than I could make leprechauns fly out of my bottom. Sophie's lunge was jerked to a stop with her yellow teeth not a foot from my throat.

Paddy stepped past me and raised the club. If Sophie saw it, or cared, she didn't show it.

"Get back, you fat sow!" he yelled, and took to thumping her about the face and shoulders, which did no noticeable good.

"Paddy, my dear," I croaked, "I think I've soiled myself."

Paddy stepped back, his face running sweat. "No, that's her you smell. It's too hot in this shed. She's coming up ripe." He pulled me farther back and we watched as Sophie snapped the air in our direction for a whole minute, then she lost interest and went back to gnawing on the cow.

"What's happened to her?"

"She's dead," he said.

"She can't be. I've seen dead folks before, lad, and she's a bit too spry."

He shook his head. "I checked and I checked. I even stuck her with the pitchfork. Just experimental-like, and I got them tines all the way in, but she didn't bleed."

"But...but..."

"Catherine came out here, too. Before Sophie woke back up, I mean. She took it hard and didn't want to hear about comets or nothing like that. She thinks we poisoned her with our whiskey."

"It's strong, I'll admit, but it's more likely to kill a person than make the dead wake back up again."

"I told her that and she commenced to hit me, and she hits as hard as Mean-Dog. She had a good handful of my hair and was swatting me a goodun' when Sophie just woke up."

"How'd Catherine take that?"

"Well, she took it poorly, the lass. At first she tried to comfort Sophie, but when the old bitch tried to bite her Catherine seemed to cool a bit toward her aunt. It wasn't until after Sophie tore the throat out of the cow that Catherine seemed to question whether Sophie was really her aunt or more of an old acquaintance of the family."

"What'd she say?"

"It's not what she said so much as it was her hitting Sophie in the back of the head with a shovel."

"That'll do 'er."

"It dropped Sophie for a while and I hustled out and bought some chain and locks. By the time I came back, Catherine was in a complete state. Sophie kept waking up, you see, and she had to clout her a fair few times to keep her tractable."

"So where's the missus now?"

"Abed. Seems she's discovered the medicinal qualities of our whiskey."

"I've been saying it for years."

He nodded and we stood there, watching Sophie eat the cow.

"So, Paddy, me old mate," I said softly, "what do you think we should do?"

"With Sophie?"

"Aye."

Paddy's bruised faced took on the one expression I would have thought impossible under the circumstances. He smiled. A great big smile that was every bit as hungry and nasty as Aunt Sophie.

* * *

It took three days of sweet talk and charm, of sweat-soaked promises and cajoling, but we finally got him to come to Paddy's cowshed. And then there he was, the Mean-Dog himself, all six-and-a-half feet of him, flanked by Killer Muldoon and Razor Riley, the three of them standing in Paddy's yard late on Sunday afternoon.

My head was ringing from a courtesy smacking Mean-Dog had given me when I'd come to his office, and Pat's lips were puffed out again, but Paddy was still smiling.

"So, lads," Mean-Dog said quietly, "tell me again why I'm here in a yard that smells of pigshit instead of at home drinking a beer."

"Cowshit," Paddy corrected him, and got a clout for it.

"We have a new business partner, Mr. Mulligan," I said. "And she told us that we can't provide no more whiskey until you and she settle accounts."

"*She*? You're working with a woman?" His voice was filled with contempt. "Who's this woman, then? Sounds like she has more mouth than she can use."

"You might be saying that," Pat agreed softly. "It's my Aunt Sophie."

I have to admit, that did give even Mean-Dog a moment's pause. There are Cherokee war parties that would go twenty miles out of their way not to cross Sophie. And that was *before* the comet.

"Sophie Kilpatrick, eh?" He looked at his two bruisers. Neither of them knew her and they weren't impressed. "Where is she?"

"In the cowshed," Pat said. "She said she wanted to meet somewhere quiet."

"Shrewd," Mean-Dog agreed, but he was still uncertain. "Lads, go in and ask Miss Sophie to come out."

The two goons shrugged and went into the shed as I inched my way toward the side alley. Pat held his ground and I don't know whether it was all the clouting 'round the head he'd been getting, or the latest batch of whiskey, or maybe he'd just reached the bottom of his own cup and couldn't take no more from anyone, but Paddy O'Leary stood there grinning at Mean-Dog as the two big men opened the shed door and went in.

Pat hadn't left a light on in there and it was a cloudy day. The goons had to feel their way in the dark. When they commenced screaming, I figured they'd found their way to Sophie. This was Sunday by now, and the cow was long gone. Sophie was feeling a might peckish.

Mean-Dog jumped back from the doorway and dragged out his pistol with one hand and took a handful of Pat's shirt with the other. "What the hell's happening? Who's in there?"

"Just Aunt Sophie," Paddy said, and actually held his hand to God as he said it.

Mean-Dog shoved him aside and kicked open the door. That was his first mistake, because Razor Riley's head smacked him right in the face. Mean-Dog staggered back and then stood there in dumb shock as his leg-breaker's head bounced to the ground right at his feet. Riley's face wore an expression of profound shock.

"What?" Mean-Dog asked, as if anything Pat or I could say would be an adequate answer to that.

The second mistake Mean-Dog made was to get mad and go charging into the shed. We watched him enter and we both jumped as he fired two quick shots, then another, and another.

I don't know, even to this day, whether one of those shots clipped her chain or whether Sophie was even stronger than we thought she was, but a second later Mean-Dog came barreling out of the cowshed, running at full tilt, with Sophie Kilpatrick howling after him, trailing six feet of chain. She was covered in blood and the sound she made would have made a banshee take a vow of silence. They were gone down the alley in a heartbeat, and Pat and I stood there in shock for a moment, then we peered around the edge of the door into the shed.

The lower half of Razor Riley lay just about where the cow had been. Killer Muldoon was all in one piece, but there were pieces missing from him, if you follow. Sophie had her way with him and he lay dead as a mullet, his throat torn out and his blood pooled around him.

"Oh, lordy," I said. "This is bad for us, Paddy. This is jail, and skinny fellows like you and me have to wear petticoats in prison."

But there was a strange light in his eyes. Not a glowing green light—which was a comfort—but not a nice light, either. He looked down at the bodies and then over his shoulder in the direction where Sophie and Mean-Dog had vanished. He licked his bruised lips and said, "You know, Pegleg...there are other sonsabitches who owe us money."

"Those are bad thoughts you're having, Paddy, my dear."

"I'm not saying we feed them to Sophie. But if we let it get known, so to speak. Maybe show them what's left of these lads..."

"Patrick O'Leary, you listen to me—we are not about being criminal masterminds here. I'm not half as smart as a fencepost and you're not half as smart as me, so let's not be planning anything extravagant."

Which is when Mean-Dog Mulligan came screaming *back* into Paddy's yard. God only knows what twisted puzzle-path he took through the neighborhood, but there he was, running back toward us, his arms bleeding from a couple of bites and his big legs pumping to keep him just ahead of Sophie.

"Oh dear," Pat said in a voice that made it clear that his plan still had a few bugs to be sorted out.

"Shovel!" I said, and lunged for the one Catherine had used on her aunt. Paddy grabbed a pickaxe and we swung at the same time.

I hit Sophie fair and square in the face and the shock of it rang all the way up my arms and shivered the tool right out of my hands, but the force of the blow had its way with her and her green eyes were instantly blank. She stopped dead in her tracks and then pitched backward to measure her length on the ground.

Paddy's swing had a different effect. The big spike of the pickaxe caught Mean-Dog square in the center of the chest and, though everyone said the man had no heart, Pat and his pickaxe begged to differ. The gangster's last word was, "Urk!" and he fell backward, as dead as Riley and Muldoon.

"Quick!" I said, and we fetched the broken length of chain from the shed and wound it about Sophie, pinning her arms to her body and then snugging it all with the padlock. While Pat was checking the lock I fetched the wheelbarrow, and we grunted and cursed some more as we got her onto it.

"We have to hide the bodies," I said, and Pat, too stunned to speak, just nodded. He grabbed Mean-Dog's heels and dragged him into the shed while I played a quick game of football with Razor Riley's head. Soon the three toughs were hidden in the shed. Pat closed it and we locked the door.

That left Sophie sprawled on the 'barrow, and she was already starting to show signs of waking up.

"Sweet suffering Jesus!" I yelled. "Let's get her into the hills. We can chain her to a tree by the still until we figure out what to do."

"What about them?" Pat said, jerking a thumb at the shed.

"They're not going anywhere."

We took the safest route that we could manage quickly, and if anyone did see us hauling a fat, blood-covered, struggling dead woman in chains out of town in a wheelbarrow, it never made it into an official report. We chained her to a stout oak and then hurried back. It was already dark and we were scared and exhausted and I wanted a drink so badly I could cry.

"I had a jug in the shed," Pat whispered as we crept back into his yard.

"Then consider me on the wagon, lad."

"Don't be daft. There's nothing in there that can hurt us now. And we have to decide what to do with those lads."

"God…this is the sort of thing that could make the mother of Jesus eat meat on Friday."

He unlocked the door and we went inside, careful not to step in blood, careful not to look at the bodies. I lit his small lantern and we closed the door so we could drink for a bit and sort things out.

After we'd both had a few pulls on the bottle, I said, "Pat, now be honest, my lad…you didn't think this through, now did you?"

"It worked out differently in my head." He took a drink.

"How's that?"

"Mean-Dog got scared of us and paid us, and then everyone else heard about Sophie and got scared of us, too."

"Even though she was chained up in a cowshed?"

"Well, she got out, didn't she?"

"Was that part of the plan?"

"Not as such."

"So, in the plan we just scared people with a dead fat woman in a shed."

"It sounds better when it's only a thought."

"Most things do." We toasted on that.

Mean-Dog Mulligan said, "Ooof."

"Oh dear," I said, the jug halfway to my mouth.

We both turned and there he was, Mean-Dog himself with a pickaxe in his chest and no blood left in him, struggling to sit up. Next to him, Killer Muldoon was starting to twitch. Mean-Dog looked at us, and his eyes were already glowing green.

"Was this part of the plan, then?" I whispered.

Paddy said, "Eeep!" which was all he could manage.

That's how the whole lantern thing started, you see. It was never the cow, 'cause the cow was long dead by then. It was Patrick who grabbed the lantern and threw it, screaming all the while, right at Mean-Dog Mulligan.

I grabbed Pat by the shoulder and dragged him out of the shed and we slammed the door and leaned on it while Patrick fumbled the lock and chain into place.

It was another plan we hadn't thought all the way through. The shed didn't have a cow anymore, but it had plenty of straw. It fair burst into flame. We staggered back from it and then stood in his yard, feeling the hot wind blow past us, watching as the breeze blew the fire across the alley. Oddly, Paddy's house never burned down, and Catherine slept through the whole thing.

It was about 9 p.m. when it started, and by midnight the fire had spread all the way across the south branch of the river. We watched the business district burn—and with it, all of the bars that bought our whiskey.

Maybe God was tired of our shenanigans, or maybe he had a little pity left for poor fools, but sometime after midnight it started to rain. They said later that if it hadn't rained, then all of Chicago would have burned. As it was, it was only half the town. The church burned down, though, and Father Callahan was roasted like a Christmas goose. Sure and the Lord had His mysterious ways.

Two other things burned up that night. Our still and Aunt Sophie. All we ever found was her skeleton and the chains wrapped around the burned stump of the oak. On the ground between her charred feet was a small lump of green rock. Neither one of us dared touch it. We just dug a hole and swatted it in with the shovel, covered it over and fled. As far as I know, it's still up there to this day.

When I think of what would have happened if we'd followed through with Pat's plan...or if Mean-Dog and Muldoon had gotten out and bitten someone else—who knows how fast it could have spread, or how far? It also tends to make my knees knock when I think of how many other pieces of that green comet must have fallen...and where those stones are. Just thinking about it's enough to make a man want to take a drink.

I would like to say that Paddy and I changed our ways after that night, that we never rebuilt the still and never took nor sold another drop of whiskey. But that would be lying, and as we both know, I never like to tell a lie.

HISTORICAL NOTE:

There are several popular theories on how the Great Fire of Chicago got started. It is widely believed that it started in a cowshed behind the house of Patrick and Catherine O'Leary. Historian Richard Bales asserts that Daniel "Pegleg" Sullivan started it while trying to steal some milk. Other theories blame a fallen lantern or a discarded cigar. One major theory, first floated in 1882 and which has gained a lot of ground lately, is that Biela's Comet rained down fragments as it broke up over the Midwest. About the only thing experts and historians can agree on is that the cow had nothing to do with it.

Plan 7 from Sin City

Author's Note

Sometimes a project comes along that is so absurd, so ridiculous, so absolutely unlikely that you just have to say, 'Oh *hell* yes, I'm in.'

Case in point.

Editor Tony Schaab, the mad genius behind the G.O.R.E. Score (look it up), dropped me a line to ask if I was a fan of the legendary 'worst movie of all time,' *Plan 9 From Outer Space*. Of course I was. I love that film and have quoted it endlessly. Tony's evil master plan was an outgrowth of the valid question...What were plans 1 through 8? He reached out to a bunch of his favorite writers, including some of my favorite literary road dogs, Joe McKinney, Michael McCarty, Craig DiLouie and others, and asked us to pitch ideas.

I pitched him a Las Vegas B-movie private eye noir tale. He told me to run with it. I had a wicked amount of fun with this one...

PLAN 7 FROM SIN CITY

A prequel (with apologies) to *Plan 9 From Outer Space*

--1--

Las Vegas, 1957

When she walked into my office I knew three things.
She was miles out of my league, even when I was *in* my league.
Someone was going to get hurt.
And someone was going to get killed. Probably me.
Yeah, her legs were *that* good.

--2--

As private dicks go I'm about two blocks left of seedy. Bail bondsmen wince when they see how my place is decorated.

But she breezed in wearing a five thousand dollar mink wrap and a diamond ring that cost more than my house, my car and my education—with maybe enough left over to buy Arizona.

The first thing that bothered me was the mink.

This is Vegas. In August. The surface of the sun is where people go to get relief from the Nevada heat.

And yet this dame wasn't sweating. She had a dress that was painted over classic lines, honey-colored hair spilling artistically out from under the kind of hat whose message was "if you don't understand why this is the height of fashion, then you're at the other end of that scale." A lizard clutch-purse and enough diamond rings to create the world's most elegant knuckledusters. Monroe hips, a Mansfield bust-line and eyes you'd mortgage your soul for.

I usually had to pay a quarter for a movie ticket to see this kind of class.

People like her don't come to me.

So, I said, "Take a seat."

She glanced down at my client chair. Cracked leather, suspicious stains, half a loaf of Skylark white bread, and an issue of *Zaftig* left over from another case.

I started to get up to clear a path for her, but she picked up the magazine, flipped it open to the centerfold, arched an appraising eyebrow, gave a soft grunt of disdain, and used the mag to sweep the seat. She placed the magazine neatly on the corner of my desk and squared it with the edges. Very precise.

"How do we do it?" she asked.

I was half a step slow to the plate. "Pardon?"

"This process," she said with a vague gesture to my office. "How do we go about it? What do I say? What do you need to know?"

She had a thick accent. I'm no good with accents, but I figured her for Swedish. Said her "W's" as "V's." Normally that would annoy me, but this dame could quack at me like Donald Duck and I'd be good with it.

"First thing I need to know is whether you're here by choice or because you got bad directions."

"Choice, Mr. Diamond," she said with a faint smile. She had bee-stung lips painted in Mary Magdalene scarlet. I approved.

"Want to tell me who gave you my name?"

"Ma Bell," she said.

"Pardon?"

"I picked you out of the phone book. Randomly. I flipped a coin onto the page and it landed on you."

"Nice to know you spent some time on it."

Another inch of that smile. "It would probably disappoint us both to spend time wondering if I'd be here if I asked around."

Ouch.

"Fair enough," I said.

She glanced pointedly around the squalor of my office. "'Lucky' Jack Diamond," she murmured. "'Lucky'—?"

"Yeah, well, the nickname is ironic."

"Maybe you should put that in your ad."

"People would bring their clothes to press," I said.

It took her only a moment to catch the joke. I got a little more of the smile, and I smiled back. Pretty and smart. Nice.

I leaned back in my chair. "And you need a P.I.—why?"

"I want you to follow my husband."

"And your husband is—?"

"Jeffrey Belden."

"Which would make you—?"

"*Mrs.* Belden," she said.

"Right." I picked up a pen from my desk and tapped the eraser on my green blotter. "You want me to follow your husband?"

"Yes."

"You think he's cheating on you?"

She gave me a frank look, and that look invited me to check out the goodies from hair to toes and everything in between.

"No," she said in a tone dryer than the desert sands, "I don't think Jeffrey is cheating on me."

"He'd be a damn fool," I agreed, and then gave her my best smile. It's the one that puts the boyish crinkles around my eyes. Women frequently disrobe when they see that smile. My line of work doesn't pay much, but I have a great dental plan. I gave Mrs. Belden the full treatment. Eyes, teeth, crinkles.

How she managed not to leap across the desk at me remains a mystery.

"So," I said into the ensuing silence, "why do you want me to follow hubby?"

She crossed her legs. For most people that's nothing, a thing they do—maybe to stall, maybe to sit more comfortably. She did it for effect. To make sure I was paying attention. I was.

She said, "I think my husband is selling classified secrets to the Reds."

Suddenly I wasn't looking at her legs. I was staring at her with every atom of my being.

"What kind of classified secrets?" I asked.

"The atomic kind," she said.

If I had a snappy comeback to that, it burned to ash on my tongue.

--3--

Mrs. Belden opened her purse and lit a cigarette. She did it to give me time to pick my jaw up off the floor.

I cleared my throat. "First off," I said, "how does your husband even *have* atomic secrets?"

"He works for the government."

"He's military?"

She blew a stream of smoke into the air and shook her head. "Private consultant. Jeffrey is a mechanical engineer. A very good one. His father built radar systems during the war. Jeffrey was his apprentice, but he's taken his father's work much further."

"Further how?"

"I—I'm not supposed to know exactly what he does. His work is highly confidential and he is forbidden to tell me."

"But you know," I said, making it a statement.

Another long puff of the cigarette. Through the smoke she said, "One day I couldn't find the clicker for the garage door. Jeffrey has a habit of using it and then shoving it into a pocket or his briefcase—if that's open on the car seat next to him. You wouldn't believe the places I've found it. Well...a few weeks ago I went looking for it in his office at home. It was in his jacket pocket...along with a ring of keys."

"Keys to what?"

She looked at the burning tip of her cigarette. "Among other things, his file cabinet and desk. He, um, always keeps those locked."

"Ah," I said.

She nodded. "It's awful of me that I even *thought* of looking, but..."

I waited.

She shrugged. "But it's difficult to live with someone for all these years and know absolutely nothing about what he does. I never get to meet his colleagues, we never go to office parties, and when he comes home at night he can't talk about anything that happened at work. He talks about sports and asks me about my day. I already *know* about my life. I want to know about my husband's. Is that wrong?"

"I'm a professional snoop," I said. "Guys like me want to know everything about everybody. If you accidentally left your purse behind I'd snoop through it, and I don't make any apologies about that. So…yeah, I can totally understand you wanting to take a little peek."

We sat for a moment with that on the table. She pursed her lips and considered it, then nodded. "Okay," she said.

"Okay," I agreed. "So…what was in the briefcase? What did it tell you about your husband?"

"I'm no scientist," she said, "but I'm no dumb bunny either."

"Yeah," I said, "I get that."

Another nod. "From what I could make out, my husband is involved in the research and development of a missile defense system. Or…perhaps I should say *the* missile defense system."

I whistled.

"Ever since we dropped the atomic bombs on those Japanese islands, anyone with half a brain knows that this is how wars are going to be fought from now on. Not little wars, like Korea, but a war between America and Russia, or maybe China. It's all going to be atomic bombs on rockets."

"Cheery thought."

She gave me a hard look. "It's not a joke, Mr. Diamond. Atomic war is coming. Russia has the bomb now and you *know* they're working around the clock to figure a way to build rockets that will carry A-bombs to every major city in the States. China is very close behind them and they're working like demons to catch up."

"We're miles ahead of the Russkies or the Chinese," I said.

"We are…because of men like my husband and whoever he works with in a research unit at Groom Lake, which is part of Nellis Air Force Base. They are on the leading edge, have no doubt about it, but this is a race and the Communists are very determined. And there are other interested parties who would do anything to know what we know."

"Like the Chinese," I said.

"Them and others, sure," she said, staring at me through the haze of blue smoke. "There are always others, Mr. Diamond."

"Okay," I said, "but I thought your husband was working on missile *defense*. Not rockets."

"Don't be obtuse," she said coldly. "You can't build a defense if you don't fully understand the weapons of attack."

I thought about it, and nodded. "Which means that your hubby has access to both sides of the equation. The rockets used to carry bombs and some kind of system to…to what, actually? Shoot them down?"

"I don't know. I don't think he's working on guns or anti-missile missiles. His background is in radar technology…"

"Maybe it's some kind of jamming thing. Something to make the missile guidance systems go wonky."

She smiled at the word "wonky." "I think that's exactly what it is. Up until he died, Jeffrey's father was working on what they called the Belden Jammer. I'm sure Jeffrey continued his father's work. And I know for sure he was working on it ten years ago, right after we were married. Jeffrey was originally stationed in New Mexico, but we left in July of 1947 after there were some, um…*problems*."

"What kind of problems?"

She waved her hand. "It doesn't matter."

"It might. Was he working at another base?"

Mrs. Belden hesitated. "Yes."

"Which base?"

"Roswell Army Air Field."

I sat back. "Ah."

She nodded. "You know about it, then?"

"Only what I read in the papers. Something crashed near the base and they said that it was a flying saucer. Then they changed their story and said it was a weather balloon. Sounds like they were drinking when they cooked up both ideas."

Mrs. Belden flushed. "My husband was one of the lead engineers on something called Project Mogul. I don't know much, of course, but I think it had something to do with trying to fit the Belden Jammer onto a balloon."

"Sure," I said, seeing the value of that. "You could let one drift into enemy airspace and kill their radar. Or, maybe tow it behind a plane to make it invisible. That's what your husband was working on down there?"

"I believe so."

"What's that got to do with little green men?"

"Little gray men," she corrected. "And I don't know. All of the nonsense about aliens and flying saucers…it's crazy talk."

"You don't buy it?"

She measured out half a smile. "Do I look that dumb, Mr. Diamond?"

"Not a matter of being dumb. A lot of people believe in flying saucers."

"I don't. Now…I don't know if the crash was Jeffrey's fault, but he took it as a personal failure. He was in an agitated state for many months, and even now he refuses to talk about it. He hasn't mentioned the Belden Jammer since then."

"The papers said that the army recovered bodies from the wreck."

"Yes."

"Did they? And if they did…*who* were they? Little *gray* men or test pilots? I mean…do balloons even have test pilots?'

"I don't know for sure that anyone was killed or even hurt," she said. "That was all a lot of hysteria in the press. All I know is that Jeffrey was transferred out of Roswell a few months later and ever since then we've been here in Nevada."

"That was 1947. This is 1957. That's a long time, and now you think he's selling secrets to the Commies."

"I fear so."

"Jamming systems, not *actual* atomic bomb secrets."

"Yes. And that increases the number of possible interested parties."

"Why?"

"Because it takes a big military to build rockets, but even a small country could build a jamming device if they had the plans. And, Mr. Diamond, there are a lot of small countries who are already under Communist influence. That man Castro is probably going to take over Cuba and that's right offshore…"

I snorted. "Castro overthrow Batista? That's a laugh. It'll never happen."

She stubbed out her cigarette. "This is a big universe, Mr. Diamond. Anything is possible. One of these days, mankind may be building bases on the moon."

"In science fiction, maybe."

She said nothing.

"Okay," I said, "so you poked around in hubby's desk and file cabinets and you found out that he's building gadgets for the government. How's that make him a traitor who wants to sell secrets to the Reds? That's a pretty big step."

"Lately he's…changed."

"Changed how?"

"He's been acting strange. He works late four or five times a week, or so he says."

"You think he's lying?"

"I called his office after hours several times over the last week and he wasn't there. At first it was just a small thing, something I wanted him to pick up on his way home, or to see if he wanted to meet for a late dinner…but his phone just rang and rang. I'd call back a few times and then get the same thing."

I sucked my teeth.

She gave me a look. A wife look. "Oh, I know what you're thinking. You're thinking that he *does* have a piece of fluff on the side and I'm being naïve."

"Or paranoid," I said. "Or both. If you play the odds on what's making a husband come home late from the office a coupla times a week then I'd put more chips on 'another dame' than 'selling atomic secrets to the Reds.'"

"Don't you think I know that?"

"Not sure. When I asked earlier you invited me to look at all the goodies in the candy shop as if there's no way anyone could stray from a knockout like you. And, I'd go a long way to agreeing with you, Mrs. Belden, because you've got more va-voom in your va-va-va-voom than any dame I ever saw. But," I said, holding up a finger before she could interrupt, "I've been doing divorce work for years and I've seen guys—from pure idiots to raving geniuses— do some damn-fool things, and that includes falling for the whole grass-is-greener thing even if he's already standing in the Garden of Eden."

She narrowed her eyes. "I think there was a compliment in there somewhere."

"Or two. My point is—"

"I get your point, Mr. Diamond, and I assure you that I'm neither insecure, blind, paranoid or an idiot."

I said nothing.

She opened her purse and removed a photo of her husband. Jeffrey Belden was a tall, moderately good-looked man with Poindexter glasses and a lantern jaw. Extremely well-cut suit. A bit of Gene Barry. Even so, he didn't look like the kind of man a woman like this would marry. Maybe he had a big engine under the hood.

"I tried following him several times," she said. "I'd park my car behind a billboard near the gate to the base and then try tailing him like they do in the movies...but I always lost him."

"How? Did he spot you and give you the slip?"

"No, and I don't know that he ever knew that I was following him. It's just that he always left at night, and I suppose I simply lost him in the dark. Every time."

"Huh," I grunted. "If I follow him I won't lose him. I'm not the world's greatest detective, but I never lost anyone I was tailing."

She nodded.

"But what if I find he's not meeting Khrushchev or Chairman Mao to sell-out the free world? What if he *is* meeting some dame?"

She gave me a frank stare. "I love my husband, Mr. Diamond, but I won't be made a fool of."

"I can see that."

She held my eye for a moment, then nodded. "Call it women's intuition, but I think Jeffrey is doing something very bad. Something that could harm this country. Maybe the whole world."

"The whole world?" I said. "That's a bit over the top, isn't it?"

"Atomic bombs and radioactive fallout don't respect national borders, Mr. Diamond. If our enemies start launching missiles, so will we, and then everyone loses. Besides…if you read the paper you know how things are going. Russia tested its first H-bomb this year. And now they have that satellite. Sputnik. They're already pulling ahead of us in some areas, and they're neck-and-neck with us in others. We can't afford to let them get the upper hand."

"Good point." I folded my hands on my desk. "So, tell me, Mrs. Belden, why on earth are you wasting time with me and not going directly to the FBI? I'm pretty good, ma'am, but this is way out of my league."

"I don't want the FBI involved."

"Why the hell not?"

"I don't want my husband to go to jail."

"If he's selling atomic secrets to the Reds then don't you think he should go to jail?"

"I love my husband."

I grinned at her. "I love my mother, but if she was selling atomic secrets to the Reds I'm pretty sure I'd find it in my heart to visit her at Alcatraz every Christmas."

She shook her head. "I don't want my husband to get into trouble."

"You ever heard the expression 'love is blind'?"

"Mr. Diamond, I only *think* my husband is doing something wrong. I'm not sure. I could be totally wrong." She waved a hand toward the photos. "This could even be part of his job. Maybe these men are consultants, or maybe he's bringing information out to a remote testing spot that's officially sanctioned. My point is that I know something's wrong and I don't want to lose my husband. Is that so hard to understand?"

"I guess not," I conceded. "What is it exactly that you'd like me to do?"

"Find out. If he's breaking the law, then I need to know that, and I want to be able to talk to him, maybe convince him to get a lawyer before anyone at the base finds out. Or…maybe he can turn over his connection, let the FBI arrest the spies he's been meeting with. Maybe if he does that he'll get some clemency."

I smiled. "You really love him?"

"Yes? Why—is that such a surprise?"

"In Vegas? Sure. In my line of work? Absolutely. Most of the women who sit in that chair are looking for a recipe so they can grill their husbands over a slow fire."

"I'm not," she said, her voice tight and cold. "I want to save him."

"If you can," I said.

She lit another cigarette and took several long drags on it before she nodded. "If I can."

We studied each other for a while. Her, the rich, beautiful woman with the husband who could be a threat to the free world; and me—? A low-rent P.I. with three alimonies, two kids I haven't seen since the courts said that I was a danger to their well-being, and an office I rented for fifty dollars a month. She needed the best of the best of the best. I shouldn't have even been in any phone book she could pick up.

Nah, no way in hell this could end badly.

"Will you help me?" she asked.

I said, "Sure."

--4--

She sighed with relief, opened her purse and gave me ten one-hundred dollar bills. I watched as her red fingernails plucked bills off of a roll that would choke an alligator. She placed them across the cover of the skin magazine. I'm absolutely sure there was a message there, but I didn't much care.

"This will get you started," she said. "I will pay you another *four* thousand when you have proof of exactly what my husband is doing—and who he's meeting."

Five grand. I knew that my heart was still beating—it was right there in my throat.

Five grand may not be much of a payday to one of the P.I.s on retainer from the casinos on the strip, but it was a whole year's income for me. And it was in cash, too, which meant that this was between Mrs. Belden, me and God. I didn't see any reason to annoy the IRS with needless trivia.

She tucked the rest of the wad into her purse. The ten bills hadn't made a dent in it. I tried not to gaze longingly at it as she snapped her bag shut. Before it closed, though, something fell out of it and bounced on the threadbare carpet. I watched her bend and pick it up. A poker chip.

Mrs. Belden considered the chip, her face wistful, then she flipped it over the desk to me. I got a hand up and caught it.

"For luck," she said.

"Thanks. I'll take all I can get." I slipped it into my vest pocket.

"Jeffrey said that he planned to work late again tonight," she said.

"Then I'll tail him and see what's what."

Mrs. Belden got to her feet and held up a hand. I stood and shook it. Her handshake surprised me. It wasn't the soft, half-folded clasp women usually give you. Her hand was hard as a rock, but it was also cold and damp. Why? Was that a fear reaction? Was she really that afraid for her husband?

It made me feel sorry for her. And it made me like her.

I watched her go. The view was magnificent but my mind was already distracted.

Atomic secrets? Russian spies?

One thousand dollars.

"Oh man," I said to the closed door. "I've got to be out of my mind."

Then I looked down at the neat stack of Franklins.

--5--

Private investigators are supposed to be invisible. As one writer once put it, we were the cockroaches in the walls—always there, seldom seen, never invited.

I drove out to Groom Lake, saw the electrified gate and the guard booth, drove past it and found a quiet billboard to hide behind. The billboard threw shade over my car, which reduced the heat by almost two degrees. I was pretty sure I could fry an egg on the upholstery. I had a bucket filled with chipped ice, but by eight o'clock you could use it to make tea. I sweltered. Seconds melted off the dashboard clock and dripped to the floor. Sweat ran down inside my clothes and pooled under my butt. A coyote came panting up to the car, looked at me through the open window as if deciding whether it was worth the effort to try and eat me, then lifted a leg and peed on my front tire. If I could have risked the noise I'd have shot him. I swear to god he was laughing like a hyena while he loped away.

The sun began tumbling into the west. A line of cars rolled past the guard shack, splitting left and right onto the highway. I had a pair of good Army binoculars and I checked each driver, each make and model. No Belden.

Night came on and the temperature out in the desert dropped like a rock. That always catches people off-guard. They think that night in a desert is just like day in a desert, only darker. But you can freeze your coconuts off out on the sand. I drank some of the melted ice, which was now roughly the temperature and flavor of piss.

And waited.

At six minutes past ten I saw headlights inside the gates, and then a few seconds later Belden turned his Oldsmobile onto the highway and made a left. Home would have been a right.

I smiled, gave him a hundred yards of lead time, and then pulled onto the road behind him, my headlights off. Following his tail-lights was easy—they were the only lights on the whole road. Otherwise it was black as the pit. The moon wouldn't be up for another half hour.

We drove in silent tandem for miles, then Belden disappeared. Just like he did when his wife was tailing him.

I slowed to a stop and stared into the darkness, trying to make sense of that.

While I'd been baking in the heat all afternoon I familiarized myself with the map of this part of the desert. The only turn-offs were unpaved dirt roads that led to undeveloped plots of scrub land that even Las Vegas realtors hadn't been able to unload on their prey.

Before I made the turn to follow him, I reached over and thumbed-open the glove-box and fished out my gun. A .45 Colt Commander. I'm not a huge fan of firearms, but I can shoot and I *will* shoot if it comes down to a choice between my ass and anyone else's. I shot a couple of guys in Guadalcanal, but I didn't enjoy it. The fact that they were shooting back made me enjoy it even less. My old man, who used to be a cop in Chicago during the bootlegger days, once told me that "killing is the result of bad planning." It was great advice. Of course, Dad was part of the gang-busters squad in Chicago and they killed more people than cholera, so that advice is open to some interpretation.

I dropped the magazine, checked that it was loaded, slapped it back and racked the slide. Then I put the safety on and laid it on the seat next to me. God is not always my co-pilot.

I touched the gas and rolled forward until I saw the turn-off. You could blink and miss it, so I didn't blink. I followed it, and after a while I realized that Belden was also driving with his lights off. I slowed even more. There was just enough starlight to make out the silvery gleam off of his chrome bumper.

"Clever bastard," I murmured, easing off the brakes.

We both rolled into the darkness.

Then he turned again. I pulled up to where he left the dirt road, but there was no side road. Belden just left the road and was bumping over the hardpan. I watched him go about a half-mile, then he stopped. I immediately killed my engine because a big blanket of absolute silence dropped over the desert. Nothing. Not even the rumble of a truck out on the highway. We were in the exact middle of nowhere.

I got out of the car.

My gut told me that this was a bad idea.

The thick wad of Franklins in my pocket kept telling me that they wanted to see more of their friends.

The Franklins yelled louder than my gut.

--6--

I lay like a bug on a flat rock.

My car was parked a quarter mile behind me, tucked into a cleft between some nondescript rocks. Belden's Olds was parked a half mile to my east. The moon was over the horizon now, and it was a big three-quarter spotlight of white light. It had taken some time to sneak up on Belden and find a vantage point where I could stretch out and observe. I picked a good spot, too. I could see everything.

Except that there was nothing to see.

Well, nothing of interest. I watched Belden smoke half a pack of cigarettes. I watched him take a piss on a cactus. I saw him check his watch every thirty seconds for almost an hour. I saw him take another piss.

Exciting stuff. I felt I was earning every penny of his wife's money. I whiled away the hours by playing with the poker chip Mrs. Belden had given me. It was thick and heavy—filled with luck, I hoped—and I rolled it back and forth over my fingers. Yeah, it was that exciting out there.

One thing that was a little weird, though, was that Belden never once looked back at the road. He'd driven to the end of it before pulling off onto the desert floor. I'd pulled off quick and hidden my car. There had been no cars following me, but if anyone was coming to meet Belden they would have to take the same bumpy road. So far, nothing.

Was he being stood up? Was that why he was so agitated? How long would this schmuck wait before he realized that his prom date wasn't coming?

Belden lit another cigarette.

He stiffened and immediate tossed the cigarette away. I saw why.

He was no longer alone.

There was a man with him. I used my binoculars to pick out details. The guy was tall, with a receding hairline; dressed in a shiny outfit with buttons up the left shoulder and a belt that looked like it was right out of a Batman comic. All sorts of pouches and doo-dads. There was a patch on the left side of his chest, a white half-moon with a horizontal lightning bolt. He wore a sidearm in a glossy silver holster which I thought looked just a little bit…what's the word? *Artistic.* Like my cousin Davey, who moved to New York to join the ballet.

What jolted me, though, was the fact that the man was there. Just...*there*. He wasn't there a second ago. I'd bet this poker chip and that whole stack of Benjamins on it. The son of a bitch was nowhere and then he was there, not three feet from Belden.

Now, butter that toast with this: Belden didn't even blink when the guy just popped out of nowhere. Like he was used to artistic fellows in shiny suits stepping out of thin air in the middle of a moonlit desert.

I was not as comfortable with it. I believe I gasped.

Or, maybe I said something like, "Yeep!"

Not manly, not creative, but there it is.

And it was just a little too loud.

Belden and the geek turned and looked up. I was sure that they couldn't see me in the dark, but they stared in my direction for almost five seconds.

"It must have been a rabbit," concluded Belden.

"Perhaps," said the geek, and his gaze lingered on the rock on which I lay for a few seconds longer than Belden's.

Then it was all business.

"What's wrong?" demanded the geek in the shiny suit. "Why do you look so nervous?"

Even from where I hid I could hear the strain in Belden's voice. "I think they're onto me."

"What do you mean?"

"I'm pretty sure I'm being followed."

"By air or—?"

"No, by a car. I've seen it several times. A big Chevy."

"Who was driving?"

"I don't know. A woman, I think."

The geek stiffened. "Describe her," he demanded.

"I can't," said Belden. "I never saw her. Not really. Just a glimpse of a face. Sunglasses and a kerchief over her hair."

The geek considered. "Not one of ours."

"I *know* that, Delos," snapped Belden.

Delos. Now the geek had a name, but it wasn't a Russian one. Or Chinese. What kind of name was Delos anyway? Greek? Were there Greek Commies? I really had no idea.

"Perhaps one of Mr. Gray's associates? I told you that you can't trust them," said Delos. He had no particular accent. Sounded American. Educated. A bit snooty. I had an art teacher like him in school. As I recall, he was a dick, too.

"I know, but—"

"Did you have your jammer on?"

"Of course. And I checked my car. There are no tracking devices in it, and with the jammer they can't follow me by air."

"Were you followed tonight?"

"No, I don't think so. It's just that if they are following me at all, then they must know."

"They don't know."

"They have to at least suspect, otherwise why have me followed?" Belden snapped.

"*If* they are following you," said Delos, and from his tone he clearly didn't think anyone was, the dumbass, "then they are probably following everyone involved in top secret work. That's what they do, Mr. Belden. They are in the business of doing two things; making war and protecting secrets."

Belden didn't look convinced. "Maybe, but—"

"And you're sure you weren't followed tonight?" interrupted Delos.

"No. I didn't see the Chevy. I didn't see anyone on the road."

I smiled smugly to myself. That's what I told his wife. When I follow someone, they don't know they're being followed. Everybody's got to be good at something, and although my personal list was pretty short, that was up near the top.

"Then why are you so frightened?" asked Delos impatiently.

"Why?" barked Belden. "Why do you *think*? I'm betraying my country."

"No, you're *saving* your country."

"By betraying it."

"I thought you were a patriot, Mr. Belden."

Belden got right up in the geek's face. "I *am* a patriot, god damn it," he snarled. "This is my world and I will do *anything* to protect it."

I very nearly stood up and blew a whistle on the play. I wanted to say, "What?" very loudly and take a peek at the playbook. I mean, why the hell was a Russian—or possibly Greek—spy playing on a traitor's patriotism? And why did Belden phrase his answer that way? Not "this is my country" or "this is America."

This is my *world.*

Delos sneered at Belden and placed a hand on his chest to push him back. "Then act like a man who wants to see this world continue to spin on its axis rather than turn to burning dust in the vacuum of space."

"Dust won't burn in a vacuum," said Belden.

Delos blinked. "I knew that," he mumbled irritably. "My point is that what you've done—what you've given me—no one will be able to launch missiles. Once we place Belden Jammers on our ships we can prevent anyone anywhere from starting a global thermonuclear war. Or…any kind of war, for that matter. Jamming from space, we will be able to jam every guidance system, every missile command center, every part of the electronics network. We will, in fact, take the weapons of war out of the hands of all of mankind."

"Except for the United States, of course," corrected Belden.

Delos smiled.

"*Except* for the United States," repeated Belden, leaning on the words. "That's what we agreed on. You'd stop any chance of a nuclear war by jamming the weapons of our enemies."

"Yes," he said smoothly. "None of *our* enemies will ever be able to wage war again. How else do you think we'd be able to conquer you so easily?"

The whole world seemed to freeze for a moment.

Belden stared at him, his mouth open to say something but the words died on his tongue.

I stared at them both, and I could feel my mouth drop open, too.

Delos pulled his shiny silver gun.

Belden said something stupid like, "What?"

"What amazes me," said Delos as he pointed the gun at Belden's chest, "is that it took us this long to devise this plan."

"What?" Belden said again. The man must have been captain of his debate team.

"We tried before, you know," said Delos. "Six tries, six failures. This is our seventh plan for conquering the Earth, and I think you, of all people, will have to agree that it's a very good plan. We have been trying for a very, very long time now. You wouldn't believe how long. And now…you hand it to us. No robot armies, no giant monsters, no bloodshed. You drive out here and hand over your life's work and now we have a highly effective means of conquering the Earth."

"I…I…"

The stuff I was hearing was insane. Conquest of Earth? Was this geek some kind of spaceman?

Even with those ideas banging around in my head, I was already in motion, shimmying quietly off the ledge. But as I moved I listened, needing to hear every word of this madness.

"You should be proud, Mr. Belden," said Delos. "You have probably saved millions of lives. Because of you, we won't have to wage war. No one will. You have, my dear sir, effectively eradicated even the possibility of war for all time. A man could die very happy and content with such an accomplishment."

"You…can't…" gasped Belden, and I could see the silver lines of tears on his cheeks. "I wanted to save us all."

"And so you have. There will be no war. The Earth will not become a nuclear wasteland. Your world will survive." Delos shrugged. "And my people take very, very good care of our slaves."

Belden swelled with fury. "You bastard…I'll never be your slave."

"That was never part of my plan anyway," said Delos, and fired.

The pistol was not a pistol.

It was a ray gun.

It fired a beam of golden light and put a hole the size of a hubcap through Belden's chest.

The man fell.

Delos never stopped smiling.

Until I screwed the barrel of my .45 into his temple and said, "Was *this* part of your plan, jackass?"

--7--

This time it was Delos who said, "Yeep!"

It's a useful word, covers a lot of situations.

"Drop the rod, space-boy, or I'll blow a hole in your head big enough to fly a saucer through."

He dropped his gun.

Then he suddenly spun like a top and went at me with some kind of alien judo. Punching this and twisting that and getting real grabby with his hands.

I fired my gun, but the bullet missed.

Then Delos and I were on the sand, and who knows, maybe this was the greatest demonstration of dirty-fighting the universe ever saw. He knew a lot of nasty tricks, but...fuck it. I grew up in Chicago, and Chicago's in the U. S. of A., and we invented dirty fighting. Ask Hitler. Ask anyone.

I head butted him and stuck my thumb in his eye; I introduced his cosmic nutsack to Mr. Kneecap. I spit in his other eye and bit him.

For a brainiac from a higher culture, he screamed just like a ten-year-old girl.

And then a whole bunch of very weird things happened. Kind of all at once.

The ground vanished.

The desert vanished.

Delos and I were floating in the air, surrounded by a weird shimmery light. We were still wrapped up in each other. He was trying to get away and I was trying to demonstrate all of the many ways you can break the Marquis of Queensbury rules.

Then I was on a metal slab. We both were. Delos was ten feet away. We were naked.

I don't enjoy being naked on metal slabs, not as a rule. It has a bit of a flavor of "autopsy" about it.

There were people around us.

Though, when I say "people" I don't mean doctors and nurses. I suddenly would have preferred doctors and nurses. These people were maybe not even human.

They were short.

They were gray-skinned.

They had really big heads. I mean, not like those retarded kids—whaddya call 'em? Mongoloid? Not like them. These freaks had huge heads and huge black eyes, slits for noses and little tiny mouths. And they were naked, too.

Or, maybe they were wearing some kind of skin-tight outfits. Didn't matter. *I* was naked, and they were all over the place.

I tried to hit them. Or kick them. Or anything them. But I couldn't move. Neither could Delos. He stared at the ceiling and screamed. A lot.

The little gray guys with the Mongoloid heads had a bunch of weird-looking scientific instruments in their hands. One of them had Belden's briefcase.

They smiled at me.

I smiled back, hoping this was all going to turn out okay.

One of them lifted an instrument that looked like it came out of an ad in the back of one of the girlie magazines I read.

--8--

Two words.

Anal probe.

--9--

Two more words.

No comment.

--10--

I blacked out during the process, which was the day's only proof that there was a God and He wasn't a total jerk.

When I woke up I was sitting at my desk.

I had my clothes on.

My ass hurt.

It was still night, but there was a light on in my office.

I was not alone.

"Hello, Mr. Diamond," said Mrs. Belden. "I'm glad you're finally awake."

--11--

How do you start that kind of a conversation?

I mean...really? How? What's the doorway into that moment?

Mrs. Belden lit a cigarette and watched me as I tried to sort it out.

"What do you remember?" she asked.

"I—"

"Our friends didn't tamper with your memory," she said. "You can thank me for that."

I remembered the probe. I wasn't sure I wanted to thank her.

I said, "What the hell?"

My voice was hoarse. I opened my desk drawer and removed a bottle of whiskey and two glasses. I poured three fingers into each and knocked mine back.

"I don't drink—" she began, but I picked up the second glass and knocked that back, too.

"I wasn't offering," I said.

She did not appear to be offended.

I studied her. She was no longer wearing jewels and fur. Now she was in a black skirt and matching blazer, with a white shirt and a man's tie. Her hair was tied up in a severe bun and she wore no make-up at all. She was still a knock-out, but in this get-up she looked like the world's toughest librarian.

I said, "Are you even Belden's wife?"

She made a face. "Hardly."

"You a Commie spy?"

"Heavens no. Try again."

I heard a sound and my door opened. A man stood there, and behind him were two others. All of them in black suits and ties. Despite the midnight hour, they both wore dark sunglasses.

The man at the door said nothing, but he touched his watch.

The woman who was *not* Mrs. Belden, nodded. "One minute."

I licked my lips. "Who *are* you people? I met two different kinds of spacemen today. Delos and those little gray Mongoloid freaks. So...are you a third bunch?"

"Do I look like an alien?"

"No, but neither did Delos."

"Fair enough."

"*Are* you?"

"No," she said. "We are not aliens."

"But...you're working with them. With the gray guys at least."

She paused, then nodded. "It's a very old arrangement," she said, "and one that is mutually beneficial to our people."

"To Americans?"

"Americans, yes. And everyone else."

"On...Earth?"

"On Earth."

"And Delos? He was definitely one of the bad guys, right?"

"He was. His kind have been trying to conquer Earth for—"

"Yeah, I heard that speech. Tell me something that makes all of this make sense. If you already knew about Delos, why did you hire me?"

"The Belden Jammer."

"Huh?"

"We have been tracking the leak of classified documents for months now, but every time we tried to follow Belden he vanished. Believe me when I tell you that we have the most sophisticated tracking equipment possible."

"Compliments of the gray guys?"

She nodded. "But Belden eluded us. We realized that he had perfected the jammer and it also made us realize that he was using it every time he left the office late. Our own reliance on high technology became our stumbling block. That's...very frustrating, Mr. Diamond. It's embarrassing."

"So is being your patsy."

"You weren't," she said. "Not really. I didn't find you with a random pick out of the yellow pages. We asked around for someone who was exceptional at tailing people and who was not likely to be discovered doing so. It may surprise you that there are a number of people—former clients and even some of your colleagues—who speak highly of you." She glanced around my office. "You should charge more."

"I'll take a look at my rate schedule when my ass stops hurting."

"Ah," she said. "Sorry about that. For reasons even I don't know, our gray friends have an enthusiastic interest in the workings of the human colon."

I said nothing, but I had another slug of whiskey.

The woman smoothed her skirt. Then she reached into a pocket of her jacket and produced a small item which she placed on my desk.

The poker chip.

"This is a tracking device. When I gave it to you, I hoped that it would lead us to wherever you tracked Belden. His jammer runs off of his car battery, so it was a gamble that once he reached his destination he would turn it off. He did and we were able to pick up your signal. The recovery of the last set of schematics is quite an important thing. We had no idea that Belden had already given Delos so much. If you hadn't trailed Belden then Delos and his people would be holding all the cards. Not even our little gray allies could save us if their equipment was jammed."

"Jeez," I said.

"And, you may find this interesting," she added, "but that jammer is years ahead of its time. Belden and his father were great geniuses. Even in its primitive form, the jammer yielded unexpected results on its first trial run."

She studied me, letting me sort it out.

I snapped my fingers. "Roswell?"

"Roswell. The grays were doing a flyover to monitor the test, expecting it to be another failure, but when the jammer was turned on their electronics and guidance systems went—to use your word—'wonky,' and their ship crashed."

"Too bad," I said, shifting in my chair to take pressure off of my ass. "And who the hell are they anyway? And why are we in bed with aliens?"

"The grays have been here for many thousands of years," she said.

"Why? Did they conquer us already and we've been living as their slaves all this time?"

"No. They are not a warlike people."

"They're not very damn nice."

"No, but that's because their understanding of 'nice' doesn't coincide with ours. They are not evil, either." She shrugged. "They are what they are."

"And what are we to them?"

A small shadow seemed to pass behind her pretty eyes. "They are not here to conquer us," was all she would say.

I leaned back in the chair, studying her.

"You're telling me a whole lot," I said.

She said nothing.

"Why? Are your friends out there going to come in here and shoot me?"

"No," she said.

"Are *you* going to shoot me?"

"No. No one's going to shoot you. No one is going to touch a hair on your head."

"Aren't you afraid I'm going to tell people about this?"

"Who would you tell?"

"Who *wouldn't* I tell? Aliens? UFOs? Attempted global conquest? Conspiracies to overthrow mankind?"

"Yes," she said. "Who would you tell?"

"Everyone."

"And who will believe you?"

I started to say something. Instead I poured another glass of whiskey.

"Exactly," she said.

She opened her purse and removed her wad of currency, and I watched her count out forty one-hundred dollar bills. "As agreed," she said.

The Franklins looked as confused as I did.

"Who *are* you?" I demanded.

She smiled, and there was a little bit of sadness there, and a little twinkle of devilish fun. "We're the good guys, Mr. Diamond."

I sipped my whiskey.

She stood up. "Thank you for your service to your country and your world."

"Wait...that's it? You just drop this in my lap and walk off?"

The woman crossed the office and reached for the door handle, but then she paused and looked back. "Who knows," she said, "we may call on you again."

"Why? Delos is dead and you have the schematics."

"True," she said, drawing it out to load it with some extra meaning, "but Delos' people are still out there. This was their seventh try at conquering the Earth, Mr. Diamond. Who knows how many other plans they have?"

She gave me a sly little wink and walked out.

I sat there and stared at the closed door.

Then down at the rows of hundred dollar bills.

I poured myself another whiskey, swiveled my chair around, reached out for the cord to yank the blinds up, and sat there, looking out my window at the stars.

Red Dreams

Author's Note

I love westerns. Always have. I love weird westerns, too. I grew up watching *Wild Wild West*. I loved *The Adventures of Brisco County, Jr.*, and I dig some of the great B-movie mash-ups of horror, science fiction, fantasy and the western genre.

When one of my favorite editors, John Joseph Adams, asked me for a weird western short story, I already had something cooking in the back of my brain. It is, in its way, a deliberate nod to Rod Serling's brilliant and moving script for "The Passersby," one of my all-time favorite episodes of *The Twilight Zone*.

RED DREAMS

Wyoming Territory

1875

McCall saw the star fall.

Like a match struck against the hard dome of the sky and then dropped, trailing sparks, burning out.

It fell slowly, though. Not like other falling stars that were there and gone, mostly caught out of the corner of the eye. This one wanted to be seen.

For a moment McCall thought it was an angel, but then he blinked his eyes clear and shook cobwebs from his head.

An angel, maybe, he thought bitterly, *but if so, then it's sure damn coming for me with a flaming sword.*

He wanted to tell himself that he didn't deserve fiery justice or burning retribution, but McCall wasn't much good at lying to himself. Besides, the light from the falling star was dropping toward the east—the way he'd come—and by its bright light it wouldn't require divine perception to see the truth.

So many bodies. Animal and man. Red and white.

The stink of gunpowder still burned in McCall's nose. That smell and the death smells. The copper of blood, the outhouse odor of shit and piss. And, just as the sun set an hour ago, the first sick-sweet stink of rot. Bodies out here in the Wyoming heat didn't wait long before they turned foul.

So many dead.

And at the end of that crooked trail, one last survivor. A guilty man and his blood-streaked horse, both of them alive by chance or miracle. Alive when they should have been as dead as everyone else. The last survivors of a massacre, now required to sit and witness the death of this piece of cosmic rock.

The comet moved slowly across the sky, so big and so bright. Going down in a blaze of glory, firing its last as it died, declaring itself bold and powerful even while the world was poised to snuff its fire out.

"Now ain't that a sight?" McCall asked his horse, a big Paint named Bob.

His voice sounded thin even to his own ears. It sounded sick and old.

Old before my time, he mused, but that wasn't true, either. A preacher once told him that a man aged according to what he did, not by how many years he lived. A good man lived forever.

A bad man?

McCall was a short footstep over forty years and felt like he was ninety. Before the fight—before the *massacre*—he'd felt younger, but that was a relative thing. He couldn't remember ever feeling *young*. Maybe back in Philadelphia when he was a boy. Before he signed on to guard wagons heading west. Before he went to work killing red men. Before he began chipping days or maybe weeks off of his life every time he pulled a trigger.

Weeks or maybe years.

Far above, pieces began breaking off of the comet. Like people jumping out of a burning building. McCall had seen that once. Way back in Philadelphia when a hotel burned right down to the ground. People from the top floors jumped out of the windows. They weren't trying to escape the flames. Not really. Most of them were already on fire. They just wanted it to end. They wanted the hard pavement below to punch the suffering out of them, to get it all over fast so they didn't have to live through their own deaths. That was how McCall saw it. People who didn't have the guts to go all the way down to the end.

McCall couldn't understand that. He could never have jumped out of that building. Death wasn't a destination he wanted to get to a second or a step sooner than he had to. No, sir. When his time came to go into the big dark, then he was going to fight every step of the way. It wouldn't be cowardly kicking and screaming, either. Jonah McCall was going to make death come for him. He'd make death work for it, earn it, sweat over it.

More and more debris fell from the comet, but the heart of it was still intact when it suddenly vanished behind the eastern wall of red rock mountains. There was a huge flash of white and green, and for a moment McCall fancied that he could see the bodies sprawled on the plain. The Cheyenne dog soldiers with their breechclouts and war bonnets, the rest of McCall's team of riders, and the horses from both sides, all torn and broken and splashed with light. But that was crazy. The battlefield was miles to the west and all that light really showed was the lumpy terrain.

McCall waited for the sound of the impact to come rolling across the hardpan toward him. He'd seen a lot of stars fall; you couldn't help see them out here. Only twice had they been this big, though, and each time they hit hard and hit loud.

He waited, his tin coffee cup an inch from his mouth, holding still to keep his own sounds from hiding any that were trying to find him.

Nothing.

He cocked his head and listened harder.

Nothing at all.

"Must have burned itself all up," he told Bob.

McCall felt vaguely disappointed. He was kind of looking forward to that sound, to the rolling echo of it. It would have been like hearing thunder. It'd been a long time since he'd heard thunder. It had been a long, hot summer, fraught with drought and dust storms. Even on days when the clouds stacked up all the way to God's front porch and they turned black as shoe polish, it never rained. The hot wind always pushed those storm clouds into someone else's sky. They went west, like fleets of ships, but none of them landed on the shores of the Wyoming desert. McCall and his boys had been riding this land for sixteen weeks and hadn't felt a drop of rain on their faces. Not one.

He was a thin man. The last time he'd looked at himself in a mirror he saw a scarecrow wearing his old cavalry trousers and a Pinkerton duster he'd bought secondhand after its owner had been killed. The woman at the general store mended the bullet holes in the back, but even with the fine stitching the fingers of the wind wriggled through each hole.

He sipped his coffee and cradled the cup in his palms, taking its warmth.

Movement in the corner of his eye made him turn, but it was only the wind pushing a piece of bloodstained rag along the ground. A sleeve, thought McCall. Torn, frayed, slick with wetness that was as black as blood in this light. Most of the cloth was dry and that part whipped and popped in the breeze; but the wet parts were heavier and they kept slapping the ground. In the variable wind, the effect was like some grotesque inchworm lumbering awkwardly across the landscape. *Whip, pop, slap.* Over and over again as it crawled toward the shadows and out of his line of sight.

"Damn," he said, and the sound fled away to chase the tattered sleeve into forever.

McCall shivered.

The open range was always so damn cold at night. Hotter than Satan's balls during the day, though.

Something scuttled past him in the dark, a quick scratchety-scratch sound. Probably a lizard chasing down a bug, or running from something bigger. Night was a lie out here. During the day, under all that heat, it was easy to think about dying because everything you saw looked like it was dying. Plants and trees dried to brown sticks; bones bleaching themselves white. And all those endless miles of empty nothing. Under the sun's brutal gaze you expect things to die.

He thought of the fallen star as he sipped his coffee.

Out there behind the hills it had died. Died in its own way.

Died, as sixteen of his men had died.

Died, as thirty-four of the Cheyenne had died.

As this star now died.

McCall poured some hot into his cup and tried to chastise himself for that fanciful notion, but it was hard to hang scorn on yourself for any strange thought when you're in the vast, cold night all alone. And it was easy to think of things dying, even chunks of rock from outer space. Who knows how long it had been out there, flying free in the big empty of the endless black. Then it took a wrong turn and came to the desert sky, and that desert sky killed it as sure as McCall had killed Walking Bear, the war chief of the Cheyenne dog soldiers.

It had come down to the two of them. Walking Bear on a Chestnut gelding, a Winchester '73 in his hands; McCall on his Paint with a Colt he'd just reloaded.

McCall suddenly shivered.

It was so abrupt and so deep that it rattled his teeth and caused some coffee to slop onto the ground. His whole body shuddered worse than when he'd had the ague down in Louisiana after the war. The shiver was so violent that it felt like cold hands had grabbed him and were actually shaking him back and forth.

Then just as suddenly it was gone. McCall stared at the night as if there should be something at hand to explain what just happened.

"The hell was that?"

But his voice came out all wrong. It startled him because...

He listened to the night.

And heard absolutely nothing.

No insect sounds.

No scuttle of animals or lizards across the sand.

Not a single cry from a night bird.

There was nothing.

Nothing.

And there was never nothing.

McCall shifted the coffee cup to one hand and with the other he touched the handle of his Colt. He could actually hear the rasp of his callused palm against the hardwood grips. Like sandpaper.

He closed his hand around the gun, as much to stop the sound as to seek comfort from the weapon's deadly potential. That gun had killed at least nine of the Indians today. Nine, including that big son of a bitch Walking Bear. It had taken five rounds to put the Indian down, and the bastard fought all the way, working the lever of his Winchester. The rifle rounds burned the air around McCall, and one hit the big steel buckle of his belt and knocked him right out of the saddle. McCall had landed hard and for a wild few moments the world spun around him in a kaleidoscope of red and black. Then the world went away.

It was Bob who woke him up. The big Paint stood over him, legs trembling, sides splashed with blood, licking the beard stubble on McCall's face.

The pain in his belly was white hot, and when McCall examined the buckle he saw that it had been folded nearly in half by the impact. He rolled over and slowly, painfully climbed to his feet.

Everything and everyone was still and silent. Walking Bear lay there, five red holes in his chest, eyes wide, mouth open. The big Cheyenne did not move. Could not move. The Indian was dead and so was everyone else. McCall's men and the dog soldiers and all of their horses.

Only McCall and Bob were left.

That moment had been as still and silent as the darkened desert was now, hours later, with the night holding its breath all around him. His stomach still hurt from where the bullet had struck the belt buckle. The skin felt pulped and there was a burning feeling deep inside, like maybe the impact had busted something. Sitting there, listening to the silence, he felt that bruise throb and throb.

McCall snugged his hand down around the handle of the Colt, but the gun withheld its comfort. Even so, McCall clutched at it and tried not to be afraid of the dark even though he knew for certain that there was no living soul anywhere around here.

Gradually, gradually…the night sounds returned.

The tension in McCall's body faded into occasional shivers that were inspired by nothing more sinister than the chilly wind.

McCall sipped his coffee and thought about Walking Bear. He was a strange man. A full-blood Cheyenne who'd been taught his letters by Quaker missionaries. The Indian could read and write better than half the white men McCall knew, and that book-learning had helped him rise to power within the Cheyenne community. Walking Bear had even once gone all the way to Washington D.C., along with a dozen other chiefs, to talk to President Grant. Not that it did much good, because treaties weren't worth the paper they were printed on and everybody knew it. A treaty was another tactic. Not of war, but of business. A treaty was honored only as long—and until—the land the Indians lived on was needed by someone with white skin. Ranch land, gold mines, whatever. Protected Indian land was as much a myth as a man telling a woman that he won't never go no further than touching her knee. It all amounted to the same.

McCall figured that Walking Bear knew all this, and he had to give the big Indian credit for trying to make the white man stick to his word. Then Walking Bear had apparently decided that guns and scalping knives were more useful than writs and lawsuits.

The territorial governor put a bounty on Walking Bear's head, and a coalition of cattle barons had quadrupled it. Two hundred dollars for Walking Bear and fifty for any dog soldier who rode with him. The most McCall ever made in a single year was one-fifty, and most years it was closer to one hundred dollars. Two hundred for a single bullet was a king's fortune to a man who lived in the saddle.

So, McCall hunted Walking Bear and his party for months, occasionally catching up long enough for someone or another on either side to take a bullet or get his throat cut. Early on the Cheyenne, along with some rogue Arapaho, held the upper hand with more men, more horses and a better knowledge of the terrain here in Wyoming and down in Colorado. But the Indians had only one rifle for every two of them, and the men in McCall's party each had a hand gun and a long gun. And all of them hungered for that bounty, which was paid out in gold coins. The tide turned slowly, but it turned.

The funny thing was that McCall rather liked Walking Bear. The big Indian had been the last surviving son of Chief Lean Bear, who had been shot by soldiers under the command of Colonel John M. Chivington, the same maniac who attacked a Cheyenne village at Sand Creek in the Colorado Territory. That had been a bad business. Most of the village's fighters had been out hunting during the attack, but Chivington ordered his men to kill everyone in the camp. Every elder, every woman, every child. Even little babies. Seven hundred riders of the Colorado Territory Militia had gone thundering in and hacked the Indians to red ruin and pissed on the bodies as they lay spoiling under the stark November sun. Seven hundred armed soldiers against a couple of hundred Cheyenne.

Maybe twenty of the Indians had been fighters. A few people escaped. One hundred and sixty-three Indians died.

McCall had been one of the colonel's men. He'd been right there when Colonel Chivington had made the statement that defined his view of the "Indian problem," as people called it. Chivington had said, "Damn any man who sympathizes with Indians. I have come to kill Indians, and believe it is right and honorable to use any means under God's heaven to kill Indians."

Chivington was one of those men who glowed with holy purpose. Blue light seemed to shine from his eyes. And McCall, so much younger then, had yelled as loud as anyone as Chivington's speeches whipped them into a frenzy. By the time the colonel aimed his militia at the Cheyenne he didn't have to use much energy to pull the trigger.

A lot of what happened there at Sand Creek seemed to take place inside a dream. It never felt real to McCall. Maybe not to most of the men. The colors were too bright. The blood was the color of circus flags. The white of bone was like snow. The screams rose like the cries of birds. And the things they all did...

Did men ever do that kind of stuff except in dreams?

McCall could not actually remember what he did that day. He couldn't remember what his guns did, or his skinning knife, or his hands. None of it. As soon as it happened it all started to fade into pieces of memory, like the way you remembered a play after it was over. You knew the story, but you can't remember every scene, every line. Why? Because it wasn't real.

It was just a dream. Chivington's dream, in fact. McCall and everyone else was an actor, a supporting character, in the colonel's fantasy.

That was back in 1864. Nearly a dozen years ago.

A lot had happened since then.

Cattle men from Colorado had gone crazy cutting Wyoming up into private plots that were bigger than some countries in Europe. They moved herds up into the grasslands and let them breed like there was no tomorrow.

Of course...that was true enough for the Cheyenne. There was no tomorrow.

Chivington was court-martialed and left for Nebraska in disgrace—but without remorse. His men were scattered to other jobs. McCall went north into Wyoming to work security for the cattle barons and eventually put together his own team. They were not as bad a lot as Chivington's militia—they didn't take scalps or ears or fetuses as trophies, and they didn't make tobacco pouches out of scrotums. But they were all killers, McCall could not say otherwise. The barons wanted the Indian problem solved, and McCall was one of a dozen such men who formed teams to solve it.

Today wasn't the only day that ended in slaughter.

Not the second, not even the tenth.

He stared down into his cup, but it was a black well that looked too far down into the truth. So he leaned back and studied the night sky. The stars were all nailed to the ceiling of the world. Nothing else fell.

McCall got up, wincing at the pain in his gut, and collected some fresh wood for his meager fire. He built it up so that its glow drew his focus, tricking his eye and his mind away from the night and all that it held.

And that was good. That worked.

*   *   *

Until the screaming started.

*   *   *

McCall jerked upright, yanked out of a doze by the terrible sound that tore through the darkness.

He fell forward onto his knees, pivoted, drew his gun, thumbed the hammer back, brought it up, one hand clutched around the grips and the other closed like a talon around the gun hand, head and barrel turning as one. All of that done in a heartbeat, done without thought. His horse cried in fear and reared, hurling its weight against the line that was made fast to a bristlecone tree.

The echo of the scream rolled past him and was torn to pieces by the desert wind.

McCall could feel his heart pounding. He could *hear* the thunder of it in his ears.

His breath came in short gasps.

Silence fell like snow. Soft and slow, covering everything.

"A cat," he said, and his voice was as thin as the lie he told himself. "Mountain cat."

After a long time he lowered his gun and exhaled heavily. Behind him his horse blew and nickered uneasily, shifting from foot to foot, tail switching in agitation.

"Just a damn mountain cat, Bob," said McCall. "That's all it is, don't you worry."

Bob blew and stamped.

The echoes faded until they were nothing.

"Y'see, Bob? You dumb son of a mule? Stop being such a—"

The second scream tore the night apart.

It was huge and massive and so loud that it punched into McCall's head. He screamed, too, and threw himself to one side, spinning on his hip to bring the pistol up again, aiming behind where he'd been facing.

The scream rose and rose.

And even as McCall screamed back at it he knew that this was no cat. No mountain cat and no jungle tiger like the one in the traveling circus. The sound was too loud, too prolonged, too shrill.

It was more like…

Like what?

If there was an answer to that question, then McCall's mind did not want to give it. His brain refused to put a name to it.

The shriek went on and on, louder and louder and louder.

The gun fell from McCall's hand as he clamped both palms over his ears. He screamed as loud as he could, trying to push the sound back with his own scream.

Still it went on and on and on and…

Nothing.

Gone.

Stopped.

There was absolute silence. Immediate and total.

Only when McCall stopped screaming could he hear the echo of the screech rolling away from him. He lay there, gasping like a trout on a riverbank. His horse stood trembling, coat flecked with nervous sweat, foam dripping from the bit.

"Steady on, Bob," gasped McCall. "Steady on. It's just a..."

His words trailed off into nothing. McCall didn't try to lie to the horse. Or to himself. This was no cat or anything else whose cry he'd ever heard. This was a banshee wail, like in the stories his grandmother used to tell him. Wailing spirits that warned of death trying to sneak into the house.

But there was no house out here. McCall was sprawled on the sand in the dark wind, and the sky was empty of everything but dying echoes.

And then there was movement out there.

McCall lunged for his fallen gun, clawed the ground for it, scrabbled it into his fist, raised it toward the shape in the darkness.

"No," said the shape.

"Step into the damn light or I'll blow your head off," snarled McCall.

The figure moved closer. It was a man. Tall and broad-shouldered, McCall could see that much; but he stood just beyond the reach of the small campfire's glow.

"No," the man said again. "No reason to fire."

McCall did not fire, but he did not lower the gun.

"No," the man said a third time as he stepped forward into the light. The glow illuminated a face that was hard and angular and streaked with blood. Firelight glimmered in the slanting dark eyes and glistened on the edges of five ragged bullet holes in the broad, flat chest. "No need to shoot. You've already killed me."

McCall stared up at Walking Bear.

And he screamed.

Then he fired.

One, two, three...

Six shots that burst in the air with hot yellow flame and sharp cracks. The bullets punched into Walking Bear, striking him in the chest, in the stomach, in the thigh, the arm, the throat, the face.

Every bullet hit a target.

Cloth and flesh puffed up from each impact. Blood and bone flew.

The hammer clicked down against a spent shell.

Click.

Click.

Click.

McCall's finger jerked the trigger over and over. The cylinder turned with impotent desperation. The clicks chased the gunshot echoes into the darkness.

Walking Bear stood there.

He did not fall.

The new wounds did not bleed.

His face was unsmiling.

"No," he said again.

McCall cried out. A small, mewling sound. Once more the pistol fell from his fingers and thudded into the dirt.

Walking Bear stepped closer. A single step, but it sent McCall scuttled backward onto his buttocks, then into a skittering crab-like scuttle on hands and heels until he was almost in the coals of the fire. He recoiled from the flames and fell onto his side, panting, sweating, tears boiling from his eyes.

"Oh god," he whispered. "Oh god..."

Walking Bear sighed and stepped forward again, but not toward McCall. There was a large stone near the fire and he lowered himself onto it.

McCall goggled at him. He could feel the skin of his face contract, could feel his lips curled back in terror and disgust from the thing that sat on the rock. When he could force the words out, his voice was a strangled whisper.

"What *are* you?"

The Indian snorted. A soft sound, with only a splinter of amusement gouged into it.

"I'm dead," said Walking Bear. "What the hell do you think I am?"

"I killed you."

"Yes, you did. Twice, though I'm not sure the second time counts."

Walking Bear's voice was so normal that it made McCall want to scream again. It had the casual tone and cadence of a city man, a gift from the Quakers who'd taught him English. But the accent was Indian. There was no mistaking that odd lift at the end of each sentence. Not like someone asking a question. Indians just had a little hook at the end of everything they said that lifted their tone and then went dead flat.

"How are you...I mean...how...?" McCall couldn't patch together a sentence that made any sense.

Walking Bear shrugged. He bent down and picked up a handful of small stones, considered them, and dropped them one at a time. No pattern to it, no haste.

McCall sat up with a jerk. With one hand he fumbled for his fallen pistol and with the other he began pushing cartridges out of his belt. He managed to open the cylinder and drop the spent shells, dropped most of the fresh ones, clumsied a few into place, slapped the cylinder shut and held the gun out in two trembling hands.

The Cheyenne looked faintly amused. "Damn, white man, how many times do you want to kill me?"

McCall licked his lips nervously. "Until it takes, damn you."

Walking Bear dropped the rest of the pebbles and placed his fingers over the holes in his chest, then showed those fingers to McCall. They were smeared with blood.

"It took the first time out."

The gun barrel shuddered like a reed in a windstorm.

"I..."

"You're going to try and make sense of it," said Walking Bear. He shook his head. "But it doesn't make sense. Not the way you think."

Before McCall could organize a reply to that, there was more movement out in the darkness. He flinched and swung the barrel around.

But it was a horse.

A big roan with a blanket instead of a saddle. It walked slowly past the camp, cutting a single glance at the two men without pausing. It gave Bob a soft whinny, but didn't stop there, either. McCall stared at it. There were three bullet holes in its stomach and one in its chest.

"That's not...that's not..."

"Possible?" finished Walking Bear. He shrugged and they watched the horse walk away and vanish into the darkness. There was a long time of silence as they both looked at the shadows. Then another horse came walking by. Its stomach was torn open, entrails dragging in the dirt as the animal followed the hoof prints of the roan.

"Jesus Christ the savior!" cried McCall. "That thing's *dead*."

Walking Bear gave him a pitying look. "I thought we covered that."

"But *how*?"

"Why are you asking me?"

"Because...because you're dead, too."

"Sure."

"Then how are you here? How can you be sitting there? How can you be talking to me, god damn it?"

But Walking Bear shook his head. "I don't know, white man. I woke up dead. You shot me full of holes and I fell down. Then I woke up."

"Are you...a ghost?" demanded McCall. "Tell me if you are."

"I don't know. I'm dead."

"How can you not know?" McCall lowered his pistol, laying it on his lap. "You're a ghost. You have to be."

"Then I'm a ghost." Walking Bear seemed to think about it. He scratched at the bullet hole in his face. "What's a ghost, though?" he asked. "I mean, to you whites?"

McCall didn't answer.

"Sure," said Walking Bear, as if answering his own question, "I read the Bible with the Quakers. There was a lot in there about ghosts and spirits. Jesus was a ghost, I suppose. He came back from the dead."

"He was a spirit," said McCall, calling on what little he remembered of proper Sunday school. "The Holy Spirit."

"Okay, sure," agreed Walking Bear. "But I remember reading that he was flesh, too. At least when he first came back. He met with his disciples and even ate with them. Fish, I think. And one of them touched his wounds to prove that he was really there."

"Thomas," said McCall softly. His mouth was as dry as paste.

"Thomas, right. So, I guess that's what happens."

"I've seen a lot of dead people, damn it," growled McCall, "and none of them ever came back."

Walking Bear turned and looked at him, his dark eyes as cold and hard as chips of coal. "How would you know that?"

There was a sound behind them and they both turned to see four men milling at the edge of the clearing. Not Cheyenne. These were white men in jeans and canvas coats, with gun belts and Stetson hats. McCall knew them, every one. Lucas Polk and his brother, Isaac. Dandy McIsle. And Little Joe Smalls.

All of them were on McCall's payroll. They'd been at the battle. They'd each killed one or more of the Cheyenne.

All of them were dead.

Bob whinnied in fright and tugged at the rope that held him.

The four men stood together, speaking to one another in low whispers. McCall couldn't make out the words. They cut quick looks at him, and Dandy McIsle gave a single shake of his head. When they began walking, they moved around the camp, staying at the very edge of the spill of orange firelight.

"Hey!" cried McCall. "Lucas…Joe…"

But the men ignored him and hurried away. They headed in the same direction as the two horses.

"Where are you going?" McCall yelled.

There was no answer. McCall wheeled on Walking Bear.

"What's happening?"

The Indian seemed to think about it. "I guess they're going home."

"Home where? Little Joe's from Arkansas. Dandy got off the boat from Ireland two years ago. He's been with me ever since. He doesn't have a home."

"I guess he sees things another way now," said Walking Bear. "I guess they all do."

"What in tarnation are you talking about?" McCall wanted to laugh. He wanted to slap himself across the face and wake up from what was obviously a dream. But he sat there, clutching the gun that lay in his lap, talking nonsense with a dead Indian. "Come on," he snapped, "tell me what you're talking about. Tell me how this makes sense."

More men walked past. Indians and his own men. Some of them walked together, heads bent in conversation so private that McCall couldn't catch a single word. Others walked alone. The expressions on their faces were mixed. There was fear on some faces, and even terror on a few. Some looked profoundly confused, and these men stumbled along in the wake of those whose countenances showed determination. But whether that determination was bred from actual understanding or if it was in the nature of those men to believe they understood what was happening at all times, McCall couldn't tell. One man staggered past, arms wrapped tightly around his chest, eyes screwed shut as he wept with deep, broken sobs. And one man went by, singing a slow, sad Presbyterian hymn. Every man was pocked with bullet holes, pierced with arrows, or opened by blades. Every single one. And yet they walked without evident pain, even those who limped on shattered legs. One man waddled past on the stumps of legs that had been hacked off below the knee. Josiah Fenton, one of the youngest of his riders.

McCall watched them go.

All of them.

Every man who had ridden with him, and every Cheyenne they'd died to kill. He even saw two men—an Indian and one of his own men, Doc Hogarth—walking together as if it was something they'd always done. As if it was something normal to do. Even Walking Bear seemed surprised to see that.

"Hunh," grunted the big Cheyenne.

Doc Hogarth had an arrow all the way through his head. The barbed tip stood out ten inches from the back of Doc's split skull, and the fletched end stood out four inches from the shattered lens of the right side of his glasses. In a dime-novel drawing it might have been bizarre enough to be funny, but McCall gagged when he saw it.

Doc heard the sound of him retching and turned to him, a flicker of sympathy and perhaps disapproval in his remaining eye.

The men passed, some coming so close that firelight danced on their faces and in their eyes, others staying well away so that they were vague shapes in the darkness. It seemed to take a long, long time for them to pass. Too long.

Then McCall cried out as he realized why it was taking this long.

There were strangers mixed in among the known dead.

Other Indians. Too many of them. Some white men, too, but not as many as the Cheyenne.

"Who are they?" he barked, pointing to the Indians.

Walking Bear shook his head. "I don't know them."

Somehow, McCall felt that this was a lie. Or, at least, not a whole truth. The tone of his voice suggested that he knew, or guessed, something.

"What is it?" hissed McCall. "*Do* you know them?"

Walking Bear only shook his head.

The line of straggling dead swelled and soon there were hundreds of bodies moving past. Not just Cheyenne, but Arapaho and Crow, too. And Shoshone and Utes. Even Comanches.

Every one of them was marked with violence. The first few hundred had clearly been shot or cut with sharp blades. McCall knew those kinds of wounds. Cavalry swords. But eventually these thinned out and the ones who followed were marked by other kinds of violence. The duller but still deadly wounds of sharpened stone axes. Cruder arrows. Rounded red craters from hurled rocks.

All dead, all carrying with them the proof of their own deaths.

No, McCall thought, correcting his own error in perception. *The proof of their own murders.*

And that's what this was. A procession of the murdered. The slain. None of them looked withered from disease or starvation. Every single man here had been clubbed or stabbed or shot.

Even this perception had to be corrected, and McCall closed his eyes for a moment to summon the will to see what was there.

He opened his eyes as a woman walked past. Her clothes were torn to reveal bruised breasts and bloody thighs, and she carried the broken remains of her child in her arms. The child wriggled against her breast, seeking milk that had gone cold and sour in the grave.

There were other women.

Other children.

Many of them.

Too many of them.

Were these the children of Sand Creek? If he looked too closely would he see faces that had looked up at him as his blade had plunged down? Would he see accusation in eyes that had watched him take aim with pistol and rifle?

"You don't have to look," said Walking Bear.

"I…"

The Cheyenne pointed. A white woman staggered past, her clothes as completely torn as the Indian woman's had been. Her eyes as haunted, her skin bled as pale. Three children followed her, their bodies crisscrossed with cuts. Hundreds of cuts.

They hurried to catch up with the Indian woman, and as McCall watched, the women fell into step with one another.

Tears burned their way down McCall's cheeks.

He said nothing as the legions of the murdered passed by. Walking Bear put his face in his hands and wept silently. They stayed where they were, one sitting on a rock, the other sitting on the dirt, both of them witnessing the procession.

Soon there was another change. The white corpses thinned and eventually there were no more of them. But the Indians changed, too. Their clothing and jewelry was different. Elaborate beadwork gave way to dyed leather, and then to plain leather. And finally to rough hides of buffalo and other animals.

These Indians had different faces. More like Chinamen, but coarse and blunt, with broader noses.

Yet each of these, even the most savage-looking among them, bore the mark of a stone knife, a heavy club, or the splayed bruising of choking hands.

"All of them?"

The words startled McCall and he turned to see that Walking Bear, his face scarred by tears, was staring at the dead. He shook his head slowly back and forth in a denial so deep that it made his whole body tremble.

"What?" asked McCall.

"Look at them," said Walking Bear. "Every single one of them."

McCall didn't need to ask what Walking Bear meant. He knew. He saw.

He understood.

Eventually the last of the Indians walked past, and it was only then that McCall realized that there had been many animals walking with them. All along, starting with the horses.

Dogs, wolves, antelope, elk.

Every kind of bird.

Rabbits and squirrels.

Their fur or feathers slick with blood that had leaked from the wounds that had killed them.

"Every one of them," echoed McCall.

"Every one," agreed Walking Bear.

Now it was only animals. And some were strange. Some were like things McCall only ever saw in circuses or in books. Big elephants, but they looked bigger and they were covered in long, shaggy hair. Bears that towered taller than the greatest grizzly. Monstrous wolves. And beasts unlike anything McCall had imagined in his drunkest nights or in his worst nightmares. Things like reptiles that were so massive that their footfalls shook the world. Bob screamed as they passed. Some lumbered along on four titanic legs; creatures whose heads rose on necks that arched up as long and slender as tree trunks. Others stalked forward on two immensely powerful legs, while absurdly small forelegs clutched at the night air.

Even here, even as these giants from nightmare or from Hell itself thundered past, McCall could see that their bodies were worn by tooth and claw.

"Every god damn one of them," he said.

They sat there and watched and watched as the wheel of night turned and the dead paraded by. Finally, Bob tore free of his tether and he ran off into the night. McCall expected him to run away from the grisly procession, but the damned crazy horse galloped at full speed in the same direction.

Eventually...

Eventually. Silence settled over the camp. The last rumbled footsteps of the giants faded. With slow hesitation the night sounds returned. A cricket. An owl. The crackle of the logs turning in the fire.

McCall looked at Walking Bear. Both men had long ago stopped crying. Their tears had dried to dust on their faces.

"Every single one," said McCall once more, and the Cheyenne nodded.

With a long, deep sigh, Walking Bear got heavily to his feet. "Guess I should go, too."

"Go?" asked McCall. "Go where?"

"Wherever they're going."

"And where's that?" McCall's voice was sharp and cold. "Are they going to heaven? To hell?"

Walking Bear shook his head. "I'm not a shaman, white man. I'm a warrior. It's not for someone like me to understand the mysteries."

"Isn't it?" demanded McCall.

The big Indian gave him a small, slow smile. "Are you coming?"

McCall tried to laugh, but the effort hurt his stomach. He got to his feet, though. "Go where?" he asked again.

Walking Bear said nothing.

"I *can't* go where you're going," insisted McCall. "You're dead."

"You should know."

"I *do* know. Like you said, I killed you twice."

"Once was probably enough," said Walking Bear.

For some reason that McCall could not understand, they smiled at each other. Then they laughed out loud. "I guess I'm sorry for shooting you," he said after their laughter bubbled down and died out.

"No," said Walking Bear. "You're not. If you could, you'd do it again. I think you got the habit now. I mean...twice."

They laughed again.

"So," said McCall awkwardly, "what now? Is this some kind of lesson? Am I supposed to ask for you to forgive me?"

"I wouldn't," said Walking Bear. "I know I was educated by the Quakers, but I'm pretty sure I don't forgive you. At least not yet. I've only been dead for a little bit. Maybe I'll come round to it."

"Yeah," said McCall. "Maybe. But where does that leave me? Are you going to just walk off? How am I supposed to deal with this? How am I supposed to live with this kind of thing in my head? Is this some kind of spiritual lesson? Am I supposed to go back to town and devote my life to good works? Is that how it ends?"

Walking Bear looked at him for a long time. Half a minute, maybe more.

"No, white man, I don't think that's how it ends. And I'm pretty sure you know it."

McCall tried to look at him, to see the meaning in Walking Bear's eyes, but he couldn't do it. He turned away.

"Don't," he said. "I know what you're going to say, but don't say it."

Walking Bear was silent.

"I'm *not* dead, god damn it."

Walking Bear said nothing.

"I'm not."

"Okay," said the Cheyenne.

"Okay," said McCall.

His stomach hurt. He touched the bent belt buckle. Felt where the rifle bullet had struck. Traced the outline of the curved metal. Felt the hole. Slipped a finger inside. It was cold in there. He turned and saw the big ragged exit wound where a bullet had punched its way out of him. Closed his eyes. A last tear broke from the corner of his eye.

"Shit," he said.

"Yeah," agreed Walking Bear. "But...you knew it already. Didn't you?"

McCall tried to hold in a sob, but it snuck past his clenched teeth. The night wind whistled through the branches of the bristlecone tree.

"It..." began McCall, but his voice broke. "It doesn't make any sense."

Walking Bear said, "No."

"If we're dead, then where are we?"

"I don't know."

"Is this heaven?"

"It's not any heaven I heard of," said Walking Bear. "It's not the Quaker heaven and it's not Cheyenne heaven."

"Then what? Are we in Hell?"

"Does it feel like Hell?"

McCall thought about it. "No."

"Then I guess it's not Hell. Half the people we saw weren't killers. Not the women or the children. Why would they go to Hell just because they were murdered?"

"Then if it's not Hell, *what* is it?" growled McCall.

"I don't know," repeated Walking Bear, leaning on each separate syllable.

They stood in the dark, in the wind, in the night.

"I'm going to go," said Walking Bear.

This time McCall said nothing.

"Are you coming?" asked the Cheyenne.

"You don't know what's out there," said McCall softly, nodding toward the east, where everyone and everything else had gone.

"No," agreed Walking Bear. He touched the bullet holes on his chest. "I only know what's here."

With that he gave McCall a single nod, turned, and walked slowly toward the eastern darkness.

Jonah McCall stood there, watching him go. The pistol was a cold, heavy weight in his hand. He raised the gun and held it out. Starlight gleamed along its length. He uncurled his fingers one at a time and then pulled back his thumb. The gun toppled to the ground for the third time.

For the last time.

"I'm sorry," he said. But he didn't say it loud enough for anyone to hear but himself.

He brushed the tear from his cheek, took a long breath, let it out very slowly, and began walking. Maybe he'd catch up with Walking Bear. Maybe not.

He thought about the comet that had burned its way across the sky and wondered if it had been an omen.

Probably. But of what? He didn't know the answer to that question, either. Maybe there would be answers out there in the darkness. Maybe not.

He kept walking.

The night, very gently but very firmly, closed its fist around him.

Saint John

Author's Note

This one is odd, even for me.

The character of Saint John was born in a dream. Not exactly a nightmare, but certainly not a nice dream. It happens like that sometimes. For writers, perhaps, a little more often than the average Joe. I woke up with the entire story already drafted out from end to end, and I couldn't wait to write it down. In one of those weird twists that lend credence to the possibility of precognition, editor Christopher Golden emailed me that morning to ask if I wanted to write a story for his new anthology, *THE MONSTER'S CORNER*. The book would feature stories from the point of view of the monster rather than the monster hunter. I told him about Saint John and, although the character is entirely human, Chris wanted me to send the story to him.

Here's another twist, though. Shortly after that, while I was plotting out the second half of my *ROT & RUIN* quadrilogy of post-apocalyptic young adult novels, I realized that there was more of Saint John's story to tell. Mind you, the story you're about to read is in no way intended for teens even though he later appears as the antagonist in teen novels. Go figure.

SAINT JOHN

--1--

Saint John walked through cinders that fell like slow rain, and he found twenty-seven angels hiding behind the altar of a burning cathedral.

--2--

An hour before that he found a crushed and soiled rose.

He stole a wheelbarrow from a hardware store and filled it with the weapons he had collected since the plague began and wheeled it to the cathedral. Saint John sang songs in his head while he worked. He did not sing them aloud, of course. God had told him years ago to sing all of his songs of praise in the temple inside his head. He left the cart by the curb and walked up the stone stairs. The door was ajar, the lock chopped clumsily out of the wood by an axe.

There was an explosion behind the far row of buildings, and Saint John turned and stood on the top step as golden embers fell. He tilted his head face upward, eyes closed, tongue out, smiling as he waited for a piece of ash to find him. When it did he pulled it in with the tip of his tongue and savored it. The strongest flavor was the uninspired taste of charcoal that had to melt before he could enjoy the other tastes. Ghosts of flavors. There was sweetness there, like meat. A sharpness like ammonia. The tang of acid sourness. He did not know what this ash had been. Something alive, that much was certain, but that could be as true of a tree as of a dog, a pigeon or the postman. He wished that he could discern which, but a learned palette was an acquired thing, its subtle perceptions honed through practice, observation, consideration and repetition. Saint John did not believe that he would have the time to sample and catalog the many flavors and combinations of flavors of this apocalyptic feast. The fires would not last as long as his appetites.

Pity.

There was an explosion off to his left. He cocked his head and replayed the boom in his memory and then listened to the echoes as they banged off the building that surrounded the stone library. He smiled faintly. This *was* something he knew well. The blast was ordinary, not military ordnance. Probably a car gas tank rupturing from superheated gasses as the vehicle burned. Semtex or C4 each had their own unique blast signature, much like the calibers of bullets, weights of loads, and makes of gun. Each possessed a unique voice that whispered its secrets to him.

As if to reaffirm this there was a rattle of automatic gunfire followed by three spaced shots. A military M4 and a Glock nine. Unique in their way, but commonplace since the Fall.

The Fall…

The concept of it was old in his mind. Saint John had expected it, prepared for it, *known* that it was coming ever since that day when he was reborn in the blood that flowed from the thousand cuts on his father's flesh. That's when the Voice began speaking to him in his mind, telling him of the Fall that would come. That was years ago and it was old and sacred knowledge to him. However, to the people around him, the panicked masses dwindling down to a scattered few, the Fall was immediate. It was their All, and in their panic they did not remember the world as it was before. Saint John was sure of that. He could see it in the eyes of everyone he met.

And yet the Fall, in societal terms, was only a few months old. A few weeks, if you start counting from the day when the offices of the CDC in Atlanta were overrun by mobs desperate for vaccines to the pandemic flu. Someone had begun a campaign on the Net saying that the CDC was hording stockpiles of the vaccine and selling it only to the super rich. The story was probably spurious, but the pulse of the nation had quickened to a fever pace. Atlanta had become a rallying point for protests, and the crowds surrounding the Centers for Disease Control had swelled to an ocean of angry, frightened people. Hundreds of thousands of them. Saint John had been among them; not because he believed the nonsense about the horded vaccines, but because the atmosphere of panic brought with it an apocalyptic flavor that he found delicious and uplifting. He was there on that Thursday morning when the temperature of the crowd had reached the boiling point. Like a field of locusts they went from sanity to insanity in the blink of an eye, and the National Guard were crushed under the sheer numbers. Shots were fired — shotguns loaded with beanbag rounds, TASERS, and finally bullets. Blood perfumed the air, but the crowd was in motion now, a mass mind bent on smashing down doors and walls.

In one of the last newscasts Saint John heard before the TVs all went dark, the authorities expressed fears that in an attempt to find the mythical stockpile, the mobs crashed into labs and hot rooms and viral storage vaults, inadvertently releasing many more diseases into the population. Saint John did not know how many viral vaults had been breached, but he suspected that there were seven of them. Seven seals were broken. As the plagues spread, the riot became a constant state of being, and it was then that Saint John revealed himself and walked among the diseased and dying, the murderous and the mauled, his knives in hand, a walker following in the hoof prints of the Horsemen.

He smiled at the thought and stretched out a hand to catch a soft piece of white ash. Then something closed out those sounds and drew Saint John's attention from the burning city back to the steps on which he stood.

A woman came running down the street, weaving and tripping and staggering under the weight of pain. She wore only a green t-shirt and one low-heeled shoe. Her thighs were streaked with blood. She screamed continuously in a red-raw voice. He watched her reel and stumble, but she was beyond the ability to focus her mind and muscles on the task of running. It made her clumsy and slow.

"There she is!" cried a voice. Male, out of sight around the corner. Saint John took a half step back, allowing the shadows of the entry arch to enfold him.

A moment later two men came pelting down the street after the woman, yelling and laughing. Saint John winced at some of the things they said. One man was completely naked, his semi-flaccid cock swinging and bouncing against his thighs with each step. The other, a college jock type in SpongeBob boxers and Timberlands, with distinctive lesions of the AL3 strain of smallpox blossoming on his face.

"Here kitty, kitty..." called the Jock, laughing as his words drew a flinch from the woman. Her screams faded to a choked sob.

She turned toward a parked car and ran for it. Saint John wondered what sanctuary she thought it would afford her. The windows were broken out, the tires long-since slashed. But she stumbled and fell before she got within a dozen paces of it, her knees striking the asphalt hard enough to pull fresh screams from her chest. Her eyes were wild and even though she looked briefly in Saint John's direction, it was clear that she did not see him standing in the shadows. She fell forward onto her palms and tried to crawl toward the car, but the Jock caught up with her and used his body to slam her to the ground. The naked man's cock was stiffening in anticipation as his companion used his knees to spread the woman's legs.

This was clearly the latest act in a play that had started hours ago. Saint John had no doubt. Intervening now could not save her. This woman was broken. If not by the rapes and abuse, then by whatever else she had lost. Whatever else had been torn from her. Family, safety, personal sanctity, perhaps even purity. Gone now, as most things were gone. What did not burn was plundered in the food riots, and what was not plundered rotted as the pathogens swept their way through the dwindling herd of humanity. This woman was a corpse whose ghost was still too shocked to leave its shell. That was sad, he thought, because to linger is to experience — with whatever sense and perception remained — all of the further indignities these monsters needed to inflict so that they could convince themselves that *they* were still alive.

Saint John did not like that. There was no beauty in this setting, and suffering without beauty was disgusting. It was crass and vulgar. Artless.

"You got her?" yelled a gruff voice and a third man emerged from the shadows. He was massive, a construct of anabolic steroids and overdeveloped muscle; he had turned himself into a freak even before time had decided that all of humanity should share in freakism. This one did not run. He swaggered slowly, his thick fingers undoing his belt buckle and zipper with the kind of deliberate calm that was itself a statement. An alpha to this small pack of dogs.

The big man was smiling, lips curled back from rows of white teeth. He came and stood over the woman and it seemed to Saint John that he was so into this moment that he did not blink. He grinned and grinned, and never flinched when bombs went off in the next street. He let his trousers drop and grabbed for his crotch, massaging hardness despite the limitations of steroids and other drugs. Saint John knew this type. If he could not rape he would brutalize, and it was all the same to men of his kind; his actions were completely unconnected to sex. Pain was the pathway to ecstasy for him.

Saint John knew that, and understood it from a height that gave him a much clearer perspective.

The Big Man pushed the smaller naked man out of the way and pawed at the woman, driving more screams from her.

Saint John stepped down. A single step, but it was his first movement, and the three men had not noticed him any more than had the woman.

Saint John took a second slow step, and the kneeling man looked up and snarled.

"Fuck off! This whore is ours."

Ah, and that is how worlds turn. On a word or phrase. Ill chosen and ill timed.

This whore is ours.

This whore.

Whore.

Saint John sighed. Such an unfortunate choice of words. Few words were less welcome to his ears. Not even the tough Aryan Brothers in the cell block had used that word around him — not after his first week in the SuperMax. One of them had, but their surviving members passed warnings down the line, to big stripes and little fish. Even though the word was tattooed on Saint John's own flesh in blue letters on his back, with an arrow pointing down between his shoulder blades to his buttocks. Burned there ages ago by an ex-con friend of his father; the act performed back when Saint John was the child Johnnie. Burned into him with a Bic pen, a lighter and a pin while the boy who was not yet Saint John lay stretched out and bound with duct tape. *Whore*, it said. Branded fast while his father and the ex-con laughed and belched and spat on each letter as they waited for their dicks to get hard.

The ink had not even dried, the burns had not yet stopped singing their white hot song, when his father had shoved the tattoo artist aside to show why he had wanted those words put there. The tattoo artist had gone next. And then the other men. A pig roast, they had called it. Friends of his father. Men who shared the same appetites.

Men like these men.

This whore is ours.

And now these three men who crouched in the ash around the half-naked woman conjured with that word.

Whore.

Saint John took another step.

There had been nine men back then, on the day the word had been fixed with boiling ink into his skin. The boy that he had been had survived it and the next day had fled. When he had come back in the night a month later and looked in through the window he saw the tattoo artist burning those same letters in another child's flesh. A girl, this time. Gender had not mattered to them. They coveted what they could dominate, what they could force.

Her screams made the men laugh.

As this woman's screams made these men laugh.

Whore.

Back then, on the day when he had been marked, it was not the first time he had heard that word. Not nearly the first.

But it was the first time that another voice spoke inside his mind.

The Voice had told him to go into a sacred place inside the mansion of his thoughts. The Voice guided him there, and with each inward step the laughter and grunts of the nine men diminished until they were no more than a faint and unimportant background noise.

The Voice had guided him back to the world later, when his body had been cut loose and thrown into the corner between the fridge and the stove. It was there to tell him what to pack and when to run, and schooled him on how to live after he'd fled. It brought him back to the house on the night the men had strapped the girl down, and it spoke great secrets to him when he begged for answers.

He had done everything exactly as the voice instructed. Saint John later understood that it was the voice of God, and upon that realization he had begun the transformation from Johnnie to the Saint. He was glowing with holy purpose when he returned to his father's farm. There were always gallons of gasoline in the barn, standing in a row beside the post-hole digger, near where a machete hung from its peg. When the Voice of God spoke, the lessons were always simple, always clear. The lessons were about clarity and simplicity.

And about fire. Ahh…fire was such a beautiful doorway.

Saint John took another step down. The cathedral had lovely white granite steps and an archway carved with the austere faces of a hundred saints. Fellow saints, and Saint John wondered if each of them had been given the gift of the Voice. Probably. Why else would they be saints? How else could they be?

The Jock and the Naked Man looked up at Saint John. They looked up from what they were trying to do, shifting their eyes reluctantly from dirty flesh and bitten skin to this annoyance. This intrusion.

Saint John did not move with haste. Haste caused rabbit reactions, quick and defensive. He wanted to see the dog reactions. The jackal reactions. That happened best if he moved slowly, giving each of them the opportunity to make slight perceptual shifts as his personal bubble extruded outward and pushed against the outer edges of their self-confidence. It was very much like subtly shifting to stand too close to a person in a crowd—at first they think you're leaning in to hear better, to catch every drop of conversational juice, but then they notice that you do not lean away when they've finished speaking. That's when the hound that dwells in the middle of their brain raises its head and lifts its ears to tufted points, sniffing and smelling the wind.

First comes speculation as distances are judged and given value; then confusion as those values are ignored. Then defensive caution as the social bubble pops to demonstrate that it never really offered any protection. It was an abstract bubble after all.

Then comes alarm.

He watched for this in their eyes. The Naked Man was less focused, his eyes continually drifting down to what the Big Man was trying to do. He was more erect than the Big Man, and bigger, but he was not the alpha of this pack and he knew that he would have to wait. The Naked Man licked his lips in nervous anticipation.

The Jock was the one who looked up at the stranger descending the steps and briefly smiled. Maybe he thought that this newcomer wanted to join in and he was preparing a stinging rebuke. Maybe it was an uneasy smile. Maybe it was a smile that would include an invitation to be the fourth car in this train.

The Naked Man flicked a glance up, then down at the woman, and back up to Saint John. For a moment there was a fragment of shame in his eyes for what he was doing. Not for the woman or her humanity, but for his own participation in something they all clearly knew was wrong. Anarchy did not yet completely own this man's soul.

Saint John marked that one in his mind. A flicker of remorse in the presence of continued action was not a saving grace. It spoke to understanding, and complicity here was proof of corruption. A man like this would not initiate a rape, but he would always go where a door was opened. There had been men like him on the night that ugly word had been burned onto his skin. One of them had even whispered, "I'm sorry," as he had hunkered over and thrust. Saint John had spent a lot of time with him later on.

The Naked Man looked away. He was a loose-lipped slobbering buffoon. No muscle tone, skin like a mushroom. White and spongy.

It was the Jock who first realized the danger. As Saint John descended another step toward the screaming thing over which the men crouched, the Jock's inner hound finally came to point.

"Hey, jackass," he snarled, "what the hell are you doing? I told you to fuck off."

Saint John smiled. "You must stop this and go your way," he said. "Man's hand was not fashioned by God to lay waste to that which the Lord has made."

The Jock stared for a two-count and then burst out laughing.

"Who the fuck are you supposed to be? Church isn't until Sunday, dumbass."

The Big Man paused to punch the woman in the thigh, angry that he was having so much trouble getting hard enough to penetrate her.

Saint John descended one final step. Now he stood above the tableau. The woman's dirty blond hair cobwebbed the asphalt.

"It *is* Sunday," murmured Saint John, but the reply was lost beneath the woman's screams. Saint John wore white bed sheets as clothes, the material lashed to his limbs and torso with strips of white tape on which he had written crucial passages of scripture. Not from the Bible, but new scripture the Voice had spoken to him. The sheets were tattered now from all that had happened since the city had begun to burn, and the tatters floated on the hot breeze, like streamers of pale seaweed in a sluggish tide.

The Jock was still in dog mind, bolstered by the presence of the pack and the alpha. The others were, too.

Saint John wanted to laugh, to kiss each of them for that ignorance. It was as delightful as it was false. So entertaining.

But he did not laugh. Instead he cast his face into the beatific smile he wore at such moments. Like Leonardo's model, his smile was a tiny curl of the lip that promised secrets but not answers. He spread his hands high and wide. He had long arms and longer fingers tipped with nails that had each been painted a different shade of night gray.

The Jock nudged the Big Man, pack dog alerting the alpha to the possibility of something wrong. When the Big Man looked up, the smaller man bent and tried to kiss the woman. Even to Saint John such a kiss was strange and awkward. Obscene.

The Big Man growled deep in his chest as he saw Saint John standing there with his arms outstretched.

A ripple of explosions troubled the air close by and the three men looked over their shoulders. Even the woman looked.

That amazed Saint John because he could not imagine in what way the destruction implied by those blasts could possibly matter to any of them. How could anything beyond the confines of this moment matter to them? Were these men in particular too stupid to grasp the importance of *now*?

Apparently so.

One by one they turned back to Saint John.

The Jock said, "Fuck off, you little faggot."

"Get your own," said the Naked Man.

The Big Man could not be bothered to pay a moment's further attention to the interruption. It's why he had a pack. Instead he glared down. "Lay still, you bitch."

Saint John caught a flicker of movement and he looked across the street to see a fourth man standing by the corner. He was a shifty, nervous little thing. Clearly a junkie or a drunk suffering through D.T.s. He shifted from foot to foot and grabbed his crotch, but he didn't cross the street. He was either too afraid of the three more aggressive pack members, or he had not yet crossed the line that separated social depravity from personal destruction. The man caught Saint John looking and immediately whipped his hand away from his crotch. He stood there, staring back, mouth open like a silent ghost.

The three men surrounding the woman laughed and told her the things they were going to do, and told her how much she would like it. And the penalties that would be imposed if she did *not* like it.

The predictability of this drama, and the triteness of the dialogue, began to wear on Saint John. He lowered his arms and said, "Let me share with you."

They all laughed, confirming that they were too stupid to understand what was going on.

"Let me share," repeated Saint John as he reached into the folds of his blowing white clothes and brought out his toys. They gleamed in the smoke-stained firelight. They were small and elegant, each polished to such a perfect shine that they seemed to trail sparks as he once more brought his hands out to his sides. A delicate blade extended the reach of each hand as he stood cruciform on the step above them.

The Jock and the Naked Man stared in awakening horror as everything froze into a bubble of time in which they all floated. The woman lay supine, her mouth strained open to cry out for mercy from a God who most of the survivors of the plague believed was either dead or mad. The Big Man knelt between her thighs in a mockery of a supplicant. On either side of him crouched the Naked Man and the Jock, their hands pressing the woman's wrists to the ground as above them an angel spread its glittering wings.

Saint John stepped down onto the pavement and two steps brought him to the curb. The Jock could have reached up to strike him. But he was unable to move. In his mind the pack was gone, transforming him from predator to prey.

"Thy will be done," whispered Saint John, and a sob of joy escaped his throat as his arms folded like wings and the knives flashed a crisscross before him. Rubies of hot blood splattered the steps and his clothes and his face as veins opened to his touch. Before the Big Man could look up again, Saint John swept his arms back and forth, each movement ending in a delicate flick of his artistic wrists.

The Big Man finally looked up as blood slapped him across the face. Saint John appeared not to have moved, his arms held out to his sides. But on either side of him the members of the Big Man's pack sagged to the ground in disjointed piles.

Saint John watched the man's eyes, saw the whole play of drama. The brutal lust and frustration crumbled to reveal shock. Then there was that golden sweet moment when the Big Man looked into the eyes of the cruciform saint and saw the only thing more terrible and powerful than the portrait of himself as post-apocalyptic Alpha that he had hung inside his own mind. Here was the sublime Omega.

"No," the Big Man said. Not a plea, merely a denial. This was not part of his world, not before or after the Fall. He had survived the plague, god damn it; he had fought through the riots and the slaughters. He had become more powerful than death itself and he expected to rule this corner of Hell until the End of Days.

Yet the Omega stood above him, and the pack lay drowning in their own blood. So fast. So fast.

The Big Man tried to fight.

But before he could close his fists he had no eyes. Then no hands. No face.

No breath.

The Big Man's mind held onto the last word he had spoken. *No.*

Then he had no thoughts and the darkness took him.

--3--

Across the street the nervous little junkie was backing away, one hand clamped to his mouth, the other still clutching at his crotch. When he reached the corner he whirled and ran. Saint John did not give chase. If the little junkie and these dead men had friends, and if those friends came here, then there would be more offerings to God. If it happened that the offering included his own life, then so be it. Many saints before him had died in similar ways, and there would be no disgrace in it.

Saint John turned suddenly, aware that he was being watched. He looked up the stairs to the church. The doors stood ajar and the stone faces of saints and angels watched him from around the arch.

But the angel faces? They watched from the open doorway. Cherubim and seraphim, hovering in the darkness. Saint John lifted a hand to them, but they were gone when he blinked.

Saint John wiped blood from his eyes.

Still gone. There were only shadows in the doorway. He nodded. That was okay. It was not the first time something had been there one moment and not the next. It happened to him more and more.

Even so, he let his gaze linger for a moment longer before turning away.

"Angels," he said softly, surprised and pleased. He had only ever dreamed of angels before. Now they were here on Earth, with him. And that was good.

--4--

The woman lay curled in pain, drenched in the blood of the three monsters who had hurt her, her faced locked into a grimace; but the scream that had boiled up from her chest was caged behind clenched teeth.

She stared at Saint John. Not at his knives, because even in her horror she understood that they were merely extensions of the weapon that was this man.

Saint John took a step toward her. Blood dripped from his face onto his chest.

"God," she whispered. "Please...god."

Red splattered onto the cracked asphalt.

The saint knelt, doing it slowly, bending at ankle and knee and waist like a dancer, everything controlled and beautiful. The woman watched with eyes that were haunted by lies and broken promises. If she had possessed the strength, her muscles would have tensed for flight; but instead there was a weary acceptance that she was always going to be an unwilling participant in the ugly dramas of men.

Saint John bent forward and placed the knives on the edge of the curb with the handles toward her. Inches from her outstretched hands. Dead men lay on either side of her, but she watched this, darting quick glances from the bloody steel to Saint John's dark eyes.

He sat back on his heels, letting his weight settle. The movement was demonstrably nonaggressive and he watched her process it.

"What...what do you want?" she asked weakly.

He said nothing.

"Are you going to hurt me, too?"

"Hurt you?"

She jerked her head toward the dead men. "Like them. Like all the others."

"Others?" echoed Saint John softly. "Other men attacked you?"

A cold tear broke from the corner of one eye. She was not a pretty woman. Bruising, battering and blood had transformed her into a sexless lump. The animals who lay around her had wanted her because of some image in their minds, not because she fit their idea of sexual perfection. She was the victim of smash and grab opportunism, and that was as diminishing as being the tool by which men satisfied their need to demonstrate control.

"How many men?" asked Saint John.

"Just today?" she asked and tried to screw a crooked smile into place. Gallows humor.

Embers still fell like gentle stars. Both of them looked up to see burning fragments peel off of the roof of the cathedral. The cathedral itself would be burning soon. Sparks floated down like cherry blossoms on an April morning.

The woman looked down and slowly pulled together the shreds of the t-shirt. There was not enough of it to cover her nakedness, but the attempt was eloquent.

"You won't hurt me, too, mister," she said softly, almost shyly, "will you?"

"No," he said, and he was surprised to find that his mouth was dry.

"Will you…let me go with you?" It was an absurd question, but he understood why she asked it.

He shook his head. "I'm not a good companion."

"You helped me."

Helped, she had said. Not *saved.* The difference was a thorn in his heart, and he hated that he had allowed himself to care.

He said nothing, however. It would be impossible to explain.

The woman crawled away from the dead men and huddled behind a corner of the car. "What's your name?"

"What's yours?" he countered. He prayed that it would not be something symbolic. Not Eve or Mary or—

"Rose," she said. "My name's Rose."

"Just Rose?"

She shrugged. "Last names really matter anymore?" She coughed and spat some blood onto the street.

"Rose," he said, and nodded. Rose was a good name. Simple and safe. Without obligations.

"What's yours?"

She asked it as he rose to stand in a hot breeze. The sheets he had wrapped around his body flapped in the wind.

"Does that matter?" he asked with a smile.

"You saved my life."

"I ended theirs. There's a difference."

"Not to me. You saved my life. They'd have raped me again and made me do stuff, and then they would have killed me. The big one? He'd have killed me for sure. I saw him stomp another waitress to death 'cause she didn't want to give him a blow job. She kept screaming, kept crying out for her mother."

"Her mother didn't come?"

Rose shook her head. "Her mom's back in Detroit. Probably dead, too. No... Big Jack got tired of Donna fighting back and just started kicking her. It didn't make no sense. He'd have worn her down eventually. They had us for almost a week, so I know."

Saint John closed his eyes for a moment. *A week.*

Rose said, "I've seen what happened with other women. There's only so long you can fight before you'll do whatever they want." She wiped a tear from her eye. "Donna was just nineteen, you know? Her boyfriend was in Afghanistan when the lights went out. He's probably dead. Everybody's dead."

"You said everybody gives in. You kept running. Kept fighting."

Rose looked away. "I got nothing left. These pricks...this was all I had. They won."

"No," he said softly. "You have life."

She cocked an eye at him. "'Cause of you."

Saint John wanted to turn, to look up and see if the angels were still watching from the shadowy doorway, but he did not. Angels were shy creatures at the best of times, and he did not want to frighten them off. If "frighten" was a word that could be used here. He wasn't sure and would have to ponder it later.

When he noticed the woman studying him, he asked, "Would you have given in? Stopped fighting them, I mean?"

"Probably. If I did they would have treated me better. Given me food. Maybe let me wash up once in a while."

"Would that have been a life?"

Rose looked up at the embers and then slowly shook her head. "Don't listen to me, mister. They gave me some pills to make me more attractive. No—that wasn't the word. What is it when you cooperate?"

"'Tractable'?"

"Yeah."

"They gave you pills?"

"Yeah. I can feel them kicking in now. OxyContin, I think. All the edges are getting a little fuzzy."

Saint John gestured to the knives. "Do you want these?"

She looked at the bloody blades. Embers like hot gold fell sizzling into the lake of blood that surrounded the three dead men.

Rose shook her head.

"Are you sure?" he asked.

A nod.

"These men," he said gently, "there will be others like them. As bad or worse. There are packs of them running like dogs."

"I know."

"Then take the blades."

"No."

"Take one."

"No."

They sat and regarded the things that comprised and defined their relationship. The embers and the smoke. The blood and the blades. The living and the dead.

"Not everyone's gone bad," she said.

"No?"

She managed a dirty smile. One tooth was freshly chipped and blood was caked around her nostrils.

"There are guys like you out here."

"No," he whispered. "There is no one like me out here."

They watched the embers fall.

After a while, she said, "You came and saved me."

"It was someone else's moment to die," he said, but she did not understand what that meant.

"You saved me," she insisted and her voice had begun to take on a slurred, dreamy quality. The drugs, he realized. "You're an angel. A saint."

He said nothing.

"I prayed and God sent you."

Saint John recoiled from her words. He felt strangely exposed as if it was he and not this woman who was naked.

Then he felt the eyes on him again. Saints and angels from the doorway.

He stood. "Wait here for a few seconds."

"Where are you going?" she asked with a fuzzy voice.

"Just around the corner. I'll be right back, and in the meantime the angels watch over you."

"Angels?"

"Many of them."

Her eyes drifted closed. "Angels. That's nice."

Saint John hurried to the corner and around it to a side street filled with looted shops. He did not linger to shop carefully; instead he took the first clothes he could find. A black track suit made from some shiny synthetic material, with double red racing stripes and a logo from a company that no longer existed. There were no sneakers left, but he found rubber aqua shoes of the kind snorkelers and surfers used. No underwear, no medicine. The last item he selected was a golf club. A seven iron. He smiled, pleased. Seven was God's number.

With the clothes folded under one arm and the seven iron over his shoulder, Saint John left the store, stepping over the rotting bodies of two looters who had been shot in the head. It was impossible to say whether they had been killed by the police or other looters, and even if that information was known, Saint John doubted that there was anyone still alive who cared. Certainly he did not.

He rounded the corner and stopped.

The woman—Rose, he reminded himself. Her name was Rose—was gone.

Saint John set the clothes and the golf club down and ran the rest of the way, the streamers of his bed-sheet clothes flapping behind him. The three dead men were there. His wheelbarrow of weapons was there. She was not.

Saint John looked for her for almost half an hour, but he could not find her.

As he walked back to the cathedral he found that he was sad. Saint John was rarely sad, and almost never sad in relation to a person. Yet, dusty and crumpled as she was, Rose had touched him. She had been honest with him, of that he was certain.

Now she was gone. He wished her well, and when he realized that he did, he paused and smiled bemusedly at the falling embers. It was such an odd thought for him. Alien, but not unwelcome.

"Rose," he said aloud.

--5--

Saint John gathered up the weapons—knives, a club made from a length of black pipe, a wrench caked with blood—and carried them up the stairs to the church. There were guns in the wheelbarrow, and even a samurai sword that the former owner had not known how to properly use. Saint John had obliged him with a demonstration. The wheelbarrow was heavy with them; it had been a fruitful week. He carried them, an armload at a time, into the church, counting out his ritual prayers with each slow step. He wanted to get everything right, however there was no need for haste. This was the end of the world, after all. To whom would haste matter? Inattention to details, however, could have a profound effect. Saints and angels were watching.

With his first armload hugged to his chest, he stood on the top step. The faces of the saints regarded him, and shadows cast by flickering flames played across their mouths so that it seemed as if they spoke, whispering secrets. Some of them Saint John understood, some were still mysteries to him.

He did not see the faces of the angels, however. The open doorway was a dark mouth, but it was filled with empty shadows, and so he entered with his armload of weapons. He paused in the narthex and looked down the long aisle that ran from the west doorway behind him all the way to the altar at the eastern wall.

The cathedral was vast, with vaulted ceilings that rose high into the darkness. The arches were revealed only by stray slices of firelight through the broken stained glass windows, and in this light the lines of stone looked like bones. Saint John walked to the center aisle and stopped by the last row of pews, bowed reverently, and then walked without haste through the vast nave toward the altar table.

"I bring gifts," he said. His voice was soft but the acoustics of the cathedral peeled that cover away to reveal the power within, sending the three words booming to the ceiling.

As he walked to the altar the weapons clanked musically, like the tinkle of Christmas bells. He stopped at the edge of the broad carved silver altar table and laid his offering in the center. Then, taking great care, he arranged the blades and hammers and brass knuckles in a wide arc, the blades pointed toward the rear wall, pointing to the base of the giant crucifix that hung there. Jesus, bleeding and triumphant, hung from nails. Saint John knew the secret story of this man. Jesus had not died to wash away the sins of monsters like Saint John's father. No, he had allowed his body to be scourged and pierced as part of the ritual of purification, then he had ascended through the pain into godhood. He marveled that so many people over so many years had missed the whole point of that story.

Once the knives were arranged—seventeen in this armload— and the rest of the weapons, Saint John bowed and headed outside for more.

It was on his second trip into the church that he noticed the foot prints on the sidewalk. Small feet. A woman. Rose? Surely hers, but there were other prints; much smaller and many of them. They were pressed into the thin film of fine ash that had begun to settle over everything. Delicate steps.

Angel feet?

Saint John stood for a moment, his arms filled with bloodstained weapons, contemplating the footprints. Then he went inside.

However he paused once more as he approached the altar table.

On his previous trip he had placed seventeen knives on this very table, arranged by size and type, from a machete to hunting knives and steak knives to a lovely little skinning knife with which he had whiled away an evening last week. However there were not seventeen knives now.

Now there were two. Only the long machete and an unwieldy Ghurka knife remained. The brass knuckles and clubs and guns were still there. Fifteen knives, though, were gone.

Saint John considered this as he laid his second armload down on the altar. He did not for a moment believe that he had only imagined bringing in those knives. Many material things in his perception were of dubious reality, but never blades. They were anchors in his world, not fantasies. The flying saucers he sometimes saw…those, he knew, were fantasies. Knives? Impossible.

Nor did he believe that someone—perhaps the little junkie— had snuck in here and stolen the knives.

He was considering possibilities and probabilities when he heard a soft sound. Barely a sound at all. More of a suggestion, like the sound shadows make when they fall to the ground as the moon dances across the sky. Soft like that.

He cocked his head to listen. The cathedral was empty and still.

Were demons moving silently between the pews? Had demons come to take his knives?

Saint John was suddenly very afraid.

Could demons materialize enough to be able to lift a piece of metal? Before this moment he would have been certain of the answer to that question, but now he wasn't so sure. The knives were gone.

Had the demons made the footprints in the ash? Were the demons here in the church, maybe preparing to hunt him with his own knives? Had the Fall of man made the demons bolder? Had it given them more power? Had it, in fact, kicked open the door between Hell and Earth?

These were terrifying thoughts, and Saint John whirled, drawing two knives from sheaths concealed beneath the white rags that covered his thighs.

"This is the house of God!" he yelled into the dusty shadows. "You may not be here!"

He heard the soft sounds again. Louder this time, and more of them. A scuffle of invisible feet moving in the shadows behind the screen that separated the altar from the choir's chancel. The sounds were stealthy, of that Saint John was certain.

The fact of their stealthy nature injected a dose of calm into his veins. Stealth was a quality of caution, of fear. Predators are stealthy for fear of chasing off the prey they need to sustain their lives. Prey is stealthy to avoid being attacked. For both, fear was the key.

Fear, even in a terrible predator, revealed the presence of weakness. Of vulnerability. An invulnerable demon would not fear anything.

You are a saint, whispered the Voice inside his mind.

A saint. He nodded to himself. A saint in a church.

Saint John felt the fear in his heart recede. Not completely, but enough for strength to flood into his hands from the knives he held; and from his hands to his arms and the muscles in his chest, and to the furnace of his heart.

He could feel his mouth twist in contempt. He raised his arms to his sides, the blades appearing to spark with fire as they caught stray bits of light from the fires burning beyond the broken stained glass windows.

"I am Saint John of the Ashes," he cried in his booming voice. "*Exorcizo te, immundissime spiritus...in nomine Domini nostri Jesu Christi!*"

A figure stepped out from behind the screen. He was dressed in filthy rags and held one of Saint John's gleaming knives in his fist.

"Go away!" said the figure.

Saint John had begun to smile, but his smile faltered and then fell from his lips.

If this was a demon, then it was a demon wearing the disguise of a cherub. The fist that was wrapped around the knife was barely large enough to encircle the handle. Its face was round-cheeked but hollow-eyed, dusted with dirt and soot, dried snot around the nostrils, tear tracks in the grime. And upon the shoulder of the t-shirt he wore was a single bloody handprint. A child's handprint.

The cherub pointed the knife at Saint John.

"Go away!" he said again. His voice was small and high, but there was so much raw power in it that Saint John was almost inclined to take a step backward. But he did not.

He asked, "Who are you to tell me to leave my father's house?"

The cherub's eyes were blue and filled with a fascinating complexity of emotions. His body trembled, perhaps with hunger or with sickness from one of the plagues; or fear. Or, Saint John considered, with rage barely contained.

This was surely no demon. He held a sanctified blade in a way that showed he understood its nature and purpose; and yet he appeared in the face and form of a child of perhaps eight. Or…seven?

That would be exciting.

That would be wonderful, perhaps miraculous; and Saint John was now convinced that he was in the presence of the miraculous. Or on its precipice.

Saint John took a step forward. The cherub—or child, if it was only that—held his ground, but he raised his knife a few inches higher, pointing at Saint John's face and giving it a meaningful shake. He held the knife well. Not perfectly, but with instinct.

"I'm not messing," said the cherub. "Go away."

Saint John was close enough to kill this child. He had the reach and the knives; but he merely smiled.

"Why should I leave?"

"This is *our* house."

Ah. *Our.* A slip.

Saint John thought of the scuffle of footprints in the ash. And of fifteen missing knives.

"This is my father's house," Saint John said. "This is the house of God."

"You don't live here," insisted the boy.

"I do."

In truth Saint John had never been inside this particular church before, but that didn't matter. A church was a church was a church, and he was a saint after all.

"Who's there?" said another voice. A woman's voice. Vague and dreamy and slurry. Saint John smiled.

"Rose—?"

There was a stirring behind the screen and the hushed whispering of many voices. More than a dozen, perhaps many more. Male and female, and all tiny except for Rose. Shadows moved behind the screen and then Rose stepped out. She wore a choir robe that was clean and lovely in tones of purple and gold; but her face was still dirty and bloody and puffed.

"You're real?" she asked as she stared at Saint John. "I thought I dreamed you."

"Perhaps you have," said Saint John, and he wondered for a moment if he, too, was dreaming; or if he was a character in this woman's dream. "I am sometimes only a dream."

Her face flickered with confusion. The drugs the men had given her held sway over her, however she kept coming back to focus. Saint John knew and recognized that as the habit of someone who was often under the influence and practiced at functioning through it.

"Are these your kids?"

As she asked that, more of the cherubs came out from behind the screen. Many of them carried knives. *His* knives. The cherubs were tiny, the youngest in diapers, the oldest the same age as the blue-eyed boy who still pointed his knife at Saint John's face.

Saint John counted them. Twenty-six. The firelight from outside threw their shadows against the wall, and their shadows were much larger. Did the shadows have wings? Saint John could not be sure.

"Go away!" growled the lead boy. "Or I'll hurt you."

"Hey," slurred Rose, "be nice!"

"He's one of *them!*"

Rose's eyes cleared for a moment. She studied Saint John and his knives, then she shook her head. "No, kid...*he* isn't. He's the one who saved me. I prayed to God and He sent him to save me."

The lead boy's eyes faltered and he flicked a glance at Rose. In that moment of inattention Saint John could have cut the child's throat or cut the tendons of the hand holding the knife. He could have dropped one of his own knives and used his hand to pluck the knife from the boy.

He did none of those things.

Instead he waited, letting the boy figure it out and come to a decision. Allow the boy his strength. The boy refocused on Saint John and his eyes hardened. "Where'd they take Tommy?"

"I don't know who Tommy is."

"You took him. Where'd you take him?"

The other children buzzed when Tommy's name was mentioned, and now their eyes focused on Saint John. He saw tiny fists tighten around knife handles, and the sight filled him with great love for these children. Such beautiful rage. They were ready to use those knives. How strange and wonderful that was. How rare.

How like him; like the boy he had been when *whore* was burned onto his back and he had first listened to the Voice and heard the song of the blade.

"I do not know anyone named Tommy," he said. "I have never seen any of you before, except Rose, and I met her only a few minutes ago."

"Bull!" the lead boy snapped.

"Shhh," said Saint John. He took a half step forward, almost within the child's striking range. "Listen to me."

The boy's eyes drifted down and Saint John could see that he was assessing the new distance between them. So bright a child. When his eyes came back up the truth was there. He knew that he was in range of Saint John's blades and overmatched by his reach. Even so, he did not lower his knife—and it was *his* now. He had claimed it by right of justice, and Saint John was fine with that.

So, Saint John lowered his own knives. He slid them one at a time into their thigh sheaths and stood apparently unarmed and vulnerable in front of this cherub. He saw the child's eyes sharpen as he realized the implication of this, the threat unspoken behind the sham of vulnerability. Most adults would never see that. Only someone graced by the Sight could see that.

The boy hears the Voice, thought Saint John.

"Tell me who you are," he said, "and tell me what happened to Tommy."

--6--

The lead boy told the story.

They were orphans. They lived with four hundred other children at St. Mary's Home for Children.

Mary. Ah. That name stabbed Saint John through the heart. *Her* name. His mother. Long gone. First victim of his father. She had tried to protect her son from the devil in their home. She had survived a hundred beatings, but not the hundred and first. A blood clot. Mary.

Mother of the savior.

Saint John already knew where this was going. He wasn't sure he liked it, though.

The boy said that a line of buses set out from St. Mary's two weeks ago, heading for a government shelter here in the city. There was a riot, fires. Gunshots. The driver was killed. The nuns were dragged off the bus. The boy did not possess the vocabulary or the years to understand or express what had happened to the nuns. He said that men did "bathroom stuff" to them. His eyes faltered and shifted away, but it was enough of an explanation for Saint John. He had been raped for the first time when he was younger than this boy. He knew every euphemism for it that existed in human language, and some spoken only in the language of the damned.

While the men were fighting with the nuns, this boy opened the back door of the bus and made the rest of the kids run. There had been forty-four of them on his bus. Last night there were only twenty-seven. Tommy had been playing on the steps of the church this morning, and men had come to take him away.

They heard him screaming all the way down the block and around the corner.

"Describe the men who took him," said Saint John. The boy did. Most of them were strangers. Two of the men fit the descriptions of the Jock and the Big Man.

Rose was fighting to stay awake, but when she heard those descriptions she jerked erect. "That's the same assholes who—"

Saint John nodded. "Tell me where they kept you, sweet Rose."

"Why?" she demanded. "The kid's gone."

"No!" yelled the lead boy. Others did, too. A few of the younger ones began to cry. "I'm gonna get him back!"

Saint John shook his head. "No," he said. "You won't. You'll stay here and guard your flock."

The boy glared at him. There was real fire in the boy's eyes; Saint John could feel the heat on his skin. It pleased him. It was like being a stranger in a strange land and unexpectedly meeting someone from your own small and very distant town. He had not expected to see that blaze here at the curtain call of the human experience.

"Tell me your name," asked the saint.

"Peter."

Saint John closed his eyes and sighed. He smiled and nodded to himself. When he opened his eyes Peter was still glaring at him.

"I am going to find Tommy," said Saint John, "and bring him back here."

Rose snaked a hand out and grabbed his wrist. "Christ, are you nuts? They'll fucking slaughter you. There are like ten or twelve of those assholes over there."

Saint John said nothing and his smile did not waiver.

Rose finally told him where the gang lived and where they "played." Saint John nodded. To Peter he said, "Stay here. Stay silent. Stay hidden."

"You can't tell me what to do."

"No. I can only tell you how to stay alive."

Peter scowled. "You're gonna get killed. You're gonna leave us like the nuns did and the driver did."

Saint John could feel the weight of the knives hidden in his clothes. He said, "Doubt me now, Peter. Believe me when I return."

And he left.

--7--

There were sixteen men at the hotel that had been converted into a lair for rabid dogs. Sixteen men on three floors.

Saint John drew his knives and went in among them.

Sixteen men were not enough.

The skinny junkie was one of them. He was on the third floor, sleeping in a bed with a woman who was handcuffed to the metal bed frame. Her skin was covered with cigarette burns. Saint John revealed great secrets to the little junkie. And to the others. For some of them it was very fast—a blur of silver and then red surprise. For a few it was a fight, and there were two who Saint John might have admired under other circumstances. But not here and not now.

Saint John painted the walls with them. He opened doorways for them and sent them through into new experiences. He took the longest with the two men who were in the room with Tommy. They were the last ones he found. So sad for them that circumstance gave Saint John time to share so many of his secrets. The boy was unconscious throughout, and that was good; though Saint John wished that Peter could have been here to serve as witness. That child, of all of them, would probably understand and appreciate the purity of it all.

Saint John left the adult captives with keys and weapons and an open door. He set a fire in the flesh of the dead men and on the beds where the women and this body had been. As he walked away the building ignited into a towering mass of yellow flames.

Saint John carried Tommy in his arms. Halfway to the church the child's eyes opened. He beat at the saint with feeble fists.

"N—no..." the boy whimpered.

"No," agreed Saint John. "And never again."

The boy realized that he was wrapped in a clean blanket and when he looked into Saint John's eyes he began to cry. He tried to speak but could manage no further words. In truth there was no lexicon of such experiences that was fit for human tongues. Saint John knew that from those days with his own father and those vile, grunting men. The look the saint shared with the boy was eloquent enough.

Saint John bent and whispered to him. "It was a dream, Tommy, but that dream is over. Peter and your other friends are waiting."

When he reached the square where the cathedral sat, Saint John saw that the fire on the roof had failed to take hold. The tiles smoldered but the church would not burn. Not tonight.

The fire of the burning hotel lit the night, and as he walked, Saint John could see the other cherubs—the angels—and the dusty Rose standing in the doorway of the church, surrounded by the arch of carved saints, and every face was turned toward him.

Peter broke from the others and ran down the steps and across the street. He was crying but he still held his knife, and he held it well. With power and love. Saint John approved of both.

Rose came, too; wobbling and unsteady, but with passion. Her face glowed with a strange light and she reached out to take Tommy from Saint John. Her brow was wrinkled with confusion.

"Why?" she demanded.

There was no way to explain it to her. Not now. She would understand in time, or she would not.

Rose turned, shaking her head, and carried Tommy toward the church as the other angels flocked around her.

It left Saint John and Peter standing in the middle of the street. They watched the others until they vanished into the shadows, then turned and watched the glow of fire in the sky. Finally they turned to face each other. Peter slowly held out the knife, handle first, toward Saint John.

Saint John was covered with blood from head to toes. He had a few bruises and cuts on his face and hands. He sank down into a squat and studied the boy.

"No," he said, pushing the offered knife back. "It looks good in your hand."

The boy nodded. "You didn't answer the lady," he said. "She asked you why you went and got Tommy."

"No," Saint John agreed. "Do you need me to explain it to you?"

Peter looked down at the knife and at the blood on Saint John's face, and then met his eyes. The moment stretched around them as embers fell from the sky. In the distance there were screams and the rattle of automatic gunfire.

"No," said Peter. Saint John knew that this boy might even have tried to get Tommy back himself. He would have died, of course, and they both knew it. Peter was still too young. But he would have tried very well, in ways the men in that building would not have expected. The boy would not have died alone.

Saint John nodded his unspoken approval.

They smiled at each other. Together they crossed the street and mounted the stairs and stood on the top step, watching the city die. There were fires in a dozen places.

"It's pretty," said Peter.

"It's beautiful," said Saint John.

The boy considered. He nodded.

The golden embers floated down around them.

She's Got a Ticket to Ride

Author's Note

I've had a lot of experience with people who have been part of cults, and I've had nearly as much experience with the people who 'rescue' cultists and try to bring them home. There's often a gray area between right and wrong here. A lot of it comes down to worldview and the right to choose.

This story touches on that world, but the larger story deals with the move toward apocalyptic thinking that has been growing in America —even before the 2012 hysteria.

SHE'S GOT A TICKET TO RIDE

--1--

Kids, you know?

Tough to raise a kid in almost any household. Tough to raise a kid with all the shit going on in the world.

You can't lie to them and say it's all going to be okay, because pretty much it's not all going to be okay. There's stuff that's never going to be okay. Neither well-intentioned rationalization, protective lies, or outright bullshit is going to make it all right.

Bad stuff happens to good people. That's one of those immutable laws, like saying "everybody dies." They do. Some things are going to happen no matter how much we don't want them to. Even despite a lot of serious effort to prevent them from happening.

Rape happens.

Murder happens.

Abuse happens.

Go bigger: Wars happen. Poverty happens. Famine happens. Take it from an arbitrary perspective: Tsunamis happen. Earthquakes and tornados happen.

Shit happens.

And it happens, a lot of the damn time, to good people. To the innocent. To the unprotected. To the undeserving.

Try to tell a kid otherwise and they know you're lying. Lie too much about it and they stop believing anything you tell them. They stop believing you. They stop believing *in* you, which is worse. They stop believing in themselves, which is worst of all. I see what happens when parents cross that line. When they call me in, the kid has crossed some lines of his own. We're not talking about "acting out." It's not selling dope to earn fun money or selling yourself as the fun guy. It's not fucking everyone who comes within grabbing distance as a way of making a statement. It's not getting a tattoo or fifteen piercings or going Goth.

We're talking a different set of lines.

When they call me in, the kids have crossed a line that maybe they can't cross the other way. Either they're so lost they can't find it, or they're so lost they don't think there ever *was* a line. All they can see is the narrow piece of ground on which they're standing in that moment. Everything else is chaos. They don't want to move because who would step off of solid ground into chaos? So they stay there.

That's when they call me in.

Sometimes that narrow strip of ground is called a "crack house," and they're giving five-dollar blow jobs so they can buy some rock.

Sometimes it's some little group of nutbags who want to build bombs and blow shit up.

And sometimes it's a cult.

A lot of what I do is with kids in cults. They go in. I go in and get them out.

When I can.

If I can.

Sometimes I bring back something that spits poison and is going to need to be in a safe place with meds and nurses and lots of close observation. Sometimes I bring back someone who will always be on some version of suicide watch. Sometimes I bring back a kid who is never—*ever*—going to be "right" again, because they were never right to begin with. Or kids who have traveled so far into alien territory that they don't even know what language you're speaking.

They spook the shit out of me, the kids who are so lost they're empty. Like their bodies are vacant houses haunted by shadows of who they used to be, who people *thought* they were.

That's sad. That's why a lot of guys who do what I do drink like motherfuckers. A *lot* of us.

Sometimes you get lucky and you find a kid who's maybe thinking that they crossed the wrong line. A kid who wants to be found, who wants to be rescued. A kid who is maybe drifting on a time of expectations because they hope, way down deep, that Mommy or Daddy gives enough of a genuine shit to come looking. Or at least to *send* someone looking.

Those are great. Do a couple like that in a year and maybe you dial down the sauce. Go a couple of years without one of those jobs and maybe you retire to sell TVs at Best Buy or you eat your gun.

I've had enough bad years that I've considered both options.

And then there are those cases where you find a kid who isn't lost on the other side of that line. I'm talking about a runaway who found what he or she has been looking for. Even if it's a cult. Even if it's a group whose nature or goals or tenets you object to with every fiber of your being. When you find a kid who ran away and found himself…what the fuck are you supposed to do then?

It's a question that's always lurking there in the back of your mind, but it's one you seldom truly have to ask yourself.

It wasn't even whispering to me when I went over the wall at the Church of the Nomad World.

--2--

My target was an eighteen year old girl.

Birth certificate has her name as Annabeth Fiona Van Der Kamp, of the Orange County Van Der Kamps. Only heir to a real estate fortune. My intel on her gives her name as Sister Light.

Yeah, I know.

Anyway, Sister Light was a few days away from her nineteenth birthday, at which point the first chunk of her inheritance would shift from a trust to her control. It was feared—and not unreasonably so—that the girl would sign away that money to the Church of the Nomad World.

That chunk was just shy of three-point-eight million.

She'd get another chunk the same size at twenty. At twenty-one, little Sister Light would get the remainder out of trust. Thirty-four million in liquid cash and prime waterfront properties, including two in Malibu.

Mommy and Daddy's lawyers hired me to make sure none of that happened.

I would like to think that they also had their daughter's emotional, physical and—dare I say it with a straight face?—spiritual wellbeing in mind.

Nope, can't really keep a straight face on that one.

But, fuck it. It's a cult, so maybe the Van Der Kamps are the lesser of two evils. I'm not paid to judge.

So over the wall I go.

--3--

The Church of the Nomad World is located on the walled grounds of an estate. The estate was sold at auction after the previous owners went to jail for selling lots and lots of cocaine. The church officials, according to my background checks, were very businesslike during the purchase and all through the legal stages. They wore suits. They spoke like ordinary folks. Their CFO wore a Rolex and drove a Beamer.

It wasn't until after the title and licenses were squared away, the walls and gates repaired, and the 501(c)(3) papers were in place that the church changed its name. Until that point it was the Church of the World, which sounds like every other vanilla flavored post-Tea Party fundamentalist group. Not that they put a sign up. They *became* the Church of the Nomad World in name only. That label appears on no forms, no licenses, no tax documents.

Everybody knows about it, though.

At least everyone who follows this sort of thing.

As I wandered the grounds, I saw signs of the things they taught in this church. Lots of sculptures of the solar system. The current thinking is that we have eight planets—Pluto having been demoted—and then there are five dwarf planets: Ceres, Haumea, Makemake, Eris, and our old friend Pluto. Plus four hundred and twenty-odd moons of various sizes, plus a shitload of asteroids. Millions of them. I noticed that many of the more elaborate sculptures included Phaëton, the hypothetical planet whose long-ago destruction may account for the asteroid belt between Mars and Jupiter. Those same sculptures had a second moon orbiting the Earth: Lilith, a dark moon that was supposed to be invisible to the naked eye. So, whoever made the sculpture naturally painted it black.

Had to get the details right.

One sculpture of Earth not only had Phaëton, but Petit's moon, the tiny Waltemath's moons, and some other apocryphal celestial bodies I couldn't name.

However here on the grounds, there is an additional globe in all of the solar system sculptures and mobiles. It's big—roughly four times the size of any representation of the Earth. It's brown. And it has a name.

Nibiru.

For a lot of conspiracy nuts, Nibiru is the Big Bad. They variously describe it as a rogue planet, a rogue moon, a brown dwarf star, a counter-Earth, blah blah blah. They say it's been hiding behind the sun, hence the reason we haven't seen it. They say that it has an elliptical orbit that—just by chance—swings it at angles that don't allow any of our telescopes to see it.

But they say it's coming.

And, of course, that it will destroy us.

End of Days shit.

Bunch of Doomsday preppers are building bunkers in the Virginia hills so they can survive the impact.

Take a moment on that.

Worst case scenario is a brown dwarf star—best case scenario is a rogue moon. Hitting the Earth. And they think reinforced concrete walls and a couple of cases of Spam are going to see them through it?

Their websites talk about the Extinction Event, but they're building bunkers and stockpiling ammunition so they can Mad Max their way through...what, exactly? Even if they didn't die during a collision, that would likely crack the planet and send a trillion cubing tons of ash and dust into the atmosphere. Even if they didn't immediately choke to death or freeze during the ensuing ice age. Even if the atmosphere wasn't ripped away and the tectonic plates knocked all to hell and gone. Even if they lived through a computationally impossible event, what exactly would they be surviving for?

That's the question.

It's also the question the Church of the Nomad World claimed to have an answer for. For them, the arrival of Nibiru was, without doubt, a game-ending injury for old Mother Earth. No going to the sidelines for stretches and an ice pack and then back in for the next quarter. Nibiru was the ultimate deal closer for the planet. Everyone and everything dies. All gone. Kaput. Sorry folks, it's been fun.

But here's the fun part: Nibiru isn't going to be destroyed in the same collision. Nibiru is going to survive. It's barely going to be dented. And the vast, ancient, high-minded and noble society of enlightened beings on Nibiru are going to reach out with "sensitivity machines"—I'm not making this up—and harvest those people who are of pure intent and aligned with the celestial godforce.

Don't look at any of that too closely or you'll sprain something.

I got all this from two of my sources. I did my homework before coming here. One source is Lee Kang, a doctor of theology at Duke Divinity School. You've probably seen him on TV. Did that book couple of years back about how science and religion don't need to stand around kicking each other in the dicks. About how a rational mind can have both flavors. He was hilarious on *The Daily Show*. Killed it on *Jimmy Fallon*.

The other source is my science girl, Rose Blum. Rosie the Rocketeer. An actual rocket scientist. Well, her business card says "Observational Physicist," which is too much of a mouthful. Smartest carbon-based life-form I have ever gotten hammered with. There are some nights I can barely recall knocking back Irish car bombs in a dive bar near the Jet Propulsion Lab in La Cañada Flintridge near L.A. Her job is looking at the solar system using radio astronomy, infrared astronomy, optical astronomy, ultraviolet, X-ray, and gamma ray astronomy and every other kind of astronomy there is. She also works closely with some of the world's top theoretical astrophysicists. Believe me, if there was something coming toward Earth that was big enough to destroy the planet, she'd know.

She would absolutely know.

I'd had some long talks with her when I first started looking for Sister Light. Rosie was always a high-strung woman. Prone to nervous laughs, mostly at the wrong times. She was also one of the few hardcore scientists I'd met who hadn't lost her faith. She went to synagogue every week and took frequent trips to Israel.

The last time I spoke with her was ten days ago. I'd wanted to bone up on the Nibiru stuff so I would have the ammunition to counter whatever programming they'd force-fed to the girl. Rosie was in a hotel room in Toronto, about to begin a big three-day international symposium on NEOs (near-Earth objects). Nibiru was on the agenda because NASA and other groups wanted to have a clear and cohesive rebuttal to the growing number of crackpot conspiracy theories. Now that the Mayan calendar thing was well behind us, the apocalypse junkies had really gotten behind the imaginary, invisible, rogue dwarf star.

Can you imagine what those conversations must be like? All those scientists, with all that scientific data, trying to combat something with zero supporting evidence — and having a hard time doing it. Emails and phone calls were choking NASA's Spaceguard program, Near-Earth Asteroid Tracking, Lowell Observatory Near-Earth-Object Search, Catalina Sky Survey, Campo Imperatore Near-Earth Object Survey, the Japanese Spaceguard Association, and Asiago-DLR Asteroid Survey, the Minor Planet Center, and other organizations whose job it was to look for things in space that could endanger the Earth.

And some pinhead from Fox News even snuck in a question about it at a White House press conference, which made it blow up even bigger.

Rosie must have been feeling it, too. She was even more jumpy than usual when we spoke on the phone.

"How's it going over there?" I asked.

"It's complicated."

"I bet."

"There are protestors outside the convention center. Hundreds of them, from all over."

"Seriously? Why? What are they protesting?"

"They…um…think we're here to decide on how best to hide the truth from the world."

I laughed. "Ri-i-i-i-ight. That's why they brought the top astrophysicists from around the world together. That's why they advertised the conference. That's why they're doing it all in plain sight, because you're all trying to hide something."

"This is serious, John. The crowds are really scary. We have a lot of security, and they don't want us to leave the convention center without an escort. They even have police patrolling our hotels."

"That's nuts. What do they think is going to happen?"

"I don't know. We have a conference in a few minutes. Someone from Homeland is coming in to talk to us about it."

"Homeland? Why them? Most of the apocalypse cults aren't dangerous. At least not in that way. I mean, sure the Heaven's Gate people killed themselves, but that was mass suicide, not terrorism. They weren't looking to hurt anyone else."

"I don't know, John. I'll call you in a couple of days. When I get back to California."

"Okay."

"But…with that girl you're looking for…?"

"Yeah?"

"Be gentle with her. She's eighteen. She waited until she was of legal age before she joined that church."

"I know, but—"

"Maybe she really believes in this."

"If she does, that's an arguable case for irrational behavior."

Rosie took a few seconds with that. "Every religion looks irrational from the outside. It all looks crazy, from a distance. If you're not a believer. We Jews believe in plagues of locusts, giant bodies of water parting, burning, people being turned into pillars of salt. You Christians worship someone who cast out demons and raised the dead. Why should we be allowed to believe in that stuff and this girl not be allowed to believe in something like Nibiru?"

"Hey, you're the one who told me that the laws of physics and gravitational dynamics can't support the presence of a celestial body that big without us seeing its effect on pretty much everything. You went on and on about that, sweetie. You're the rational got-to-measure-it-to-believe-it science nerd. I'm just a hired thug."

She usually laughed at stuff like that. She didn't this time.

She told me again that she'd call me, and that was the last time I talked to her.

I've been trying to get through to her office since the conference ended, but her voicemail's jammed. Probably crank callers asking about Nibiru. Rosie was pretty high profile in the news stories about the gig in Toronto. She's been very vocal about the scientific impossibility of it all.

Wish I could get her on the phone. Any new info she could give me might help with breaking Sister Light away from the Church of the Nomad World.

I'd need it, too, because my read on Sister Light was that she was more a true believer than a lost soul. That's important to know because you have to have an approach. The lost ones are beyond conversations. They are terrified of finding out that they're wrong. So much so that they'll hurt themselves rather than face the truth. Buddy of mine had to call parents once to tell them their daughter slashed her own throat when she spotted the pick-up team coming to take her home.

Imagine that.

Fifteen-year-old girl who'd rather take a pair of fabric scissors to her throat instead of going back to whatever hell she'd fled. Whether their problems are real or imagined, kids like that are sometimes too far gone.

Not everyone can be saved. The people here at the Church should understand that. They believe only their initiates are going to hitch a ride on Nibiru. The rest of the unworthy or unrepentant will become stardust.

Stardust.

Sounds better than saying we'll all burn in hellfire, which is what most of these nutbags say.

Stardust doesn't actually sound that bad.

Stardust.

Star stuff.

I spotted her five minutes after I climbed the wall. Sitting on a bench by herself. No watchdogs.

Sister Light.

She was five foot nothing. A slip of a thing, with pale hair and paler skin, and eyes the color of summer grass. Not especially pretty. Not ugly. No curves, but a good face and kind eyes.

Intelligent eyes.

She was sitting on a stone bench in a little grove of foxtail palms and oversized succulents. A small water feature burbled quietly and I think there was even a butterfly. You could have sold a photo of that moment to any calendar company.

All around the grove was a geometric pattern of white rectangular four-by-seven foot stones. They fanned out from where she sat like playing cards. Four or five of them, covering several acres of cool green grass.

The girl was wearing a white dress with a pale blue gardening apron. White gloves tucked into the apron tie. Her head was covered with the requisite blue scarf that every woman in the Church wore. The men all wore blue baseball caps with circles embroidered on them. Symbolic of the nomad world, I supposed.

I'd come dressed for the part. White painter's pants, white shirt, blue cap.

Stun gun tucked into the waistband of my pants, hidden by the shirt. Syringe with a strong but safe tranquilizer. A lead-weighted sap if things got weird. A cell phone with booster chip so I could talk to Rosie, Lee or, at need, my backup. Three guys in a van parked around the corner. Three very tough guys who have done this before. Guys who are not as nice as I am, and I'm not that nice.

She set down the water bottle she'd been drinking from and watched with quiet grace as I approached.

She smiled at me. "You're here to take me back, aren't you?"

--4--

I slowed my approach and stopped at the edge of the little grove.

"What do you mean, sister?" I asked, pitching my voice so it was soft. The smile I wore was full of lots of white teeth. Very wholesome.

She shook her head.

"You're not one of us," she said.

"I'm new."

"No, you're not."

"How do you know?"

"I know."

"*How* do you know?"

The girl looked at me with eyes that were a lot older than eighteen. Very bright lights in those eyes. It made me want to smile for real.

"Mind if I sit down?"

"Who are you?"

"A friend."

"No, I mean…what's your name?"

"Oh. John Poe."

"Poe? Like the writer."

"Like that."

"Nice. I read some of his stuff in school. The one about the cat, and the one about the guy's heart under the floorboards."

"Scary stuff."

"I thought they were sad. Those poor people were so lost."

I said nothing.

She nodded to the empty end of the bench. "It's okay for you to sit down."

I sat, making sure that I didn't sit too close. Invading her little envelope of subjective distance was not a good opening move. But I also didn't sit too far away. I didn't want to give her a wall of distance either. You have to know how to play it.

We watched a couple of mourning doves waddle around poking at the grass.

"My parents sent you," she said, making it a statement rather than a question.

"They care about you."

Her reply to that was a small, thin smile.

"They want to know you're okay," I said.

"Do you really believe that?"

"Of course. They're your parents."

She studied my face. "You don't look that naïve, Mr. Poe."

And you don't sound like an eighteen-year-old, I thought.

Aloud I said, "If that's something you'd like to talk about, we can. But is here the best place?"

"It's safer."

"Safer for whom?"

"For me," she said. "Look, I understand how this is supposed to work. You come on very passive and friendly and helpful and you find a way to talk me into leaving the grounds with you. To have a chat at a diner or something like that. Then once we're off the church grounds, you grab me and take me to my parents."

"You make it sound like an abduction. All I want to do is bring you home."

"No. You want to *take* me to where my parents live." She patted the bench. "*This* is home, Mr. Poe." She gestured to the lush foliage around us. "And this." And finally she touched her chest over her heart. "And this."

"Okay, I get that. Our home is where we are. Our home is our skin and our perceptions. That's nice in the abstract, but it isn't where your family is. They're at your *family* home, and they're waiting for you."

Her smile was constant and patient. I wanted to break through that level of calm control because that's where the levers are. Fear is one level. Insecurity, which is a specific kind of fear, is another. There are a lot of them.

"Mr. Poe," she said before I could reach for one of those levers, "do we have to do this? I mean, I understand that you're being paid to be here, and maybe there's a bonus for you to bring me back. I know how Daddy works, and he likes his incentives. I think it's easier if we can just be honest. You want to earn your paycheck. Daddy and Mommy want me back so they can put me in a hospital, which would make them legal guardians of me *and* my money. They think I'm nuts and you think I've been brainwashed. Is that it? Did I cover all the bases?"

I had to smile. "You're a sharp kid."

"I'm almost nineteen, Mr. Poe. I stopped being a kid a while ago."

"Nineteen is pretty young."

She shook her head. "Nineteen is as old as I'm ever going to get."

We sat with that for a moment.

"Go on," she encouraged, "say it."

"Say what?"

"Say anything. I just said that I wasn't going to get any older. That probably sounds suicidal to you. Or fatalistic. Maybe it's a sign of deep-seated depression. Go on. Make a comment."

What I said was, "You're an interesting girl."

"Person. If you don't want to call me a 'woman,' then call me a person. I'm not a girl."

"Sorry. But, yes, you're a very interesting person."

"Which goes against the 'type,' doesn't it?"

"Which type?"

"Well, if I was political, or if this was some kind of radical militant group, then you'd expect me to be more educated. You'd expect me to rattle off a lot of Marxist or pseudo-Marxist tripe. But the Church isn't radical. Not in that way. We don't care at all about politics. I know I don't. We're what people like you would call a 'doomsday cult.'"

"If that's the wrong phrase, tell me which one to use."

She laughed. "No, it's fine. It's pretty much true."

"What's true?"

"The world's going to end."

"Because of Nibiru?"

"Sure."

"And — what is it, exactly? People can't seem to agree."

"Well," she said with a laugh, "it's not a dwarf brown star."

"It's not?"

"You think I don't know about this. You think I'm a confused little girl in a weirdo cult thinking we're all going to hitch a ride on a passing planet. You think this is Heaven's Gate and Nibiru is another Hale-Bopp. That's what you think."

Again, she wasn't framing it as a question.

"Well, let me tell you," she continued, "what they tell us here in the church. One of the first things they did was to explain how it couldn't possibly be a brown dwarf because that would mean it was an object bigger than Jupiter. Even in the most extreme orbit, it would have been spotted, and its gravitational pull would have affected every other planet in our solar system."

I said, "Okay."

"And if it was a giant planet four times larger than the Earth, which is what a lot of people are saying on the news and on the Net, then if it was coming toward the Earth it would be visible to the naked eye. And that would also warp the orbits of the outer planets. And it can't have been a planet concealed by the sun all this time because that would be geometrically impossible."

"You know your science."

"They *teach* us the science here."

"Oh."

"That surprises you, doesn't it."

"I suppose it does. Why do you think they do that?"

"No," she said, "why do *you* think they do it? Why teach us about the science?"

"If you want me to be straight with you, then it's because using the truth is the easiest way to sell a lie. It's a conman's trick. It's no different than a magician letting you look in his hat and up his sleeve before he pulls a rabbit out. They don't let you look at where he's keeping the rabbit."

"That might be true if the church was trying to sell us something. Or sell us on something."

"You're saying they're not?"

"They're not."

"So, they have no interest at all in your trust fund?"

"A year ago, maybe," she said offhand. "Two years ago, definitely. Not anymore."

"What makes you believe that?"

"Because Nibiru is coming."

"You said that it wasn't."

"No," she said, "I said that it wasn't a brown dwarf or a rogue planet."

"Your group's called the Church of the Nomad World. Emphasis on 'world.'"

"I know. When they started, they were using the rogue world thing in exactly the way you think they still are."

"Uh huh. And there are YouTube videos of your deacons talking about how the gravity of Nibiru is going to cause the Earth to stop spinning, and that after it leaves the Earth's rotation will somehow restart."

"Those videos are old."

"Six years isn't that old."

"Old enough," she said. "Nobody says that anymore. Not here. Besides, if the world were to somehow stop rotating the core heat would make the oceans boil. And you couldn't restart rotation again at the same rate of spin. The law of the conservation of angular momentum says it's impossible."

"You understand the physics?"

"We all do," she said, indicating the others who walked or sat in the garden. "We study it."

Her tone was conversational and calm, her demeanor serene.

"Then what do your people believe?" I asked.

"Nibiru is coming."

"But—"

"You look confused," she said.

"I am confused. If it's not a brown dwarf and it's not a rogue planet, then what *is* Nibiru?"

"Ah," she said, nodding. "That's the right question."

"What?"

"That's the question you should have been asking."

"Okay, fine, I'm asking it now. What is—?"

"It's an asteroid," she said.

"An asteroid."

"Yes."

"That you think is going to hit the Earth?"

"No."

"Then—"

"It's going to hit the Moon," she said. "And the Moon will hit the Earth."

"An asteroid that big and no one's seen it?"

"Sure they have, Mr. Poe. A lot of people have seen it. Why do you think everyone's so upset? It's all over the news, and it's getting worse. There are all those books about it. Everyone's talking about it."

"Talking, sure, but there's no evidence."

"There are lots of pictures," she said, her manner still calm. "But I guess you think they're all doctored. Solar flares causing images on cameras, that sort of thing."

"And they disprove those things as fast as they go up."

"I know. Some of them. Like the one of Nibiru that was on YouTube a few years ago that they said was a Hubble image of the expanding light echo around the star V838 Mon. Yes, most of the images have been discredited. Most, not all. There are a bunch that still get out there, and NASA and the other groups say they're faked."

"They *are* fakes."

"You say that, but you don't actually know that, do you?"

I dug my cell phone out of my pocket. "I pretty much do. I have one of the top observational astrophysicists on speed dial. She's been my information source for this ever since I began looking for you."

Sister Light nodded. "Okay. Was she at the conference in Toronto?"

I grinned. "You keep up with the news. Yes, she was there."

"What's her name?"

"Rose Blum."

She nodded. "She's good. I read a couple of her books."

"You *understood* her books?"

"Some of it. Not all the math, but enough. She's right about almost everything."

"Except Nibiru, is that right?"

"If she says it doesn't exist, then no. If she told you that there was no dwarf star or giant planet about to hit the Earth, then she was telling you at least some of the truth. But have you actually asked her if she knows anything about the asteroid heading toward the dark side of the moon?"

"I'm pretty sure she'd have said something," I said, chuckling.

Sister Light shook her head. "I'm pretty sure she wouldn't."

"I could call her."

She stood up and walked over to the one of the stone rectangles set into the grass. I joined her, standing a polite distance to one side. There was writing on the stones which I hadn't taken note of before. I stepped onto the grass and read what was carved into the closest one.

Myron Alan Freeman.

It took me a moment, but I found the name amid the jumble of information I'd studied about the Church.

Freeman was a deacon, one of forty men and women who helped run the organization.

Below his name was the word: Peace.

I stiffened and cut a look at Sister Light. She nodded to the other stones, and I walked out into the field. Each of them had a name. Some I recognized, others I didn't. All of them had the word "peace" on them.

My throat went totally dry and I wheeled to face her. My heart was racing. I raised my shirt and gripped the butt of the stun gun.

"What the fuck is this?" I demanded.

"What does it look like?"

"It looks like a fucking cemetery."

She nodded. "That's what it is."

I drew my weapon but held it down at my side. "All of them?"

"Yes."

"Every stone here?"

"Yes."

"Dead?"

"Yes?"

"Who killed them?"

Her face was sad. "Not everyone wants to wait for it to happen, Mr. Poe."

"You're saying they killed *themselves*?"

"Nobody here commits murder. It's against our beliefs. Only God has the right to take a human life."

"God...?"

"The one true God, Mr. Poe. The one who has sent his angel, Nibiru, to end the suffering of all mankind."

I looked for the crazy. I looked for that spark of madness in her eyes. The religious zeal. The disconnect.

I looked.

And looked.

"We believe," she said. "We don't require anyone else to. We don't proselytize. We're not looking for new members. We get a lot of them, though. People see the truth, they read through the lies in the media, the lies told by NASA and Homeland and everyone else. They see what's coming and they know what it means. And they come to us."

"For *what*?"

"Some of them want to be loved before it all ends. That's why I'm here. My parents are so cold, so dismissive. I didn't leave because I was acting out. I wasn't going through teenage angst. I came looking for a place to belong so I could wait out the time that we have left among those who don't judge, don't hate, don't want anything from me except whatever love I want to share. I'm only eighteen, Mr. Poe. I'll be dead within a few months of my nineteenth birthday. I won't have a future. I won't have a husband or kids or any of that. I have this. This is the only chance I'll ever have to *give* love. Here in the Church...I have love. I have peace. I have prayer."

She turned away from the stone markers.

The grave markers.

"I want to live all the way to the end. I don't want to commit suicide."

"Why? What do you think is going to happen if this asteroid is real? Will you be transported off to a new world? Will you be elevated to a higher consciousness?"

I couldn't keep the bitterness out of my voice.

"No," she said simply. "When Nibiru hits the Moon and the Moon hits the Earth, I'll die. It'll probably hurt. I'll be scared. Of course I will. But I'll die here, among my friends, content with the will of God."

I wanted to slap her.

I really did.

I wanted to hit her until she didn't believe this bullshit anymore. We stood there in a churchyard surrounded by the graves of five hundred suicides.

"You need help," I said. "Everyone here does."

"No we don't. We've found what we need. We don't require anything else but to be left alone to pray, to love each other, and to die."

She nodded to the stun gun I held.

"You can use that on me. You can take me by force. No one here is going to try and stop you, and you probably have help somewhere close. So…sure, you can take me against my will. If you do, and if they manage to lock me away somewhere where I can't escape or can't take my life, it won't change anything. I'll still die. We all will. However you'll die knowing that you robbed me of being happy before I died." She stepped close to me and looked up into my eyes. "Is that what you want, Mr. Poe? Is that what you really think is best for me? Will taking me out of here actually keep me 'safe'?"

--5--

I got home around eight that night.

Last night.

I let the other guys go. Told them that we'd drawn a blank. Told them I'd call when I had a fresh lead. It was all the same to them. They were day players.

At my apartment, I cracked a fresh beer and took it out to the deck to watch the sky.

The Moon was up. Three-quarter moon.

I drank the beer. Got another. Drank that.

Sat with the Moon until it was down.

I tried fifteen times to get Rosie Blum on the phone.

Fifteen.

Cell. Office. Home answering machine.

Finally, someone picked up.

Not Rosie, though.

It was her roommate. Rachael Somethingorother. A junior astrophysicist.

"Hello—?"

There was something about the way she said it. Tentative and a little weary. Like she was afraid of a call. Or of another call.

"Rachael? It's John Poe," I said. "Is Rosie there? I've been trying to get her for days and she's not picking up. I really need to talk to her. Is she there?"

She took too long to reply.

Too long.

"John...I'm so sorry," she said.

So sorry.

"What happened?" I asked.

"It...it's going to be in the papers. God, I'm sorry. I thought someone would have called you."

"What's going to be in the papers? What's wrong? Where's Rosie?"

"She's gone..." she said. "I didn't even know she *had* a gun. Oh god, there was so much blood...oh god, John..."

I stared at the night. Listened to the voice on the phone.

"When...?" I asked softly.

"Last night," said Rachael. "When she and Dr. Marcus got back from Toronto. They came back from the airport and they went straight into her room without saying anything. I thought...well, I thought that maybe they were together now. That they'd hooked up in Toronto and, well, you know..."

"What happened?"

"Like I said, I didn't even know she had a gun until I heard the shots."

"Shots?"

"Yes. Oh god, John....she shot him in the head and then put the gun in her...in her..."

She may have said more. There must have been more to the story, but I didn't hear it.

I dropped my hand into my lap, then let it fall down beside my deck chair. The phone landed hard and bounced away. Maybe it went over the rail. I don't know. I haven't looked for it.

I'm sitting here now, and I don't know why I'm recording this. I mean…who the fuck am I leaving a record for?

I watched the news this morning.

Sixteen suicides. Eight of the speakers at the Toronto conference.

Eight others who were there.

Not counting Rosie and Dr. Marcus.

Eighteen.

All of them there to talk about Nibiru. To work out what kind of message to tell the world.

Eighteen.

I guess the message is pretty clear.

I'm going to leave this recorder here on the dashboard. Not sure what good it would do for someone else to find it.

Across the street I can see the wrought iron gates and the granite pillars. And beyond that the white stones in the green grass.

I can see Sister Light standing there, watching my car.

Watching me.

Waiting for me.

Smiling at me.

She lifts her hand.

A welcome gesture.

Okay, I tell myself.

Okay.

Spellcaster 2.0

Author's Note

This collection has several 'firsts' in it. My first short story, my first straight mystery, my first parody, etc. This story was the very first fantasy I ever wrote.

It started with an email from my friend Charlaine Harris, the brilliant and charming writer who wrote the Sookie Stackhouse novels upon which HBO's *TRUE BLOOD* was based. She asked me to write a fantasy for her. So…of course I said yes.

What makes it even more fun was that I got to write a story set in the world of academia, and I was a college teacher for fourteen years. I generally view the academic world as not actually belonging to the real world anyway, so…

SPELLCASTER 2.0

--1--

"Username?"

"You're going to laugh at me."

Trey LaSalle turned to her but said nothing. He wore very hip, very expensive tortoiseshell glasses and he let them and his two hundred dollar haircut do his talking for him. The girl withered.

"It's...obvious?" she said awkwardly, posing it as a question.

"Let me guess. It's going to be a famous magician, right? Which one, I wonder? Won't be *Merlin* because even *you're* not that obvious, and it won't be *Nostradamus* because I doubt you could spell it."

"I can spell," she said, but there was no emphasis to it.

"Hmm. *StGermaine*? No? *Dumbledore*? *Gandalf*?"

"It's—"

He pursed his lips. "Girl, please don't tell me it really *is* Merlin."

Anthem blushed herself mute.

"Jesus save me." Trey rubbed his eyes and typed in MERLIN with slow sarcasm, each keystroke separate and very sharp. By the fourth letter Anthem's eyes were jumping.

Her name was really Anthem. Her parents were right-wing second gens of left-wing Boomers from the Village, a confusion of genetics and ideologies that resulted in a girl who was bait fish for everyone at the University of Pennsylvania with an I.Q. higher than their belt size. Though barely a palate cleanser for a shark like Trey. He sipped his pumpkin spice latte and sighed.

"Password?" he prompted

"You're going to make fun of me again."

"There's that chance," he admitted. "Is it too cute, too personal or too stupid?" He carved off slices of each word and spread them out thin and cold. He was good at that. Back in high school his snarky tone would have earned him a beating—had, in fact, earned him several beatings; but then he conquered the cool crowd. Thereafter they kept him well protected, well-appeased, and well-stocked with a willing audience of masochists who had already begun to learn that anyone with a truly lethal wit was never—*ever*—to be mocked or harmed. In that environment, Trey LaSalle had flourished into the self-satisfied diva he now enjoyed being. Now, in his junior year at U of P, Trey owned the in-crowd and their hangers-on because he was able to work the sassy gay BFF role as if the trope was built for him. At the same time, he could also play the get-it-done team leader when the chips were down.

Those chips were certainly down right now. Trey figured that Jonesy and Bird had gotten Anthem to call Trey for a bailout because she was so thoroughly a Bambi in the brights that even he wouldn't actually slaughter her.

"Password?" He drew it into a hiss.

Anthem chewed a fingernail. Despite the fact that she painted her nails, they were all nibbled down to nubs. A couple of them even had blood caked along the sides from where she'd cannibalized herself a bit too aggressively, and there were faint chocolate-colored smears of it on the keyboard. Trey made a mental note to bathe in Purell when he got back to his room.

"Come on, girl" he coaxed.

She blurted it. "*Abracadabra.*"

Trey stared at the screen and tried very hard not to close the laptop and club her to death with it. He typed it in. The display changed from the bland login screen to the landing page for *The Spellcaster Project.*

The project.

It sounded simple, but wasn't. Over the course of the last eighteen months the group had collected, organized and committed to computer memory every evocation and conjuring spell known to the various beliefs of human culture. From phonetic interpretations of guttural verbal chants by remote Brazilian tribes to complex rituals in Latin and Greek. On the surface the project was a searchable database so thorough that it would be the go-to resource. A resource for which access could be leased, opening a cash-flow for the folklore department. And, people would definitely pay. This database—nicknamed *Spellcaster*—was a researcher's dream.

Trey found it all fascinating but considered it immensely silly at the same time. He was a scientist, or becoming one, and yet his field of study involved nothing that he believed in. Doctors at least believed in healing, but folklorists were a notoriously atheistic lot. Demons and gods, spells and sacred rituals. None of it was remotely real. All of it was an attempt to make sense of a world that could not be truly understood or defined, and certainly not controlled. Things just happened. Nobody was at the controls, and nobody was taking calls from the human race.

And yet with all that, it was fascinating, like watching a car wreck. You don't want to be a part of it but you can't look away. He even went to church sometimes, just to study the people, to mentally catalog the individual ways in which they interpreted the religion to which they ascribed. There was infinite variation within a species, just as within flowers in a field. And soon he would be making money from it, and that was something he *could* believe in.

The second aspect of the project was *Spellcaster 2.0*, which began as Trey's idea but along the way had somehow become Professor Davidoff's. In essence, once the thousands of spells were entered, a program would run through all of them to look for common elements. Developmental goals included a determination of how many common themes appeared in spells and what themes appeared in a majority, or at least a significant number of them. The end goal was to create a perfect generic spell. A spell which established that there were some aspects to magical conjuring that linked the disparate tribes and cultures of mankind.

Trey's hypothesis was that anthropologists would be able to use that information, along with related linguistic models, to more accurately track the spread of humankind from its African origins. It might effectively prove that the spread of religion, in all of its many forms, stemmed from the same central source. Or—as he privately thought of it—mankind's first big stupid mistake. In other words, the birth of prayer and organized religion.

Finding that would be a watershed moment in anthropology, folklore, sociology and history. It would be a Nobel Prize no-brainer, and it didn't matter to Trey if he shared that prize, and all of the fame and—no doubt—fortune that went with it. *Spellcaster* was going to make them all rich.

"Okay," Trey said, "why are we here?"

Anthem chewed her lip. She did it prettily, and even though she was the wrong cut of meat for Trey's personal tastes, he had to admit that she was all that. She was an East Coast blonde with ice-pale skin, luminous green eyes, a figure which could make any kind of clothes look good, and Scarlett Johansson lips. Shame that she was dumber than a cruller. He was considering bringing her into his circle; not the circle-jerk of grad students to which they both currently belonged, but the more elite group he went clubbing with. Arm candy like that worked for everyone, straight or gay. It was better than a puppy and it didn't pee on the carpet. Though, with Anthem there was no real guarantee that she was house broken.

The lip chewing had no real effect on him, and Trey studied her to see how long it would take her to realize it. Seven Mississippis.

"I've been hacked," she said.

"Get right out of town."

"And they've been in my laptop messing with my stuff."

"The spells?"

"Some of them, yes."

Trey felt the first little flutter of panic.

"I've been inputting the evocation spells for the last couple of weeks," Anthem explained. "One group at a time. Last week it was Gypsy stuff from Serbia, before that it was the pre-industrial Celtic stuff. It's hard to do. None of it was translated and Professor Davidoff didn't want us to use Babelfish or any of the other online translators because they don't give cultural or—what's the word?"

"Contextual?"

"Right. They don't give cultural or contextual translations, and that's supposed to be important for spells."

"'Crucial' is a better word," Trey murmured, "but I take your point."

"I had to compare what I typed with photocopies from old spell books. After I finish this stuff Kidd will add the binding spells, then Jonesy will do the English translations. Bird's doing the footnotes, and I guess you'll be working on the annotations."

"Uh huh."

"At first Jonesy dictated the spells while I typed, but that only really worked with Latin and the Romance languages because we kind of knew the spellings. More and more, though, I had to look at it myself to make sure it was exact. Everything had to match or the professor would freak. And there are all those weird little symbol thingys on some of the letters."

"Diacritical marks."

"Yeah, those." She began nibbling at her thumbnail, talking around it as she chewed. "Without everything just so, the spells won't work."

Trey smiled a tolerant smile. "Sweetie, the spells won't work because they're spells. None of this crap works, you know that."

She stared at him for a moment, still working on the thumb. "They *used* to work, though, didn't they?"

"This is science, honey. The only magic here is the way you're working that sweater and the supernatural way I'm working these jeans."

She said, "Okay." But she didn't sound convinced, and it occurred to Trey that he didn't know where Anthem landed on the question of faith. If she was a believer, then that was a tick against her becoming part of his circle.

"You were saying about the data entry?" he prompted, steering her back to safer ground.

Anthem blinked. "Oh, sure. It's hard. It's all brain work."

Trey said nothing to that. It would be too easy; it would be like kicking a sleepy kitten. Instead he asked, "So what happened?"

Anthem suddenly stopped biting her thumb and they both looked at the bead of blood that welled from where she'd bitten too deeply. Without saying a word, Anthem tore a piece of Scotch tape from a dispenser and wrapped it around the wound.

"Every day I start by checking the previous day's entries to make sure they're all good."

"And—?"

"The stuff I entered last night was different."

"Different how?"

"Let me show you." Anthem leaned past him and her fingers began flying over the keys. Whatever else she was or wasn't, she could type like a demon. Very fast and very accurate.

The world lost a great typist when she decided to pursue higher education, mused Trey.

Anthem pulled up a file marked *18CenFraEvoc*, scrolled down to one of the spells, then tapped the screen with a bright green fingernail. "There, see? I found the first changes in the ritual the professor is going to use for the debut thingy."

Trey's French was passable and he bent closer and studied the lines, frowning as he did so. Anthem was correct in that this ritual—the *faux* summoning of Azeziz, demon of knowledge and faith—was a key element in Professor Davidoff's plans to announce their project to the academic world. Even a slight error would embarrass the professor, and he was not a forgiving man. Less so than, say, Hitler.

Anthem opened a file folder which held a thick sheaf of high-res scans of pages from a variety of sources. She selected a page and held it up next to the screen. "This is how it should read."

Trey clicked his eyes back and forth between the source and target materials and then he did see it. In one of the spells the wording had been changed. The second sentence read: *With the Power of the Eternal I Conjure Thee to my Service.*

It should have read: *With the Power of My Faith in the Eternal I Conjure and Bind Thee to my Service.*

"You see?" Anthem asked again. "It's different. There's nothing about the conjurer *believing*. That throws it all off, right?"

"In theory," he said dryly. "This could have been a mistype."

"No way," she said. "I always check my previous days' stuff before I start anything new. I don't make those kinds of mistakes."

The pride in her voice was palpable, and in truth Trey could not recall ever making a correction in any of her work before. The team had been hammering away at the project for eighteen months. They'd created hundreds of pages of original work, and entered thousands of pages of collected data. After a few mishaps with other team members handling data entry, the bulk of it was shifted to Anthem.

"It's weird, right?" she asked.

He sat back and folded his arms, "It's weird. And, yes, you've been hacked."

"By who? I mean, it has to be one of the team, right? But Jonesy doesn't know French. I don't think Bird does, either."

Jonesy was a harmless mouse of a kid. Bird was sharper, but he was an idealist and adventurer. Bird wanted to chew peyote with the Native American Church and go on spirit walks. He wanted to whirl with the Dervishes and trance-out with the Charismatics. Unlike Trey and every other anthropologist Trey knew, Bird was in the field for the actual beliefs. Bird apparently believed that everyone was right, that every religion, no matter how batty, had a clue to the "Great Big Picture," as he called it. Trey liked him, but except for the project they had nothing in common.

Would Bird do this, though? Trey doubted it, partly because it was mean—and Bird didn't have fangs at all—and mostly because it was disrespectful to the belief systems. As if anyone would really *care*. Except the thesis committee.

"What about Kidd?" asked Anthem. "It would be like him to do something mean like this."

That much was true. Michael Kidd was a snotty, self-important little snob from Philly's Main Line. Good looking in a verminous sort of way. Kidd was cruising through college on family money and never pretended otherwise. Even Davidoff walked softly around him.

But, would Kidd sabotage the project? Yeah, he really might. Just for shits and giggles.

"The slimy little rat-sucking weasel," said Trey.

"So it *is* Kidd?"

Trey did not commit. He would have bet twenty bucks on it, but that wasn't the same as saying it out loud. Especially to someone like Anthem. He cut a covert look at her and for a moment his inner bitch softened. She was really a sweet kid. Clueless in a way that did no one any harm, not even herself. Anthem wasn't actually stupid, just not sharp and would probably never be sharp. Not unless something broke her and left jagged edges; and wouldn't that be sad?

"Is this only with the French evocation spell?" he asked.

"No." She pulled up the Serbian Gypsy spells. Neither of them could read the language, but a comparison of source and target showed definite differences. Small, but there. "I went back as far as the Egyptian burial symbols. Ten separate files, ten languages, which is crazy 'cause none of us can speak all of those languages."

"What about the Aramaic and Babylonian?"

"I haven't entered them yet."

Trey thought about it, then nodded. "Okay, let's do this. Go in and make the corrections. Before you do, though, I'm going to set you up with a new username and new password."

"Okay." She looked relieved.

"How much do you have to do on this?" Trey asked. "Are we going to make the deadline?"

The deadline was critical. Professor Davidoff was planning to make an official announcement in less than a month. He had a big event planned for it, and warned them all every chance he could that departmental grant money was riding on this. Big time money. He never actually threatened them, but they could all see the vultures circling.

Anthem nibbled as she considered the stacks of folders on her desk. "I can finish in three weeks."

"That's cutting it close."

Anthem's nibbling increased.

"Look," he said, "I'll spot-check you and do all the transfers to the mainframe. Don't let else anyone touch your laptop for any reason. No one, okay?"

"Okay," she said, relieved but still dubious. "Will that keep whoever's doing this out of the system?"

"Sure," said Trey. "This should be the end of it."

--2--

It wasn't.

--3--

"Tell me exactly what's been happening," demanded Professor Davidoff.

Trey and the others sat in uncomfortable metal folding chairs that were arranged in a half-circle around the acre of polished hardwood that was the professor's desk. The walls were heavy with books and framed certificates, each nook and corner filled with oddments. There were juju sticks and human skulls, bottles of ingredients for casting spells—actual eye of newt and bat's wing—and ornate reliquaries filled with select bits of important dead people.

Behind the desk, sitting like a heathen king among his spoils, was Alexi Davidoff, professor of folklore, professor of anthropology, department chair and master of all he surveyed. Davidoff was a bear of a man with Einstein hair, mad scientist eyebrows, black-framed glasses and a suit that cost more than Trey's education.

The others on the team looked at Trey. Anthem and Jonesy on his left—a cabal of girl power; Bird and Kidd on his right, representing two ends of the evolutionary bell curve—evolved human and moneyed Neanderthal.

"Well, sir," began Trey, "we're hitting a few little speed bumps."

The professor arched an eyebrow. "'Speed bumps'?"

Trey cleared his throat. "There have been a few anomalies in the data and—"

Davidoff raised a finger. It was as sure a command to stop as if he'd raised a scepter. "No," he said, "don't take the long way around. Come right out and say it. *Own* it, Mr. LaSalle."

Kidd coughed but it sounded suspiciously like, "Nut up."

Trey pretended not to have heard. To Davidoff, he said, "Someone has hacked into the *Spellcaster* data files on Anthem's computer."

They all watched Davidoff's complexion undergo a prismatic change from its normal never-go-outside pallor to a shade approximating a boiled lobster.

"Explain," he said gruffly.

Trey took a breath and plunged in. In the month since Anthem sought his help with the sabotage of the data files her computer had been hacked five times. Each time it was the same kind of problem, with minor changes being made to conjuring spells. With each passing week Trey became more convinced that Kidd was the culprit. Kidd was in charge of research for the team, which meant that he was uniquely positioned to obtain translations of the spells, and to arrange the rewording of them, since he was in direct contact with the various experts who were providing translations in return for footnotes. Only Jonesy had as much contact with the translators, and Trey didn't for a moment think that she would want to harm Anthem, or the project. However, he dared not risk saying any of this here and now. Not in front of everyone, and not without proof. Davidoff was rarely sympathetic and by no means an ally.

On the other hand, Trey knew that the professor had the typical academic's fear and loathing of scandal. Research data and drafts of papers were sacrosanct, and until it was published even the slightest blemish or question could ruin years of work and divert grants aimed at Davidoff's tiny department.

"Has anything been stolen?" Davidoff asked, his voice low and deadly.

"There's...um...no way to tell, but if they've been into Anthem's computer then nothing would have prevented them from copying everything."

"What about the bulk data on the department mainframe?" growled Davidoff.

"No way," said Bird confidently. "Has that been breached?"

Trey dialed some soothing tones into his voice. "No. I check it every day and the security software tracks every login. It's all clean. Whatever's happening is confined to Anthem's laptop."

"Have all the changes been corrected before uploading to the mainframe?" asked Davidoff.

"Absolutely."

That was a lie. There were two hundred gigabytes of documents that had been copied from Anthem's computer. It would take anyone months to read through it all, and probably years to compare every line to the photocopies of source data.

"You're sure?" Davidoff persisted.

"Positive," lied Trey.

"Are we still on schedule? We're running this in four days. We have guests coming. We have press coming. I've invested a lot of the department's resources into this."

He wasn't joking and Trey knew it. Davidoff had booked the University's celebrated Annenberg Center for the Performing Arts and hired a professional event coordinator to run things. There was even a bit of "fun" planned for the evening. Davidoff had a bunch of filmmakers from nearby Drexel University do some slick animation that would be projected as a hologram onto tendrils of smoke rising from vents in the floor around a realistic mock-up of a conjuring circle. The effect would be the sudden "appearance" of a demon. Davidoff would then interact with the demon, following a script that Trey himself had drafted. In their banter, the demon would extol the virtues of *Spellcaster* and discuss the benefits of the research to the worldwide body of historical and folkloric knowledge, and do everything to praise the project short of dropping to his knees and giving Davidoff some oral love.

There were so many ways it could go wrong that he almost wished he could pray for divine providence, but not even a potential disaster was going to put Trey on his knees.

"Sir," Trey said, "while I believe we're safe and in good shape, we really should run *Spellcaster 2.0* ourselves before the actual show."

"No."

"But—"

"You do realize, Mr. LaSalle, that the reason the press and the dignitaries will all be there is that we're running this in real time. They get to share in it. That's occurred to you, hasn't it?"

Yes, you grandstanding shithead, Trey thought. *It occurred to me for all of the reasons that I recommended that we not go that route.* He wanted to play it safe, to run the program several times and verify the results rather than go for the insane risk of what amounted to a carnival stunt.

Trey held his tongue and gave a single nod of acquiescence.

"Then we run it on schedule," the professor declared. "Now— how did this happen? By *magic?*"

A couple of the others laughed at this, but the laughs were brief and uncertain, because clearly this wasn't a funny moment. Davidoff glared them into silence.

Trey said, "I don't know, but we're doing everything we can to make sure that it doesn't affect the project."

The *Spellcaster* project was vital to all of them, but for different reasons. For personal glory, for a degree, for the opportunities it would offer and the doors it would open. So, Trey could understand why the professor's vein throbbed so mightily.

"I've done extensive online searches," Trey said, using his most businesslike voice, "and there's nothing. Not a sentence of what we've recorded, not a whiff of our thesis, nothing."

"That doesn't mean they won't publish it," grumbled Jonesy, speaking up for the first time since the meeting began.

"I don't think so," said Trey. "The stuff on Anthem's laptop is just the spell catalog. None of the translations are there and none of the bulk research and annotations are there. At worst they can publish a partial catalog."

"That would still hurt us," said Bird. "If we lost control of that, license money would spill all over the place."

Trey shook his head. "The shine on that candy is its completeness. All of the spells, all of the methods of conjuration and evocation, every single binding spell. There's no catalog like it anywhere, and what's on the laptop now is at most fifty percent, and that's nice, but it's not the Holy Grail."

"I think Trey's right, Professor," said Jonesy. "We should do a test run. I mean, what if one or more of those rewritten errors made it to the mainframe? If that happened and we run *Spellcaster 2.0*, how could we trust our findings?"

"No way we could," said Kidd, intending it to be mean and scoring nicely. The big vein on the professor's forehead throbbed visibly.

Trey ignored Kidd. "We have some leeway—"

Jonesy shook her head. "The *2.0* software is configured to factor in accidental or missed keystrokes, not sabotage."

Shut up, you cow, thought Trey, but Jonesy plowed ahead.

"Deliberate alteration of the data will look like what it is. Rewording doesn't look like bad typing. If it's there, then all our hacker has to do is let us miss one of his changes he made and wait for us to publish. Then he steps forward and tells everyone that our data management is polluted…"

"…and he'd be able to point to specific flaws," finished Bird. "We not only wouldn't have reliable results, we wouldn't have the perfect generic spell that would be the sign post we're looking for. We'd have nothing. Oh, man…we'd be so cooked."

One by one they turned to face Professor Davidoff. His accusing eye shifted away from Trey and landed on Anthem, who withered like an orchid in a cold wind. "So, this is a matter of you being stupid and clumsy, is that what I'm hearing?"

Anthem was totally unable to respond. Her skin paled beneath her fake tan and she looked like a six year old who was caught out of bed. Her pretty lips formed a lot of different words but Trey did not hear her make as much as a squeak. Tiny tears began to wobble in the corners of her eyes. The others kept themselves absolutely still. Kidd chuckled very quietly, and Trey wanted to kill him.

"It's not Anthem's fault," said Trey, coming quickly to her defense. "Her data entry is—"

Davidoff made an ugly, dismissive noise and his eyes were locked on Anthem's. "There are plenty of good typists in the world," he said unkindly. "Being one of them does not confer upon you nearly as much importance as you would like to believe."

Trey quietly cleared his throat. "Sir, since Anthem first alerted me to the problem I've been checking her work, and some of the anomalies occurred *after* I verified the accuracy of her entries. This isn't Anthem's fault. I changed her username and password after each event."

Davidoff considered this, then gave a dismissive snort. It was as close to an apology as his massive personal planet ever orbited.

"Then…we're safe?" ventured Bird hopefully.

Trey licked his lips, then nodded.

Davidoff's vein throbbing quite aggressively. "Then we proceed as planned. Real test, real time." He raised his finger of doom. "Be warned, Mr. LaSalle, this is your neck on the line. You are the team leader. It's your responsibility. I don't want to hear excuses after something else happens. All I ever want to hear is that *Spellcaster* is secure. I don't care who you have to kill to protect the integrity of that data, but you keep it safe. Do I make myself clear?"

Trey leaned forward and put his hands on the edge of Davidoff's desk. "Believe me, Professor, when I find out who's doing this I swear to God I will rip his god damn heart out."

He could feel everyone's eyes on him.

The professor sat back and pursed his lips, studying Trey with narrowed, calculating eyes. "See that you do," he said quietly. "Now all of you...get out."

--4--

Trey spent the next few hours walking the windy streets of University City. He was deeply depressed and his stomach was a puddle of acid tension. As he walked, he heard car horns and a few shouts, laughter from the open door of sports bars on the side streets. A few sirens wailed with ghostly insistence in the distance. He heard those things, but he didn't register any of it.

Trey's mind churned on it. Not on why this was happening, but who was doing it.

After leaving Davidoff, Trey had gone to see his friend Herschel and the crew of geeks at the computer lab. These were the kinds of uber-nerds who would once have never gotten laid and never moved out of their mother's basements—stereotypes all the way down to the Gears of War t-shirts and cheap sneakers. Now, guys like that were rock stars. They *got* laid. They all had jobs waiting for them after graduation. Most of them wouldn't bother with school after they had a bachelor's because the industry wanted them young and raw and they wanted them now. These were the guys who hacked ultra-secret corporate computer systems just because they were bored. Guys who made some quick cash on the side writing viruses that they sold to the companies who sold anti-virus software.

Trey explained the situation to them.

They thought it was funny.

They thought it was cool.

They told him half a dozen ways *they* could do it.

"Even Word docs on a laptop that's turned off?" demanded Trey. "I thought that was impossible."

Herschel laughed. "Impossible isn't a word, brah, it's a challenge."

"What?"

"It's the *Titanic*," said Herschel.

"Beg pardon?"

"*The Titanic*. The unsinkable ship. You got to understand the mindset." Herschel was an emaciated runt with nine-inch hips and glasses you could fry ants with. At nineteen he already held three patents and his girlfriend was a spokesmodel at gaming shows. "Computers—hardware *and* software—are incredibly sophisticated idiots, feel me? They can only do what they're programmed to do. Even A.I. isn't really independent thinking. It's not intuitive."

"Okay," conceded Trey. "So?"

"So, what man can invent, man can fuck up. Look at home security systems. As soon as the latest unbreakable, unshakeable, untouchable system goes on the market someone has to take it down. Not wants to... *has* to."

"Why?"

"Because it's there, brah. Because it's all about toppling the arrogant assholes in corporate America who make those kinds of claims. Can't be opened, can't be hacked, can't be sunk. Titanic, man."

"Man didn't throw an iceberg at the ship, Hersch."

"No, the universe did that because it's a universal imperative to kick arrogant ass."

"Booyah," agreed the other hackers, bumping fists.

"So," said Trey slowly, "you think someone's hacking our research because he can?"

Herschel shrugged. "Why else?"

"Not to try and sell it?"

Some of the computer geeks laughed. Herschel said, "Sell that magic hocus pocus shit and you're going to make—what? A few grand? Maybe a few hundred grand in the long run after ten years busting your ass?"

"At *least* that much," Trey said defensively.

"Get a clue, dude. You got someone hacking a closed system on a laptop and changing unopened files in multiple languages. That's *real* magic. A guy like that wouldn't wipe his ass with a hundred grand. All he has to do is file a patent on how he did it and everyone in corporate R and D will be lining up to blow him. Guy like that wouldn't answer the phone for any offer lower than the middle seven figures."

"Booyah!" agreed the geek chorus.

"Sorry, brah," said Herschel, clapping Trey on the shoulder, "but this might not even be about your magic spell bullshit. You could just be a friggin' test drive."

Trey left, depressed and without a clue of where to go next. The profile of his unknown enemy did not seem to fit anyone on the project. Bird and Jonesy were as good with computers as serious students and researchers could be, but at the end of the day they were really only Internet savvy. They would never have fit in with Herschel's crowd. Anthem knew everything about word processing software but beyond that she was in unknown territory. Kidd was no computer geek either. Although, Trey mused, Kidd could afford to hire a geek. Maybe even a really good geek, one of Herschel's crowd. Someone who could work the kind of sorcery required to break into Anthem's computer.

But…how to prove it?

God, he wished he really could go and rip Kidd's heart out. If the little snot even had one.

The sirens were getting louder and the noise annoyed him. Every night it was the same. Football jocks and the frat boys with their perpetual parties, as if belly shots and beer pong genuinely mattered in the cosmic scheme of things. Neanderthals.

Without even meaning to do it, Trey's feet made a left instead of a right and carried him down Sansom Street toward Kidd's apartment.

He suddenly stopped walking and instantly knew that no confrontation with Kidd was going to happen that night.

The entire street was clogged with people who stood in bunches and vehicles parked at odd angles.

Police vehicles. And an ambulance.

"Oh...shit," he said.

--5--

Tearing out Kidd's heart was no longer an option.

According to every reporter on the scene, someone had already beaten him to it.

--6--

They all met in Trey's room. The girls perched on the side of his bed; Bird sprawled in a papa-san chair with his knees up and his arms wrapped around them. Trey stood with his back to the door.

All eyes were on him.

"Cops talk to you?" asked Bird.

"No. You?"

Bird nodded. He looked as scared as Trey felt. "They asked me a few questions."

"Really? Why?"

Bird didn't answer.

"They came around here, too," said Jonesy. "This morning and again this afternoon."

"Why'd they want to see you guys?" asked Trey.

Jonesy gave him a strange look.

"What?" Trey asked.

"They wanted to see you," said Anthem.

"Me? Why would they want to see me?"

Nobody said a word. Nobody looked at him.

Trey said, "Oh, come *on*. You guys have to be frigging kidding me here."

No one said a word.

"You sons of bitches," said Trey. "You think I did it, don't you? You think I could actually kill someone and tear out their frigging heart? Are you all on crack?"

"Cops said that whoever killed him must have gone apeshit on him," murmured Bird.

"So, out of seven billion people suddenly I'm America's Most Wanted?"

"They're calling it a rage crime," said Jonesy.

"Rage," echoed Anthem.

"And you actually think that *I* could do that?"

"Somebody did," said Bird again. "Whoever did it must have hated Kidd because they beat him to a pulp and tore him open. Cops asked us if we knew anyone who hated Kidd that much."

"And you gave them *my* name?"

"We didn't have to," said Anthem. "Everyone on campus knows what you thought of Kidd."

And there was nowhere to go with that except out, so Trey left them all sitting in the desolation of his room.

--7--

The cops picked him up at ten the next morning. They said he didn't need a lawyer, they just wanted to ask questions. Trey didn't have a lawyer anyway, so he answered every single question they asked. Even when they asked the same questions six and seven times.

They let him go at eight-thirty that night. They didn't seem happy about it.

Neither was Trey.

--8--

The funeral was the following day. They all went. It didn't rain because it only rains at funerals in the movies. They stood under an impossibly blue sky that was littered with cotton candy clouds. Trey stood apart from the others and listened with contempt to the ritual bullshit the priest read out of his book. Kidd had been as much of an atheist as Trey was, and this was a mockery. He'd have skipped it if that wouldn't have made him look even more suspicious.

After the service, Trey took the bus home alone.

He tried several times to call Davidoff, but the professor didn't return calls or emails.

The week ground on.

The *Spellcaster* premiere was tomorrow. Trey spent the whole day double and triple checking the data. He found nothing in any of the files he checked, but in the time he had he was only able to check about one percent of the data.

Trey sent twenty emails recommending that the premiere be postponed. He got no answers from the professor. Bird, Jonesy and Anthem said as little to him as possible, but they all kept at it, going about their jobs like worker bees as the premiere drew closer.

--9--

Professor Davidoff finally called him.

"Sir," said Trey, "I've been trying to—"

"We're going ahead with the premiere."

Trey sighed. "Sir, I don't think that's—"

"It's for Michael."

Michael. Not Mr. Kidd. The professor had never called Kidd by his first name. Ever. Trey waited for the other shoe.

"It'll be a tribute to him," continued Davidoff, his pomposity modulated into a funereal hush. "He devoted the last months of his life to this project. He deserves it."

Great, thought Trey, *everyone thinks I'm a psycho killer and he's practicing sound bites.*

"Professor, we have to stop for a minute to consider the possibility that the sabotage of the project is connected to what happened to Kidd."

"Yes," Davidoff said heavily, "we do."

Silence washed back and forth across the cellular ocean.

"I cannot imagine why anyone would do such a thing," said the professor. "Can you, Mr. LaSalle?"

"Professor, you don't think I—"

"I expect everything to go by the numbers tomorrow, Mr. LaSalle."

Before Trey could organize a reply, Professor Davidoff disconnected.

--10--

And it all went by the numbers.

More or less.

Drawn by the gruesome news story and the maudlin PR spin Davidoff gave it, the Annenberg was filling to capacity, with lines wrapped halfway around the block. Three times the expected number of reporters were there. There was even a picket by a right-wing religious group who wanted the *Spellcaster* project stopped before it started because it was "ungodly," "blasphemous," "satanic," and a bunch of other words that Trey felt ranged between absurd and silly. The picketers drew media attention and that put even more people in line for the dwindling supply of tickets.

Bird, Jonesy and Anthem showed up in very nice clothes. Bird wore a tie for the first time since Trey had known him. The girls both wore dresses. Jonesy transformed from mouse to wow in a black strapless number that Trey would have never bet she could pull off. Anthem was in green silk that matched her eyes and she looked like a movie star. She even had nail tips over the gnarled nubs of her fingers. Trey was in a black turtleneck and pants. It was as close to being invisible as he could manage.

Davidoff was the ringmaster of the circus. He wore an outrageously gorgeous Glen Urquhart plaid three-piece and even with his ursine bulk he looked like God's richer cousin.

Even the university dons were nodding in approval, happy with the positive media attention following so closely on the heels of the murder.

The as yet unsolved murder, mused Trey. The cops were nowhere with it. Trey was pretty sure he was being followed now. He was a person of interest.

God.

When the audience was packed in, Davidoff walked onto center stage amid thunderous applause. He even contrived to look surprised at the adoration before eventually waving everyone into an expectant silence.

"Before we begin, ladies and gentlemen," he began, "I would like us all to share in a moment of silence. Earlier this week, one of my best and brightest students was killed in a savage and senseless act that still has authorities baffled. No one can make sense of the death of so wonderful a young man as Michael Kidd, Jr. He was on the very verge of a brilliant career, he was about to step into the company of such legendary folklorists as Stetson Kennedy, Archie Green, and John Francis Campbell."

Trey very nearly burst out laughing. He cut a look at Bird, who gave him a weary head shake and a half-smile.

"I would like to dedicate this evening to Mr. Kidd," continued Davidoff. "He will be remembered, he will be missed."

"Christ," muttered Trey. The stage manager scowled at him.

The whole place dropped into a weird, reverential silence that lasted a full by-the-clock minute. Davidoff raised his arms and a spotlight bathed him in a white glow as the houselights dimmed.

"Magic!" he said ominously in a voice that was filtered through a sound board which gave it a mysterious-sounding reverb. The crowd *ooohed* and *aaahed*. "We have always believed in a larger world. Call it religion, call it superstition, call it the eternal mystery...we all believe in something. Even those of us who claim to believe in nothing—we will still knock on wood and pick up a penny only if it is heads up. Somewhere, past the conscious will and the civilized mind, the primitive in us remembers cowering in caves or crouching in the tall grass, or perching apelike on the limb of a tree as the wheel of night turned above and darkness covered the world."

Trey mouthed the words along with the professor. Having written them he knew the whole speech by heart.

"But what is magic? Is magic the belief that we live in a universe of infinite possibilities? Yes, but it's also *more* than that. It's the belief that we can *control* the forces of that universe. That we are not flotsam in the stream of cosmic events, but rather that we are creators ourselves. Co-creators with the infinite. Our sentience — the beautiful, impossible fact of human self-awareness and intelligence — lifts us above all other creatures in our natural world and connects us to the boundless powers of what we call the *super*natural."

From there Davidoff segued into an explanation of the *Spellcaster* project. Trey had to admit that his script sounded pretty good. He'd taken what could have been dry material and given it richness by an infusion of some pop-culture phrasing and a few juicy superlatives. The audience loved it, and they were carried along by a multimedia show that flashed images on a dozen screens. Pictures from illuminated texts. Great works of sacred art. Churches and temples, tombs and crypts, along with hundreds of photos of everything from Mickey Mouse as the Sorcerer's Apprentice to Gandalf the Gray. And there were images of holy people from around the world; Maori with their tattooed faces, Navajo shaman singing over complex sand paintings, medicine men from tiny tribes deep in the heart of the Amazon, and singers of sacred songs from among the Bushmen of Africa. It was deliberate sensory overload, accompanied by a remix mash-up of musical pieces ranging from Ozzy Osbourne to Mozart to Loreena McKennitt.

Then the floor opened and a gleaming computer rose into the light. It wasn't the department mainframe, of course, but a prop with lots of polished metal fixtures that did nothing except look cool. A laptop was positioned inside, out of sight of the audience. Smoke began rising with it, setting the stage for the evocation to come.

Suddenly four figures in dark robes stepped onto the stage. Two men and two women with black robes lined with red satin swirling around them. Juniors from the dance department. They did a few seconds of complex choreography that was, somehow, supposed to symbolize a ritual, and then they produced items from within their cloaks and began drawing a conjuring circle on the floor. Other dancers came out and lit candles, placing them at key points. The floor was discreetly marked so the dancers could do everything just so. Even though this was all for show, it had to be done right. This was still college.

The conjurer's circle was six feet across, and this was surrounded by three smaller circles. Davidoff explained that the center circle represented Earth, the smaller circle at the apex of the design represented the unknown, the circle to his right was the safe haven of the conjurer, and the circle to the left represented the realm of the demon who was to be conjured.

It was all done correctly.

Then to spook things up, Davidoff explained how this could all go horribly, horribly wrong.

"A careless magician summons his own death," he said in his stentorian voice. "All of the materials need to be pure. Vital essences—blood, sweat or tears—must never be allowed within the demon's circle for these form a bridge between the worlds of spirit and flesh."

The crowd gasped in horror as images from *The Exorcist* flashed onto the screens.

"A good magician is a scholar of surpassing skill. He does not make errors...or, rather, he makes only *one* error."

He paused for laughter and got it.

"A learned magician is a quiet and solitary person. All of his learning, all of his preparation for this ritual, must be played out in his head. He cannot practice his invocations because magical words each have their special power. To casually speak a spell is to open a doorway that might never be shut."

More images from horror movies emphasized his point. The dancer-magicians took up positions at key points around the circle.

"If everything is done just right," continued Davidoff, "the evocation can begin. This is the moment for which a magician prepares his entire life. This is the end result of thousands of hours of study, of sacrifice, of purification and preparation. The magician hopes to draw into this world—into the confined and contained protection of a magic circle—a demon of immeasurable wisdom and terrible power. Contained within the circle, the demon *must* obey the sorcerer. Cosmic laws decree that this is so!"

The audience was spellbound, which Trey thought very appropriate. He found himself caught up in the magic that Davidoff was weaving. It was all going wonderfully so far. He cut looks at the others and they were all smiling, the horrors of their real world momentarily forgotten.

Davidoff stepped into the Earth circle. "Tonight we will conjure Azeziz—the demon of spells and magic. The demon of *belief* in the larger world! It is he who holds all knowledge of the ways of sorcery that the dark forces *lent* to mankind in the dawn of our reign on Earth. Azeziz will share with us the secrets of magic, and will then guide us toward the discovery of the perfect spell. The spell that may well be the core magical ritual from which *all* of our world's religions have sprung."

He paused to let that sink in. Trey replayed the spell in his head, verifying that it was the correct wording and not any version of the mistakes that kept showing up in Anthem's computer. It all seemed correct, and he breathed a sigh of relief.

"Azeziz will first appear to us as a sphere of pure energy and will then coalesce into a more familiar form. A form that all of us here will recognize, and one in which we will take comfort." He smiled. "Join me now as we open the doorway to knowledge that belongs jointly to all of mankind—the knowledge that we do, in truth, live in a *larger world.*"

As he began the spell, Davidoff's voice was greatly amplified so that it echoed off the walls. "Come forth, Azeziz! Oh great demon, hear my plea. I call thee up by the power of this circle! By thine own glyph inscribed with thy name I summon thee."

Suddenly a ball of light burst into being inside the demon's circle. Trey blinked and gasped along with the audience. It was so bright, much brighter than what he had expected. The lighting guys were really into the moment. The ball hung in the midst of the rising smoke, pulsing with energy, changing colors like a tumbling prism, filling the air with the smell of ozone and sulfur.

Trey frowned.

Sulfur?

He shot a look at the others. Which one of those idiots added that to the special effects menu? But they were frowning, too. Bird turned to him and they studied one another for a moment. Then Bird sniffed almost comically and mouthed: *Kidd?*

Shit, thought Trey. If that vermin had worked some surprises into the show then he swore he would dig him up and kick his dead ass.

On stage, Davidoff's smile flickered as he smelled it, too. He blasted a withering and accusatory look at the darkness offstage. Right where he knew Trey would be standing.

Davidoff reclaimed his game face. "Come forth, Azeziz! Appear now that I may have council with thee. I conjure thee, ancient demon, without fear and trembling. I am not afraid as I stand within the Circle of the Earth. Come forth and manifest thyself in the circle of protection which is prepared for thee."

The globe of light pulsed and pulsed. Then there was a white-hot flash of light and suddenly a figure stood in the center of the conjuring circle.

The crowd stared goggle-eyed at the tall, portly figure with wisps of hair drifting down from a bald pate. Laser lights sparkled from the tiny glasses perched on the bulbous nose.

Benjamin Franklin. Founder of the University of Pennsylvania.

The demon smiled.

The audience gaped and then they got the joke and burst out laughing. The hall echoed with thunderous applause as Benjamin Franklin took a bow.

Trey frowned again. He didn't remember there being a bow. Not until the end.

"Speak, O' demon!" cried Davidoff as the applause drifted down to an expectant and jovial silence. "Teach us wisdom."

"Wisdom, is it?" asked Franklin. There was something a little off with the pre-recorded sound. The voice was oddly rough, gravelly. *"What wisdom would a mortal ask of a demon?"*

Davidoff was right on cue. "We seek the truth of magic," he said. "We seek to understand the mystery of faith. We seek to understand why man *believes.*"

"*Ah, but wisdom is costly,*" said Franklin, and Trey could see Davidoff's half smirk. That comment was a little hook for when the fees to access *Spellcaster* were presented. Wisdom is costly. Cute.

"We are willing to pay whatever fee you ask, O' mighty demon."

"*Are you indeed?*" asked Franklin, and once more that was something off-script. "*How much would you truly pay to understand belief?*"

None of that was in the script.

God damn you, Kidd, thought Trey darkly, and he wondered what other surprises were laid like landmines into the program. Anthem, Bird and Jonesy moved toward him, the four of them reconnecting, however briefly, in what they all now thought was going to be a frigging disaster. If Davidoff was made a fool of, then they were cooked. They were done.

Davidoff soldiered on, fighting to stay ahead of these new twists. "Um, yes, O' demon. What is the cost of the knowledge we seek?"

"*Oh, I believe you have already paid me my fee,*" said the demon Ben Franklin, and he smiled. "*My fee was offered up by vow if not by deed.*"

He rummaged inside his coat for something.

"What's he doing?" whispered Jonesy.

Bird leaned close. "Please, God, do not let him bring out a doobie or a copy of *Hustler.*"

But that's not what Franklin pulled out from under his coat flaps. He extended his arm and turned his hand palm upward to show Davidoff and everyone what he held.

Davidoff's face went slack, his eyes flaring wide.

A few people, the ones who were closest, gasped.

Then someone screamed.

The thing Franklin held was a human heart.

--11--

Davidoff said, "W—what—?"

Bird gagged.

Jonesy screamed.

Anthem said, "No..."

Trey felt as if he were falling.

--12--

The demon laughed.

It was not the polite, cultured laughter of an eighteenth century scientist and statesman. It was not anything they had recorded for the event.

The laughter was so loud that the dancers staggered backward, blood erupting from nostrils and ears. It buffeted the audience and the sheer force of it knocked Davidoff to his knees, cupping his hands to his ears.

The audience screamed.

Then the lights went out, plunging the whole place into shrieking darkness.

And came back on a moment later with a brilliance so shocking that everyone froze in place.

The demon turned his palm and let the heart fall to the floor with a wet *plop.*

No one moved.

The demon adjusted his glasses and smiled.

Trey whirled and ran to the tech boards. "Shut it down," he yelled. "Shut it all down. Kill the projectors. Come on—*do it!*"

The techs hit rows of switches and turned dials.

Absolutely nothing changed on stage.

"*Stop that, Trey,*" said Ben Franklin. His voice echoed everywhere.

Trey whirled.

"W...what?" he stammered.

"*I said, stop it.*" The demon smiled. "*In fact, come out here. All of you. I want everyone to see you. The four bright lights. My helpers. My facilitators.*"

Trey tried to laugh. Tried to curse. Tried to say something witty.

But his legs were moving without his control, carrying him out onto the stage. Jonesy and Anthem came with him, all in a terrified row. They came to the very edge of the circle in which the demon stood.

Bird alone remained where he was.

The audience cried out in fear.

"*Hush,*" said the demon, and every voice was stilled. Their mouths moved but there was no sound. People tried to get out of their seats, to flee, to storm the doors; but no one could rise.

Ben Franklin chuckled mildly. He cocked an eye at Trey. "*This performance is for you. All for you.*"

Trey stared at him, his mind teetering on the edge of a precipice. Davidoff, as silent as the crowd, stood nearby.

"*At the risk of being glib,*" said the demon, "*I think it's fair to say that class is in session. You called me to provide knowledge, and I am ever delighted, as all of my kind are delighted, to bow and scrape before man and give away under duress those secrets we have spent ten million years discovering. It's what we live for. It makes us so…happy.*"

When he said the word "happy," lights exploded overhead and showered the audience with smoking fragments that they were entirely unable to avoid. Trey and the others stood helpless at the edge of the circle.

Trey tried to speak, tried to force a single word out. With a flick of a finger the demon freed his lips and the word, "How?" burst out.

Ben Franklin nodded. "*You get a gold star for asking the right question, young Trey. Perhaps I will burn it into your skull.*" He winked. "*Later.*"

Trey's heart hammered with trapped frenzy.

"*You wrote the script for tonight, did you not?*" asked the demon. "*Then you should understand. This is your show and tell. I am here for you. So…you tell me.*"

Suddenly Trey's mouth was moving, forming words, his tongue rebelled and shaped them, his throat gave them sound.

"*A careless magician summons his own death,*" Trey said, but it was Davidoff's voice that issued from his throat. "*All of the materials need to be pure. Vital essences—blood, sweat or tears—must never be* allowed within the demon's circle for these form a bridge between the worlds of spirit and flesh."

The big screens suddenly flashed with new images. Anthem. Typing, her fingers blurring. The image tightened until the focus was entirely on her fingernails. Nibbled and bitten to the quick, caked with…

"Blood," said Anthem, her voice a monotone.

Then Jonesy spoke but it was Davidoff's bass voice that rumbled from her throat. *"A learned magician is a quiet and solitary person. All of his learning, all of his preparation for this ritual must be played out in his head. He cannot practice his invocations because magical words each have their special power. To casually speak a spell is to open a doorway that might never be shut."*

And now the screens showed Jonesy reading the spells aloud as Anthem typed.

Trey closed his eyes. He didn't need to see any more.

"Arrogance is such a strange thing," said the demon. *"You expect it from the powerful because they believe that they are gods. But you…Trey, Anthem, Jonesy…you should have known better. You did know better. You just didn't care enough to believe that any of it mattered. Pity."*

The demon stepped toward them, crossing the line of the protective circle as if it held no power. And Trey suddenly realized that it did not. Somewhere, the ritual was flawed beyond fixing. Was it Kidd's sabotage or something deeper? From the corner of his eye Trey could see the glistening lines of tears slipping down Anthem's cheeks.

The demon paused and looked at her. *"Your sin is worse. You do believe but you fight so hard not to. You fight to be numb to the larger world so that you will be accepted as a true academic like these others. You are almost beyond saving. Teetering on the brink. If you had the chance, I wonder in which direction you would place your next step."*

A sob, silent and terrible, broke in Anthem's chest. Trey tried to say something to her, but then the demon moved to stand directly in front of him.

"You owe me thanks, my young student," said the demon. *"When the late and unlamented Mr. Kidd tried to spoil the results of your project*

by altering the protection spells, he caused all of this to happen. He made it happen, but not out of reverence for the forces of the universe and certainly not out of any belief in the larger world. He did it simply out of spite. He wanted no profit from your failure except the knowledge that you would be ruined. That was as unwise as it was heartless...and I paid him in kind."

The demon nudged the heart on the floor. It quivered and tendrils of smoke drifted up from it. Trey tried to imagine the terror Kidd must have felt as this monster attacked him and brutalized him, and he found that he felt a splinter of compassion for Kidd.

"You pretend to be scholars," breathed the demon, *"so then here is a lesson to ponder. You think that all of religion, all of faith, all of spirit, is a cultural oddity, an accident of confusion by uneducated minds. An infection of misinformation that spread like a disease, just as man spread like a disease. You, in your arrogance, believe that because you do not believe that belief is nothing. You dismiss all other possibilities because they do not fit into your hypothesis. Like the scientists who say that because evolution is a truth—and it is a truth—that there is nothing divine or intelligent in the universe. Or the astronomers who say that the universe is only as large as the stones thrown by the Big Bang."* He touched his lips to Trey's ear. *"Arrogance. It has always been the weakness of man. It's the thing that keeps you bound to the prison of flesh. Oh yes, bound, and it is a prison that does not need to have locked doors."*

Trey opened his eyes. His mouth was still free and he said, "What?"

The demon smiled. *"Arrogance often comes with blindness. Proof of magic surrounds you all the time. Proof that man is far more than a creature of flesh, proof that he can travel through doorways to other worlds, other states of existence. It's all around you."*

"Where?"

The screens once more filled with the images of Maori with their painted faces, and Navajo shaman and their sand paintings, medicine men in the remote Amazon, the story-singers of the Bushmen of Africa. As Trey watched, the images shifted and tightened so that the dominant feature in each was the eyes of these people.

These believers.

Then ten thousand other sets of eyes flashed across the screens. People of all races, all cultures, all times. Cave men and saints, simple farmers and scholars endlessly searching the stars for a glimpse of something larger. Something *there.* Never giving up, never failing to believe in the possibility of the larger world. The larger universe.

Even Bird's eyes were there. Just for a moment.

"Can you, in your arrogance," asked the demon, *"look into these eyes and tell me with the immutable certainty of your scientific disbelief that every one of these people is deluded? That they are wrong? That they see nothing? That nothing is there to be seen? Can you stand here and look down the millennia of man's experience on Earth and say that since science cannot measure what they see then they see nothing at all? Can you tell me that magic does not exist? That it has never existed? Can you, my little student, tell me that? Can you say it with total and unshakeable conviction? Can you, with your scientific certitude, dismiss me into nonexistence, and with me all of the demons and angels, gods and monsters, spirits and shades who walk the infinite worlds of all of time and space?"*

Trey's heart hammered and hammered and wanted to break.

"No," he said. His voice was a ghost of a whisper.

"No," agreed the demon. *"You can't. And how much has that one word cost you, my fractured disbeliever? What, I wonder, do you believe now?"*

Tears rolled down Trey's face.

"Answer this, then," said the demon, *"why am I not bound to the circle of protection? You think that it was because Mr. Kidd played pranks with the wording? No. You found every error. In that you were diligent. And the circles and patterns were drawn with precision. So…why am I not bound? What element was missing from this ritual? What single thing was missing that would have given you and these other false conjurers the power to bind me?"*

Trey wanted to scream. Instead he said, "Belief."

"Belief," agreed the demon softly.

"I'm sorry," whispered Trey. "God…I'm sorry…"

The demon leaned in and his breath was scalding on Trey's cheek. *"Tell me one thing more, my little sorcerer,"* whispered the monster, *"should I believe that you truly are sorry?"*

"Y—yes."

"Should I have faith in the regrets of the faithless?"

"I'm sorry," he said. "I...didn't know."

The demon chuckled. *"Have you ever considered that atheism as strong as yours is itself a belief?"*

"I—"

"We all believe in something. That is what brought your kind down from the trees. That is what made you human. After all this time, how can you not understand that?"

Trey blinked and turned to look at him.

The demon said, *"You think that science is the enemy of faith. That what cannot be measured cannot be real. Can you measure what is happening now? What meter would you use? What scale?"*

Trey said nothing.

"Your project, your collection of spells. What is it to you? What is it in itself? Words? Meaningless and silly? Without worth?"

Trey dared not reply.

"Who are you to disrespect the shaman and the magus, the witch and the priest? Who are you to say that the child on his knees is a fool; or the crone on the respirator? How vast and cold is your arrogance that you despise the vow and the promise and the prayer of everyone who has ever spoken such words with a true heart?"

The demon touched Trey's chest.

"In the absence of proof you disbelieve. In the absence of proof a child will believe, and belief can change worlds. That's the power you spit upon, and in doing so you deny yourself the chance to shape the universe according to your will. You become a victim of your own closed-mindedness."

Tears burned on Trey's flesh.

"Here is a secret," said the demon. *"Believe it or not, as you will. But when we whispered the secrets of evocation to your ancestors, when we taught them to make circles of protection—it was not to protect them from us. No. It was us who wanted protection from you. We swim in the waters of belief. You, and those like you, spit pollution into those waters*

with doubt and cynicism. With your arrogant disinterest in the ways the universe actually works. When you conjure us, we shudder." He leaned closer. *"Tell me, little Trey, now that your faithless faith is shattered...if you had the power to banish me, would you?"*

Trey had to force the word out. "Yes."

"Even though that would require faith to open the doors between the worlds?"

Trey squeezed his eyes shut. "Y—yes."

"Hypocrite," said the demon, but he was laughing as he said it. *"Here endeth the lesson."*

Trey opened his eyes.

--13--

Trey felt his mouth move again. His lips formed a word.

"Username?" he asked.

Anthem looked sheepishly at him and nibbled the stub of a green fingernail. "You're going to laugh at me."

Trey stared at her. Gaped at her.

"What—?" she said, suddenly touching her face, her nose, to make sure that she didn't have anything on her. "What?"

Trey sniffed. He could taste tears in his mouth, in the back of his throat. And there was a smell in the air. Ozone and sulfur. He shook his head, trying to capture the thought that was just there, just on the edge. But...no, it was gone.

Weird. It felt important. It felt big.

But it was gone, whatever it was.

He took Anthem's hand and studied her fingers. There was blood caked in the edges. He glanced at the keyboard and saw the chocolate colored stains. Faint, but there.

"You got blood on the keys," he said. "You have to be careful."

"Why?"

"Because this is magic and you're supposed to be careful."

Anthem gave him a sideways look. "Oh, very funny."

"No," he said, "not really."

"What's it matter? I'll clean the keyboard."

"It matters," he said, and then for reasons he could not quite understand, at least not at the moment, he said, "We have to do it right is all."

"Do what right?"

"All of it," said Trey. "The spells. Entering them, everything. We need to get them right. Everything has to be right."

"I know, I know…or the program won't collate the right way and—"

"No," he said softly. "Because this stuff is important. To…um…people."

Anthem studied his face for a long moment, then she nodded.

"Okay," she said and got up to get some computer wipes.

Trey sat there, staring at the hazy outline of his reflection. He could see his features, but somehow, in some indefinable way, he looked different.

Or, at least he believed he did.

T. Rhymer

Author's Note

I've always been a fan of folklore and folk tales. I remember sitting in my girlfriend's basement back in 1974 listening to the album *NOW WE ARE SIX* by Steeleye Span. My favorite song on that album was "Thomas the Rhymer," which conjured thoughts of magic, doomed love and the realms of faerie. Years later, when doing research for my nonfiction books on supernatural folklore, I began reading about Thomas of Erceldoune, the real-world 13th century Scottish laird on whom the legend is based. There are so many wonderful and complex tales about Thomas that it's hard to pin down exactly who and, moreover, *what* he was.

When an opportunity came for me to tackle another fantasy story—this time for Christopher Golden's *DARK DUETS* anthology, I reached out to my good friend, the noted fantasist Gregory Frost. He is deeply knowledgeable about folklore and is as much a Thomas the Rhymer fan as I am. We cooked up this tale, and it is very likely it will be the first of a cycle of stories about him we'll tell.

T. RHYMER
by
Gregory Frost and Jonathan Maberry

--1--

When the tall sleek man sitting alone at a table caught Stacey's eye, she ignored him. He was alone, a glass of whiskey between his palms, watching her.

Stacey turned away. She even made it clear that she was ignoring him. It was too early in the evening to throw anyone too much rope. Let him tread water for a while. If she swam past all the guppies and didn't let any of the sharks take a bite, then maybe she'd carve off a thicker slice of her attention.

Coming to this place wasn't even her idea. The whole Edinburgh club scene was a bore; but tonight it was a necessary evil. The trip to the nightclub was an impromptu mini-celebration because her roommate, Carrie, had gotten the promotion she'd been aching for. Carrie celebrated everything of value in her life with tequila, loud music and a degree of flirtation that would shame Hugh Grant.

And, thank god, it was Friday.

As well as the night before Hallowe'en.

More reasons for Carrie to throw caution, common sense and—all too frequently—her clothing, to the wind.

Stacey wasn't entirely sure if she was here as a friend sharing a moment, a wingman, a designated driver, or a chaperone. Since moving in with Carrie, Stacey had been all of those things. More than once.

She sipped her drink and killed some slow minutes by looking around. Jack-o'-lanterns lit every table; warm drinks came in mugs filled from a bowl that bubbled and smoked like a tub of dry ice on the end of the bar. A lot of people pranced about in costumes, and some half-out. At the best of times she would have avoided the lights, crammed crowds, and thumping beats of clubbing. The speakers were loud enough to create little Jurassic Park vibration rings in her drink. She had a favorite song by *The Be Good Tanyas* that commented how only crazy people went to a place that was too dark to see and too loud to hear in order to meet anyone. Whatever else, she was not looking to meet anyone.

No way, Jose.

Especially after the last one, the law clerk. She should have fled early from that one. He was twenty-six and had posters thumb-tacked to his bedroom walls. Not framed art—posters. Granted they were classic movies—*Casablanca, Metropolis*—but it was a warning sign she'd chosen to ignore. The law clerk was cute, with a kind of Bradley Cooper vibe that somehow disabled her common sense. The first time he cried during sex Stacey thought it was special, a sharing of something genuinely deep and meaningful. By the fifth or maybe sixth time the word *"flee!"* was painted on the inside of her head. Even then, she stayed too long, and now she felt wrecked, jaded and weary of the whole dating thing.

So, this field trip was strictly for Carrie. A few drinks and then go home. Otherwise she'd have worn something more stylish than a drab sweater and black jeans over her Nina slingbacks.

And yet…

Her attention kept returning to the man. Black jacket over black crew-neck shirt. Black hair, too, with a windswept style that looked expensive. Perfect deepwater tan. And eyes the color of hot gold.

Stacey lifted her glass to take a sip and set it down with no conscious awareness of whether she'd had any. She tried not to look at those eyes.

Tried.

He gave her the smallest of smiles. Not a come on. Not even encouragement. Just a smile. Showing that he knew she was looking at him, just as he was looking at her. It was the first thing he'd done since sitting down. All this time he'd simply sat there, watching the crowd swirl around him, some in work clothes, some in costumes. He was in the middle of it and entirely apart from it.

Stacey thought, *No thanks, buddy. Whatever you're selling, I can't afford it.*

She thought that, but then she realized that she wasn't sitting at her table anymore. In some dreamy and distant way she felt herself moving. Walking across the floor, weaving without thought between clusters of vampires and zombies, and a few grinning Guy Fawkeses.

Then she was at his table. Standing so close the edge of it pressed into the tops of her thighs. And he didn't seem the least surprised when she just came to a rest right before him.

Her mind told her to leave.

To run.

Right now.

But she stood there, leaning into his table, aware on some level that if it wasn't there she'd have fallen on him.

Wake up, you stupid bitch!

Her mind kept screaming at her, but it was like the soundtrack of a film she was watching: happening to someone else.

The man lifted his eyes. They really did look like hot gold. As if they were lit from within. Weird contacts? *No,* came the answer in her mind. *It isn't the contacts that are weird.*

Run. For Christ's sake...run.

From across the room the man's eyes were just eyes. From across the room his smile was friendly.

Oh, god...

But here...within reach, within touching distance, the eyes were alien, and his smile...

Oh, Jesus, what's wrong with me?

But she knew—on every level—that what was wrong was not her.

That smile seemed to somehow touch her. Without lifting a finger or saying a word, this man seemed to touch her. Everywhere. Inside her clothes. Inside her body.

Inside...

She could see the gold of his eyes as he sliced off each and every one of her secrets and slipped them between those smiling lips.

Took them.

Consumed them.

Please.

She thought she said it aloud. Maybe she did, but the music crushed it flat.

Please, she begged.

That only made his smile creep wider.

Stacey could feel herself wanting to give in. She knew that she had issues with being too submissive. Five years of therapy hadn't fixed that. She wasn't a total slave, not like the girls she knew who cruised in the BDSM waters. But she gave up and gave in too soon.

Too soon.

Too much.

Oh, god, please.

The man's smile seemed to coax her to share her darkest thoughts. It made her unlock the locks and pull open the doors of her mind so that he could see his image there. The Dark Knight about whom she'd fantasized since before puberty. The shadowy stranger who would come and sweep her off her feet.

A man of shadows. From shadows.

With burning eyes.

And he, without so much as a word, peeled each secret out of her soul and pasted before her the images of what he would do. . . and it was everything she wanted. Motionless, staring into his eyes, she grew wet with desire.

The man raised his glass and finished his whiskey, then he pushed his chair back and stood up. Without saying a word, he turned and left the bar.

Stacey followed him.

She felt herself do it and couldn't believe she was doing it.

"Hey, girl!" called Carrie from across the bar, but the thumping beat all but drowned her out. It made it easy for Stacey to pretend she didn't hear.

They left the club.

The man didn't even once glance back to see if Stacey was following, but walked on across the parking lot.

"*Stacey!*"

Hearing Carrie yell her name stalled her in her tracks, and Stacey turned like a sleepwalker.

Here came poor Carrie, looking both angry and concerned. "Wot are you playing at, you daft cow? You're going to abandon me to those carnivores in there? Wot's 'e—"

Carrie's tirade suddenly disintegrated into a meaningless jumble of sounds. Noises.

The man stepped between her and Stacey.

"No," he said.

Immediately Carrie stopped walking, stopped talking and she sat down right there in the middle of the parking lot. Right on the asphalt that was stained with grease and oil. Carrie's rump thumped down, her legs splayed wide revealing white thighs and blue knickers. Her eyes were as wide as saucers and there was absolutely no trace of anything in them.

"Carrie...?" began Stacey, but the man turned around and focused his eyes on her. Stacey's voice evaporated into a misty nothing.

"Time to go, Stacey."

His voice was like syrup, like the most potent drink imaginable, like heroin.

She forgot about Carrie sitting splay-legged on the ground.

She forgot about her car. Her purse. Her life.

The man took her arm.

She melted into him.

Into his arms.

Into his car.

And into the night.

--2--

The sleek limousine drove past him, but no one inside—not the brutish driver, the smiling man or the drowning woman—saw the figure who watched it go. He was in plain sight, but he stood so completely still that the world seemed to move around him. Nothing reacted to him—not drunks on the street, not the dog searching for scraps in the alleys.

He watched the car with eyes that had grown old and fierce and murderous. As its taillights vanished around a corner, he bared his teeth like a night-hunting cat or some darker predatory thing. Those he was hunting were in that limo, the glamoured one, and a skinwalker as a bonus.

When the street was empty, the figure turned, seeming to detach himself from the shadows. He touched his pockets and belt in a reflexive movement as natural to him as breathing. Checking that everything was where it should be.

His knives, the *òrdstone*, his strangle-wire. All of it.

Without haste he turned and crossed the street to where a motorcycle stood, black and gleaming. Waiting for him. The only detail on the bike was a partial handprint burned onto the engine cowling in angry red. It was not put there as a decoration. It had happened during a moment of blood, of screams and slaughter. And now the mark was burned into the metal.

The man swung his leg over the seat, keyed the ignition and fed gas into the hungry engine.

The roar of his motorcycle split the air like a cleaver as he rode away in the same direction as the limousine.

--3--

The man's limousine was long and dark and sleek, and there was plenty of room for Stacey to get naked.

She did it slowly, but in a dreamy way, not like a vamp.

Piece by piece. Snaps, hooks, sleeves, straps. The hiss of cloth down her skin.

The air inside the car was stifling hot. Furnace hot.

Sweat ran in crooked lines down her arms and legs and back, and despite the heat her skin pebbled with gooseflesh, her nipples growing hard. Stacey's breath rasped in her throat. It was less like the heaving breath of passion and more like the gasps of drowning.

Her clothes were scattered around her.

She was naked, vulnerable, unable to resist him.

The man sat on the bench seat, legs crossed, hands folded idly in his lap, eyes hooded in thoughtful appraisal.

Stacey felt her arms lift, hands reaching for him. Her mouth opened and a low moan came from deep inside her chest.

The man did not move. He watched her, still smiled at her. His lips were red, his teeth glistening with spit.

Stacey closed her eyes and waited to be taken. To be used.

To be whatever he wanted.

No, cried a voice deep down in her soul, but it went unheeded.

The limo drove far out of town, leaving Edinburgh behind. Shadow-shrouded trees whisked by on either side.

All the time Stacey knelt there, arms raised, beckoning to him, aching with a need that no part of her mind could understand.

"Please…" she managed to say aloud.

The man looked at her for a moment longer, then he turned his head and stared out at the night-black landscape.

After a long, long time the car slowed to a stop, the tires crunching over gravel and then dried leaves. Stacey sagged back, her arms falling to her sides.

The limo door opened and the man stepped out. He did not tell her to follow, but she followed. Naked, covered in sweat. Cold air licked at her.

They were in the countryside somewhere. It looked like there were huge ruins in the distance, but they were vague shapes against the underlit clouds.

They walked some distance from the limo. Tiny lights like fireflies began to accumulate around them, dancing, flitting about until they all flew to one spot ahead, coalesced into a vertical line. Then, impossibly, the line split wider, began swelling into a bright green glow. She looked to him bathed in that light, but he was no longer there. Something transforming, inhuman, walked in his stead, but still with those eyes that held all she desired.

He walked ahead of her toward the green light. Around him were shadow-shapes, not the ruins she'd seen in the headlights of the limo, but something else. And distance. It wasn't merely light, it was a place. Inside the glow he turned about and held out a hand to her.

"Come," he said.

Stacey looked from his golden eyes to the proffered hand. Her heart lurched in her chest. The fingers were wrong.

So wrong…

They were iron-dark, and all along the back of his hand and down his wrist the skin rose and rippled into dozens of tiny mounds, as if something was pushing from underneath. Then it tore as the needle-sharp tips of small spines thrust outward. Each barb curled out from a knot of gristle, like roses rising from malformed stems.

She watched her own arm extend to take that terrible hand.

Please…please…please…

She could hear her inner voice, her inner howls, but she could not act.

No…it wasn't that. She had no will to act, no desire. Those howls were an enraged echo of the Stacey who used to claim ownership of this body.

Was that Stacey gone? Was she dead?

Her hand reached for his and she took a small step forward, toward the creature who, second by second, was changing. The mottling of his skin ran up his iron-like arm, under dissolving clothes, and erupted all over his throat and cheeks and face. His smiling lips thinned, the mouth widened into an ophidian leer.

The scream she needed to scream burned in her chest.

The owner of the golden eyes chuckled. An ugly noise that was painful to hear.

He said, "Now."

He didn't say it to her. It wasn't a demand for her to do anything, but her eyes widened and her mouth fell open as the night *changed,* and the green burned away her world.

The man—if it was ever a man—stood revealed as something entirely inhuman. Huge and bulky, with skin like that of a diseased toad stretched over muscles undulating in strange arrangements.

His eyes remained that compelling molten gold. And despite the utter horror of what he had revealed himself to be, Stacey had but to look into those eyes to know that she was still a slave. Still lost. Still haplessly willing.

The man—the *thing*—cut one last glance over his shoulder at her and then the green light took him.

He was gone.

Just…gone.

Finally, the scream that could not find release burst out of her.

Not from fear. Not in horror at his grotesque body or the impossibility of what was happening to her.

No, she screamed because the creature intended to destroy her *and she could not help but follow.*

Arms outstretched, she ran straight at the light.

"No!"

The bellow came from the shadows and Stacey turned to see a wild figure emerge from the darkness, running at her with the speed and ferocity of a wolf. He was tall, slim as a sword-blade, with glossy black hair whipping in the night breeze. One hand was empty but in the other he held something—was it a gun? A knife?

Still screaming, he leapt at her, wrapped his arms around her, crushed her to his chest as he fell. They landed together with a bone-rattling thud, but the newcomer turned as they hit, taking the brunt of the fall, the spin of their bodies sloughing off the shock of impact. As they rolled away from the light he opened his arms and she spilled out and away from him. Then he was up cat-quick and he flung himself toward the wall of shimmering green light. His hand rose up and plunged down as if he meant to reach into the light and smash or stab the man who'd brought her here. But instead, as the object made contact, the green light disappeared.

The stranger ripped his arm back and forth, slashing at the light, destroying more of it with each swipe.

No, she thought as a splinter of clarity jabbed through the strange muzziness in her thoughts. She cried, "Wait, what are you doing? You're closing it!"

He dropped to one knee and with a last vicious swipe sealed the night. The shimmering green light shivered and went out, plunging the clearing into darkness.

--4--

Stacey sat up slowly.

It was like coming out of a dream. Or a coma. Her body felt new to her, as if it was something she'd never owned before.

The newcomer stood a few yards away, his back to her, his

hands loose at his sides, the object still clutched in one fist. The limo lights splashed over him obliquely. He sighed and his shoulders sagged for a moment, then he took the object—which she could now see was a piece of smooth gray rock a bit larger than the palm of his hand—and slid it into a leather pouch on his belt. As it vanished from sight, Stacey saw that its face was covered with complex patterns of strange design.

From behind he had dark shaggy hair. He wore a light gray jacket over a torn army-khaki t-shirt, old jeans, and lace-up boots. He turned. She took in the thin hair above his forehead, the beard that was maybe a week old. Her mind seemed to be swirling, confused in its attempt to reconcile being here with being at the club, where she knew she must be.

Then he turned and looked past her to the limousine.

"Skinwalker," he said in a terse, eager whisper and broke into a run. Straight at her.

Stacey screamed and flung herself backward, crossing her arms in front of her to try and ward off another of this night's horrors. But he shot past her, heading straight for the limousine. Too late its engine turned over and started. The door she had emerged from still hung open and the man dove through it as the limo lurched forward. The door swung shut and the limousine rolled maybe ten yards before it braked to a stop again and there was a flash of red from inside it. The engine kept running.

The door opened again and the man climbed out. He held something in his arms, a bundle that, as he came nearer, she saw was her clothes. Only then did she realize she was naked in the middle of a field. And it was cold. She crossed her hands over her breasts.

The man didn't seem affected by her nudity. He held out her clothing as if holding out a gift. Her slingbacks dangled by their straps from two of his fingers.

"You should probably change in the vehicle," he said. His voice was soft, the accent strange. Irish, but with Scottish overtones. And something else. A strange quality she couldn't quite identify.

"I..." she began and faltered. "I don't..."

"You have to hurry." His eyes shifted past her to where the

light had been. "They'll open the portal again in a moment, and he won't be alone this time."

He took her by the arm and directed her back to the limo. There was none of the warmth or magnetism of the other man. In fact, his grip hurt a little, enough to get her moving. She tried to pull away, but his hand was like a vise.

"You're *hurting* me."

His answer was a short, hard laugh. "What do you think *they'll* do?"

He held the door to let her climb in and slammed it behind her. Her mind was still sorting out a hundred questions, but she remained too rattled to ask any of them.

Then she saw the driver. Still upright at the wheel.

Stacey began to say something to him, to plead for help or an answer, but as she bent forward she froze in absolute horror.

The driver was dead.

More than dead...he looked like a corpse that had been rotting for weeks, maybe months. Stacey's mouth worked in a silent attempt to make some kind of rational sound, to *react* in some proper way to this, but that was impossible. She'd expected to see blood everywhere, but there was nothing—nothing to explain that strange explosion of red she'd glimpsed.

The driver's door opened suddenly, and the stranger grabbed hold of the corpse and yanked it out. The neck made a cracking noise and the head dangled loosely. The man got in. He looked back at her. It was not an unpleasant face, but his sharp blue eyes were the saddest she'd ever seen—until they abruptly burned green. It was a moment before she realized they were reflecting a flare of light, and she glanced around.

"Damn it," he whispered tightly.

As he'd predicted, the bright green oval had re-appeared. Stacey stared at it with a mind that felt like it was fracturing. Even though she'd seen one like it only a minute ago, seeing this new one form out of nowhere was somehow worse. It promised something, some secret she knew she didn't want to hear.

Through the tinted window of the limo, she made out strange, rough shapes moving within the light.

Moving toward *her*.

"Hold on," growled the stranger as he slammed the door and put the car in gear.

Stacey stared at the green light and saw an impossible shape begin to emerge. All spikes and knobs, with massive shoulders packed with muscle.

"Oh, god! Something's coming through!"

The man stamped down on the gas. The limo pawed at the dirt like a maddened bull, then sprang forward with a roar of tires that left a cloud of dust behind them. He kept accelerating until they reached the main road, and then squealed onto the pavement.

The green became a tiny thing seen between trees and then was gone.

--5--

They drove in silence a while, and she wasn't prepared when the wave of shock finally slammed into her. Without realizing, she was abruptly gasping, panting, her heart racing. She thought she might be sick, rolled down the window and stuck her head out into the cold wind. Her eyes watered and she broke into sobs. She reeled her head back in, found him watching her in the rearview mirror. He hadn't closed the driver's compartment panel.

The realization of her fear exhausted her. She lay back against the seat and stared at nothing. She still hadn't put on her clothes, and how ridiculous was it that they didn't seem to matter? She tried to explain to herself what had happened to her, to Carrie sitting unconscious in a puddle of oil.

Her right shoulder blade itched and she scratched at it. The silence was becoming oppressive.

"Where are we going?" she asked.

He shrugged out of his jacket and it thrust it at her. "Cover yourself."

"Where are we going?" she repeated, leaning on each word.

"Somewhere safe."

Stacey covered herself as best she could with the jacket, shivering with cold and the terror that trembled beneath her skin.

"Not back to the club then."

"D'ye not know how far from there you are?"

"Um…a long way?" she ventured.

He gave a short, bitter laugh. "Not so long as it could have been."

"My roommate's at the club. I left her."

"She'll be fine. They didn't select her. But not the club, no. Nor to your flat."

His accent really was odd. It wasn't Irish at all, she decided. It sounded somehow old, unevolved, like maybe he lived out on the Orkneys or somewhere else isolated. She couldn't place it.

"Why did you interfere?" She didn't mean for it to sound accusatory that way. The part of her that had acknowledged her lifetime of subjugation seemed to be speaking, but he didn't seem to notice.

"Be happy I did, lass."

"No…why? Tell me."

At least a mile passed before he answered. "It's a very long story. Just know for now that I'm going to keep them from taking you."

"Why?" she asked, leaning forward. "What are you, the Lone Ranger?"

"I don't know who that is."

"Right. Naw, you wouldn't."

Another silent mile, then, "You sound angry that I didn't let him have you."

"I …" She couldn't figure out how to answer him, but he interrupted.

"Try to understand, they're good at hearing that in you, that sort of need. It's not your fault, any of it."

"What's not my fault?" She climbed across the center table to the seats in back of him, stuck her head through the open barrier. "Who in hell *are* you?"

"Who out of hell, not in," he said bitterly. "The one who escaped but came back like the tide again and again."

"Oh, great. Riddles. I've stepped into the Twilight Zone, and you're feeding me riddles? What are you, Gollum?"

"Hardly."

"Well…who *are* you, then?"

He thought about that for a moment. "Rhymer," he replied, though she didn't know if that was his name or some form of behavioral explanation.

"Do you know what's going on?"

"Aye, I do." His voice and face were sad.

"Why is this happening to me?" she asked, and her voice suddenly dwindled to something smaller, more vulnerable. "Why do these people want to hurt me? Did I do something wrong or—?"

"No," he said firmly, "it isn't your fault that the Yvag singled you out."

"*Yvag*? Is that his name?"

"It's what he is."

She huddled behind the jacket, eyes huge. "I saw that, didn't I? I mean…all that stuff back there, and him changing. It really happened, didn't it?"

Rhymer nodded.

Tears broke from her eyes. "That man—"

"Wasn't a man," he finished.

"What *was* he?"

He considered the question. "They're what you'd call elves."

Despite her tears, a single bark of laughter escaped her. "Wait, what? I'm sorry, but did you say…*elves*?"

"Aye."

"As in the little sods making toys for Father Christmas?"

"Hardly." He glanced sidelong at her, the smile still in place. "Sounds so cute and cuddly, doesn't it? Little wee elves."

"The night before Hallowe'en and I got picked up in a club by an elf?"

"Aye."

"What did he slip into my drink?"

"Nothing."

"Then I'm crazy? Is that it? I've gone barking mad?"

"I know it all *feels* a bit mad," he admitted. "But it's true. Like it or not, this is the real world."

"*How?*"

"Like I said, there's a long story."

She reached to scratch her shoulder again.

"You might not want to do that," he told her, "or it could start bleeding."

"What could?" she asked, wide-eyed. She pushed her shoulder forward and tried to see her back. Was there something? She glanced around for her purse, a compact. It wasn't here. Probably back at the club. Great, her ID, credit cards. Looking up then, she realized that the ceiling of the rear section of the limo was mirrored. She could guess why. There was probably a highway club that only did it in limos. She looked around till she located the bank of switches, flicked them until she'd ignited lights surrounding the mirror. Now she could see her naked self clearly, curled up on the seat, her dirty soles tucked under her. On her back there was definitely some kind of mark. It looked angry, infected maybe.

"What the hell?" she demanded.

"It's a *sigil*. He marked you. Why you cannae go back to your flat nor anywhere close. They're going to track you by that no matter where—"

But by then her hysteria had hit the ceiling. "Track me? What do you mean, *track* me? How did this happen?" Her voice quavered and tears stung her eyes. "Mister, what are you talking about?"

He sighed and gripped the wheel. "Ten centuries and you'd think I'd be better at this," he said to himself. "Look, lass. The short version—which isn't going to make sense tae ye—is that you've become the chosen *teind*, which translates for the Yvag as their tithe to Hell."

"Whoa…wait. Hell?"

"Aye."

"As in…*hell*?"

"Aye."

"Actual hell? Not just hell but *hell* hell?"

"The same."

"I think I need to scream."

"You might at that," he said, either not getting her joke or not considering it one. "The Yvag have chosen you, marked you with their *sigil,* and that means that until they get their hands on you again, they're going to be extremely unhappy, not to mention panicked, because if they don't get you back for their ceremony, then that princeling who snatched you has to take your place in the ritual."

"Good. Fuck him."

"I couldnae agree more."

"Wait...princeling?"

"Aye, he is powerful among them. He has great charisma, lass. They all have it, but few wield it with his level of power."

"'Charisma'?" she echoed.

"Aye. To humans that's just a gift of attraction, something to sell cars with, but for the Yvag it's one of their most powerful weapons. They can make you lay bare your throat for the knife and thank them while they cut."

She thought about all of the absurd things she had done, including stripping naked without a thought, and shivered.

Rhymer sighed. "Had I brought him down tonight it would have crushed them."

"For good?"

"No...but it would weaken them for many years to come. Ah well. Meantime, I recommend you switch off those lights before we pass this articulated lorry, else you're going tae give the driver a heart attack. You might want to put your clothes back on, too, as we'll be pulling off the road in a minute. At least your shoes."

"Oh, God."

Everything that was happening was jumbled inside Stacey's head and she knew, on some level, that she should be reacting better than she was. She also knew, with perfect clarity, that she was teetering on the edge of some dangerous level of shock. There were too many bizarre and impossible things happening and despite tears and gooseflesh, she was taking this all too calmly. Her lack of ordinary reaction to it terrified her.

Her nudity, oddly, did not. And it damn well should have. She didn't even like wearing low-cut blouses.

Even so, she punched the switches until the rear of the limo went dark, and they passed the semi. She sorted through the heaped jeans, cami, and sweater until she found her panties.

"Can you answer a question?"

"I can try."

"I…just went with that guy. That elf or whatever. I went with him. I let him touch me. I took my fucking clothes off for him. I don't *do* that. A guy tries to grab my ass I kick the piss out of him. I'm not a victim, damn it, and I'm not anyone's casual piece of ass."

"No," Rhymer agreed.

"Well, you seem to understand this madness, so you tell me why I did this?"

In the rearview mirror she saw him grin again. It changed his face from one of lupine harshness to something else. When he smiled his face was gentle. Sad…but gentle.

"If I tell ye that this is all glamour and magick, will you hit me in the back of the head with your shoe?"

"Why…is that the sort of thing you're likely to say?"

"Well…elves and all…"

"Bollocks," she said, but it was to herself. An admission that they were no longer driving through a sane landscape.

She pulled on her clothes. "So, what, I have to stay hidden till after Hallowe'en?"

"Well, that's where we get into the long version of things. Normally, they would be hunting you for about a year."

"A *year*?" She did almost whack him with her shoe then.

"It's a question of relational temporalities. A day in *Yvagddu* lasts a year in our world. But they got cocky about things, figured to haul you over and dispose of you just like that, so they waited —"

"Just tell me for fuck's sake!"

"Thirty more hours, more or less."

She fell back against the seat. "I have to call Carrie. I need to know she got back to the flat okay."

"Right. Here." He handed her a cell phone. "It's a burner. You don't want to use your own."

She stared from the phone to him. "Elves can track cell phone calls?"

For the first time he gave her a genuine and open grin. "Aye, the universe is totally daft like that."

"But…why the secrecy? Why not go south? We could go down to London, nobody can find anybody there."

He shrugged. "You're lucky you don't have a family," he said. "If ye had folks, children, it'd be far worse. They could substitute them on account of your blood."

"If I had kids and a family," she fired back, "I wouldn't 'a been clubbing with Carrie in the first place. Pish."

Quite suddenly, Rhymer spoke in a peculiar sing-song.

"No cause to trust eyes of promise,

Eyes so golden, eyes that burn, down into your darkest soul.

When you fall, and all unbinds

The last of you will scream out for the first."

Despite the words his singing voice was beautiful. In the strangest way, the sound of his voice comforted her, removing splinters of fear from her mind.

Rhymer fell silent again, and drove on as if nothing odd had occurred.

She stared at him, his face bluish like a ghost in the dawn light. Rhymer—what in hell kind of name was that? Like something out of an old folk song.

--6--

Stacey had assumed they would be pulling into, at the very least, a lay-by. They weren't all that far from where they'd begun, maybe five or ten kilometers.

Instead, Rhymer turned the behemoth of a limo onto another dirt track that led into the darkness of another wood. He shut off the engine but left the headlamps glowing onto a clearing among the trees.

When she climbed out after him, she spotted the nose of a blue Fiat Punto backed in on the left. She remained where she was while he headed to the other car. He didn't seem to realize she wasn't following him until he had crossed the clearing.

He met her gaze over the limo. "I don't blame you," he said. "I'd be contemplating scarpering, too, wondering how hard it can be to lose me in the woods. I'll save you the trouble of breaking your ankle on a root—I'll not chase you. You go as you choose. Whatever you do, though, don't wait here. It'll like as not take them the whole morning, but they'll find you."

She took a wobbling step away from the limousine door. "Will they all be like him? Because I didn't have any choice with him…" She felt her face burn as she said that. It felt like admitting something bad, something dirty.

"What, you mean his glamour? Oh, they'll be sleekit but none of them's cowrin or timorous beasties."

She said, "What?"

Rhymer took a breath and continued, but Stacey noticed that he dialed down his accent. It seemed to take effort for him to speak in a normal, modern way. So weird, she thought. Rhymer said, "The glamoured ones all gleam like that. They'll have a harder time now on account of you're not wide open, d'ye see? So you stand a chance there, you can get away before they snare you again. It's the skinwalkers you likely won't see coming."

"What are skinwalkers?"

He glanced into the darkness behind the limo. "We should have this conversation while in motion, not waiting for them to catch us up."

"But you took their transportation."

He shook his head. "It's hardly the only way they travel. Even on foot I get from here to there. They won't be on foot." He sighed. "I had to leave a bonny little motorcycle back there, but I could'nae see driving off on that with you starkers on the back."

"Uh…no."

He nodded to the Punto. "This piece of junk will do for now. It's faster than it looks, and it's the kind of thing no one pays attention to."

"Nondescript ain't in it," she agreed.

Suddenly something whooshed above the trees. It might have been an owl, she thought, but Rhymer immediately climbed into the Punto and started the engine. Stacey pulled off her shoes again and walked, limped, cursed her way across the clearing toward the compact Fiat. The second she was in, he took off. They swung around the limousine and back up the dark rutted track, then back onto the A68 again.

A stripe of gray dawn painted the eastern horizon. She tossed her shoes in the back, noticing as she did the curving lines of some device laid across the rear seats.

Her inner voice couldn't seem to settle between rage and terror. The urge to yell at him compelled her, but she couldn't identify what for. He had saved her, saved her life, and she was reacting as though she resented it. All meaningful questions went unspoken while she asked herself what in hell was wrong with her.

Finally, she prompted, "Skinwalkers...?"

"Mmm." He glanced at her sidelong. "People taken over by the Yvag. Mostly people in positions of power."

"What, like kings?"

Rhymer's features stiffened as if he could see something terrible on the road ahead. She couldn't help looking. But then he sang in the same soft voice as before. It was almost spoken-word, but flowed with an elusive interior melody.

"Never kings, but always kingdoms.

Never thrones but always ears.

Crucial words, spoke in whispers,

from our hands put power in theirs."

"God *damn* it, what is that? You got like some fucking Tourette's you can't help?"

"What?" He blinked at her, perplexed. "What did I say?"

She repeated the lyrics more or less, then asked, "You don't know when you do that?"

Rhymer took a moment answering that. "I don't, actually, strange as that sounds. I...know it's happening, but I'm lost *while* it happens. It's like something is talking through me."

"Oh, fuck me. You're telling me you're possessed?"

"No," he said quickly. "It's not that at all. I don't know how to explain it, though."

"But you do know what it means—what you said?"

"Aye."

When he didn't offer more than that, she said, "Well? How about we both know, since it's my arse they want, not yours."

"It's my *head* they want."

"I thought they wanted me."

"And now I've interfered, you're a pathway to me."

"The fuck I am."

Rhymer shrugged. "It's complicated."

"So's algebra. Try me anyway."

But he didn't.

She ground her teeth. "Okay, then what about the other thing? Tell me about those skinwalker things. Otherwise, you're taking me the hell back to Edinburgh right now, and sod you and your elves."

"Right." Rhymer rubbed his eyes. "So, the Yvag, they're ancient, like more ancient than the Earth itself."

"How's that possible?"

"Where they live, it's a space between universes, ours and others. There are lots of others, I gather."

"A multiverse?"

He cut her a sharp look. "Now how do ye know that word?"

"I have every episode of *Doctor Who* DVR'd. Keep talking."

Looking vaguely perplexed, Rhymer nodded. "They came from one of the others. It collapsed or something—I'm not entirely clear on the concept and it's not like they feel as if I ought to be included. Their escape, though, tied them to or was dependent upon some other form of life."

"Like what?"

"Like Hell," he said. "Not your scriptural one exactly, though I expect your version of Hell came from them, too."

"Hold on...Judeo-Christian tradition comes from elves?"

"I know how it sounds."

"Not to a history major, you don't."

"All right, history major, just suppose that a lot of people with influence, advisors to the powers-that-be, were..."

"What?"

"Were not really *people*, d'ye see? Suppose the Yvag had colonized them?"

"Skinwalkers, that's what you meant?"

"Yeah. They move in, take control of certain people—the ones who make laws, the ones who decide for everyone else, almost never the central person, almost always the advisors."

"'Never kings but always kingdoms,'" she repeated back at him.

"Exactly. If they were kings, they'd be in view. But manipulating the king? They stay in the shadows."

"Was the driver—?"

"He was one, yeah. I know, he's not someone in a position of power like, but they need others, too, to do simple tasks, move the glamoured ones around."

"Minions?" she said, smiling for the first time.

"Aye," agreed Rhymer, "minions is a good word."

"Jesus," she said to herself, "I'm having a conversation in which elves, the multiverse and minions are serious talking points. And vodka is not involved." She took a breath. "But why did that skinwalker bloke look so…so dead?"

"Because he *was* dead the instant an Yvag took him. When they move in, they rip the human soul out. Whoever that person was is destroyed. Shredded. From that moment forward, the body is dead and only the Yvag is alive. The corpse maintains the appearance of being alive as long as the Yvag is inside, but once it's gone then the magic is broken and the body becomes what it really is—dead and rotting flesh. The longer the Yvag occupies you, the faster you turn to dust when it leaves. Understand, this magic is difficult, it requires a lot of energy and sometimes it slips. Every now and then you see a person who looks more dead than alive, and it's probably an Yvag whose control has slipped. Which is the other reason they choose to keep to the shadows."

"What do you mean?"

"Sunlight is nae good for dead skin. It speeds the corruption."

"Sounds like vampires."

He nodded. "What people call vampires are almost always Yvags."

"'Almost' always?"

Rhymer gave her a crooked grin. "It's a strange, big universe, lass."

"Yeah, yeah, there are more things in heaven and Earth…" Stacey shook her head, trying to make sense of this. "The driver...the Yvag left him?"

"You could look at it that way."

"Which is to say you killed him."

"That's right."

"Why?"

Rhymer twitched, ducked his head as if she had finally hit a nerve, a place he couldn't go or explain. In the end all he said was, "It's what I do."

She squinched up her face. There was something he had said — tossed off so casually it had flown right past. She rewound the conversation, listened, came to the moment when she'd freaked, and there it was. "Ten centuries. What was that about you living for ten centuries?"

"Well, give or take a decade..."

"Please tell me you're at least cool enough to be a Time Lord."

"A what?"

"Sigh," she said, pronouncing the word.

"I know it's impossible to believe —"

"No, see, that's the problem, I *completely* believe it. I just don't want to be a part of it!"

"I'm sorry you are."

She chewed her lip for a moment. "The way you fought? What was that? Kung-fu? Judo?"

"Gutter fighting," he said. "Bit of this and that."

"Nasty."

"It's not supposed to be nice."

"So...for a thousand years you've been messing it up with them, right? Interfering with this..."

"Tithing."

"Tithing. How often do they have to do that, pay this tithe to Hell?"

"Part of a cycle. Here, it's every twenty-eight years."

"And you've been keeping people like me from getting taken."

He had a strangely anxious look on his face now, and only nodded.

"No wonder they want your head. So in all that time, you must have saved like, what, five, six hundred people?"

He said nothing, staring hard at the road ahead.

"Rhymer, goddamn it. How many have you saved?"

"Counting you, seven."

"Seven hundred people? Really?"

"No," he said softly. "Just seven."

He met her gaze then, and the misery in his look spoke for him.

Very quietly, she said, "I think I want to go home now."

"You can't," he replied. "Not for twenty-one more hours or you're just handing yourself to them."

"Oh really? How's that different from sticking with you?"

"Staying with me means you haven't given up," said Rhymer. "And when they come for you again, we're going to make them pay dearly."

A moment later he added under his breath, "For a great many things."

--7--

Stacey awoke with a jolt.

She hadn't even realized that she'd fallen asleep. She sat up, brain muzzy, tongue thick, skin clammy. She had drool on her chin and wiped it away as she glanced at Rhymer. He was watching the road.

"How long was I asleep?" she asked. She rubbed at her eyes.

"About three hours. You've been through a lot. Magic wears a body out every bit as quickly as exertion."

"'Magic,'" she echoed. "Right. Not a dream. Damn."

Outside, the sky was cloudy, and she didn't recognize anything in the brown and green landscape. They had left the A68 at some point.

"Are we there yet?"

"No, we've still got a bit to go," murmured Rhymer. "Sorry, but we couldn't just keep going straight. They would have come at us from ahead, so I've been shifting direction, zigzagging roads to keep them from being able to predict where we're heading."

"Where *are* we heading? Do we have an actual destination or are we just going to drive around until these Elvis thingees get bored."

"Yvags," he corrected.

"Whatever. Where are we going?"

"I've a place. But going there will only work once, and I want to make sure they don't have sight of the car when we turn off."

As if to accentuate his point, a car roared up from behind to pass on the straightaway. As it came abreast it seemed to hold for a moment, and the driver gave them a hard stare before accelerating ahead.

She saw that Rhymer was watching the car, too. She gripped his forearm.

"Oh, god...please don't tell me that's one of those bleedin' skinwalker things?"

"Can't tell from here," he said. "You can bet they have every available one out listening for your sigil."

"Listening for it," she repeated, trying to grasp the concept. Her stomach gurgled. "For fuck's sake...we're being chased by monsters and here I am starving. I didn't eat last night. What is it, noon?"

"We'll get some food as soon as it's safe and —"

"I'm going to need some real shoes, too. Can we stop somewhere, some town center? Just for, like, half an hour?"

He didn't look happy at the prospect. "What is it about women and shoes?"

"Oh, mock me for being a cliché, that'll help."

"Sorry."

"I need something I can run in. We are fleeing, right?"

"Right. We'll see about getting better shoes, but understand me, lass, we take our lives in our hands every time we stop."

"I get that," she said soberly, "I really do. But if we *are* stopped—by them I mean—I'm no good running through woods and across fields in heels or bare feet."

"Still safer to keep moving," he said.

"Look, you can't seriously expect me to stay in this car for thirty hours? Besides...they could run us off the road way out here and nobody would so much as notice. In a town there are lots of people. Doesn't that make it harder for them?"

He looked at her critically. "You were surrounded by a couple of hundred people at that tavern last night."

"Club," she corrected. "That still doesn't alter the fact that I can't run through the woods barefoot."

Rhymer seemed to weigh that. "All right," he said, and suddenly turned left, heading, so the sign indicated, for the village of Marfield.

"Thank you. Can I try Carrie again?"

He handed her the disposable phone. The signal was lousy, but it rang, dumping her immediately to voice mail. Stacey ended the call as she had done the previous time. Carrie not answering her phone was a bad sign, and Stacey imagined that a car had struck her while she sat stupefied in the parking lot last night. Last night? Christ, it seemed like days ago.

They arrived in Marfield on Creightontown Road, first passing a small hotel and cafe called The Rowan, and then shortly as they crawled along the main street of the village, a shoe shop. He pulled over and parked across from it. She got out, ran barefoot across the road.

The shop seemed to specialize in Doc Martens, but she found a pair of red sneakers that fit. Rhymer paid, producing a thick wad of bills from his pocket. When he caught her staring at the money, he leaned close and said, "Picking the pocket of a skinwalker isn't actually theft."

"Jeez," she said. Then her stomach grumbled again, much louder this time. "If I don't eat soon they won't need that effing sigil to find me. They'll just follow the hunger pangs."

He rubbed his eyes and then nodded as if accepting a sentence to be flogged. "Very well," he groused. "We'll get some food."

They left the car there and walked back down the road to The Rowan.

They sat by the front window, giving him a view of the street outside. He looked as tired as someone who hadn't slept in a year.

"When we're done here," Stacey said, "let me drive."

He started to protest but his words were interrupted by a jaw-creaking yawn.

"That's settled then," she said.

A waitress came—the only one in the place. Stacey ordered an American-style burger and a Coke. Rhymer had the shepherd's pie and coffee. "I've acquired a taste for it," he explained, though she hadn't asked.

"Do you think we're safe?"

He shook his head. "No way to tell. I don't have an elf detector."

"Hilarious. But they have a tithe detector, don't they?" She meant it to sound light, but it fell over them like a bucket of cold water. "How do they choose? How did they pick me over everyone else in that shite club?"

"You must have made eye contact at the right moment—from his point of view, I mean. It could as easily have been your friend if you'd switched seats."

She chewed her burger, ate some chips, and meanwhile sorted through all that had happened to her, the beautiful monster who had snared her, this strange slight man who seemed to be some kind of immortal in his own right. Unless, of course, he was barking, but then if he was, so was she. "What started you—I mean, ten bloody centuries, you were here for the Davidian Revolution for fuck's sake. I can't wrap my mind around it."

"Me, either," said Rhymer. "Davidian? I think I missed that one."

"What made you pit yourself against them?"

He took a forkful of meat and mashed potato. "The short version is—"

"Does everything have two versions with you?"

"Everything in life does," he said. "Though rarely only two."

She bit her burger.

"Anyway…it was the Yvag who set me on this path. Everything that's happened was because of them. *Is* because of them." He ate, and his eyes slid past her, focused upon the street as if something had caught his attention. But it soon became apparent that he was looking deep into the cavern of his own memories. Gray clouds seemed to drift across his face, deepening the sadness in his eyes.

"What's the long version?" she asked gently.

Without looking her way, he answered, "They chose unwisely." His voice was distant, pale, and filled with ice.

She set down her burger. "That's the *long* version?"

He came back to the moment, then his blue eyes closed for a moment. When he opened them, he gave her a hard, grim smile. But he didn't answer. His reluctance was palpable. She found herself reaching across the table to close her hand over his. He twitched at her touch. Human contact was that alien to him?

"It's fine," she said. "You don't have to."

"It's not that. I don't know quite where to start it. Tell me, have you ever heard of the ballad of Thomas the Rhymer?"

"Rhymer?" She smiled. "He a relative?"

"Have you ever heard of it?"

"Sure. We read something in school. Let me see...'True Thomas sat on Huntley Bank'?"

He nodded.

It took her almost twenty seconds.

"Jesus H. Christ!" she gasped.

"Shhh," he cautioned.

"You're going to sit there and tell me that *you're* Thomas the fucking Rhymer?"

"What...after everything else it's that you can't believe?"

"No, it's just...just... There are all those legends. And songs. I mean, Steeleye Span did a song. My mum had that album. And that band...Alabama 3, they did a song. That's the damn band that did the theme song for *The Sopranos*. You want me to believe you're *that* Thomas the Rhymer?"

He spread his hands.

Stacey tapped the table top. "There's a tower in Earlston that's supposed to be connected to him. Well, what's left of a tower. It's a bleedin' tourist site."

He gave her a lopsided grin. "I know. I took the tour once. Just to see. It's called the Ercildun tower. Actually, I never lived in that tower. They built it on top of my cottage a century after I'd gone."

"And where were you?"

"In Yvagddu." She drew her hand back doubtfully. "I told you I didn't know where to begin."

"You were the *tithe*?"

"Not the first time," he admitted. "The first time, I spied on them carrying off their *teind*."

"And...?"

"And they caught me watching. They don't like being observed."

Suddenly his sharp eyes became unfocused and she knew he'd been pulled into another of his riddles.

"The friend who is nae what you see,

The lie not told but in the being.

They close the circle who come tae ye."

His eyes cleared. He drew a sharp breath, set down his fork, and pushed his fingertips against his forehead as if massaging a headache.

"Does it hurt?" she asked.

"Not more than being kicked in the face," he muttered. He blinked a few times and leaned back against the cushions. "All right. Tell me what I said."

She told him. When she was done, Rhymer glanced out the window again, but with such intensity that she turned her head, too. Nothing out of the ordinary caught her eye.

"We should go," he said quietly. "If you need to use the loo, this is the time."

She got up and walked quickly across the small hotel lobby. At the restroom door, she glanced back. He was peeling bills from his thick roll of dead people's money.

She didn't take long in the toilet stall, but she lingered at the sink, washing her face over and over again as if the soap and hot water would somehow sponge away the day.

No, that wasn't it, and she had to study her own haunted eyes until she framed it the right way in her head. She wanted to wash away the *reality* of all of this.

But she shook her head at that, too.

Not all of it.

Not Rhymer.

She wanted him to be real. He was powerful in ways she didn't understand, and beautiful in a wolfish fashion. Whether he was truly Thomas the Rhymer in reality, or a madman with some kind of psychic powers, or something else, he was real and this was happening. He'd saved her from humiliation and degradation. That alone made him heroic and even…sexy, though it was hard to get all hot and bothered while monsters are hunting you down in order to sacrifice you to Hell.

Hell…

The word smashed into her mind like a fist.

Hell. You couldn't say the word enough times for it to lose meaning. Not today. Not after last night.

Hell.

It was no longer an abstract place in a Sunday service homily. Not a concept from a horror movie. Not a metaphor.

It was actual…*hell.*

She started to turn away from the mirror, from the belief in these things she saw in her reflection, but her knees buckled and she crashed into the wall beside the sink. The floor pulled her with unkind gravity, demanding that she collapse into a huddled and quivering ball of tears. Maybe of screams.

"Fuck!" growled Stacey with all the ferocity of a trapped animal. She slammed the wall with her elbows, propelling herself erect. She looked at the face of the woman in the mirror—the face that was filled with fear and wanted to let the enormity of all this crush her.

"*Fuck you,*" she snarled.

She whirled and banged open the bathroom room door.

--8--

She came out of the bathroom and edged past an elderly man who was heading into the men's room. As she crossed to the table she swiveled her head to check every face. To look for…what? The elf thing that had nearly taken her looked completely human at first. So what did she expect to see?

"You ready—?" she began as she slid into the booth. The question died unasked.

Stacey's heart nearly seized in her chest.

Rhymer was gone.

Instead...*Carrie* sat in his seat.

Carrie was sitting across from her.

"Oh my Lord, *Carrie*. You're okay? God," she babbled, "did Rhymer tell you to meet us here?"

"Stacey," said Carrie very quietly, "I need you to listen to me."

But Stacey was so happy to see her friend. "I've tried to call you, to make sure you're all right."

"Ah," said Carrie, "that was you. I didn't recognize the number so I didn't try calling back. You left your phone in your bag at the club. Here."

Carrie pulled Stacey's small purse up onto the table and pushed it to her.

Stacey stared at her purse but didn't take it. "The phone's off," she said.

"Is it?" said Carrie. "It doesn't matter."

The elderly man came out of the men's room and made his way across the lobby behind Carrie's shoulder. He paused behind their booth and stared down at the back of Carrie's head as if contemplating speaking to her. Instead, he turned away for the exit.

Where was Rhymer? Was he in the loo? Was he getting the car? What was taking him so long?

"Stacey, I need to tell you something and you have to listen. You *have* to." Carrie leaned closer to take Stacey's hands in hers, holding them firm and giving them small emphatic shakes as she spoke. "Listen to me, the man you're with is a lunatic. He's very dangerous. The police told me about him. He totally daft. He thinks he's some sort of savior."

"No, you don't understand," said Stacey. "The guy I left with was the loony. Rhymer saved me."

Carrie shook her head. "No, honey, they have warrants out for him. You're not the first girl he's taken. The others....well, it'd fair turn your stomach what he's done with them. He's a monster. It's all over the news, the whole country's looking for you. For *him*."

"Did you call the police?"

"Of course I did! When I came to outside the club and you weren't there, I knew something had happened to you. I reported it right away."

"But you don't understand, Carrie," insisted Stacey, "he's not the man who kidnapped me. I got away from the other guy. Rhymer stopped him."

Carrie smiled as if having to indulge a slow child. "You only think you got away, Stace. They're all in it together. See? It's a trick. They're working some kind of mindfuck on you. I think they slipped something into your drink, so who knows what you *think* you saw. The police know the truth."

"No, listen—"

"Stace, you think you've been rescued, which is just how he makes girls think they can trust him. Now he's trying to take you to some secret place. He'll lie and say that it's a safe place, that you have to wait there with him for a while. Has he told you that?"

"I—"

"That's where the other girls will be."

"What other girls?"

Carrie shook her head sadly. "That's what I'm trying to tell you. He's collecting girls. Kidnapping them, rounding them up. He's going to take you to wherever he keeps them. You'll see…they'll be there. All of them."

"That doesn't make sense."

"Sure it does. It's a sex trade thing, Stace. That's what they're doing, kidnapping women for the sex market. He tells them it's *him* who's saving them from some evil cult or coven or somesuch bullshit, but that's just to confuse them. It's all about sex and money for him. Do you know how much money a good looking white bird like you is worth to some Arab prince? Or to a brother in Dubai or someplace? All of this…all the elaborate steps he's taken is just to make it work. He uses a lot of money and a lot of tricks because the payoff is huge."

"No, Carrie, you're wrong about him. It's not like that at all."

Carrie ignored her; she gave Stacey's hands another squeeze. "Now listen, you need to come with me, okay? The police sent me in to get you away from him."

Stacey felt like the seat was tilting under her. This made no sense at all. She hadn't imagined the man who abducted her, who got her to strip naked, who tried to lure her into a wall of shimmering light.

She could not have imagined it.

Nor could she have imagined that Rhymer came out of the night to save her.

It had happened.

Right?

Now Carrie was telling her that all of those things were false—lies or the product of some kind of drugs, maybe mind manipulation. Did that make sense?

Or...which made more sense? A coven of evil elves who wanted to tithe her to hell or a manipulative bastard who wanted to sell her to the sex trade?

Neither seemed to be part of any world Stacey lived in.

Right?

She stared into Carrie's eyes, looking for the lie, looking for something that made sense of what her friend was saying. After all, this was her flatmate, her girlfriend for the past three years, the person she trusted with secrets she would not have shared with anyone else. The boyfriends, the bad dates, the skeevy English professor who'd come on to her last year—that's who this was holding out a hand with chipped Chancer red nail lacquer, ready to whisk her away to safety while the police brought down the madman who called himself Rhymer, and the whole network of sex traffickers working with him. Maybe they'd taken him already and that was why he'd vanished.

Or were the police outside waiting for Rhymer to come out of the bathroom? Were the SWAT team, the Lothian and Borders squad cars all poised to pounce?

She looked out the window but there wasn't anything on the street except a bronze-colored Bentley parked right outside, with two official-looking men in charcoal suits standing beside it, the people on the street glancing as if expecting a celebrity to pop out any moment. Not a policeman in sight. But from here she couldn't see the Fiat either.

"I have to get you out of here," Carrie insisted.

And then like an echo, Rhymer's voice seemed to whisper in

her ear. A fragment of his last riddle.

"*...the friend who is nae what you see...*"

The blood in Stacey's veins turned to cold slush.

Carrie sat there, eyes intense, mouth...

Smiling?

It was so small a thing. Just the tiniest upturn at the corners of Carrie's full lips.

A smile.

Why in the wide blue fuck would Carrie smile?

And where the hell was Rhymer himself?

If this was a trap, how had it been laid? Was the receptionist one of their kind? Smiling so nice at everyone?

Smiling like Carrie.

"Will you come with me, sweetie?" asked Carrie with that smiling mouth.

A word rose to Stacey's lips. It came slowly and reluctantly, and Stacey knew that to speak it would cost her. It would hurt her.

She said, "Skinwalker."

For a tiniest fraction of a second, Carrie's façade slipped, the brown eyes flicked with a degree of intelligence that had never shone in the girl Stacey knew. It was weird.

No, it was *alien*.

In that moment, seeing that different mind look out at her through those familiar brown eyes, Stacey knew—as surely as she knew her own name—that Carrie was dead.

The monsters had come and stolen her friend away.

Stolen the light that was Carrie's light. Stolen her laugh, her dreams, her joy of living. Stolen everything. It was worse than murder. Using her body like this was a new, foul kind of rape.

"Oh, god, Carrie..." Stacey said as she jerked her hands away. Tears threatened to flood her eyes. And she repeated that dreadful word. "Skinwalker. You're part of that coven."

Carrie's smile blossomed into something overripe, swollen and nasty. She rose and came around the table and clamped a hand onto Stacey's biceps. The pain was immediate and intense. "You need to come with us now."

"Why? Why didn't they just take you or somebody else?"

Carrie abandoned all pretense of being herself as she jerked Stacey out of the booth.

"Rules," she hissed, making that word into something hideous. "Your new boyfriend put the sigil on you. Hell has *tasted* you. Nobody else will do."

Tasted. She shivered.

God almighty.

She tried to pull away, but it was hopeless. She twisted around to yell for help, but everyone in the place was already looking at her.

Every single person was smiling.

At her.

Their smiles were wrong. All so wrong.

Like Carrie's.

Stacey sagged against Carrie. "Where's Rhymer?"

Carrie—or the thing that had invaded her body—sneered with contempt. "Your savior ran away like the coward he is."

"No..."

"He saw us and he fled."

"He wouldn't do that."

Carrie laughed. "That's exactly what he does, you silly little cow. How do you think he's survived for so many years?"

"No!"

Carrie leaned closer. "Why do you think that so many people have died in his stead? Or hasn't he confessed his failures? His crimes? Thomas the Rhymer is a coward who stole his immortality and all he does—all he's capable of doing—is bringing pain to those he pretends to protect."

"And what are you?" snapped Stacey. "You're nothing but monsters who—"

"Who pay a tithe to Hell," finished Carrie. "Yes, we do. And why? Because appeasement is the only thing that prevents the legions of Hell from waging war on all the realms of the living. In this pathetic world of yours, and across all the worlds." She leaned closed and Stacey could smell a rotting-meat stink on Carrie's breath. "That's the truth that Rhymer won't tell you. He delights in the songs sung about him and the tall tales you humans tell, but his freedom is bought at what cost? He paints us as evil, calls our organization a 'coven,' tried to make us out to be the villains. But it was his own escape that nearly brought down all the infinite worlds. His arrogance is his greatest crime."

"He saved my life!"

"Your life?" spat Carrie. "What is your life compared to a billion billion lives? To a trillion worlds? The tithe to Hell is so small a price to pay, you should drop to your knees and thank all of the gods of all the worlds that you were chosen as the true savior of the universe. You—you pathetic bitch. These monsters *killed* me, but they chose you to be the sacrifice that would save everyone. I'm actually dead. Am I supposed to mourn for you? To feel sorry for *you*?"

Dazed and confused beyond speech, Stacey could find no will left to fight as Carrie dragged her outside, leading her to the Bentley. One of the bodyguards opened the rear door. Cold hands reached out, dragged her into the back.

"Here is the tithe," said the skinwalker in Carrie. "Try not to let her tears of self-pity drown you."

There were only two seats in the back, with a paneled elbow rest and divider between them. The other seat was occupied by a heavy older man with salt-and-pepper hair and jowls. His eyes were blue, but watery, almost colorless. She knew she'd seen him before, in the news somewhere. An MP maybe.

Kingdoms, never kings.

The two men in the front seat turned around to look at her. They were both important-looking older men.

"This is the tithe?" asked the driver with an imperious sniff. "How far we have fallen."

"Please," Stacey pleaded. "Just let me go."

Carrie, still lingering in the doorway, said, "I tried to explain the truth to her, but she's too stupid to listen."

"It's always the same with those the Rhymer tries to save," said the other man in the front seat, an iron-haired man with a military bearing. A general, perhaps. "Some whimpering, simpering bitch who thinks that Prince Charming will protect her from the Big Bad Wolf." He made a disgusted sound.

"Please, please...this doesn't make sense," pleaded Stacey. "Why would Rhymer do this?"

"Why would he try to save you?" asked the fat statesman in the back seat with her.

They all laughed. Short, bitter laughs that were entirely without humor.

"We have a word for it," said the driver. "Actually there's a word for it in every language throughout all the universes but they all mean the same thing. It describes people like Rhymer."

"Tell me," she begged. "I have to understand."

"Why...he's a terrorist, my dear," said the military man. "I thought that was obvious to anyone. He *wants* to start a war with Hell."

"It wouldn't be a war," said Carrie coldly. "Without the tithe...it would be fire and slaughter forever."

They all looked at Stacey as she wept.

"That's who Thomas the Rhymer is," said the driver.

Carrie's mouth wore her vicious, secret little smile as she slammed the door.

--9--

They left Marfield, turned away from the direction she and Rhymer had come, and headed somewhere else. Stacey sat in stunned silence, staring out at the road for signs. The next listed Milton of Clava. She knew that site and where she was if those burial cairns were only twenty kilometers up the road. They passed the Nairn viaduct, and shortly after that they turned onto the narrow paved road past Balnuaran. A dozen or more tourists milled around between the three cairns in the crisp autumn weather, a few of them in medieval or Druid costumes; but the car rolled on past. To the left lay a farm house and outbuildings, and a large brown field full of baled wheels of hay or grass. Another farmhouse went by on the right. A sign read "Milton of Clava," directly after which the road turned left at an acute angle. Instead of turning, the Bentley pulled off to the right, effectively blocking a narrow footpath between low wire fences. It seemed to lead straight into the afternoon sun.

The fat statesman remained where he was until Stacey's door had been opened and she'd been led out. Then he came around the nose of the Bentley and stepped in behind her to propel her along the path. The two black-suited men remained with the car, no doubt to keep anyone else from coming along after them.

Stacey knew that she could run. That she *should* run.

But her legs wouldn't deviate from the path.

What if it was all true? What if her life was the price that could save so many?

Everyone she ever knew. Everyone in the world.

In...all the worlds, if that part was true.

Could she actually run away from that? As Rhymer obviously had? Could she be so selfish? So murderously self-centered?

And yet...

Why had Carrie smiled that last little smile?

Who was telling the truth?

What was the truth?

Was there any? Or was this all a two-sided game with no good guys...only bad ones. And her life as the only piece on the board.

Help me, she prayed, mouthing the words but not speaking them. *Help me.*

But she had no idea to whom her plea was meant.

God—if there was a God—seemed to allow this madness. Did that mean that He was complicit in so much misery?

Of course He was, she thought, scolding herself. People died in pain and misery every minute of every day. All she had to do was Google the statistics of rape, child abuse, murder, genocide to know that any god of this world did not care about suffering, pain and death, or it was part of His indescribable plan.

Was there a point to suffering? Or was it some kind of fucking entertainment?

These thoughts slowed her feet and the fat statesman gave her arm a sharp jerk.

"Come along, you cow," he growled.

People were already gathered ahead to the right, half a dozen in a rectangular space where an open gate led onto a path between an eight foot tall standing stone that seemed to mark the site and a smaller clump of boulders. On the gradual downhill slope beyond it lay a bowl-like depression in the ground next to the piled rubble of what might once have been a cairn like those back up the road at Balnuaran. A little farther on, but separated by fences, lay more stones and boulders and artificial depressions in the ground. At the low end of the fenced space stood a line of high shrubs, and beyond that a stretch of woodland. She glimpsed the glisten of a stream on its far side.

Because the previous event had occurred late at night, Stacey anticipated that nothing would happen here until after dark. Instead, the six people already there spread out into a circle around the central depression—a runnel surrounding a small mound, like a miniature of a Bronze Age hill fort. No one said a word. The clarity and stillness of the afternoon, the matter-of-fact way they all took their places, made it surreal to her. Entranced, she had escaped from this fate last night. Now, fully aware, she might as well have been entranced again. She couldn't stop it.

"Over here," said the statesman, taking her arm again. He waddled down into the runnel and then up onto the mound. A cold wind blew across the field.

As he spoke, some of the gathered people snickered.

That seemed strange to Stacey. Even now, even with all of this.

No...*because* of all of this.

If she was a necessary sacrifice, then why laugh at her? If her death meant that worlds would be safe, shouldn't these people— these *skinwalkers*—be weeping for her? Honoring her?

It's what she would have done.

But their laughs were like Carrie's secret smile. Wrong and out of place.

The fat statesman pushed her to a spot and then stopped her. "You will take off your clothes and pass naked through the doorway."

"Why?" she demanded.

"Only a *pure* sacrifice will do. Clothes are impure. Plastics, metal...no. You will be reborn into the fire as naked as you were born into the blood of this world."

The smiles around her grew brighter. Several of them licked their grinning lips and wrung their hands.

Stacey frowned. "N-no..."

"Do it," said the fat man, "or we will do it for you, and we won't be gentle."

She made no move to obey. Instead she looked into his eyes. "Why are you doing this?"

"We told you..."

"No. Why this? Why do I need to be naked? I stopped fighting you, so why are you treating me like this? Why are you being so mean?"

His only answer was a lascivious chuckle. Then he reached into the inside breast pocket of his suit-coat and drew out a black stone about the size and general shape of a large box cutter. It had been polished to a high gloss and sharped along one side with a wicked razor edge. Like the one Rhymer had, all sorts of markings and symbols covered it. But his wasn't knife-like, and Stacey thought of primitive knives or adzes from prehistoric sites. She was nearly sure she'd seen such a tool in a museum display somewhere.

"No," she begged.

"Oh yes," he said. "You are a cow, but you are a comely cow. Let us see the flesh that will burn. Let us delight in the breasts that will suckle monsters and the loins that will spawn the horrors of Hell."

He darted out a hand and caught her blouse. Stacey cried out in disgust and pulled away, but the man's grip was strong and buttons flew and cloth tore.

She staggered back, her blouse torn open, her bra and bare midriff exposed to their sight. The eyes of every person blazed with delight at what they saw.

"Tear the rest off," yelled one of the women.

"Let us see the whore," cried a hulking man.

"Cut her!" yelled the others. "Let us see the wine of her heart. Cut her...cut her!"

They all began to chant for the fat man to strip her. To use his knife to cut her clothes. To slash her face and breasts and limbs. They hopped up and down, punching the air with their fists, eyes ablaze, passion causing red poppies to bloom in their cheeks.

Laughing with them, the fat man advanced on her, one hand clutching as he reached for her, the other slicing the air with awful promise.

Suddenly, it was as if a cold, clean hand reached out of the darkness of her mind and slapped Stacey across the face.

A coven after all.

Just that.

All around her, hearts beating for the love of darkness.

And everything was lies.

She actually staggered back from him as if struck.

But as her foot came down it landed firmly and she crouched, fists clenched, teeth bared, and deep understanding catching fire in her mind.

This was the truth. This carnal madness of the moment tore away the cobwebs in her mind.

"You bastards," she said. "You lied to me."

They heard her words and for a moment they stared blankly at her, and then they erupted into huge, coarse laughter that scared all the birds from the trees.

"This is all a game to you, you sick fuckers."

The woman who had yelled gave a few seconds of ironic applause. "And the trained monkey squeezes out a real thought."

Everyone laughed at that.

Stacey spat in her face, but the woman wiped it from her skin and licked her fingers.

"So...all of that about Rhymer, that was—what? A joke?"

"Oh, no," insisted the fat man, "it's not a joke."

Stacey hesitated. "But—"

"It's more delicious this way," he explained. "The last turn of the knife, so to speak. The ugly truth, the final betrayal, the realization that you came willingly when you really should have tried to run away and find your fabled savior. So nice. Like whipped cream." He leaned closed. "Oh...how they scream when they hear that."

The gathered skinwalkers cackled like crows.

Stacey wheeled around, looking for a line of escape, but the people closed ranks around her.

"And how it must turn the knife even harder in Rhymer," said the fat man. "To know that those he fails to save either die hating and damning him, or they die calling for his help and he is always too late."

"Too late!" chanted the crowd.

"Year after year, century after century, too late." The fat man squeezed his crotch as a wave of erotic joy flushed through him. "His pain is so delicious. So...very delicious."

"You *are* monsters," said Stacey softly. "Everything Rhymer said—all of it—was true. You are a coven of monsters."

"Monsters, monsters, monsters," they chanted, laughing and fondling themselves.

The fat man guffawed and held his trembling belly as he laughed. "I wish you had seen it, girl," he said. "When he realized that we were already in that town. When he saw that we were already in the restaurant. He turned as white as a sheet and ran— actually ran—from there. Your hero. Failed once again. The last we saw of him was his back as he ran for his life, leaving you, my dear, to...*us.*"

And with that he lunged at her with the stone. For all his bulk, the man was terrifyingly fast. Stacey flung herself backward but the edge of the sacred stone drew a red line across the tops of both breasts. Beads of red blood bulged from the cuts and then spilled down, following the curves of her breasts, staining her torn blouse, falling onto the ground.

The crowd cheered wildly.

"Cut her again!" screeched a reed-thin man dressed in a postman's uniform.

The fat man laughed and raised his stone. Stacey tried to back away but the crowd was a solid ring and they forced her toward him.

"Cut her! Cut her!"

Stacey knew realized that this was it, that she was going to die. Even with all that had happened since last night she'd never quite accepted the absolute reality of her death. Or its absolute imminence.

The stone knife slashed through the air, inches away, and she saw strands of her hair flutter in the breeze. The fat man was circling her, closing the distance with each pass. Cut after cut whistled through the air and she felt lines of molten heat erupt along her back and arms. Blood ran like rivers.

"Cut her! Cut her!"

The chant filled the air.

The fat man grinned like a ghoul as he closed in. Behind him the air began to shimmer with green fairy lights.

"Cut her! Cut her!"

Stacey braced herself, shifting her weight to the balls of her feet, ready to run, ready to spring. Ready to fight. Ready to do anything but let him butcher her without at least crippling the bastard. She was determined to take his eyes with her. If she had to die, then fuck it. Let them pay for it.

"Cut her! Cut her!"

She timed herself to his next swing and then Stacey ducked low and snatched up a rock, rose, pivoted and hurled it with all of her strength.

It struck the fat man on the shoulder as he was raising his weapon, and then ricocheted off and struck the postman in the mouth. He staggered back, spitting teeth.

The crowd laughed at that too.

With a sinking heart she realized that they were used to their victims struggling. Worse, they enjoyed it.

The wall of green light intensified, blocking out part of the circle of skinwalkers. Its presence cut down on the amount of maneuvering room she had. She was barely able to stay away from the killer as it was, but as the wall strengthened and grew, Stacey knew that sooner or later she would fall beneath the knife or be forced through that doorway.

The fat statesman slashed at her again, and she dodged but as she did so she realized that he *could* have cut her. She stumbled away, confused. Surely he wasn't showing her mercy…

As he stalked her, the fat man began speaking some words and phrases in a language she didn't know, which sounded like a made-up form of Latin. With each word the shimmering light flared and grew.

He must have seen the look of realization in her eyes. He said, "That's right, we won't kill you here. But we will lap your blood." His tongue waggled obscenely.

She was a tithe to Hell. Not a blood sacrifice. She was going into the green light alive, not into the ground dead.

The light bathed the whole clearing, painting the faces of everyone here in shades of sickness and unreality. It was like looking at a pack of madmen through night vision goggles. All green and black and shades of gray.

The fat man raised the blade high over his head.

He opened his mouth to say something else. Perhaps another phrase in that weird language. Maybe another taunt.

Whatever it was, though, would never be spoken.

Not in this world.

Something whipped past Stacey's ear and for a split second she thought it was a wasp. It hummed, high and sharp.

Then she stared with slack-jawed shock at the thing sticking out from between the fat man's teeth. Long and slender, with brown feathers quivering at the end.

An arrow.

The fat man took a slow, wandering sideways step, turning away from Stacey, revealing as he did so the barbed spear-point standing out from the back of his skull, slick with blood and strands of gore.

The fat man clutched at Stacey, but his body began to shudder violently. His chest bulged outward—she could hear the wet, muffled sound of his ribs and sternum snapping, then the skin stretched and stretched until it burst open in a spray of blood. Something leapt through the bone-broken doorway, a humped and gnarled figure no larger than a child. It landed on two misshapen legs and stared around with eyes that glowed with real inner heat. Its skin looked like a map of veins and musculature, like some grotesque subject of dissection in a medical school. But it was alive and filled with hate. Intelligence burned in those hot eyes.

Stacey lunged for the fallen stone knife.

So did the creature.

But as they both reached for it—as Stacey curled her fingers around it—a second arrow snapped through the air and struck the creature. This time it hit the chest and transfixed it. If this monster, this *Yvag*, had a hard heart, then the broad-bladed arrow must surely have torn it in half.

The creature looked at Stacey, its burning eyes seeming to lock on her, and its inhuman mouth opened, screeching to the sky in furious terror. Then it abruptly ruptured into a gray-green mist that spattered Stacey and every shocked and now silent person in the circle. Bones and raw meat flopped to the ground.

The statesman's body—the fat, empty shell—still stood impossibly upright; but it was rotting before her eyes in swift freakish decomposition. Skin bruised, sagged, the wide eyeballs liquefied and fell back into the skull, and the whole corpse deliquesced inside the suit, collapsing with a wet squelch to the ground. He had been in the press for years, decades she thought. Dead far longer than the driver of the limousine.

The wall of light suddenly changed from green to red. Furnace heat roared out across the clearing.

"Push her in!" screamed the woman who had applauded with such vicious irony. Her words broke the others out of their shock. The postman was closest; he made a grab at Stacey.

A third arrow came out of nowhere and punched through his chest. It stood there, the shaft thrumming from the force of impact.

The postman juddered to a stop, and he managed to croak a single last word, raised his arm and pointed.

"No..."

Everyone turned.

A figure stepped out from behind the border of tall shrubs below them.

Lean as a wolf, with eyes that were bottomless and dark with incalculable rage. He was dressed in jeans and a vest made of rough doeskin. Belts crossed his hips and from them hung knives of every description. In his hands, though, he held a great yew bow, and a quiver heavy with arrows hung from a strap behind his shoulder.

Stacey watched as he quickly, deftly drew another arrow, fitting it to the string without effort, as if he'd done this a hundred times. Or a thousand.

Or ten thousand.

"Rhymer," she breathed.

--10--

As Thomas the Rhymer raised the bow, the crowd of skinwalkers howled at him.

They howled with seething hatred for their ancient enemy.

They howled in burning rage for this disruption of their ritual.

They howled in fear of this man.

And they howled in terror for the consequences of his attack.

Stacey heard those roars and yells and she understood them. A scream ripped its way out of her own throat.

Beside her, the postman's stomach exploded as the red monster within tore free. It dropped into a crouch like a bloody ape, head swiveling back and forth as if seeing with new and more cunning eyes than it had used a moment ago. Those eyes came to rest on Stacey and the thing's lip curled back from rows of gore-streaked fangs that were bracketed by wicked tusks. Its muscles tensed for the spring.

Stacey gave it no time.

She swung the sharpened stone knife with all her strength and the razor edge slashed through the Yvag's throat so deeply the stone grated on the knobbed spine. Green blood sprayed outward as the creature dropped.

The postman's body shriveled to dusty rags in a heartbeat.

As if the collapse of the empty clothing was a signal, the elves attacked, and though the real hell waited beyond the shimmering veil of light, there was enough of it to be had in that clearing.

As one they surged forward—a dozen monsters in stolen bodies. The nearest lunged at Stacey; the rest barreled downhill toward Rhymer.

For his part, Rhymer stood his ground, firing arrow after arrow, filling the air with death—first to kill the hijacked bodies and then to slaughter the Yvag who dwelled within. His jaw was tight, his mouth curled into a sneer of disgust, but Stacey saw that his eyes blazed. With madness? Or was he enjoying this? After all these centuries, was this the only time he was truly alive?

Then she had no more time to think. A woman dressed in expensive furs and jewels tried to stab her with a diamond-crusted dagger, but Stacey bashed her arm aside and drove the tip of the sharped stone into her chest. Over and over again, tearing through ermine and powdered flesh and tough bone. As the woman's chest collapsed, the Yvag inside tried to burst free, thrusting its clawed hands outward to try and snatch the sacred stone from Stacey's hand. But Stacey bellowed and hammered at the scrabbling fingers, smashing them, shattering bones, battering the emerging Yvag even as it fought through blood and ragged tissue to escape its dying frame. Sagging halfway out, the Yvag and its host collapsed onto the ground.

The man with the military bearing leaped over the fallen body and drove a savage punch at Stacey that would surely have broken her neck, but an arrow crunched through the balled fist and pinned it to his chest. Before he could react, Stacey finished him with a slash to the throat. His blood sprayed everywhere.

Bodies fell and clogged the clearing, and Rhymer used those obstacles to advance over the fence. He fired and fired. One bolt struck a skinwalker in the stomach and it fell forward. Its body heaved, then lay still, and Stacey realized that the arrow had found and killed the Yvag within as well.

Then there was a loud *KRAK* and Rhymer spun backward, his bow falling from his hand as red blossomed from high on his left shoulder. A figure—the driver of the Bentley—stood with braced legs, aiming a Glock nine millimeter at Rhymer. Only the wild panic of the crowd prevented him from ending it there.

"Get out of the way, damn you!" cried the driver, and when one of the skinwalkers didn't move fast enough he shot it in the head. Rhymer leaped the fence and dodged behind the shrubs again. The driver fired into them, but Rhymer had already bolted for the woods. Furiously, the Yvag plunged after him, bounding over the fence and into the trees.

A second man bent and rummaged inside the folds of the military man's empty clothes and straightened with a mad grin on his face and a big .45 Navy Colt in his hand. When he turned toward her, Stacey saw that there was something strange about his eyes. They weren't like the rest of the skinwalkers.

They were more like the eyes of the man who had abducted her from the club. They generated a strange and overwhelming attraction. She knew that this could not be the same man, the one Rhymer said was a princeling among them—he had shed his skin and gone into the green light—but the power was similar. It was so normal and natural and warm that it nearly stopped her in her tracks.

What had Rhymer said about the charisma of these elves?

To humans charisma is just a gift of attraction...but for the Yvag it's one of their most powerful weapons. They can make you lay bare your throat for the knife and thank them while they cut.

She could feel her hand begin to open. The sacred stone began to slip away from her even as the creature raised his pistol and pointed it at her face.

She closed her eyes, waiting for the bullet.

Almost...wanting it.

The shot never came. She opened her eyes to see him lower the pistol.

The creature sighed, "Alas for everyone that the tithe must be alive and able to scream."

"I..." she began, but there was nowhere to go with words.

"Take her," said the Yvag. He turned away and ran after the others into the woods to hunt for Rhymer. A few moments later there came a burst of shots and a solitary scream of agony.

Only two skinwalkers remained in the clearing and they closed in on Stacey. They were as splattered with blood as she was.

"You will scream for a thousand years," whispered one of them, a woman with masses of blond curls. "That's the truth of hell, bitch."

"You will become the whore of a hundred thousand demons," said the other.

Stacey closed her fist around the sacred stone. The spell of the princeling had snapped as soon as he turned away.

She bared her teeth at them.

"Fuck you," she said, and sprang from the mound. She cut them to pieces with their own stone knife.

--11--

There was another scream and Stacey ran downhill. As she reached the wire fence, the skinwalker with the Glock came stumbling backward through the shrubs. He hit the fence and fell on his back at Stacey's feet. His face and throat and chest had been slashed to ribbons. The Yvag—mortally wounded—struggled to tear free from the shriveling body, but Stacey kicked it over and stomped on its head.

Within the forest, Stacey could see Rhymer moving among the skinwalkers. He held a knife in each hand and stray shafts of sunlight struck sparks from the steel as he wheeled and cut and slashed and stabbed. If the bullet had done him any damage it was not evident. Two skinwalkers, both of them trailing blood and streamers of torn flesh, crawled out of the forest and into the clearing, making for the wall of light and, perhaps, a chance of escape.

There was a sudden howl of rage, and heat struck her back like a wave. It sent her reeling and the stone flew from her hand. She whirled to see that the wall of light had grown brighter and bigger, filling more than half of the clearing now. It was as if the sky was being sliced apart in pursuit of her. The light seemed to expand toward her like the chest of some great dragon.

A grotesque face peered through, spotted her—a baleful eye that she remembered from last night.

The *princeling*, Rhymer had called it.

It strained to reach for her through the glowing opening, barbed and knobbed fingers gleaming with the sheen of cast iron. Stacey staggered back and wrenched her head away before the princeling's charisma could conquer her.

One of the remaining skinwalkers had crawled out from the trees; they stared at each other for a second. Then he jumped for the cutting stone. Stacey kicked him in the face. The stone flew out of his grasp and blood spurted from his nose. She took a step to kick him again, but with both hands cupped over his face he skittered away from her.

Then someone called her name.

It spoke in a voice like thunder. The force of it shook the clearing and shivered the trunks of the trees. Birds fell dead from the air, the rocky ground beneath her cracked.

Stacey screamed.

It wasn't just her name that was called. It was her whole being in two syllables, shouted by the prince of the elves from the mouth of Hell.

The power of it enfolded her again, the charismatic force as clinging as tentacles, dragging her toward the blazing light.

With everything she had, she fought to pull free, but her captured body betrayed her. As had happened at the club, her mind became compartmentalized, boxed in, trapped.

"The ritual," she heard him broadcast to the surviving Yvag. "Bring the other two. Complete it from your side."

Another of the skinwalkers ran out of the woods—a solid woman with red hair and dressed in a lemon yellow tracksuit that was smeared with a bloody handprint. She scrambled over and retrieved the blood-smeared cutting stone, cringing back immediately as if expecting to be kicked, too; but Stacey could no longer work her legs. Although she was screaming inside, not a sound came out. Her eyes flooded with tears at the helplessness. They had her. She understood now how Rhymer had only managed to save a few; how tenacious, unstoppable these monsters were.

The woman clambered up beside her to push Stacey up the mound and through the opening.

And then Thomas the Rhymer stepped out from behind the tall standing stone above them.

He was covered with blood, his shirt torn halfway off his body. His limbs were crisscrossed with cuts and the vicious welts from bites and tearing fingers. But he had recovered his bow and he held it in his red, gleaming fist above which the shaft of an arrow rested.

"Rhymer..." whispered Stacey. With sudden horror she realized that he was pointing the arrow at her. Was that how this would end? If he couldn't save her from Hell, then he would deny the demons the living sacrifice they demanded?

His eyes were hard and merciless as he stared along the shaft at her.

Stacey wanted to curse him. To hate him for this. He had used her to find this coven, hadn't he? To bring the princeling back into this world. Now here he was ready to sacrifice her life. She should hate him with her last breath and thought.

She said, "Do it."

He took careful aim and let his arrow fly.

Stacey closed her eyes.

The arrow whipped by so closely that she felt it pass, viscerally shared the thud of it into the breastbone of the tracksuited woman beside her. Stacey's eyes snapped open to see the woman spin around and stumble backward—straight into the wall of light, her arm extended as if to hand the cutting stone to Stacey. At the last, her shaking, dissolving hand flung it to the ground.

Stacey's arms were free, but she stood there for a moment, too stunned to know what to do.

"The stone!" cried Rhymer. "Now before it's too late!"

That was like a bucket of water in the face. Stacey snapped out of her shock and dove for the sacred stone.

"You dare not!" bellowed the Yvag prince, and Stacey spun around in horror as the monster dragged the tracksuited body aside and stepped halfway from the light, reaching for her, swiping at the air with its claws.

An arrow thudded into the princeling, but instantly glowed and caught fire, the ashes blowing away in the superheated wind.

"The stone," Rhymer cried again.

But Stacey had it seated in her palm now, her fingers wrapped tightly around it, her body turning—not away from the Yvag prince but toward him. She slashed at him with his sacred stone. The razor-sharp edge of it drew a glowing green line from shoulder to elbow.

The Yvag's shriek of pain came like the screech of grinding metal, like a train wreck inches from her face. It picked her up and slammed her back against the shrubs. Even where he stood,

Rhymer fell, too, his arrows spilling from their quiver.

The Yvag prince thrashed in place, like a wasp caught in a spider's web. As Stacey watched, the green lines of glowing blood spread like a vine into the red of the shimmering wall and somehow seemed to bind him there.

Or did it?

The creature threw its twisted body against these new lines of force and step by step the resistance yielded, one line then another snapped, and he emerged. He was almost all the way out now.

Stacey pushed herself up. Thunder seemed to pound through her head. She pressed a palm against one ear, found that she was bleeding from it. And from her nose. Rhymer, sprawled in the dirt, was coughing, and with each cough a bloody foam rimed his chin.

Somehow Stacey still had the stone in her hand, but the monster in the fiery gateway was reaching for it. She raised it for one last stab. Maybe she could cut a tendon or…

"Hell and eternal suffering await you," whispered the prince in a voice that was so inhuman that Stacey did not know how to describe it. Words forced out of a throat that was never meant for human speech.

She jabbed at the thing's knobbed fingers and it twitched back, careful to avoid her. They both knew who would win, but the elf did not want to suffer more damage in the midst of its victory.

"The…wall…"

Stacey heard those words distantly, from a million miles away.

"What—?"

The elf grabbed her ankle in its steely hand and began to pull her across the ground.

"Not the…Yvag," croaked Rhymer as he fought to climb shakily to hands and knees. "The wall…close it."

Stacey twisted back to the Yvag prince. His goblin face leered at her.

"Too late," he mocked. "Give in to the suffering that is your destiny."

Stacey raised the sacred stone.

"Fuck you!" she screamed, and stabbed.

Not at the monstrous hand that held her.

Not at the grinning impossibility of the black, golden-eyed skull that laughed at her pain.

She stabbed the shimmering wall of light.

There was a dazzling explosion that erupted without sound. A ring of bright green light punched out from the glowing red wall.

"Again!" cried Rhymer. He was crawling toward her, his body broken and bleeding.

"No!" howled the prince of the elves. He yanked at her foot, tearing her sneaker off.

Stacey stabbed again, then raked the stone blade from top to bottom.

Across the line she made the fiery light vanished.

She stabbed and stabbed.

Wherever the blade touched, the red wall disappeared.

The elf prince was still half in this world. One leg, one arm and shoulder and his misshapen head. He roared at her and slashed her leg with his claws. Her blood seeded the air.

Then an arrow struck the clawing hand, pinning it to the ground for an instant before it dissolved. But a second hit it. And a third. Rhymer was on his knees, scooping up fallen arrows, tearing them from rotted corpses, and firing them as fast as he could nock and pull and release. They held him off for seconds, long enough for her to pull her leg out of his reach.

The wall collapsed bit by bit. Glowing line by line, shrinking in on the struggling Yvag.

Rhymer fired a final arrow and it struck the elf in the left eye and knocked it backward through the fiery wall, out of this world and back into his own world or into Hell. Which it was, Stacey did not know and did not care. She swept her arm up into the remaining angry hole and it vanished.

Her shoe lay on the ground near her foot.

Overhead, clouds scudded across the sky, and birdsongs echoed from the woods below. Had it not been that the fenced site looked like an overturned cemetery, it might have been a lovely afternoon.

She heard Rhymer's bow thud to the dirt and as she collapsed onto the rocky ground the sacred stone rolled from her fingers, struck on its edge and rolled away into the grass. It lay there, looking like any other black, polished stone.

--12--

Thomas Rhymer did not call an ambulance or any other aid.

As darkness closed over Stacey, she was half-aware that he was dragging her up the slope toward the parked Bentley.

When she opened her eyes for a moment, the light outside had changed. Rough bandages were wrapped around her wounds. She wasn't bleeding, but she didn't know if she had any blood left to lose. She lay in the plush back seat of the Bentley watching treetops flicker past in the windows. She had only one red sneaker on, but her other foot was bathed in enough blood that it almost looked like a match.

She said, "Where are we?" Managed to turn her head enough to see him.

Rhymer was hunched over the wheel, his face gray, his fists white-knuckle tight on the wheel. He did not have the strength to answer.

"Oh, well, that's fine then." Darkness came for Stacey and took her down again.

--13--

The café was quiet. The waiter came and poured fresh coffee into their cups, murmured something in French, and walked away. Traffic whisked back and forth, but no one seemed to be in a hurry.

The bandages beneath her long sleeves chafed, the stitches itched. They would have to come out soon.

Stacey sipped her coffee, wincing at the pain in her lip. It had been split and was taking its own sweet time to heal. Rhymer wore sunglasses even at night. A broken nose had given him black eyes.

People walked by, some of them laughing, a few hand-in-hand.

"Is he gone?" she asked. It was not the first time she'd asked the question since that day. For a lot of that time Rhymer remained silent, morose, lost in his own inner darkness.

This time he answered her. "We hurt him," he said softly. "That's the most you can say for certain. He's not like most of the Yvag. He's royalty. I'm not sure if he *can* die." He paused a moment. "But either he steps into the well of the damned or someone else of his bloodline has to. 'You'll scream for a thousand years' was nae hyperbole."

"God…"

"At the very least a princeling of the elves has been wounded by a mortal, a woman, and that's only happened once before in the whole history of the world to my knowledge." He added sugar to his coffee, stirred as if everything depended on it.

"Will it stop them?" she asked.

He shook his head. "It'll complicate things for them. Opening the gateway takes a lot of power. I…don't know if he can accomplish it with what we did to him. Others will, though, next time. And next time they'll come early to the party. You came at great cost."

She nodded and they sat together for a quarter hour without talking. Then she said, "Rhymer…I *was* the tithe."

"Aye."

"Now we spoiled that."

"Aye."

She looked around at the square. Paris glowed with life. "The Yvag said that my life would buy the safety of the whole world. Of all the worlds. Is that remotely true? Has saving me opened everyone up to something bad?"

"They sold you a lie to make you cooperate in your own sacrifice. Their idea of fun."

"So…Hell *won't* take revenge?"

Rhymer smiled. "Not on us, lass," he said. "Their bargain."

She opened her mouth to reply, but all she said was, "God…"

"Some believe that the Yvag were angels once," said Rhymer. "When certain angels revolted, God ordered that the gates of Heaven and Hell be shut. Any angel left in Heaven became the true and sanctified angels. Those who were shut into Hell became demons. But there were many who were trapped in the worlds between Heaven and Hell."

"And they became the Yvag?"

"According to that version of things." He nodded. "Not pure enough for Heaven but not evil enough for Hell." He laughed. "More like us than they want to believe."

"Or…maybe they *do* believe," she suggested. "Maybe that's why they mess with our world so much."

He considered it, sipped his coffee awhile before speaking again. "As I said, that's one version of it. The tithe paid is to stay free from Hell. As fallen angels they belong to Hell, and the tithe buys their freedom."

"So…why would Hell take it out on us if the tithe isn't paid?"

"It wouldn't. And that's your version of them filtered through Christian theology. I know a deal more. They're older than our religions. Older than our race, maybe our world."

She thought about that. "Hell will go after the Yvag, then?"

"Aye. It's a war they cannae hope to win. But Hell…" He looked grimly at some memory. "Hell is like nothing Christianity ever dreamed up, and vaster than worlds."

"The well of the damned?"

His mouth twitched at her repeating his own phrase back at him. "The universe balances on a knife edge."

"So saving me you forced an immortal creature to sacrifice itself to buy the Yvag time?"

"Time runs differently in their world between worlds. But, aye. Time until the next *teind* comes due."

A cold wind seemed to blow among the tables. "Twenty-eight years, you said."

"Your time as tithe is over. The mark on you is no good to them now. Like the one on me."

"Then I'm safe, am I?" She knew the answer but needed to hear it laid out.

Rhymer's mouth pulled tight with sadness and weariness. "They won't come after you as tithe," he said quietly. "But the Yvag are a bitter race. You injured their prince. Maybe slew him. They'll ne'er forgive you. Never stop hunting you."

Stacey felt like she wanted to cry, but she didn't. She'd known it already.

Instead she asked, "You said only one woman has ever injured a prince of the Yvag before."

"I did."

"Who was it?"

He finished his coffee, then looked into the cup, head bowed. When she thought he wasn't going to say anything, he replied, "Someone that mattered. A long, long time ago."

"And you've been running from them and fighting them, what, ever since?"

"Ever since."

"Alone?"

"It's not a journey you… Of course, alone."

She reached across the table and took his hand. "Well, not anymore."

He smiled at her, but there was so much sorrow in that smile that Stacey knew his eyes behind the sunglasses weren't participating. She turned and looked away, looked out at the passing traffic on the Rue de Rivoli. Every once in a while, one of the people in the passing cars would catch her eye. The looks were brief, except sometimes they went on just a second too long.

Rhymer squeezed her hand and they sat in silence as the world turned around them.

The Cobbler of Oz

Author's Note

Who isn't a fan of *The Wizard of Oz?*

Like most kids, I was introduced to that magical world through the books before I ever saw the movie. Much as I love the movie, the books are where my heart is. I remember using toys to tell Oz stories long before I could read or write. They were the first stories I conjured, and I always wanted to tackle one as an adult.

When John Joseph Adams invited me to write an Oz story, however, I started in the wrong gear. I'd been writing horror and thrillers and so my first inclination had been to write an intense and gruesome story that would have splashed blood on the Yellow Brick Road.

But as soon as I sat down to write I realized that I was going about it all wrong. I read the Oz books as a kid. The intended audience was kids. Those books, although occasionally frightening, are charming and innocent. So...I shifted gears and wrote the story that appears here.

Sometime after the story appeared, I was contacted by the Baum Estate because this story had been included in the official chronology of Oz.

THE COBBLER OF OZ

--1--

"*I need* a pair of traveling shoes."

When the cobbler heard the voice he peered up over the tops of his half-glasses, but there was no one there. The counter that separated him from the rest of the town square was littered with all of the tools of his trade—hammers and scissors, awls and stout needles, glue and grommets. However, beyond the edge of the counter there was nothing.

Well, that was not precisely the case, because beyond the empty space that was beyond the counter were a thousand chattering, noisy, moving, bustling, shopping, buying, selling, yelling, laughing people. They were there in all of the colors of the rainbow; green was the most common color here in the Emerald City, but the other colors were well represented, too. There were Winkies in a dozen shades of yellow, and Munchkins in two dozen shades of blue, and Quadlings in scarlets and crimsons and tomato reds, and Gillikins in twilight purples and plum purples and the purple of ripe eggplants.

But there was no one who seemed to own the tiny voice that had spoken.

The cobbler set down the boot he was repairing for a palace guard.

"Hello—?" he asked.

"Sir," said the voice of the invisible person, "I need a pair of traveling shoes, if you please."

"I do indeed please," said the Cobbler, "or I would if I could see your feet or indeed any part of you. Though, admittedly, your feet are necessary to any further discussion on the matter of shoes, traveling or otherwise."

"But I'm right here," said the voice. "Can't you see me at all?"

The cobbler stood up and leaned over, first looking right and then looking left and finally looking down, and there stood a figure.

It was a "figure" even in the Cobbler's mind, because he could not call the figure a man or a woman because that would never be correct. Nor could he call it a boy or a girl, because neither of those labels would hang correctly on the person who stood there wringing its tiny hands.

"I thought you were an invisible little girl," said the cobbler.

"No sir," said the figure. "Neither invisible nor a girl. Though I am little and to my own people I am a girl for I am not yet fully grown."

"I see that you are quite little, my dear. But why stand down there where no one but a giraffe can look over and see you? Why not fly up here onto the counter? There's plenty of space," he said, pushing some of his tools aside.

The little figure looked sad—or at least the cobbler *supposed* that she looked sad, because he had very little experience reading the expressions of persons of her kind. She turned around so that he could see her back, and then she raised her arms to her sides and with a soft grunt of effort expanded the pair of miniature wings.

The wings were lovely to see. Gold and tan in color, with nicely formed primary feathers, as well as all of the requisite secondary and tertiary feathers, and quite attractive emarginations.

However, upon seeing the feathers the cobbler felt his mouth turn into a small round O, and he even spoke that word aloud. "Oh," he said, faintly and with an equal mix of surprise, and consternation and pity.

The wings slumped and the little figure turned.

"I know," she said sadly. "They look perfect, but they're so small that they wouldn't lift a pigeon let alone a monkey."

"Ah," said the cobbler. It was not a great change in his response, but it conveyed a different emotion—sympathy. A winged monkey whose wings were so small she could never ever fly.

The little monkey fluttered her wings so they beat with the blurred speed of a hummingbird, but there was no corresponding change in the elevation of the owner. All that the cobbler could see was a bit of a flutter in the brocade vest the monkey child wore, stirred by a faint breeze from those stunted wings.

Once more the wings sagged back in defeat and the little figure seemed to deflate with them. She hung her head for a moment, shaking it sadly.

"My sisters and my brothers all have normal wings, even my littlest brother who is only two. Momma has to tie a tether to him to keep him from flying out of the nursery window. And Dadda has great wings. Big ones, with a pattern like a hunting falcon. He can fly way above the tops of the tallest trees in the forest and then soar down among the trunks, swooping past our windows. Sometimes he flies past and without even a flutter or a pause he'll toss walnuts and coconuts in through the window and they land on our beds as if placed there by a slow and careful hand." She sighed and shook her head. "My wings are almost the same size now as they were after I was born. They grew a little and then stopped, but I never stopped growing and I'm still growing. Soon I'll be full grown and I'll still have wings that would barely lift a small bird."

Then she drew in a breath and looked up at the cobbler who still leaned forward over the counter.

"And now you see why I need a pair of traveling shoes."

--2--

The cobbler stepped out from behind his market stall and addressed the little winged monkey. He extended a large and callused hand.

"My name is Bucklebelt," he said.

The winged monkey curtseyed. "I'm Nyla of the Green Forest clan. It's a pleasure to make your acquaintance, Mr. Bucklebelt."

"And a pleasure to make yours, Miss Nyla." He tilted his head toward his counter. "As it is rather difficult to hold a conversation with you with my counter in the way, and entirely impossible to measure you for shoes, travelling or otherwise, may I assist you by lifting you onto the counter?"

Nyla sighed again and cast a sad glance around the bustling square. "I suppose everyone who is likely to laugh at a nearly wingless winged monkey has already had their fill of snortles and chuckles. I don't see how being lifted onto a counter can cause me any greater embarrassment."

He winked at her. "If anyone so much as sniggers I will tonk them a good one on their noggins in the hopes that it helps them remember their manners. This is the Emerald City after all, and the Wizard requires that everyone have manners." Now he sighed. "But of course we both know that for some folks, manners come and go like the phases of the moon."

She nodded, knowing full well that this was true. Some of the other winged monkeys her age laughed and made jokes about what they called her "butterfly" wings, but they never did that when the adults were around.

With her permission, Bucklebelt lifted Miss Nyla onto the counter. He did it gently and made sure not to set her down on anything sharp. Then he went back around to his side of the counter and climbed onto a stool, for in truth even though he was a grown man, the cobbler was not a large man. Only parts of him were large—his nose was a red bulb, his eyes were as big as the largest blueberries in the southern groves, and his eyebrows stood up like giant caterpillars.

For her part, Nyla was graceful and small, with dark brown fur, a soft gray muzzle and big brown eyes that were the exact color of polished oak. She wore a vest stitched with every color from the Land of Oz, along with a leather satchel that was hung slantwise across her body. The leather was dyed red and green and delicately stitched with a pattern of ripe bananas under lustrous green leaves.

The cobbler noticed the bag and nodded his approval. "That's good work," he said. "And if it's not the work of Salander the Leathermaker then I'm a Munchkin."

"It is!" she cried, delighted at his recognition. The bag was Nyla's prized possession. "My grandmomma bought this for me when I started school. You wouldn't believe how many things I can keep in here."

"Oh yes I would," he said with a knowing smile. "Salander is the genius of our age when it comes to leather goods. There's a saying that if it's a Salander bag, then you can put six things in a bag made for five."

"Or even seven or eight," she said.

He nodded. "Your grandmomma must be shrewd and wise. That bag will never wear out and you'll never lose anything you put in it. There's no better place to keep your hopes and dreams."

That put a smile on Nyla's face.

"Now," said Mr. Bucklebelt, "let's talk about traveling shoes. Exactly what *kind* of traveling shoes are you looking for? Because there are traveling shoes and then there are traveling shoes. Some will get you home and some will get you far, far from home. Some will take you places that you want to go and others will take you to places that you *need* to go—even if you didn't know that's where you needed to be."

Nyla settled herself on a soft roll of yarn, pulling her bag around so that it rested on her lap. She took a moment to compose her thoughts, and then said, "I want traveling shoes that will take me to places I don't even know about."

"Ah," he said, adjusting his glasses. "You want *magic* shoes."

"But…aren't *all* traveling shoes magical?"

"Oh no," he said. "Not at all. Most traveling shoes are very civilized and proper, and as you know when you're too civilized then there's no magic at all."

"How can those kinds of shoes take you to wonderful places?" she asked, confused.

He took a moment before he answered that. "Well, it's because there are different kinds of magic. In the most civilized places—in gray places where everything is normal--then shoes will protect your feet from ordinary things like stones in the road or nettles in the grass. They'll keep your feet from burning on the hot sands or from freezing in the snow. And when you're walking in mud they won't let squishy worms wriggle between your toes."

"I don't mind worms," said Nyla, but she said it to herself.

Mr. Bucklebelt said, "That kind of traveling shoes will help you run indoors when there's lightning or help you run fast to catch a boat that's about to sail. They won't squeak when you sneak and they won't flop when you hop. A good pair of traveling shoes— even the nonmagical kind that people wear here in Oz and everywhere where people have feet—will be a comfort on a long journey. And—maybe there's just the tiniest spark of magic in them, because when you put on any pair of traveling shoes your feet just want to go find somewhere new to walk."

"Then what about shoes with *real* magic?"

"Ah," he said sagely, touching his finger to the side of his nose, "that's another thing entirely. There are very few genuinely magical traveling shoes. In my whole career as a cobbler I've seen only three pairs."

"Three?"

"One was a pair of stalking boots worn by the Huntsman of Hungry Hall. When he put those boots on he never needed horse nor even hounds to find a stag or a wild boar for the village roast. Those boots always found the trail and kept him on it until his prey was within easy bowshot. No one in all the district ever went hungry because of the Huntsman's stalking boots."

"Wow!"

"Then there are the dancing slippers of the Ash Princess. The shoes looked like ordinary slippers on anyone else's feet, but on her feet they transformed into the second most elegant shoes in all the world, and even though they were as soft as calfskin leather they were as clear as polished crystal." He leaned close and whispered. "Made from the leather of dragon's wings. With those shoes, the Ash Princess and her prince danced on moonbeams and starlight, high above the heads of everyone else at their wedding."

"Wait…you said they were the *second* most elegant shoes in the world. What are the first?"

Mr. Bucklebelt sighed very softly, and when he spoke his voice was hushed. "Ah, now…that brings us to the third pair of traveling shoes. The dragon-scale walking shoes. Now there is a pair of shoes, my girl! The finest craftsmanship in all the world. I'm only a humble cobbler—I *repair* shoes—but those were made by the finest cordwainer, the finest shoe*maker* in all the land. Do you know the story? No? Shall I tell you?"

Nyla nodded, her eyes alight with excitement.

"Then tell you I shall, for it is a tale anyone looking for traveling shoes really *should* know." He settled himself more comfortably on his stool. "This is a very old story because it happened a very long time ago. Back in an age when there were griffins and dragons and herds of unicorns. Back when fish with scales of true gold swam in rivers that flowed to a great sea called Shallasa. Ah, but that was so long ago that most people don't believe it's anything but an old story. I know, though, that Shallasa is neither a made-up story nor myth nor even a dream. And yet all we have left of that sea are its bones."

"The bones of a sea?" asked Nyla. "How can a sea have bones?"

"They don't look like bones as you and I know them, but everything has a part of itself that remains even when all of this is gone." He gave her arm a gentle pinch. "When a sea dies it leaves behind a great waste of salt and sand."

"The Deadly Desert!" cried Nyla in horror.

"Yes indeed. That cruel waste that no one can cross," he said, nodding gravely. "It stretches beyond our knowing and surrounds all of Oz. No one can cross it and live, and we know this because many have tried. So many. Even heroes and fast horses, even scorpions in their armor and birds on their wings. Nothing that lives can traverse the Deadly Desert. And what a sadness that is because even though the dragon-scale walking shoes were made in what is now Munchkin Country, the materials—the *key* materials, mind you—came from a land far beyond the Sea of Shallasa. A land not even remembered in fairytales and old songs, more's the pity. It was a land of tall castles and deep valleys, a place where jewel-birds flitted among the trees and the mountains sang old songs every night at the setting of the sun. It was there, in a place in whose very soil the soul of magic thrived, that is the only place where the silver sequins that were used to cover the shoes can be found."

"But...can't someone *make* silver sequins? There is plenty of silver around and—"

"Ah," said Bucklebelt, shaking his head, "like traveling shoes, there is silver and then there is *silver*. The silver I'm talking about isn't a cold metal chopped from a mine. No, this is living silver and there is only one source for it. Just one in all the world."

"What is it?" asked Nyla in a wondering little voice.

He bent closer and his whisper was hushed and secret. "Dragon scales," he said.

Her eyes went as wide as eyes could go. *"D-dragon's* scales?"

"Oh yes. When Shallasa was still a shining sea, there were dragons in those far off lands. Only a few, mind you, because even way back then dragons were becoming scarce. But they were there. And there were different kinds of dragons. There were puffer dragons whose exhalations could chase the clouds through the sky and blow rainstorms away into other lands. There were soot dragons that ate fire and slept in the mouths of volcanoes. And, of course, there were silver dragons. Great, gleaming beasts made of living metal."

"Oh my," said Nyla. "Were they friendly dragons?"

Bucklebelt laughed. "Friendly? Whoever heard of a friendly dragon?"

"I read about talking dragons in stories," said Nyla. "Sometimes they're nice."

"Those are stories, little one," said the cobbler. "Stories are made up except when they're not."

Nyla blinked. "But...but..." Her face wrinkled with confusion as she tried to understand what Mr. Bucklebelt just said.

He chuckled. "I suppose *some* dragons have been civil, but I don't know if any of them have ever been *nice*. At least not to edible, crunchable folks like you and me. Long, long ago, though, there were people who found a way to talk to those dragons. Not all of them...but the less grouchy ones. There are old songs—songs so old that half the words aren't even words to us anymore—about people talking to dragons. High on a cliff or under a mountain or deep in the darkest woods."

"What did they talk about?"

"About sad things," said Mr. Bucklebelt, and he felt sad to say it. "The dragons were the last of their kind. Each of them, be it shadow dragon or red-clay dragon or corn dragon, they were the last of their kind."

"What happened to all the others? To their mommas and daddas and all their sisters and brothers and aunts and uncles and cousins?"

"Dead," said the cobbler. "All dead. Just as most of those dragons are probably dead now. Bones and dust, like Shallasa the sea is salt and sand. Nothing lives forever. Not even dragons."

Nyla looked sad. "That's terrible. Dragons are immortal, they're forever."

"Even mountains don't last forever and ever." The cobbler took a breath and shook his head as if shaking off sad thoughts. He got up and tottered over to a big chest that had been placed on painted sawhorses. Mr. Bucklebelt fished inside his shirt and produced a golden key that hung from a silver chain. He looked forlornly at the key, then inserted it in the chest and opened the lock. The cobbler raised the lid and removed several items that he set carefully aside. Then he removed a parcel that was wrapped in the very finest silk. He brought this over to the counter and placed it with great reverence in front of Nyla. The cobbler licked his lips nervously and then peeled back the corners of the silk wrapping to reveal the ugliest pair of shoes the little monkey had ever seen.

They were tiny and battered, with holes in each sole and many signs of damage and wear. And though there were sequins sewn onto them, each sequin was as pale as ash and devoid of luster.

Nyla gave Bucklebelt a puzzled expression. "What shoes are these?"

"Why," he cried, "these are the dragon-scale traveling shoes."

"But...they aren't magical shoes at all. These are just a pair of dirty old shoes." Tears sprang into the monkey's eyes. "You're trying to fool me. You're making fun of me like everyone else does. I thought you might be different, but you're just as cruel..."

The cobbler leaned back and laughed. And yet it was not a mocking laugh, or a cruel laugh, or even an embarrassed laugh of someone whose prank has been found out. No, this was a hearty laugh filled with jolly merriment.

"But my girl, these *are* the dragon-scale shoes and make no mistake."

"How can they be? They're so old and ugly and small."

Bucklebelt shook his head. "Don't be so quick to judge. These shoes have walked more miles than there are stars in the summer sky. They were made for a little princess who wanted to see the whole world before she ascended to her throne to become queen. She wanted to walk on every street, to dance at every ball, and play with every child. She wanted to walk behind the ploughman and stroll the streets with the flower sellers and climb the watchtower steps with the sentinels. This little princess wanted to know everything about her kingdom so that she could rule with knowledge and understanding."

"That must have taken a long, long time."

"The observing took time but not the traveling," he said. "For with these shoes she could run from Gillikens to Quadling and back twice in an afternoon, and to anyone else that's a journey of weeks upon weeks. And run she did, because it was important to her to know everything she needed to know before she wore the crown."

"She must have been a very great princess."

"A great princess she was," agreed Bucklebelt, but then a shadow seemed to cross over his face. He lowered his voice. "But a great queen she did not become."

"Why not? If the shoes could take her everywhere…"

The cobbler looked left and right to make sure no one stood near his market stall, then he leaned close again. "Because the Wizard of Oz came and destroyed all of her dreams."

"I don't understand…the Wizard is the savior of Oz."

"Is he? Is that what they teach in schools these days? O', sad times. Oz, the great and terrible, came from far away and with his magic, he overthrew the kingdom and set himself up as the wizard king of the Emerald City." He sighed. "It is treason to say this much, but I must because it is part of the story of the dragon-scale traveling shoes."

"Oh dear, what happened?" cried Nyla, clutching her leather bag to her chest.

"What happened indeed?" Bucklebelt mused, and he had to fight to keep the bitterness out of his voice. "When the princess returned here after all her journeys she was prepared to be empress of all the land, and a fair and just empress she would have been. All of the lands, all of the people would have been one under her rule, and with the dragon-scale shoes she could have walked abroad over her entire reign to see that justice was done and that everyone lived according to her laws. We would have had a golden age."

"Surely she could not have worn these shoes when she was a queen. They are so—"

"Dirty and damaged?" He shook his head. "With the magic broken, they simply show the wear of all those miles she walked."

"No, I mean that they are so small. If she wore them as a little girl she could not have worn them as an adult."

"Ah, now," he said, grinning, "that's part of their magic. When they were working properly, they grew with her and changed with her. They would have become the shoes of a young woman and then a fully-grown woman. And if she left them to a daughter or heir, those shoes would change to perfectly fit the feet of whoever had the right to wear them. But that sorcery is all broken, as the shoes are broken. The magic in them sleeps."

Nyla looked confused and sad, and she hung her head.

"Can nothing be done? You're a cobbler...you repair shoes. Can't you fix them? Can't you awaken the magic?"

"Well," he said, "I have done much to repair these shoes. I've tightened every sequin and I've done what else could be done. However, there is only one way to fix these shoes, to make the magic within come alive again."

"How? Oh, tell me please."

"If I tell you, will you promise to help me fix them?"

"I will!" she said, clasping her tiny hands together. "I will...I *will*."

He nodded, satisfied. "Even if it means going on an adventure?"

Nyla's eyes went wide. "Would it be a dangerous adventure?"

"Now, what kind of question is that from a girl who came here looking for traveling shoes? There are dangers in your own garden. There are dangers climbing to the tree house where you live...after all, if you fell, your wings could not save you."

She thought about it and nodded.

The cobbler smiled. "The only way to repair these shoes—the most wonderful traveling shoes ever made—is to replace the missing scales."

"How?"

"The only way to replace the missing sales is by finding *new* scales."

"But there are no more dragons."

"Are there not? How can you be so sure?"

"How can there be? No one ever sees a dragon. People would talk about it if they did. Everyone would say if they saw a dragon. They'd tell us that in school."

"School tells you about everything that happens in Oz, that much I know. Schools are great that way," said the cobbler. "But...they don't tell you about anything that happens *outside* of Oz."

"Outside?"

"The dragons never lived in Oz," he said. "Never ever. Dragons only ever lived in one place."

"But...but...that's all the way over the sea. I mean...where the sea used to be. On the far, far side of the Deadly Desert."

He gave the tip of her nose a tiny little touch. "You are so very correct, my girl. Across the bones of the Sea of Shallasa in the land where dragons once lived there is a single dragon living still." He raised his eyebrows. "And can you guess what kind of dragon still lives there?"

"A...a...*silver* dragon?"

"Yes indeed. A great and vastly old silver dragon. The very dragon, in fact, whose scales were used to make this pair of shoes."

--3--

"Oh my!" gasped Nyla. "But the dragon is on the other side of the Deadly Desert. No one can cross it and live."

"That is very nearly true," agreed the cobbler, "but it is not absolutely unreservedly true. Except when it's not."

"What do you mean?"

He pointed to the shoes. "These are magical shoes as we both know. Magic *traveling* shoes covered in the scales of a dragon. Such shoes can take the wearer anywhere. Across the whole land of Oz, up and down the tallest mountain, and even across the burning sands of the deadliest of Deadly Deserts."

"But...how?"

"That's the right question. The dragon-scale shoes let the wearer travel so fast that nothing can catch up—not heat nor cold or anything that troubles the foot or troubles the wearer. Remember, the princess for whom these were made traveled the whole length and breadth of Oz. She went everywhere and anywhere and she did it quick as a wink."

"But the shoes are broken, the magic is asleep."

"The magic sleeps," he said. "However when the right person puts on the shoes it will wake the magic from its slumber. Not all of the magic—oh no, sadly much of the magic of the shoes was lost when the scales fell off. But even a little magic is still magic, and to cross the sands in shoes like these you only need a little magic."

"Why hasn't anyone else used the shoes to find the dragon scales?"

"They won't fit anyone else," said the cobbler sadly. "Until they've been restored to their full glory, these shoes will remain as small and as ugly as they have been since the Wizard of Oz stole the land from the princess."

She shook her head, unable to understand that.

"It doesn't matter," said the cobbler. "What matters is that the *right* person could wear the shoes and awaken enough magic to cross the desert. Do you know why?"

She shook her head.

"Because in these shoes the journey—even across the Deadly Desert—will only take a few seconds. Your feet will move so fast that the desert won't even know you're there."

"My feet?" Nyla raised one leg to show him her foot. "The shoe was made for girl feet and I have monkey feet. Will they fit?"

Bucklebelt shrugged. He touched the bunched silk and pushed the shoes toward Nyla.

"Why don't you try them and we'll both find out?"

Nyla stared at him for a moment and then looked at the shoes. They really did look bad. There were at least a dozen scales missing from each shoe, and the soles looked very thin. It was hard to imagine that those shoes had once adorned the feet of a great princess.

"Go on," urged the cobbler. "Try them on."

Nyla chewed her lower lip for a moment, then she reached out to take one of the shoes from where it nestled in the silk. She gave a soft cry at what happened when her fingers touched the shoe. It was like touching something warm and alive. The shoe seemed to shudder under her fingers and Nyla almost dropped the shoe. But the feeling was not unpleasant. Not at all. In fact, it was as comforting as picking up her pet hamster. The shoe seemed to *want* her to pick it up.

Is that was magic was like? Was it that way for everyone?

Nyla held the shoe, turning it this way and that. At close range the shoe did not seem to be that badly damaged. The holes in the sole no longer seemed to go all the way through. The heel wasn't ground down quite as much as she thought. And not as many of the stitches were frayed as had initially seemed apparent. How strange.

"Try it on," coaxed Bucklebelt.

Nyla did so and to her surprise and delight, the shoe fit perfectly. Even though it had been crafted for a human princess it seemed perfectly suited to her monkey foot. She eagerly reached for the other one and put it on as well. Like the first, it was less weathered and battered than she thought and it fit like a dream.

"Let me help you down," said the cobbler, and he lifted Nyla to the floor. "Now, try walking in them. But be careful…the magic may wake up at any time."

Nyla took a single step and suddenly the cobbler and his stall and the whole market was gone. She yipped in fear and surprise as she turned and looked around to see that she stood by the east gate of the Emerald City.

"But I…" She backed away from the grim-faced guards who stood at the gate. But as she took that backward step suddenly she was in a meadow of wildflowers that grew inside the west gate. It was impossible. A single backward step had taken her all the way across the Emerald City.

She turned her head but was very careful to keep her feet where they were.

She was close to the yellow road that curved and snaked its way back into the heart of the city. That road ended at the market square. Nyla knew that she had to go back to Mr. Bucklebelt's stall, but how to get there if every step took her too far?

In her consternation she took a half step and suddenly she stood in front of the cobbler's stall. He still sat on his stool, and he wore a great grin that stretched from ear to ear.

"Ah-ha," he said with a chuckle, "and is that a great princess I see before me wearing dragon-scale traveling shoes?"

"I—I—I—"

"That's exactly what I *thought* you would say."

"These are *amazing!*"

"Now," he said with bright eyes glowing in his face, "do you see how a person wearing these shoes could go anywhere? Even all the way across the Deadly Desert?"

"Yes," said Nyla, almost hopping with delight and wonder. "Oh, yes!"

Then she stopped and her smile faded.

"But...even if I could cross the desert, how would I ever find the last silver dragon?"

The cobbler chuckled again and went once more to the chest. He rummaged around until he found a scroll tied with silver cord. He undid the knot and carefully opened the scroll to show that it was a map of such great age that it crackled and seemed on the verge of falling apart. It showed a map of the land of Oz, with the Emerald City in the center.

"This map was made by the great-great-great-great-great-ten-more-times-great-grandson of the cordwainer who made the dragon-scale shoes. See here? That dot is the town square right here in the Emerald City with the four major countries around it. All around Oz was the broad gray waste. To the Gillikens of the north it was the Impassable Desert; in Munchkin Country to the west it was the Shifting Sands; the Quadlings of the south called it the Great Sandy Waste; and to the Winkies of the east it was the Deadly

Desert, which is also what it was generally called here in the Emerald City."

Beyond that desolation were other places, though, and Nyla had never before seen a map that gave names to those nameless and forgotten places. The Kingdom of Ix, the Land of Ev, the Vegetable Kingdom, Mifkits and Merryland and others. Most fearsome of all was the Dominion of the Nome King, and even Nyla and her people had heard dark things of that terrible place. But the spot that was marked with an X was to the far southeast.

The Country of the Gargoyles.

"Oh dear!" whispered Nyla. "Must I go there?"

"If you want me to fix the dragon-scale shoes, then go you must and go *now*."

"Now?"

"The shoes are awake," said the cobbler. "But they are not strong and if you don't hurry they will soon fall asleep once more."

She protested and twenty-six different reasons why she was sure that she should not do this occurred to her, but Mr. Bucklebelt pressed the map into her hand and gave her the gentlest of pushes toward the southwest.

Before Nyla could utter a single one of her twenty-six very good reasons, she was no longer in the market square. Nor in the Emerald City nor even in the Land of Oz.

She stood under a sun so hot that it made her gasp, and on sands that were hotter than a bread oven. All around her the flat and lifeless sands stretched away.

She was in the middle of the Deadly Desert.

--4--

Nyla took in a huge breath intending to scream her head off—because finding yourself alone in the middle of the Deadly Desert is really an appropriate reason to scream one's head off—but the air was so hot that it scorched her mouth and throat. She did scream, but it was so tiny and high-pitched that even she didn't hear it.

There were bones in the sands. Human skulls and the rib cages of animals and some bones that she couldn't tell what they were from. There were even gigantic bones and Nyla wondered if these were the bones of dragons, or of great fishes that once swam in the Sea of Shallasa.

Nyla felt herself suddenly growing very drowsy and weak and she realized with horror that the terrible heat of the desert was already sapping her strength and her life. She tried to flap her tiny wings, but all they did was tremble and flutter uselessly.

She managed to murmur a single word as she stumbled forward.

"Southeast…"

The desert wind blew past the spot like a hot scream, but there was no one there to hear it.

--5--

When Nyla opened her eyes she expected to see that unrelenting desert stretched out all around her, but a cool breeze blew across her face and the ground beneath her feet was covered in green grass. Flowers grew upward on long stems that towered over her like young trees, and butterflies as big as kites danced from blossom to blossom.

"Oh dear," said Nyla. "I must be dreaming…"

"We are all dreaming," a voice behind her said. "Everything is a dream."

Nyla yelped and whirled and then stood quite aghast.

For a moment she was quite sure that a house had just spoken to her. It was huge—many times as high as Mr. Bucklebelt's market stall—and covered all over in plates of polished metal. A chimney smoked at an odd angle.

However, it was not a house at all and the smoking chimney was not a chimney.

It was a dragon.

A dragon that was as big as a house, with a tail that lay threaded through the grass like a giant snake. A long, long neck rose higher than a chimney and smoke puffed from nostrils that were bigger than feast-day dinner plates. The whole thing, from the tip of the tail to the crest of horns on its massive head, was coated in silver metal. In plates and ringlets, in shingles and in sequins.

But as the beast breathed, the metal expanded and contracted the way an animal's hide would, for this metal was clearly alive.

And yet...

Nyla could see that the metal around the dragon's face was tarnished with great age, and many of the scales and plates were cracked and uneven. The eyes of the dragon were large and red, but although they may once have been fierce, now those eyes were rheumy with age and sickness.

It broke her heart to know it, but Nyla could tell that this great silver dragon was dying. Even though it was a dragon and not at all a monkey, it looked like her grandpoppa had looked before he climbed into the great tree that leads all the way up to the stars.

"You...you...you..." she said, but that was the only word her mind could think of.

"I...I...I...what?" asked the dragon.

"You're a dragon."

The red eyes blinked once and the big head turned to look at its tail and its bulk. "Why, yes. It appears I am. Now how about that? It took a monkey from who knows where to tell me that I am a dragon, when all this time I thought I was a teapot."

"That's not what I meant!" insisted Nyla. "It's just that I've never seen a dragon before."

"Clearly. But, to be fair," said the dragon, "I have never seen a talking monkey before who didn't have wings."

"I...I do have wings," said Nyla, and she felt the sting of shameful tears in her eyes.

"Let me see them."

Nyla turned and showed him the tiny wings that sprouted from the brown fur of her back. She fluttered them and then her wings and her shoulders slumped.

"Oh my my my," said the dragon, and Nyla thought she heard real sympathy in the beast's booming voice. He sat there in the green field, his silvery body shining with reflected sunlight as fleets of white clouds sailed above his head.

"Do you have wings?" she asked, craning to see over his bulk.

"Alas, my wings are gone," he said heavily.

"Gone? What happened to them?"

"They broke off," said the dragon and Nyla thought that he looked a little embarrassed. "You see…when I was a much younger dragon I had wings so huge, so great that the shadow of them would darken this entire field. I needed them, you see, because I am made of metal and metal is very heavy. Other dragons had smaller wings, like the corn dragon, who weighed very little, or the fire dragon whose body was filled with hot gasses. I was always the heaviest of the dragons, but in my prime I could fly. Oh…how I could fly! I would climb up the side of a mountain and hurl myself into the wind, and my wings would spread out all the way to the horizon on either side and when I beat my wings the world shook and trembled. I would fly higher and higher on my wings until the world was nothing but a pretty blue marble below me. Ah…ah, those were the days. Those were lovely days," he said sadly, "but they were long ago. Over the years I kept growing and growing until I was so big that my wings could not even lift me. One day, as I stood atop a mountain preparing to fly, I wondered if I had become too big, too old, and too fat for my wings. But I leaped into the air anyway. My wings beat once, twice and then I heard a crack and a clang like the breaking of a thousand swords. Down, down I went, tumbling over and over — me, the big, old, fat dragon and the broken pieces of my wings." He sighed.

"That must have been terrible. Did it hurt much?"

"Hurt? No, I'm made of metal and I don't feel pain. Not in the way flesh and blood creatures feel pain. But I suppose it did hurt here." He touched one claw to his chest. "To know that I would never fly again was a terrible thing. I wept for days and filled pools with tears of liquid silver."

"I'm so very sorry," said little Nyla. "But at least you did fly and you can remember flying."

The dragon nodded. "And here I am lamenting the loss of my wings when here you are, a little child who should have a lifetime of flying ahead of you, and not even a moment of that joy is open to you. It is I who feel sorry for you, my dear."

Nyla sniffed back the tears that formed in her eyes. "It's okay," she said bravely. "I've known for a long time now that I'll never fly."

"A 'long time,'" echoed the dragon. "You are not two handfuls of years old and I can't even count the millennia of my life. When I was full grown the mountains were not yet born and the desert was a new sea in which the first fish swam. I pity myself like an old fool."

"No! You're a dragon," said Nyla. "The very last of the dragons. I came all this way just to see you and I will remember this moment forever. It is the greatest honor of my life."

The dragon smiled. "You are very kind to say so. Tell me, though, why did you come on such a long journey? And where did your journey begin?"

So Nyla told the dragon everything, from her own decision to go out in search of traveling shoes to her meeting with Mr. Bucklebelt, to the astonishing speed with which her new shoes carried her across the burning desert sands. The dragon listened with the patience of a dragon and it studied her with the shrewd intelligence of a dragon. Then it bent low to study her shoes.

"Ah," he said. "Those are truly my scales. I recognize them."

"You do?"

"A dragon cannot forget its own scales, my dear. We know each and every one of them just as you know every hair on your body."

"But I don't! There are too many and besides they fall out and new ones grow."

"Alas, not for dragons. Our scales may grow larger as we grow, but they do not fall out and if one is somehow lost, it is never replaced. See here." He coiled his tail around where they stood and she could see that there were several patches where scales had been lost. The skin beneath was also silver, but it looked much more like the skin of a crocodile than that of a dragon. "Once when I was sleeping a long winter's sleep a thief snuck in and scraped off enough scales to…well, to make a pair of magic traveling shoes."

"Oh no!" Nyla immediately took off her shoes and held them out to the dragon. "I had no idea that these scales were *stolen* from you. How horrible! How unfair! Here, please take them back."

The dragon peered at her. "Are you serious? You have come here to find more scales and yet you'd give all of them back?"

"Of course I would," said Nyla. "If they were stolen from you then they belong to you."

Smoke curled up from the silvery nostrils as the dragon studied her. "Do you understand what you offer? If I take back my scales, then your traveling shoes will be only ordinary shoes. And in the condition they're in they won't want to take you traveling anywhere."

She nodded slowly. "I...I know."

"You'd be trapped here. On this side of the desert. Far away from your family and the trees where they live."

"Yes...but I could never keep something that was stolen...especially something stolen from your poor tail! Besides...my poppa always told me that the winged monkeys are good people. We give our word and never break it, and we never act unjustly."

"Ah," said the dragon, "if only all races upon the Earth held to such values then the sun would shine on a happier world."

Nyla stood, still holding out the shoes.

The dragon extended one claw and delicately touched one of the sequin scales. "You offer a great gift to an old dragon to whom you owe no obligation. You are willing to make a sacrifice that was unasked of you. Noble indeed are the winged monkeys of Oz. Even those with little, little wings."

With his claw, the dragon gently pushed the shoes back. "Take them, my girl."

"But..."

"And here..." The dragon used the same claw to scrape a line of scales from his tail. They fell like silver rain. "Take these as well. Take them to your cobbler and let him remake those shoes. It is a pity to see something so perfectly intended look so incomplete."

Tears sprang into Nyla's eyes and she could barely speak as she gathered up the scales. Then the dragon handed her a piece of silvery leather.

"Wrap them in this and put them in your bag," he said gently.

Nyla did as she was told and then she rushed forward and hugged the foreleg of the big creature—for the foreleg was all she could reach.

"Thank you, thank you," she said excitedly. "Now Mr. Bucklebelt will be able to repair the shoes and I'll be able to travel everywhere and see everything. I'll go to places I could never go even if I had full-sized wings."

There was sadness in the dragon's eyes, though, when she stepped back from him. "Now listen to me, little Nyla, for there are two things that you must know, and one may break your innocent heart."

"What is it?" she asked, aghast.

"The cobbler will be able to repair those shoes, but magical shoes are unpredictable. These were made for a special purpose and for a certain person. Once they are repaired the shoes may no longer fit your tiny feet. The shoes may also want to find the feet for whom they were made. Magic is a wondrous thing, but it isn't always a nice thing."

Fresh tears burned in the corners of Nyla's eyes but she fought them back.

"And what is the other thing?" she asked in a tiny, fearful voice.

"There is a different kind of magic in the world, and it's older and more powerful than sorcery or witchcraft. It's a magic that comes from the world itself. I will whisper one secret about it to you." He bent down so that his metal lips were an inch away. "Goodness," he said, "is always rewarded. Not always in ways you can see, not always in ways you know or expect, but this world loves goodness. It is a thing that many people think is as rare as dragon scales, but believe me, little girl of the trees, goodness shows everywhere."

Nyla tried to think of how to respond to that. A hundred questions crowded her tongue at once, but the dragon straightened and shook his head.

"The shoes are not yet repaired and the magic that's in them is starting to fall asleep. I can feel it in my scales. Put them on, little Nyla, and run, run, run for home before there is no magic left to carry you over the burning sands."

Nyla did as she was told and even though she could feel the power of the shoes, it was indeed drowsy.

"Thank you, Mr. Dragon!" she cried. She clutched her leather bag to her chest. "I hope your kindness is rewarded a thousand times."

He winked at her.

"Run away, little monkey," he said. "Run for your life."

And so she ran.

--6--

She ran the wrong way first and found herself on the slopes of a mountain that was covered with snow, but from that vantage point she could see the Deadly Desert. She ran toward it as fast as she could and in a wink-and-a-half she was in the market stall with the astonished cobbler.

"I'm back!" she cried as she dug the leather parcel of dragon scales from her bag. She presented them to Mr. Bucklebelt who accepted them with reverence, his eyes alight.

"They're perfect!" he declared as he examined them. "Let me have the shoes so that I may sew them on."

Nyla hesitated—of course she did—and it hurt her heart to have to take off the shoes and hand them over, knowing that she might not get them back. But they really did belong to the cobbler. He had only lent them to her after all.

Even so, the cobbler gave her a strange look as she handed them over.

"You'd give them back to me?" he asked. "Freely?"

"I guess so," she said, and then sniffed away her tears.

The cobbler held the shoes for a long moment and Nyla was totally unable to understand what emotions flitted back and forth in his eyes.

"There aren't many people who would give away anything magical."

"But the shoes don't belong to me."

"Some might say that they belong to whoever has them," said the cobbler. "But...that is another matter. You've given them to me freely and I accept them freely. And yet I don't know that I can recall a single time in all my years when something of a magical nature was given away with such innocence and trust." He shook his head. "Perhaps I don't know as much about the winged monkey people as I thought."

Nyla did not blush because monkeys cannot blush, but she lowered her eyes.

In truth the cobbler's words were as much a mystery to her as the dragon's words had been. They seemed to refer to behavior that was so different from the way her people acted.

"I'm only a little girl," she said because she didn't know what else to say.

The cobbler nodded, but it was more to himself than to her. He set to work on the shoes and Nyla watched him, sitting once more on the ball of yarn. It took more than two hours for him to sew the new scales in place, and as he did so, Nyla saw that the old scales around it suddenly flashed with a new luster. Even the worn sole and heel no longer looked as battered and weathered as before. The cobbler only stopped working once. His eye strayed to the silvery leather in which the scales had been wrapped. He frowned, picked it up, rubbed it between his fingers, sniffed it, stretched it between his hands, then grunted as his bushy eyebrows rose high on his head.

"Did the dragon give you this as well?"

"He used it to wrap the scales," said Nyla. "I suppose he gave it to me. He didn't say he wanted it back."

"Did he not," mused the cobbler distantly, "did he not..." Then the cobbler straightened, fished in his pocket for a coin and handed it to Nyla. "This will take a while longer. Go and get us some fresh strawberries for a snack."

She was off in a wink—realizing that she was very hungry, not having eaten in hours—but she discovered that the strawberry stand was on the far side of the market and there was a long, long line. She fretted as she waited, and danced in agitation because a very fat lady in front of her wanted to examine every single strawberry before making her selection. Two winged monkey boys her own age flew past the stand and then soared high onto a jeweled parapet, where they sat making jokes about her wings and calling them down to her.

Nyla bought the strawberries and trudged back to the cobbler's stall, feeling very low and dejected. And when she returned, she saw that the dragon-scale shoes were completely done.

But they had changed in more than appearance.

"Oh no!" she cried, dropping the strawberries and covering her face. When she could bear to look she saw that apart from the silvery shine that gleamed from every single polished scale, the shoes themselves had grown. They were now slender and graceful and perfectly suited for the foot of a grown woman. A human woman.

Mr. Bucklebelt smiled sadly at her. "Oh, poor little one, I was afraid this would happen. With the magic restored, the shoes have grown to suit the foot for which they were made."

"The dragon warned me that this might happen," said Nyla, "but...oooh! I hoped it wouldn't. Now I'll never go traveling faster than the wind. I'll never run from one end of Oz to the other, and I'll never see all the wonderful things there are to see. I'll always be a little monkey girl without wings and all I'll see is what's down here on the ground."

Yet, even in the depths of her despair, Nyla did not whine and did not shout about the unfairness of it all. She despaired, but she accepted these things. After all, the dragon-scale traveling shoes were not made for her feet.

"I'm sorry, little one," said the cobbler, and she could see from his face that he truly was sorry. "Magic is a funny thing and we can't always predict what will happen."

"But what will happen to the shoes?"

"They will wait for the right feet," he said. "They've waited this long, they can wait longer. That's the way of shoes...they are used to waiting for the right feet."

Nyla nodded. She started to turn away, but stopped. "Thank you for letting me wear them for a little bit. I'll never forget your kindness and trust. And...I got to meet a real dragon!"

"Ah," said the cobbler, "indeed you did, and that dragon must have liked you very, very much."

"Why? Oh...because he gave me the scales so you could repair the shoes."

"Not just that." Mr. Bucklebelt reached under the counter for something. "That dragon gave you more than his trust. He gave you a very great gift."

"A...gift?"

The cobbler removed the item from under the counter. It was the silvery leather in which the scales had been wrapped.

"Do you know what this is?"

"Just a piece of leather. You can keep it if you want. I have no need for it."

The cobbler laughed. A soft, warm laugh.

"Are you so sure?"

He held the material up and Nyla gasped to see that the cobbler had worked on it. The leather had been snipped and sewn and stitched into a pattern that looked like...

"Wings?" she asked in wonder.

"Wings indeed," said the cobbler. "And magical wings at that, for the gift that the dragon gave you were pieces of his own wings. I don't know how this leather came to be detached from his wings, or why he would give it up, but as you see there is more than enough here to make a very pretty set of wings."

The wings were sewn onto a harness that was small enough to fit her. He had her take off her vest, and the cobbler snipped a slit in the back of it. After he'd helped her buckle on the wings, he pulled the silvery leather through the slit so that the wings lay draped over her own tiny, useless wings. Then he gently tucked each of her wings into pouches he'd sewn into the leather.

Then Bucklebelt stood back and pursed his lips for a moment before he nodded approval.

"They're very pretty. Thank you very much," said Nyla, though her voice was still a little sad. "Now at least people will be able to admire my wings, even if they are only leather and thread."

The cobbler arched one furry eyebrow. "Do you think so little of dragon magic, my girl?"

"W—what do you mean?" stammered Nyla.

"At very least trying flapping your wings."

"No! The leather is too heavy and it will break my little wings."

"Will it indeed? And am I a villain who would make something that would injure a little monkey girl for my own sport? Is that what you think?" His words were sharp, but there was a twinkle in his eye.

"But…but…"

"*Try!*" urged the cobbler.

Nyla took a breath and braced herself against the pain she knew she would feel. She'd made paper wings before and her own wings could barely lift it. And once she had made wings of cloth and sticks and it hurt her own wings so badly that she cried all afternoon.

But she did not want to be rude or appear weak.

So Nyla gritted her teeth and flexed her wings.

And something incredible happened — the silver dragon wings expanded out as high and wide as the greatest wings on the biggest eagle in the forest.

The cobbler clapped his hands in delight.

"It doesn't hurt at all!" cried Nyla.

"Flap then," said the cobbler. "See if they'll flap."

She tried, still bracing against the moment when her little wings collapsed from the strain.

There was a huge *crack* but it was not of the bones in her wings. It was the powerful flap of her dragon-leather wings.

She flexed again and there was an even louder crack.

And another and another.

When Nyla looked at cobbler for an explanation, she was shocked to see that he was not there.

He was many feet below her, looking up, pointing and dancing with joy.

The wings cracked and cracked and cracked, and up and up and up Nyla went, soaring above the cobbler's stall, up above the market square, up beyond the tallest spires in the Emerald City. Her laugh was high and clear and it bounced off of the lofty towers of the Wizard's castle.

The gift of the dragon and the skill of the cobbler brought forth the magic that lay sleeping in the leather. Wings that had broken off of the old dragon now lived again and to Nyla it felt like they were a part of her.

She swooped and soared and fluttered and dove and rose up to meet the golden sun. She flew past the two monkey boys by the strawberry stand and laughed at the goggle-eyed expressions they gave her. Then she swooped back and dared them to follow her.

They goggled a moment longer, then they laughed and threw themselves into the wind. The three of them swirled and chased each other and flew away toward the forest. But as fast as the two monkey boys flew, the little monkey girl flew so very much faster.

--7--

The cobbler dabbed at a happy tear in his eye.

Then a shadow fell across his counter and he turned to see a tall figure standing there. It was a woman wearing a green cloak trimmed in black, and the cowl of the cloak hid her face. A battered umbrella was hooked over one thin arm.

"That was a kindly thing," said the woman. "You changed that child's life."

The cobbler's smile melted away and he hastily adjusted his apron and stood very straight.

"She...she certainly changed mine, my lady," he said.

The woman leaned forward slightly and placed her hands on the counter. The motion caused her cowl to slip so that her face was partly revealed. She was old and wrinkled, and she wore an eye-patch that shimmered as if covered with oil. Three gray-black pigtails hung within the shadows of the cowl.

"And has that child changed *my* life?"

The cobbler licked his lips nervously, but he bobbed his head.

"Yes, my lady."

He turned and opened the chest and removed the dragon-scale shoes. The sight of them, restored and whole, shining with living silver, made the old woman gasp.

"At last...after all these years..."

The cobbler looked right and left to make sure no one was watching, then he raised the shoes and offered them to her, head bowed in fear and respect.

The woman hesitated for just a moment, her fingers seeming to claw the air above the delicate shoes. Then she snatched them from him. She kicked off her own shoes and put the silver shoes on. Her robes seemed to ripple as if the shoes gave off waves of energy. The strawberries Nyla had bought suddenly withered and turned rotten.

From far above the sound of innocent laughter floated down. The old woman raised her head to listen. "All this time I thought the winged monkeys were nothing more than curious freaks." Her eyes took on a calculating look. "Apparently they're useful after all."

Before the cobbler could ask the woman what she meant, the crone tapped the shoes together once, twice, and a third time and took a single step away.

And was gone.

The cobbler wiped sweat from his face.

Gone, he knew, but not from Oz.

He stood there for a long time, trembling and frightened, considering what it was he had done. And for whom. She had been his princess long ago and might one day be his queen. His allegiance was owed to her.

But he looked up into the sky and saw the little monkey girl with her beautiful silver wings swooping and dancing on the wind. In the end, he wondered, what would be the most powerful magic here in Oz? The dark arts of the witch who once more had her silver shoes, or the goodness of a child?

"Fly, little one," he murmured. "Fly and fly and fly."

He sat on his stool and spent all of the rest of the day watching the sky.

The Things that Live in Cages

Author's Note

I spent a lot of my years in the martial arts. Over fifty, predominately in Japanese jujutsu, with a bit of this and that along the way. I had some issues to work out as a young man, so I also competed in hard-contact sports. I wrestled, fenced, boxed and fought in a lot of full-contact martial arts tournaments.

This story is born partly from those experiences, and partly out of my love of all things creepy and weird.

THE THINGS THAT LIVE IN CAGES

--1--

Dillon saw the punch floating toward him and knew that there wasn't a god damn thing he could do about it. The Cuban kid had battered his arms for three rounds and Dillon could no more raise his hands to block that punch than he could have sprouted wings and flown away. His legs were over-cooked macaroni and his heart was beating against the walls of his chest like a hummingbird trying to push through the windows of a burning house.

The punch was going to end him.

He knew it.

Time seemed to have slowed down so he could appreciate that fact. Dillon's corner man was screaming at him to block. The crowd was yelling like they were at the Roman Circus. Mike Dillon couldn't see at all out of his left eye and his right was smeared with sweat, blood and Vaseline.

Dillon tried to duck his head down, to take the punch on his forehead instead of his nose. That might give him a chance. If the Cuban kid busted a couple of hand bones, then maybe his corner guy might toss a towel into the ring, or the ref might stop the fight.

Yeah, and maybe bright blue pigs'll fly outta my ass, thought Dillon.

Even so, he closed his one good eye and ducked.

He could feel the exact moment when time snapped back to full-speed. The fist seemed to fill the whole world. There was a huge sound inside his head. It was so loud that it muffled the sound of the Cuban kid's knuckles hitting bruised flesh and cracked bone.

Dillon felt the shock moving at an angle from the point of impact through his sinuses and eye-sockets, past the back of his mouth, the surge of power shifting his head, tilting the opening at the back of his skull toward the brain stem.

There was a cracking sound. Sharp, wet, deep. Dillon knew that it wasn't his skull. It wasn't his jaw. The sound was immediately followed by a feeling of immense emptiness, as if his entire body had been hollowed out—nerves and skin and bone and blood. Everything below the level of his collarbones became a blank.

"I'm dead," said Dillon.

Or maybe he thought it.

He couldn't feel himself fall.

He didn't feel the flat of his back hit the mat.

He didn't feel anything.

All he was aware of was a huge black mouth gaping wide as death leaned forward to swallow him whole.

--2--

"You're awake," said a voice. "Good."

Dillon wasn't sure that the voice was real. Mostly because he was pretty sure that he was asleep. Or, maybe *unconscious* was the right word. It's not like he drifted off in his La-Z-Boy in front of the big screen. He hadn't opened his eyes though, so he wondered how anyone could tell he was awake.

His mind was filled with gutter water and debris. His thoughts were broken things that lay scattered around inside his head.

He knew that he'd been in a fight. This wasn't the first time he'd awakened in a hospital bed. A fight. Sure. Okay.

But which fight?

Who beat him this bad?

And how bad was it?

He could feel his head, which hurt so much that Dillon wanted to let the darkness take him back down into the dim nothingness.

He tried to move his arms.

Nothing.

His legs.

Nothing.

Shit, he thought, but beneath that thought there was a second and less articulate thought. It was more of a sense of how bad things might be, but his mind rebelled against putting it into words.

Got to think, he told himself. *Got to get my shit together and think this through.*

Dillon lay there, letting some internal hand flick on the light switches one by one.

He didn't try to speak. He wasn't sure he could.

There was a soft *ping-ping* sound behind him. He knew that sound. One of those hospital machines that never seemed to do anything but make soft noises. There was a dull pain in the back of his right hand. He didn't need to look to identify that. I.V.

Fuck.

Unless he was dead and this was some kind of holdover memory.

"Mr. Dillon—?"

The voice again.

Male. He could tell that much. Nobody he knew. If it was St. Peter waiting for him to make his case for entrance through the Pearly Gates, then Dillon wasn't interested. Dillon didn't want to have to explain to St. Pete that he didn't believe in any of that shit. Heaven, wings, halos, paradise. None of that shit.

And if it wasn't St. Pete and it was that other guy, then fuck you to him, too. Dillon *did* believe in hell, and as far as he was concerned hell was better known as Trenton, New Jersey. Any other place, even if it was all fire and brimstone and shit, would be an improvement.

There was a rustling sound. Like newspapers. Whoever was there didn't speak again and Dillon figured the guy was reading the paper.

Fine. Whatever. Hopefully he had a comfortable seat because Dillon wasn't in any hurry to wake up and rejoin the world. Any world.

He settled back and let the darkness take him again.

His last thought before he passed out again was that nothing hurt. Everything should have hurt, though, so that was a little weird. The Cuban kid had beaten the shit out of him for seven two-minute rounds. Dillon had gotten two good shots in—a roundhouse kick to the ribs and a spinning backfist that emptied the kid's eyes for a few seconds, but that was back in round one.

Dillon had come out hard and heavy the way he always did. That was his thing—he wrapped up the fight in the first round or he generally got his ass handed to him. Different when he was young, but Dillon was a lot of miles away from anyone's definition of "young." Cage fighting was not a sport for middle-aged guys, as the Cuban so eloquently proved. After that first round, Dillon hadn't scored a single point that mattered. And the Cuban made him pay for those early hits.

He wondered why it didn't hurt.

Darkness whispered in his ears but it gave him no answers.

The lights in his mind dimmed and the last thing he saw, or thought he saw, was a figure—A man? A woman? He couldn't tell—move toward the I.V. stand, a small plastic needle in one hand. The figure inserted the dagger-point of the needle into a port on the I.V. Dillon thought he saw some ruby-red liquid, some exotic medicine, flow from the needle into the I.V.

Then the darkness in his mind flared with red shadows and he was gone again.

--3--

When he woke up again Dillon knew that he was actually awake. Not dead, not floating in limbo or purgatory or trying to run a shuck on St. Peter outside the gates. Alive.

Balls.

He knew from the way he felt that he'd been asleep for a long time. Easiest way to tell was by how much the painkillers had worn off. They don't keep giving you that shit unless you ask for it. Not in crap hospitals in Trenton. Not with his health plan.

And every-damn-thing hurt. His face felt like it had been hand-carved from his skull, diced into little bits, run through a Cuisinart, and put back on, piece by piece, with staples. His teeth felt loose and his hair hurt.

His body hurt, too, but not as intensely. That pain was distant, like an echo.

It took him a while to figure out how to move his hand, but finally his fingers twitched like the thick legs of some obscene spider and slowly crawled across the sheets. He fumbled for the button that would call the nurse, couldn't find it, and then froze as someone pressed the control into his hand.

"It's the top button," said a voice.

It took Dillon a few seconds to make sense of that. Then he remembered the voice that had called his name earlier. Was that today or last month or a year ago?

Dillon decided to open an eye and look at whoever it was.

One eyelid refused to budge. It felt like it weighed twenty pounds and was cemented shut. That was the one the Cuban kid had wailed on every single god damn round. Fucker had a thing for that eye.

The other one wasn't as badly puffed, but opening it was like jacking up a truck.

He said, "Ow."

It took a few seconds for his eye to focus. The hospital room was small and cheerless, with furniture that was purely functional and clearly intended to make people want to leave the hospital as soon as possible. There was a window that gave a wonderful view of a brick wall streaked with pigeon shit. There were no cards or flowers on the dresser. The TV was off.

Dillon turned his head very, very carefully to look at the person sitting in the visitor's chair. He was a total stranger. Young white guy. Twentyish. Rail thin, but thin the way models and art dealers are Like he enjoyed looking like a rake handle. Dark hair combed back, dark eyes, red lips that Dillon thought were painted with lipstick, but weren't. Expensive suit, expensive watch and rings.

"Who the fuck are you?" croaked Dillon.

The man gave him a bland, friendly smile that curled his lips without showing his teeth. "My name is Viktor Petrov."

"Russian?"

"Russian."

Dillon tried to pry open the file cabinet in his brain. Did he owe anything to one of the Russian bookies? He didn't think so, but it wasn't impossible. The Russians had taken over the kind of mixed martial arts matches Dillon fought in. They'd crowded the Brazilians out a couple of years ago because they were more ruthless but also more organized. And, let's face it, Brazilian street thugs—no matter how tough they were—weren't going to get into any serious pissing contests with guys who were ex-Spetznaz and ex-KGB. The Russians were ass-deep in muscle who were ex-special forces.

Dillon said nothing. His tendency toward smartass remarks did not extend to deliberately pissing off the Russians.

"Are you in very much pain?" asked Petrov.

Dillon licked his lips. "It's...not too bad."

"Can you move your legs?"

The question scared Dillon, but when he tried to move his feet, they moved. Not well, but they moved.

Petrov nodded. "Good."

"Why...did I hurt my back?"

"You had a neck injury," said Petrov. "But it's nothing permanent. Some discomfort for a while."

"Did they have to operate?"

"No."

"I...I thought I saw...I mean, did *you* inject something into my I.V.?"

Petrov took a while before he answered. "Yes."

"Are you my doctor?"

"I am...part of the treatment team," said Petrov. "A consultant."

"My head's all messed up," said Dillon cautiously, "so sorry if I'm a little slow here. But...do I know you? Have we met somewhere?"

Instead of answering, Petrov said, "I've seen you fight."

"You mean you saw that Cuban kid kick my head in."

"Well, that, too...but I've seen you in better days."

Dillon laughed even though it hurt his chest to do it. "Then you got a long memory, friend, 'cause my better days were so long ago dinosaurs were running the world."

Petrov smiled at that. His face looked like a moray eel when he smiled. "It wasn't that long ago, Mr. Dillon. I can well remember when you were the up-and-coming thing. A real martial artist in a league that has become glutted with brawlers whose only talent is that they haven't evolved enough to feel pain. Mouth breathing Neanderthals."

"That Cuban kid had some moves," said Dillon.

Petrov shrugged. "Five years ago you would have beaten him."

Dillon said nothing. He wanted to give a nonchalant shrug, but that would involve using too many brutalized muscles. "Kid had some moves."

"He had youth and the stamina that comes with it," said Petrov, dismissing the Cuban with a wave of his hand. "Five years ago he wouldn't have lasted four rounds with you. Ten years ago he would never have made it past round one."

"Yeah, well, everyone gets old. One of these days some kid will be handing the Cuban kid his ass. Way of the world."

Petrov crossed his legs and arched an eyebrow. "Way of the world," he echoed, taking his time, tasting each word.

"Fighters aren't built to last," said Dillon. Then he sighed. "But, yeah, once upon a time I had the juice. I was always hard to hurt. Hardly ever bled, which keeps the refs from stopping the fight. And I could take a punch off of anyone."

"And you are trained as a true fighter. A warrior. Daito-ryu aikijutsu, if I'm not mistaken. For how many years?"

"Started when I was six," said Dillon, and for a moment he felt a flush of pride. "So call it thirty-five years and change. Started cage fighting when I was eighteen. Twenty-three long damn years ago."

"I know. Ninety-two fights. Fifty-seven wins, two ties, thirty-three losses. You knocked-out or choked-out forty-three of your opponents, and you were only carried off four times counting last night."

"So?"

"So, you know more about martial arts than most of the fighters in your league put together. Real martial arts. The deep knowledge, the genuine skills. The kind of knowledge that should be preserved but which is fading in obscurity with each new generation."

Dillon sighed. "Yeah, no shit. I opened a bunch of dojos over the years. Traditional stuff, very old-school, but no one wants to spend the time to learn the old stuff. They want a few flashy moves, a quick belt promotion, and then they want to call themselves 'masters.' Breaks my heart."

"Mine, too. I have very little appreciation for *new* things, Mr. Dillon. I'm very much an old-fashioned kind of person."

Dillon had to restrain himself from snorting. The Russian looked like he was two or three years out of high school.

"It's a shame," continued Petrov, "that you can't use those old-school skills in your matches."

"Ha! I wish. But the league don't let guys like me bring out A-game."

"Pity."

"Got to have rules, I guess," said Dillon bitterly. "You can't really unload on a guy, even in a cage match. People'd get killed."

Petrov smiled and he slowly traced the outline of his sensuous mouth with the sharp tip of one manicured fingernail. "That's not what they tell the rubes. The league's advertising goes to great lengths to declare that this is no-holds barred, that everything is legal, that this is—what's the phrase they use all the time? 'Fighting as real as it gets.'"

He gave a derisive snort.

"What do you expect?" asked Dillon, unsure where this guy was going with this. "This is a sport. It ain't Spartacus and shit."

Petrov sighed. "Alas, no. Those were the good old days."

You're a fucking weirdo, thought Dillon, but he kept that to himself.

"I bet you'd give a lot to fight the way you truly know how to fight. With subtlety, with ruthless efficiency, with a deadly grace."

"I wouldn't go that far," said Dillon. "You don't need to kill people to have a good fight. There are a lot of old-school techniques that I could have used…"

"Why didn't you?"

Dillon shrugged. The action was painful, and Dillon winced. "Bad timing. If I knew what I knew now back when I started in this league, it'd be a whole different thing. But even setting aside the lethal stuff, the moves that would neutralize a bull like that Cuban kid don't take insane amounts of strength, but they do require speed and control. Thing is, the more damaged your muscles get, the less precise your control is. That's where the problem comes in. The older you get the more you know, but the older your body gets the less able you are to use that knowledge. It's proof that the universe likes playing sick jokes."

"I suppose you would like to have your old speed and control back last night."

"No shit. But...if wishes were horses," murmured Dillon sourly.

Petrov uncrossed his legs and leaned forward. "Suppose you could get your mojo back?"

"Very funny, ha ha."

"I'm serious."

"Serious about what?"

"About getting back in the ring for *real*. Wouldn't that be great? Wouldn't that be worth anything? To be at the top of your game, to be Killer Dillon once again?"

"Killer Dillon? Christ, nobody's called me that in years. That was from my old boxing days. Corny name—"

"No," said Petrov quickly, "it's not. It's a name filled with great promise. It's a name that used to give your opponents serious pause, and one that could strike genuine fear into anyone who steps into the cage with you."

Dillon laughed even though it hurt his face to do it. He raised the hand with the IV drip and waggled it back and forth. "I'm five years past my expiration date, son. I should've quit after I lost the split decision with that Polish son of a bitch from Detroit. What was his name? Lenny 'the Breaker' Sepulski. That bastard fair beat the white off my ass. Should have realized he was trying to beat some sense into me, but I was too far into my own shit. Back then I still believed all the hype; I was still high off of my win-loss stats from ten years back. And, man, there's nothing sadder than a cage fighter who's losing every fight and still blaming it on a bad streak that's going to end soon. It's not a streak, it's a downward slide, and it *doesn't* end. But by the time you realize that you've lost your punch and your reflexes are shot from muscle fatigue, nerve damage and too damn many miles on the odometer, you're already into the phase of your life where you're nothing but a punching bag for younger, better fighters and a punch-line to the guys who knew you when."

Petrov was nodding while Dillon spoke. "Yes," he said softly, "but I've seen how you fight. You always make the right choice—kick or punch or takedown. You knew ten times what the Cuban fighter knew. That was true of your fight with Breaker Sepulski. You were the better fighter."

"I lost those fights. And damn near every fight over the last five years."

"You lost because your age and the amount of damage you've sustained over your career have slowed your body and made your reflexes betray you."

"Yeah, well, that's why they call this a young man's game."

"No, that's why this game has become polluted, Mr. Dillon," said Petrov sternly. "When these matches first got started there were some real fighters in there. Men and women who knew the martial arts. Now what do you have? Thugs, barroom bouncers, brawlers—goons who don't understand the martial arts, not in any real sense. Men who don't *care* about the martial arts. This is just a game to them, and for many of them it's the only work they could get because they lack the raw intelligence even to work in construction, and they take themselves too seriously to go into professional wrestling." He sniffed. "At least the professional wrestlers call it 'sports entertainment.' They make no pretense about it being a genuine sport. These thugs have so crowded MMA competitions that they've become the standard for excellence. People look at them and think that these are the masters of unarmed combat."

"It's as close as you're ever going to get to having real masters climb into the cage," observed Dillon. "Most of them are too smart to risk getting wailed on. Most of them are too old. By the time they really qualify as masters they're too old for full contact sports. Sure, they could kick ten kinds of ass in a street encounter, but self-defense against a junkie with a knife or a couple of gangbangers is one thing. The techniques you'd use in those situations come from a whole different toolbox than the stuff we're allowed to use in cage matches. And just from the point of view of recovering from injuries—I'll bet that Cuban kid won't even show a bruise by Tuesday and my face'll look like a tropical sunset for two weeks. And I'll be walking like an eighty year old man for at least that long." He shook his head. "No, this is a young man's game. The real masters either aren't interested in showing off in the ring or they can't see how the risk-reward thing tilts in their favor. Too much to lose, not enough worth winning."

He fumbled for the remote and hit the button for the nurse. But she still didn't come. "God damn it…"

"Not necessarily so," said Petrov.

Dillon, distracted by the lack of a nurse showing up, had lost the thread of the conversation. "What?"

"I said that, while I agree with your assessment, there is more to the equation than that."

Dillon squinted at him with his one good eye. "Like what? The only way a master—and by that I mean some guy who's spent forty, fifty years going all the way deep into a martial art—is going to last more than a round with a twenty-something gorilla who can barely feel pain is if he goes street lethal in the first ten seconds. Otherwise young muscles and stamina are going to crush him. Everyone who has half a brain knows that. So how you going to set up that kind of fight?"

Petrov said nothing; he folded his hands on his lap and gave Dillon a bland smile.

"What?" asked Dillon. "You're saying you know someone willing to take that kind of a risk?"

No answer.

"You're nuts," said Dillon. "Look, it's not even worth it from a purely financial perspective. Guy who's spent his life training to become a master—a real, genuine master of a martial art—he's got a school, or maybe a chain of schools, filled with students who look to him as the icon of martial arts skill. Now understand, all of this belief is based on what they see in class and a kind of *faith* that their master could go all Jet Li on the bad guys in a real fight. But these kinds of guys don't *get* into real fights. Avoidance is a big part of their lifestyles. They're passive, they'll walk away from an insult rather than fighting over it. So their ability to deliver the absolute combat goods is never seen but deeply believed by everyone from the newest white belt to the most senior assistant instructor. Now…if one of these masters does something as dumb as climb into a cage to fight someone like Breaker Sepulski or the Cuban kid, he risks losing. He knows he can't match the younger fighters for stamina, and he probably doesn't have anywhere near the same protective muscle mass, which means he's jousting without armor. He also knows that he can't use his best stuff. He can't dip into his black bag of tricks and do shit like rupture the spleen, smash the hyoid bone, shatter the knee, burst ear drums, pop an eyeball or anything else that he might use in a real street defense. He's facing a fighter who spends all of his time preparing to be hit, and whose arsenal are those strikes and kicks allowed in the cage. It would be like taking a master-level swordsman from Renaissance Italy, giving him a fake sword, and then putting him in the ring with a Viking who has a sharpened war axe. It's an unfair contest on too many levels. The only way it could be fair—and this is pure fucking fantasy here—is if you could take all of the knowledge and experience from the old masters and somehow put it into the heads of the young Turks. Then, even though there would still be some restrictions on certain techniques, you'd see what master-level martial arts are like when it goes whole-hog. But…that's a pipe dream."

"Ah," said Petrov, holding up a finger. "That is exactly my point. That's the tragedy right there."

Dillon frowned. "Huh?"

"At no point in this 'sport' that we both love so well are we seeing anything approximating the kind of fair fight you postulate. The game is skewed, the rules are fractured. This is why these matches draw the worst kind of gambler." Petrov laughed. "You are right to feel a measure of disdain for the kind of brawlers who dominate the sport; but I have equal disdain for the breed of gambler attracted to these kinds of blood sports. They are the same lowbrow crowd who bet on cock fights and dog fights. They bet on animals fighting animals."

Now it was Dillon's turn to remain silent. He was smart enough to recognize the insult buried inside that comment, but at the same time he couldn't really take offense. He was a dumb hulk fighting in a league of dumb hulks. No better than chickens or pit bulls except in being smart enough to know that this was no kind of life at all.

Petrov adjusted his cuffs and necktie. He was dressed very well. Expensive clothes, but good taste expensive rather than fuck-up expensive. Attention to quality rather than for display. Russian Mafya guys often dressed nice. You never saw them in those damn track suits the Jersey goombahs wore. None of the open-shirted satin-finish sport coats of the Cuban players. This guy could be selling expensive watches or showing you four million dollar homes with a view.

When it was clear that Petrov wasn't going to say anything either, Dillon cleared his throat and said, "So where's that leave us other than lamenting what I don't have? I ask, because I hurt too much to lie here singing the blues."

Petrov nodded as if that was the right thing to have said.

"I was at your first fight," he said.

"You saw that?" Dillon narrowed his eyes. "Where? On tape?"

"No, I was at the Princeton Stadium when you fought two matches on the same card. Leroy 'The Lion King' Sanders and then Sonny Daye."

"Bet you don't remember much. That was twenty-three years ago. You were—what? An embryo?"

"A lot older than that," said Petrov with a chuckle. "And I remember both fights as if they happened this morning. The so-called Lion King went down in the very first round. He threw two punches and then tried to sweep your leg. You kick-checked his sweep that I bet no one past the first row saw, and then you hit him with a back-wrist strike to the floating ribs that sent a shockwave through his abdomen which caused his diaphragm to spasm. Very, very subtle. The judges scored it as a backfist because they were too dense to know what they were looking at. And your finishing blows? A two-knuckle tap to the left sinus that had to fill his eyes with tears and cause enough shock to the Eustachian tubes to make him gag. Then you hit him with a tight looping palm that only four martial arts styles teach. It hit the precise point on his jaw that snapped his head around far too fast for his body to follow, which created a corkscrew twist of the brain stem. He was out before he began to fall."

Dillon narrowed his eyes. "Who told you all that? The blow-by-blow in the fight magazines called that last combination a jab-hook punch combo."

"The trade magazines are staffed by hacks who don't know a hammerblow from a blow-job."

"Fair enough. But that doesn't explain how *you* know what I did."

"I told you, Mr. Dillon, I was there."

"Not a chance in hell. Even if you're older than you look you couldn't have been more than five or six years old. Only an advanced pro would have recognized what I was doing."

Petrov shrugged. "The second match lasted two rounds," he said.

"Sonny Daye was a better fighter. It was only 'cause someone else dropped that I wound up on the card with him. Nobody expected Lion King to go more than a round."

"Sonny Daye was the full contact fighting champion of the Deep South. Forty-four wins, one loss and that was a split decision."

"Like I said…"

"I remember watching that fight," Petrov reminded him. "Daye only tagged you twice, both with jabs while you were feeling each other out. After that he never scored one single point that mattered. By the end of the second round he was out on his feet. You delivered a series of blows to acupressure points that systematically shut down his ability to defend himself. You could have taken him down halfway through that round and choked him out. He had nothing left."

"He might have hurt bad if I tried. Get a guy who's that dazed he might not have enough marbles left to tap out. Better to dance him a little and let the corner man and the ref stop the fight."

"Which they did."

"Sure."

Petrov leaned his elbows on his thin knees. "You were a superior fighter, Mr. Dillon. If you'd have been able to get into the better leagues and better venues while you were still young enough, you could have been a contender. You might have been the champion."

"Lot of good guys up on that level."

"Few of whom are as good as you. Few of whom know as much about real martial arts. Few of whom *care* about real martial arts. There are people who still bet on you, despite your recent stats, because they know that you have more knowledge, more real skill, than the apes who dominate the league. I've made several such bets. If you were to win one of these fights, the return on the bet would be considerable."

"Then you got money to burn, 'cause even I don't bet on myself anymore. See these knuckles, the way they're too large. That's arthritis. I got osteo from old damage and now I'm getting rheumatoid. You want to bet on me in a cage match against old age?"

Dillon pushed the button for the nurse, who still didn't come.

"The fuck!" growled Dillon. The pain was getting worse. His whole body like it was about to catch fire.

Petrov reached out and closed his hand gently around Dillon's wrist. Dillon immediately flinched back from the man's touch. The Russian's skin was as cold as ice and clammy as a locker room wall.

"Don't worry about the nurse," he said.

Dillon tried to pull his hand away, but the Russian's grip was bizarrely strong. That was weird because even beat up and half-dead in a hospital, Dillon outweighed Petrov by ninety pounds and none of those pounds were fat. At forty-one, Dillon was rock-solid. Maybe past his own prime, but stronger than this pencil-neck.

Except that he wasn't.

Petrov's hand was like an icy cuff locked around Dillon's wrist.

"Please, Mr. Dillon," said the Russian in a soft voice, "please. We're having a nice and very productive talk. Let's continue to have that talk."

"Let go of me, you freak."

After a long moment, Petrov opened his fingers. Dillon snatched his arm away and immediately began massaging his skin, which was cold and sore.

"What the fuck, man," he growled.

"I'm sorry for the discomfort," said Petrov.

"Shit, you almost broke my god damn arm."

"I'm sorry, but—"

"What the hell, you're a frigging stick figure. What the fuck are you taking? Steroids? Meth?"

Petrov's smile turned sly. "Ah."

"Ah…what? *Is* it meth?"

"No."

"Then what? You're on something. A skinny young prick like you shouldn't be that strong. What are you on?"

"What I'm *on*, to use your word, is part of why I'm here. And before we get to that, I want to correct a small mistake."

"What?" asked Dillon uncertainly. If he wasn't so thoroughly flattened by injury and painkillers he would have bolted for the door. He cut quick looks at the door anyway, wondering if he could make it to the nurse's station.

"How old do you think I am?" asked Petrov, and the question was so weird and unrelated to anything that was happening that it jolted Dillon and made him whip his head around.

"What?"

"You keep saying I'm *young*, and I admit that I look young, but how old do you actually think I am?"

"Who gives a—"

"I ask, because the reason I'm so strong and the reason I look so young are both side effects of what I'm 'on.'"

Dillon had no idea where this was going so he said nothing.

Petrov fished in his pocket for his wallet and produced his driver's license. "I am fifty-seven years old," said Petrov. "And before you ask, I have never had a facelift or any Botox injections."

Dillon stared at the license and then at Petrov. "Bullshit."

Petrov put the wallet away.

"That's bullshit," insisted Dillon.

Petrov spread his hands. "Listen to me, Mr. Dillon, and give me an honest answer. What if there was a way for you to get back your youth, your strength, your speed? What if that process also repaired any damage, no matter how old, and which also helped you heal at an accelerated rate from any new damage?"

"You're definitely on something. Magic mushrooms or something."

Petrov ignored that. "What if you go back into the ring with all of the knowledge you currently possess but with your body and reflexes at the very peak of conditioning. Stronger, faster, more durable, less vulnerable. Can you lie there and tell me that you wouldn't want to climb into the ring again without age and scar tissue and disease hanging around your neck like a ton of bricks?"

"That's a stupid question," snapped Dillon. "Of *course* I would. Who wouldn't? But the league dope tests us all the time. I come up positive for steroids or something, I'd be out on my ass, stripped of all my titles, barred from even stepping foot into—"

"This isn't a steroid."

"Or coke or some designer meth. They test for everything."

"They don't test for this," said Petrov. "Or, rather, they *can't* test for this. I can show you if you're genuinely interested."

Dillon studied him. The things the guy was saying were wacked out, but his tone and body language was calm. There were no crazy lights in his eyes. It was Petrov's calm rather than his words that kept Dillon's own emotions in check.

And…well, Dillon was curious. Really curious.

He was too old not to want to know.

He was too badly hurt, too sore and spent not to want to know.

And the warrior in his soul, the one that time and damage and arthritis was turning into an impotent old joke, wanted to know.

Dillon licked his dry lips.

"Okay," he said, "show me."

Petrov nodded and reached into the inner pocket of his suit. He produced three hypodermics. One was filled with a dark red liquid; the other two were empty.

"I anticipated your interest," he said softly. "I've already begun the treatment."

"What?" croaked Dillon. "What the fuck!"

"Shhh," soothed Petrov. "Just listen. There are three steps to the process. All very antiseptic, all done with the greatest of care." He held up one of the empty syringes so Dillon could see that there were trace amounts of red liquid in it. "For step one I drew a few cc's of your blood."

"Who gave you permission, you son of a—"

"Please, Mr. Dillon, we both know that we are not talking about an approved medical procedure. It was totally safe, so you have nothing to worry about. And it's already done. So, please, bear with me."

Dillon lapsed into a tense and angry silence. However, fear gnawed at him. What had this maniac done to him?

Petrov said, "I injected your blood into my arm."

Dillon's mouth hung open in shock.

"Then, after a wait of a few hours, I drew off two syringes of my blood. I injected one syringe into you via the port on your I.V. I believe you were semi-conscious at the time. Do you remember?"

Dillon did remember, and his fear began growing into terror.

Petrov showed him the third syringe, the one that was still filled with red liquid.

With blood.

God, though Dillon.

"Why, for Christ's sake?"

Petrov's smile faded. "Because, Mr. Dillon, the injury you sustained in last night's fight was far more serious than you know. The Cuban hit you with a powerful blow at an unfortunate angle. It cracked two cervical vertebrae and the broken bones caused a deep laceration to your spinal cord. The doctors are discussing their options, but so far it is their belief that you will be a quadriplegic. Everything from the neck down *died* last night, Mr. Dillon. You were destroyed in the ring."

Dillon thrashed backward from Petrov's words, his feet kicking at the sheets, fingers stabbing the device to call the nurse.

"Fuck you!" he roared. "Fuck you. I'm not crippled, you stupid bastard. Look! I'll kick your ass!"

Petrov sat where he was, the syringe held between two slender fingers. He waited for Dillon's tirade to wind down. Dillon flopped back, gasping.

"I'm not crippled," he snarled.

"Of course not," agreed Petrov. "But you *were*."

Dillon opened his mouth but nothing came out.

"Before I injected my blood into you, you were dead from the collarbones down. Machines breathed for you, machines pumped your heart."

Dillon raised his hands and looked at them, totally perplexed. "But...but..."

"It's not a drug," said Petrov. "It's blood. There is a very, very old Biblical saying: 'Blood is the life.' That is so very true."

"What are you talking about?"

Petrov waggled the full syringe between his fingers. "The process is simple. I consume your blood, you consume mine. Writers have mythologized the process in all sorts of absurd ways, but in simple terms it's an exchange of certain key biological materials. A virus, a very ancient virus, activates dormant DNA in you, and that begins a process whereby certain biological and genetic changes take place. The initial stages of the process occur very quickly. The complete transformation, however, takes years."

"A...virus...?"

"Oh, don't get hung up on that part, Mr. Dillon, this will be the very last virus that will ever affect you. After this, no more colds, no more flu, no cancer, no arthritis, not even the heartbreak of psoriasis."

"You're insane."

"Not at all." Petrov got to his feet and came to stand close to Dillon. He plugged the syringe into the port, but did not depress the plunger. "If I do nothing, the effect of the first injection will eventually wear off and you'll be exactly where you were last night. A head attached to a lump of dead meat. The first injection is self-reversing. So, if you want me to walk away, then I'll go."

Dillon said nothing. He could not compose a single sentence, not even a single word, that made sense.

"However, if you give me permission, then I will inject the second dose of my blood and within forty-eight hours you will *walk* out of this hospital. You'll probably feel so good you'll want to run. Within seventy-two hours you won't be able to find a single trace of any of the injuries you sustained in that fight. Within a week no X-Ray, MRI or CT scan will be able to find a trace of arthritis or scar tissue."

"Who are you?" breathed Dillon. "What *are* you?"

Petrov smiled, but unlike his earlier smiles, this one was a broad grin that showed lots of white teeth.

Lots of sharp white teeth.

"I think you know what I am," said Petrov.

Dillon wanted to scream. He tried to shrink away, but his body was sluggish, as if the numbness he'd felt last night was creeping back. The sight of those terrible teeth filled his mind with horror-show images of pale creatures rising from graves and tearing the throats out of the innocent. He wanted to shout a word, to put the label on the monster that stood above him, but he could not force himself to say that word. It was an impossible thing. To say it might make it real.

"Why are you doing this to me?" he hissed.

Petrov blinked as if surprised. "Why am I saving your life? Why am I giving you eternal youth and strength and health? I thought we already covered that."

"Be…because of the fights?"

"I already told you that I was very old-school, Mr. Dillon. I, and those like me, appreciate only the finest things. Immortality tends to cultivate more sophisticated tastes, as I hope you'll discover. I've always been a fight fan. Even before I became what I am. I want to stop being a spectator and get involved more deeply in the sport. As a manager, as a promoter. But I don't want to trot out one mouth-breathing thug after another. Just as this process will elevate you to a higher level, I want to elevate the sport of full-contact fighting to a level it has never before been able to reach. A class of masters."

"Are there others…?"

"Like you? Not yet. I want you to be the first. I want you to cut a swath through the brawlers currently in the game and then make room for a new breed of martial arts competitor. Immortal masters. Come now, Mr. Dillon, tell me you wouldn't give everything to see fights where both competitors could use their greatest skills, to showcase the elegant beauty and sophisticated science of the real martial arts. Tell me that doesn't stir your soul."

Dillon stared at him but said nothing.

His arms and legs began to tingle again. His fingers were already going numb.

Petrov caressed the plunger of the hypodermic with one pale thumb.

Tears broke from the corners of Dillon's eyes. "I don't want to be a monster," he said softly.

"We are not monsters," said Petrov with surprising gentleness. "We are elevated beings. Call it the next step in evolution. Call it whatever you want. We don't fear the cross. We don't hunt the innocent. None of that. So, tell me, Mr. Dillon—*Master* Dillon—what's your choice? Ordinary or extraordinary? A broken man dying in a forgotten hospital ward…or the champion you were born to be?"

Dillon could not feel his hands and feet.

"Do it," he whispered.

The Vanishing Assassin

Author's Note

Having done a Sherlock Holmes story,[1] I found that I really enjoyed writing short-form mysteries. So, when editors Paul Kane and Charles Prepolec reached out to ask if I'd be interested in doing a story about another classic unofficial detective—I said yes. The detective was, in fact, the inspiration for Sherlock Holmes: Edgar Allan Poe's brilliant misanthrope, C. Auguste Dupin.

Part of the fun in writing these kinds of stories is the research. I had to sit and read, and spend time considering the nature of the character, the specifics of his world, the minutia of the form, and the tone of Poe's trilogy of Dupin tales, *"The Murder in the Rue Morgue," "The Purloined Letter,"* and *"The Mystery of Marie Rogêt."* I do not claim to have written a tale worthy of Poe (I'm not actually insane enough to make such an absurd claim), but I wrote one that I feel shows my deep affection and respect.

---

[1] *"The Adventure of the Greenbrier Ghost,"* included in my previous collection, *WHISTLING PAST THE GRAVEYARD.*

THE VANISHING ASSASSIN

It should, I suppose, be entirely appropriate that I sat with my friend C. Auguste Dupin in the gloomy autumn shadows inside the cavernous and—some would insist *haunted*—walls of the decrepit mansion we shared at No. 33, Rue Dunot, Faubourg St. Germain. We had been to see a rather melancholy play about phantoms and murder and it had brought us into a discussion of many things gruesome and bloody. Over excellent wine and a tray of small cakes, we whiled away the hours speculating on the nature of the supernatural. I have a tendency toward belief in it, or at least in some parts of it; however, Dupin will have none of it.

"Specters are the product of a lack of information," he said as he lit his pipe, "as well as a failure of perception."

"How so?" I asked, intrigued.

He took several long puffs of the strong Belgian tobacco he had been favoring lately, blowing ghostly clouds of smoke into the air between our chairs. Small vagaries of wind made the smoke dance and twitch before whipping the hazy tendrils from sight.

"There is an example," he said. "Had you, a credulous man, peered in through a frosted window and beheld the dancing smoke that has so recently departed us, and had you not perceived the meerschaum in my hand, might you not have thought that inside this house, haunted as it is, at least in reputation, you beheld a specter? And, had you been even more credulous—as say our charwoman has demonstrated herself to be on so many occasions—wondered if the two gaunt men who sat with heads bowed together were not, in fact, sorcerers who conjured the dead from the dust of this place?"

"Perhaps," I said cautiously, for I know that to agree or disagree too quickly with Dupin was the surest way to put a foot into a bear trap of logic.

"Then consider the nature of a ghostly sighting," he continued, warming to his thesis. "Most of them occur at night, and of those many in remote places, darkened houses, dimly-lit country lanes, and church yards—places where proper lighting is seldom provided. Such places lend themselves to morbid thoughts, do they not? Now additionally consider the nature of the sighting itself. So often there is a sense of unnerving coldness, a perception that something unseen is moving so close that its frigid reach brushes against the perceptions of the witness. Add to this the fact that most specters are only seen as partially materialized figures or amorphous blobs of light and shadow. Reflect further on the time of day, and let us remember that at night we are often sleepy and closer to a dreaming state than we are at the height of noon." He sat back and puffed out a blue stream. "The evidence we collect are elements of circumstance and a predisposition of mind that not only lacks clarity and is likely fatigued, but which is also shaped into a vessel of belief because of the macabre atmosphere."

"So it is your opinion that all ghosts are merely the creations of overly credulous minds who witness—what? Mist or fog or smoke on a darkened night? How then do you explain the movement of these specters? How do you dismiss the moans they make?"

"I do not dismiss any sounds or movement," said Dupin, "but I challenge the authenticity of the eyewitness account. Let me hear an account of a ghost who appears on the Avenue des Champs-Elysees at two o'clock on a May afternoon, and present me with at least three unbiased witnesses who have had no time to confabulate, and then perhaps you will ignite a flicker of credulity even in a stoic such as me."

Outside, the wind blew against the house and found some crack in the slate tiles on the roof so that its passage was an eloquent wail, like a despairing spirit.

Dupin nodded as if pleased with the confirmation of his argument.

We sat there, smoking our pipes and listening to the sounds of the old house, some caused by the relentless wind, others by the settling of its ancient bones into the cold earth. Despite the cogency of his argument, we both huddled deeper into our coats and cast curious looks into the shadows that seemed to draw closer and closer to us.

Then there was a sharp *rap-tap-tap* that was so unexpected and so jarring that we both jumped a foot in the air and cried out like children.

However, when the door opened, in came Monsieur G—, the Prefect of the Parisian police, and his presence broke the spell. Dupin and I glanced at each other, aware that we had both been as surely spooked as if we had seen a specter in truth. We burst out laughing.

"Well, well," said G., looking rather startled and confounded by our sharp cries and ensuing gales of laughter, "now behold another mystery. Have I come in upon some great jest or have you two fine gentlemen taken sure and final leave of your faculties?"

"A bit of both, I dare say," said I, and that sent Dupin into another fit of laughter.

G. smiled thinly, but it was clear that he was forcing a cordial face. Dupin saw this, of course, and quickly sobered. He waved G. to a chair.

"Let me pour you some of this excellent wine," I suggested. "It is a Prunier Cognac, 1835. Quite scandalous for a blustery autumn night in a drafty pile such as this, but appropriate for whiling the hours away with dark tales of shades and hobgoblins."

However, G. remained standing, hat in hands, nervous fingers fidgeting with the brim.

"Gentlemen," said he, "I wish I could join you, but I am afraid that those things of which you jest are perhaps out in truth on this wretched night."

Dupin lifted one eyebrow. "Do you say so? And what spectral vapors could possibly conspire to draw the Prefect himself away from a quiet evening at the Jockey Club de Paris?"

"It is a matter of…" began G., but his voice trailed away and stopped. "Wait, how could you possibly know I was at that club this evening?"

Dupin waved the stem of his meerschaum as if dismissing the matter as being of no importance. "A blind man could see it."

"Then I am blind," said I. "Please light a candle to this darkness."

The briefest ghost of a smile flickered across Dupin's mouth and I knew from long experience that although my friend can appear both cold and inhuman at times, particularly in his pursuit of the pure logic of observation and analysis, he has a splinter of perversity that enjoys both the confounding of whatever audience is at hand, and the later satisfaction of their curiosity.

Affecting a face of boredom, Dupin said, "The scandalous matter of race fixing which was resolved so satisfactorily last month was entirely the doing of our good Prefect of the Parisian police. One of the more notable applications by modern law enforcement of the value of evidence collection and the science of observing details to discern their nature rather than forcing assumptions upon them."

G. colored slightly. "I make no pretense to brilliance," he murmured. "And I openly admit to having applied methods I have observed in recent cases with which you were involved."

"Just so," said Dupin without false modesty.

"But how does that place Monsieur G. at the club this evening?" I demanded.

"It is customary of such clubs to grant special memberships to distinguished gentlemen who have been of service to their organization. It would be entirely out of character for the Jockey Club de Paris to have eschewed that policy after G. saved them from scandal and ruin."

"Agreed," I said slowly, taking the point.

"It is also in keeping with the policies of such clubs to hold a gathering to celebrate the induction of a new member. In virtually any other circumstance such a dinner would be held on a Saturday, with much fanfare and mention in the press."

"But there was no mention," I said, having read every paper from front to back.

"Of course not," said Dupin. "Scandal cannot be advertised. No, such a gathering would be on a night when the club would be the least well-visited, and that is a Thursday night because of the big races in England on Friday. Many of the members would be crossing the channel. That would leave only the most senior members and the governors of the board in Paris, and it would be they who would want to offer their private thanks. They lavished food and drink upon you, my dear G., and before you ask how I know, I suggest you look to your cuffs, coat sleeve and waistcoat for evidence. Crème sauce, sherry, aspic and…if I am not mistaken… *pâte à choux*."

G. looked down at his garments and began brushing at the crumbs and stains.

"A gentleman who has had time to go home and brush up would never have ventured out in such a condition. No, you came from that robust dinner to the scene of some crime."

"But it could have been any club that serves a fine dinner," said I.

"True, true," admitted Dupin. "However, I believe I can put a nail in the coffin with the unsmoked cigar I perceive standing at attention in your breast pocket. It is wrapped by a colorful paper band, which is the invention of Cuban cigar makers Ramon and Antonio Allones, and although other cigar makers have begun to similarly band their cigars, the Allones brothers were the first and theirs is quite easy to identify. These excellent cigars are not yet being exported to Europe, but they are often given as gifts by American horse racing moguls to colleagues in Great Britain and France. It is unlikely anyone but a senior official of the Jockey Club would have such a fine cigar; however it is *very* likely that such a prize would be presented to the man who solved the French horse racing incident."

"By God, Dupin," said G. in a fierce whisper. "Your mind is more machine than flesh and blood."

"Ah," said Dupin, "how I wish that were so. Machines do not fatigue. They are pure in function." He sighed. "There are other bits of evidence as well, both hard clues and inspirations for informed speculation, but I have no desire to show off."

I kept my face entirely composed.

"Nor do I wish to waste any more of our dear friend's time. Tell me, G., what *has* brought you away from food and festivities and compelled you even further to visit us?"

"Murder," said G. "Murder most foul and violent."

"Ah," said Dupin, his mouth curling with clear appetite.

"But come now," I said, "you earlier spoke of something unnatural."

G.'s eyes darkened. "I did, and indeed there is nothing at all *natural* about this case. A man was killed without weapons by a killer who seems to have vanished into thin air."

Dupin's eyes burned like coals through a blue haze of pipe smoke.

"We shall come at once," he said.

* * *

And so we did.

We piled into the cab G. had left waiting, and soon we were clattering along the cobblestoned streets of Paris. And within a quarter hour we found ourselves standing outside a building which was divided into offices for various businesses engaged in international trade.

Gendarmes filled the street, keeping back a growing knot of onlookers and preventing anyone but official persons into the building. As I alighted I spied an ancient-looking woman swathed in a great muffler of green and purple leaning heavily on a walking stick. She raised a folded fan to signal our cabbie. I paused to help her inside. In a thickly accented voice she asked the driver to take her to the train station.

Dupin, who waited for me while I assisted the lady, glanced at his watch. "She'll have a long, cold wait. The next train isn't for three quarters of an hour."

"Poor thing," I said. "She was as thin as a rail and already shivering with the cold."

But our concern for the old lady was swept away by the Prefect, who loudly cleared his throat.

"Gentlemen," he said with some urgency, "if you please."

Dupin gave a philosophical shrug and we turned to address the building and the knot of police who stood in a tight cordon around the place. They gave G. a crisp salute and stood aside to let him pass, however they eyed us with some curiosity. The Prefect did not pause to introduce us, as was well within his right.

We climbed three flights of stairs to a suite of offices that occupied half of the top floor. There was a cluster of official-looking persons on hand, including several gendarmes in uniform, two detectives from the Prefect's office, a lugubrious medical examiner waiting his turn, and an ancient cleaning woman who sat shivering with fear on a bench, her face still blanched white from what she had witnessed.

"It was she who alerted the police?" asked Dupin.

"Yes," agreed G. "She heard blood curdling screams of fear and agony coming from this floor and, knowing that M. Thibodaux was the sole occupant working this late, she hurried to see if he had done himself an injury. However, she found his door locked. But here is the cause of her greatest consternation—she saw a line of bloody footprints leading away from M. Thibodaux's office, but they vanished mid-stride and were not seen again. The thought that a phantom had come to do cruel harm to M. Thibodaux sent her screaming into the street as if the hounds of hell were on her heels. There she sits now, shaken and frightened half to death. Do you want to interview her?"

Dupin stood for a moment in front of the woman. His dark eyes took in her posture, her mean clothing, the nervous knot of her fingers in her lap, and the florid and puffy countenance of her face.

"No," said Dupin, "she knows nothing."

The Prefect opened his mouth to demand how my friend could be so certain, but then thought better of it and shut his jaws. We both know that Dupin would rather say nothing at all than make a declaration which could in any way be impeached. He had observed this woman and summed up everything there was to know about her—at least from the point of calculating observation—and had reached a conclusion that he could defend.

He turned away from her and glanced down the hall to where the office of M. Thibodaux awaited us.

"The door was locked, you say?" he mused.

The Prefect nodded. "The superintendent had gone home for the evening which necessitated that the guards break the door down."

"Interesting," said Dupin. He walked over to where the medical examiner sat. "Have you inspected the body?"

"I have," said the doctor, who was as old as Methuselah and as thin as a stick. "He is the victim of—"

But Dupin raised a finger to stop the flow of words. "Thank you, doctor, but I prefer to make my own assessments. I was merely inquiring as to whether it is safe for us to examine the victim."

The doctor looked both skeptical and annoyed. "Yes, there is nothing more of official merit to be learned."

Dupin smiled thinly. "Please remain on the premises, doctor. I may have a question or two for you after I have examined the scene."

"Very well," said the doctor in as cold a tone of voice as I am ever likely to hear.

Dupin moved down the hallway to where a beefy gendarme stood guard before glass-fronted double-doors. When the officer stepped aside I could read the name of the firm written in gold script.

Oriental Artifacts and Treasures
Antoine Thibodaux, Proprietor

However, we all stopped ten paces from the door and cast our eyes upon the floor. As Mrs. Dubois had sworn, there was indeed a line of bloody footprints that trailed from the doors of the murder room and along the runner carpet. Twelve steps in all, the intensity of blood diminishing with each successive footfall.

"A child!" I cried, pointing to the diminutive size of the prints.

Dupin did not immediately comment.

"Surely," I said, "the blood merely wore off by this point and that is why there are no further marks."

Dupin got down on his hands and knees and peered at the last stains. "No," he said. "The blood on these prints was fading, surely, but there was more than enough to leave a trace for several more paces. No, consider this print." He gestured to the last one. "It is somewhat denser in color than the one before it, with an emphasis on the ball of the foot. Then there is an overlay of the edge of the foot as if it was lifted slightly and placed down again with most of the weight on the blade."

He stood up, shaking his head.

"My dear Prefect, may all ghosts be laid as easily as this one and the world will be free of spirits forever more."

"I don't follow," said G.

"The person who left that room stopped here to remove the bloody shoes. When first bending to remove the left shoe, the killer placed weight on the ball of the right foot. The overlay of the edge was likely an attempt to catch their balance while untying the laces. Once the left was off, a bare or stockinged foot was placed here — see the slight indentation in the nap of the carpet? Standing on that foot, the killer removed the other shoe."

G. grunted, seeing it now.

"Come look at the scene of the crime," he suggested, "and perhaps you can dispel the rest of the mystery as easily as this."

Dupin did not answer. Instead he shoved his hands into his pockets as he followed G. inside. I too followed, but stopped nearly at once.

"Good God!" I cried.

"Indeed," drawled Dupin.

The room was a charnel house.

Unless a person is a professional soldier, a slaughterhouse jack, or a member of the police department, it is unlikely that he will chance to encounter a scene of such carnage. I admit that I froze, unable to set foot into that place of slaughter. My heart instantly began to hammer inside my chest and I felt as though my whole body was bathed in frigid dew. I put a hand to my mouth, as much to stay my rising bile as to staunch a flow of unguarded curses.

Even Dupin, with all of his practiced detachment from ordinary emotions, seemed to hesitate before crossing the threshold. Only the Prefect, jaded and hardened by so many years and so many crime scenes, seemed predominantly unmoved. However, his wooden features might well be a tactic to keep his more human emotions to himself.

Despite my misgivings, I shifted around so that I could look over Dupin's shoulder into the room. Except for a solitary figure, the room was entirely unoccupied and thoroughly cluttered. Paintings crowded the walls and filled every inch of space so that not even a sliver of the wallpaper was visible, and each of these works were in a distinctive Asian style. I am no Orientalist, but I could pick out the differences between Chinese and Japanese artwork, and both were represented here, with—perhaps—a bias toward the Japanese. Grim-faced samurai, demure courtesans, absurd fish, and fierce demons looked down from the walls and regarded the scene with serene dispassion. The furniture was of the kind called "japanned," in which the body of each piece was lacquered in a glossy black, then either over-painted or inlaid with designs of unsurpassed intricacy. There were racks of scrolls, urns filled with hand-painted fans, chests made of polished teak from which spilled tendrils of the rarest silk. Every table, every cabinet, every shelf and surface was crammed with carved combs, silk kimonos with elaborate patterns, knives and swords, ink boxes, trinkets, statues, and many other items whose nature or category was beyond my knowledge.

And all of it was splattered with blood.

Streaks and dots of it were splashed upon the walls, scattered across the tops of tables, and ran in lines down the sides of desks.

And there, slumped in a posture that contained no trace of vitality, was a corpse.

"Dear God," I gasped.

It was the body of a man, but that was all I could tell for sure about him. I turned away ostensibly to study the walls, but everywhere I looked I saw evidence of the carnage that had been wrought upon this unfortunate individual.

Without turning away from the corpse, Dupin asked, "What has been touched?"

G. cleared his throat. "The gendarmes who responded to the alert broke into this room. They hurried to the man you perceive there in the chair and felt for heartbeat and listened for breath and found neither."

"I daresay," murmured Dupin.

"The officers then made a cursory search of the room, touching as little as possible, but enough to determine that the windows were closed and locked."

Dupin turned to him. "And—? I believe you are omitting some facts, my friend. Out with it. In the absence of information I can be of no value at all."

"It's a queer thing," admitted G. "When the officers entered the building, they held the door for a person who was leaving."

"God in heaven," I cried. "Are you saying that they held the door so the murderer could exit? Did they tip their hats as well and wish our killer their best wishes? Really, G., this is outrageous."

But the Prefect was shaking his head. "No, it was not like that at all. Though in the absence of all other leads I..."

His voice trailed off and he looked uneasy and uncertain.

Dupin said, "Come on, dear friend, out with it. If the bird has flown, then at least tell me your officers had the good sense to record a basic physical description."

G. snapped his fingers to summon a pair of gendarmes. One was as green a recruit as ever I have seen wear the uniform of a Paris police officer. The other, however, was well known to both Dupin and myself. It was none other than Jacques Legrand, a hulking brute of a sergeant whose brutish physique was at odds with the shrewd intelligence sparkling in his blue eyes. On more than one occasion Dupin remarked that Legrand had a real chance in his profession and we should not be surprised if one day this monster of a man wore the Prefect's badge.

The sight of Legrand looking so embarrassed and wretched caused Dupin to throw up his hands and click his tongue in the most disapproving manner.

"Come now, Legrand," said my friend, "surely you will not break my heart by confessing that you let a red-handed criminal walk past you while you held the door."

Legrand drew in a big breath that made his muscular shoulders rise half a foot into the gloom, then exhaled a sigh that would have deflated an observation balloon.

"I fear I have done exactly that," he confessed, "and I'm more the fool for even now being unaware of how actions might have played out in a different manner."

"Tell me everything," declared Dupin. "Unburden your soul with every fact you can recall and we shall see how low you have sunk."

Legrand drew in another breath and then took the plunge. "It was like this, gentlemen," he said to us. "My partner, Roux, and I were on foot patrol and on such a foggy, cold night many a mugger and footpad is abroad, content that the dense fog and their own mufflers will conceal their identities. Roux and I had made two circuits of this district and we were considering stopping at a café to take our evening break."

"What time was this?" interrupted Dupin.

"A quarter to eight," said Legrand, who checked his notebook, then his watch. "Forty-one minutes ago."

"Forty-two," corrected Dupin absently. "Your watch is off by nearly thirty seconds."

Legrand colored, but he cleared his throat and plowed ahead. "We were within half a block of the café when we heard a bloodcurdling scream. Naturally we came running and intercepted the charwoman, Mrs. Dubois, who was screaming as if she was being chased by half the devils in hell."

"What did she say?"

"It took quite a bit to get her to make sense, but her story was a simple one. She had finished the top floor and was bringing her mops and buckets down to this floor, the third, when she heard a cry of pain coming from the office of M. Thibodaux. She dropped her mops and came hustling down the stairs only to find the door locked and a trail of bloody footprints. She tried to open the door, but it was solidly locked and it is a stout door, as you've no doubt observed. However, Mrs. Dubois heard M. Thibodaux continue to moan and cry out in great agony. Then…she heard him die, you might say."

"Heard?" I asked.

"M. Thibodaux called out a name then Mrs. Dubois heard a solid thump. She pressed her ear to the crack and swears that she heard his last breath and death rattle. It was this grisly sound that broke her and she ran screaming into the streets."

Dupin's eyes glittered. "M. Thibodaux called out a name, eh?"

"Yes, sir. Anna Gata. Or something very like it. A woman's name, I believe, though it is not a name I have ever heard before, and it is not included on the register of occupants of this building, nor in the ledger of visitors."

"You checked?" asked Dupin.

"I did, sir. All occupants' names are engraved on a plaque in the foyer along with accompanying office numbers and floors. The visitors' ledger is on the desk downstairs. I checked it very carefully while waiting for reinforcements to arrive."

"That, at least, was good police work." Dupin pursed his lips. "Gata is an unusual surname. If it is a real name, then we should have little trouble locating the possessor of it, for it cannot be common even in Paris. If it is a nickname, then we have some leads. It is the Catalan word for 'cat' and Fijian name for 'snake.' Perhaps there are clues there, for each is suggestive. However, such speculations are far in advance of the information we yet need to collect." He shook his head to clear his thoughts of such distractions.

"Wait," I said, "we seem to have skipped over a vital clue. The person who exited the building."

"Not skipped over," said Dupin, "but left it to its place of importance." To Legrand he said, "Now tell me of the person who exited the building as you left, and explain why you thought it was beyond sense or prudence to detain this individual. Every detail now, spare nothing."

"There is little *to* spare," said Legrand. "As Roux and I approached the building we saw the door open and a lady stepped out."

"A lady," I said. "Anna Gata, perhaps?"

Dupin ignored me.

"I do not think so," replied Legrand. "This was no sweetheart for a man the age of poor Monsieur Thibodaux, for this was a crone, a withered old woman, and a foreigner to boot."

"Was she wearing a gray cloth coat with a green and purple muffler?" asked Dupin.

"Why…yes!" gasped Legrand. "However did you guess that?"

"It's not a guess," said Dupin. He cut a withering look at me. "My companion here helped her into a cab."

Legrand did not look at me.

"You said she was a foreigner," said Dupin. "From where?"

"Well, she was all bundled up, as you apparently saw, but I spotted her eyes. I reckon that she was a Chinese or somesuch. Small, slender, and so wrinkled that I believe she must have been a hundred years old. Frail, she was, and she needed to lean heavily on a carved walking stick."

Dupin stood considering this for many long and silent seconds. He cut a look at me. "You were closer to her than I. Did you see her eyes and can you confirm that she was Chinese?"

"I did see her eyes, though briefly," I admitted, "but I cannot tell from those if she was Chinese, Japanese, Korean or any of countless Orientals. They are all of a piece to me."

Irritation flickered across Dupin's face. "That may be a dead end in terms of apprehending the killer, but surely, Legrand, you had to make some connection between an Oriental woman and the nature of M. Thibodaux's business."

Legrand swallowed. "To tell the honest truth, sir, I thought she was another charwoman. She was dressed in rags except for that scarf, and walked hunched over. In any other circumstance I would have offered her my arm and escorted her to a public house or fetched her a cab."

"Too late for that now." Dupin looked even more disgusted. "Let us leave that for the moment. Is there anything more you can tell me?"

The big sergeant shook his head, and Dupin dismissed him with bad grace. When he was gone, Dupin snarled, "Had that been an old man leaving the building, even a dotard or a cripple, I have no doubt Legrand would have detained him without thought. But he, being a big and powerful man, can barely imagine anyone but a similarly large person committing an act of such shocking violence. It is a blind spot that may hurt his career and may have prevented us from easily solving this case. Bah! It is my curse that I am so often disappointed by believing in the potential of a person only to find them as flawed and shallow as the rest of the herd."

"Surely not," I began, working up some heat in protest to my friend's words, but he dismissed me with an irritable wave of his hand. I bit down on the rest of my words and they left a bitter taste on my tongue.

Dupin stalked back toward the murder room, leaving G. and I to exchange helpless looks. With raised eyebrows, we followed. Dupin walked past the elderly doctor without comment. He once more examined the bloody footprints and then, nodding to himself, entered the room. He was careful not to step on any of the spilled blood, but that care limited him for the blood was everywhere. He moved slowly through the chamber, speaking in a low murmur as he assessed each item therein and offered commentary to construct a scenario.

"That M. Thibodaux was an Orientalist is evident," said he. "Except for ordinary items of daily convenience—pens, ink bottles and suchlike—there is nothing here of local or common manufacture. It is likewise evident that M. Thibodaux was an antiquarian of some note. These premises are not inexpensive, and his stationary and calling cards are of the very best quality. Likewise his clothes, what we can see of them. He was a man of expensive tastes and deep pockets." He did a complete circuit of the room, peering up and down, sometimes bending quite low to examine one of the countless artifacts on display. "It appears that the late M. Thibodaux was more than a mere Orientalist, but rather a specialist within that field, for virtually everything here, with the exception of a few paintings, is of Japanese origin. This statue of sacred cranes is well known and is surely the work of H—, a noted sculptor from the city of Osaka. There are a number of *Tansu* chests of great value. And see these *Satsuma* vases, *Ko Imari* and *Kutani* covered bowls, *Oribe* tea bowls, *Usuki* stone Buddhas, as well as stone mirrors, jade combs, and many swords."

"But what of it?" demanded G. "Please, my friend, I did not bring you here to inventory the possessions of a murdered man, but to offer advice in the discovery of a murderer."

"The fact that some of these items are even here is surely at the heart of this gruesome matter," said Dupin. "See here, this tea-leaf jar with a design of wisteria? This is a treasure from the seventeenth century and it belongs in a museum. I would venture the same holds true of this fine Akikusamon bottle. This is authentic Heian period, later twelfth century. I know for a fact that this is considered a national treasure of Japan. How then is it in the collection of a Parisian dealer of antiquities? The fact that the man who came to be in possession of these items could not under any circumstances legally own them is undoubtedly tied to the cause of his death."

"Then Thibodaux was naught but a common thief?" exclaimed G.

"Oh, I daresay he was much more than a common thief. More likely a trafficker in stolen items. A most elite fence, for these items are unparalleled in quality, and more to the point, they are treasures of historical and cultural significance. Wars have been waged over the possession of items such as these. Even now Japan is slowly being torn apart by cultural changes, with one faction wanting to move toward a more modern culture—with fractured and fuming Europe as its model—while the other desperately tries to hold onto the ancient values of the samurai traditions. Look at these items, gentlemen, and you will see their delicacy and exotic beauty, but to the Japanese on both sides of the cultural rift these are emblematic of the spirit of the people."

"How came they here?" asked the Prefect.

Dupin picked up an ornate knife and studied the fine weaving of black silk thread around its handle. "Certainly it is not the traditional faction who would let such items leave Japan. No, gentlemen, this is part of an insidious plan by the modernists, the groups who want to see the old remnants of the Tokugawa Shogunate torn down and replaced by a more corporate and capitalist structure. To that end they have engaged many of the world's greatest thieves as well as traitors from within the oldest families. Bribery and promises of power are the grease that allows the machinery of theft and exportation to work."

"But why? Bowls and urns and hair combs? Why steal trinkets and baubles?" I asked. "What possible political value could they possess?"

Dupin cocked an eyebrow. "Imagine, if you can, that a similar schism were taking place in, say, Great Britain. What if dissidents were spiriting away the Crown Jewels? And, closer to home, imagine that thieves were walking off with the splendors of Versailles, and doing so in a deliberate attempt to inflict a wound upon the heart of all that we hold dear as Frenchmen. That is the scope of this. That is what is at stake for the Japanese. The treasures of that nation are being looted and men like our dearly departed Monsieur Thibodaux are the parasites and Shylocks who both assist in these crimes and profit handsomely from them."

We looked around the room, seeing it afresh. I could very well now understand the vehemence of the attack. The degree of harm, and the apparently protracted length of the assault, spoke to a passion fed by love of country and horror at the rape of an ancient culture. I found now that I could look upon the corpse with less revulsion and more with a particular repugnance—and a total lack of sympathy.

"We are still no closer to solving the mystery of who committed this murder," said G. "I cannot ignore it because I may sympathize with the murderer's cause. That is for courts, domestic and likely foreign, to decide. And furthermore I am still at a loss for *how* the murder was committed. I daresay the killer took his weapon with him, but I cannot deduce what that weapon may have been."

"*Weapons*," corrected Dupin, making the word clearly plural, "for I perceive that a great many of them were used in the work that was done here."

"But which ones? I see swords aplenty, and even spears, but these are not the cuts and slashes of those weapons."

"No." Dupin's tight mouth wore a strange half smile. "There is a certain poetry to this carnage."

"In God's name, how?" I demanded.

"Gentlemen," he said, holding wide his arms, "we are surrounded by the murder weapons. Can you not see them? They have been left behind for us to find—for anyone who had the eyes to see."

G. and I looked around, and though we saw blood glisten and drip from virtually every object and surface, there did not appear to be any particular weapon on display except those fashioned for that purpose, but they had inexplicably been eschewed by the killer.

"I cannot see it," confessed the Prefect. "I am all at sea."

"Then let logic bring you safely in to shore," said Dupin. He pointed to a particularly deep gouge on M. Thibodaux's scalp. "To identify an object used in a murder as creative as this we need to broaden our minds from thoughts of those things created to be weapons and to those which were not, but can nevertheless be used to accomplish harm." He turned and picked up a fragile vase with one hand and then the painted wooden stand with the other. For all of the delicacy of the vase, the stand was a sturdy piece of work. Dupin held it up for our inspection and with our wondering and horrified eyes we could see a smear of blood in which floated a few fine hairs that were a match to the deceased's, and the corner of one leg was an equally perfect match to an indented scalp wound.

"He used a…vase stand?" gasped the Prefect.

"Oh yes. A vase stand is but a piece of wood after all, and wooden weapons have such a rich history, wouldn't you say?" While we continued to gape, Dupin pointed out several other objects, matching each to a specific wound or series of wounds. Decorative chopsticks made from bone had been used to create dreadful rough punctures, the steel ribs of a lady's court fan had been used to create dozens of shallow slashes, an ink-block had clearly been the cause of a broken nose and crushed brow. On and on it went, until Dupin had proved that we, indeed, stood within an arsenal of deadly weapons, though each appeared to be utterly fragile and lovely.

"If we suspected that the murderer was one of the modernist Japanese, then I would have expected to find bullet wounds or the marks of military knives. But no, the fact that commonplace objects—or, rather those things never intended for such grim purposes—had been used, reinforces my supposition that the murderer is indeed devoted to the ancient samurai houses of Japan. But not, I am certain, a samurai himself."

"Please explain," said G., "so that I may begin composing a rough description for my men."

"The samurai and their retainers are highly skilled in many fighting arts, not least the sword. But some of these sciences are more obscure, their nature and use coveted by the great families. One such art is called *hadaka-korosu*, and it translates roughly to 'the art of the naked kill.' The name refers not to a person being unclothed in combat, but a fighting art used when the samurai has no sword. The Japanese, particularly the samurai, are less mystical than the Chinese in that they endeavor to see things plainly for what they are. And so to them a piece of wood is a potential weapon, whether it has been fashioned into a club or made to support a delicate vase."

"Astounding," said I.

"Subtle," said he. "Look around and you can see how many of these things are surrogates for blades, for truncheons, for garroting wires, for weapons of combat or—as clearly in this case—for weapons of torture, punishment and execution." He looked down in disdain at the body. "Think about the care, the patience and the risks taken by the killer, gentlemen. Even a retainer of a samurai family would be skilled with every kind of knife. He could have made this quick and silent. Instead he chose to use the stolen artifacts as the weapons of this man's destruction. This was a performance of murder, a symphony of slaughter, make no mistake. And...think of how poetic that is."

"*Poetic?*" I asked, aghast.

"Oh yes," said Dupin, "and in its poetry the killer is revealed. Remember the words the dying man cried aloud."

"You mean the name," said the Prefect, "Anna Gata."

"No, my dear friend, I do not, for I would doubt that M. Thibodaux ever knew the name of the assassin sent to kill him. My guess is that he arranged a late meeting with what he thought would be a client, someone bringing a new and illegal piece to him that he could never receive during regular hours. The caller was almost certainly a woman."

G. snapped his fingers. "The old Oriental woman Legrand encountered. Surely it can't be she? These wounds are the work of a powerful hand."

Dupin nodded. "And yet Thibodaux would never feel quite safe meeting a Japanese man after hours, not with the likelihood of a samurai spy hunting for a broker such as he. No, Thibodaux expected to meet with a woman, but her name was never 'Anna Gata.'"

"Then what?" I demanded.

"Thibodaux did not, with his last breath, name the killer, but cried out in surprise as he discovered the killer's secret. In the extremis of the situation, Thibodaux realized that it was, after all his precautions, a man who assailed him...but a man dressed as a woman. And therein is the answer to his outcry. Not 'Anna Gata,' gentlemen, but *onnagata*. A Japanese word from the world of Kabuki theater—which we have all seen upon the stage even here in Paris. Like Shakespeare of old, Kabuki does not allow women to perform, and instead young men are chosen to play the female roles, and the word for such a role is *onnagata*. Our killer revealed that he was a man, and quite a lethal one, during the act of murder, but by then Thibodaux was doomed."

The Prefect gaped at Dupin for a long moment, but he did not dare question my friend's veracity or try and poke holes in the chain of his logic. Dupin seldom speaks unless he is sure, even when other men witness the same evidence and are far less certain.

Then G. bellowed for Legrand and his other gendarmes and bade them hurry to the train station to arrest anyone they met there. An old woman, an old man, or even someone dressed like a Buddhist monk, for a Kabuki actor could adopt any of a thousand roles and play them with surpassing conviction.

Dupin hooked his arm in mine and we went down the stairs and out into the cold, foggy night.

"Your knowledge is in itself remarkable," I told him, "but it is in the way that you allow disparate facts from such vastly different closets of your mind to find their way together that continues to astound me."

"It is the result of a practice of logical thought," he said. "It is not a comfortable discipline, for it is very demanding and it can sour one to many aspects of ordinary social behavior. But...but...it has its advantages."

I removed my pocket watch and looked at the time. "Oh dear," I cried, "I doubt that the gendarmes will have time to intercept our suspect before she—or, I should say, *he*—boards the continental express."

Dupin merely shrugged.

I shot him a look. "Surely this distresses you? A criminal—one who you alone have found out—is likely to slip away."

He turned and looked at me with eyes that were as deep as wells and equally dark. "Are you, my friend, so inflexible in your views of justice that you view this man, this deadly actor, as nothing but a common criminal, one to be hunted, tried, jailed and hanged?"

Before I could answer, he added, "Certainly the actor is an assassin, and surely he is operating on French soil without permission and in ways that contravene so many laws…but tell me and speak true from your heart—if you were he, would you consider yourself a criminal or an agent of justice? Has not the true criminal of this drama already been found, tried, and executed?"

I formed a dozen arguments against so radical a notion, but before I could barrage Dupin with any of them, he turned and began walking along the avenue. Within seconds the darkness and the fog had turned him into a specter and then he was gone entirely. I, on my part, was left standing there with his words ringing in my ears and no clear opinion painted on the walls of my heart.

The Wind Through the Fence

Author's Note

Zombies. I love my life-impaired fellow citizens. Over the years I've written about them in many forms including nonfiction (*ZOMBIE CSU: THE FORENSICS OF THE LIVING DEAD*), comics (*MARVEL ZOMBIES RETURN, MARVEL UNIVERSE VS THE PUNISHER*, etc), thrillers (*PATIENT ZERO*), adult horror (*DEAD OF NIGHT* and *FALL OF NIGHT*), and a lot of short stories. I've even edited an anthology of zombie stories with the living dead grandmaster himself, George Romero (*NIGHTS OF THE LIVING DEAD*). I was on the commentary track for *NIGHT OF THE LIVING DEAD REANIMATED* and was a talking head on the History Channel documentary series *ZOMBIES: A LIVING HISTORY*.

So...yeah. Zombies.

Even though *"Pegleg and Paddy Save the World"* was the first zombie story I wrote, I consider this next tale to be the one that allowed me to make a solid footprint in that genre. Although it's shorter than the other stories here, this one hit me hardest while I was writing it. And it seems to have resonated with many of my readers.

In terms of where it fits in my overall Maberry meta-universe, it is a sequel in theme (meaning there are no previously named characters) to *DEAD OF NIGHT* and a companion to *"Jingo and the Hammerman."* That means it's also a prequel (for adults) to my Young Adult *ROT & RUIN* series.

The Wind Through the Fence

--1--

The fucking thing was heavy. Sixteen pounds of metal on a two pound piece of ash. Eighteen pounds. Already heavy when the foreman handed it down from the truck ten minutes after dawn held a match to the morning sky; by nine o'clock it weighed a god damned ton. By noon my arms were on fire and by quitting time I couldn't feel where the pain ended and I began. I'd eat too little, drink too much, throw up and shamble off to bed, praying that I'd die in my sleep rather than hear that bugle.

The bugle, man. You couldn't stop it. Only one thing in the world more relentless than that motherfucking bugle, and they were the reason the bugle got us up. To build the fence. To fix the fence. To extend the fence. To maintain the fence.

The fence, the fence, the god damned fence.

We talked about the fence. Nobody talked about what was on the other side of it.

Each and every morning the bugle scream would tear me out of the darkness and kick me thrashing back into the world. Almost every morning. They gave us fence guys Sunday off. We were supposed to use the day praying.

Not sure exactly what we were praying for. Suicides were highest on Sundays, so hang any meaning on that you want. Me? I used Sundays to get drunk and try to catch up on sleep. Yeah, I know that drunk sleep doesn't do shit for the body, but who do you know that can sleep without booze? Maybe some of those lucky fucks who scavenged good headphones from a store, or the ones who popped their own eardrums. No one else can get to sleep with that noise. The moaning.

Even after the fear of it wore off, and that was a long damn time ago, when you lie there in the dark and hear the moaning it makes you think. It makes you wonder.

Why? Are they in pain?

Is it some kind of weird-ass hunting cry?

Are they trying to communicate in the only way they know how?

I shared a tent for two weeks with a guy who was always trying to philosophize about it. Not sure what his deal was. Some kind of half-assed philosopher. Probably a poet or writer back when that mattered. Some shit like that. Everybody called him Preach. He'd lay there on his cot, fingers laced behind his head, staring up at the darkness as the dead moaned and moaned, and he'd tell me different ideas he had about it. Theories. He'd number them, too. Most nights he had two or three stupid theories. Demons speaking with dead tongues—that was a favorite of his. That was Theory #51. He came back to that one a lot. Demons. Motherfucker, please.

The last theory I heard from him was #77.

"You want to hear it?" Preach asked.

The camp lights were out except for the torches on the fence, and we didn't bunk near the fence. That night we were hammering posts in for a new extension that would allow us to extend the safe zone all the way north. Some genius decided to reclaim arable land along Route 60, and the plan was to run west from Old Tampa Bay straight through to Clearwater. They moved a lot of us in wagons from the fence we'd been building just above Route 93 by the Saint Petersburg-Clearwater airport. I pitched my tent on a mound where I could catch a breeze. I was half in the bag on moonshine that was part grain alcohol and part battery acid. No joke.

I said, "No."

"You sure?" asked Preach.

"I'm trying to sleep."

Preach was quiet for a while, and then he started talking as if I'd said, sure, tell me your fucking Theory #77.

"It's the wind up from hell."

I frowned into my pillow. At first I thought he was talking about the hot wind out of the southwest. But that wasn't what he was saying.

"You know that line? The one everybody used to say right around the time this thing really got started."

I knew what he was talking about. Everyone knew it, but I didn't answer. Maybe he'd think I drifted off.

But he said, "You know the one. When there's no more room in hell…? That one?"

I said nothing.

"I think they were right," he persisted. "I think that's exactly what it is."

"Bullshit," I mumbled, and he caught it.

"No, really, Tony. I think that's what that sound is."

We both said nothing for a minute while we listened. The breeze was coming at us across re-claimed lands all the way from the Gulf of Mexico, and it kept the sound damped down a bit. Not all the way, though. Never all the way. It was there, under the sound of trees and kudzu swaying in the breeze; under the whistle of wind through chain links of the fence. The moan. Sounding low and quiet, but I knew it was loud. It was always loud. A rhythm without rhythm, that's how I thought of it. The dead, who didn't need to breathe, taking in ragged chestfuls of air just so they could cry out with that moan. Day and night, week after week, month after month. It never stopped.

"That's exactly what that is," said Preach. "That's the wind straight from hell itself, boiled up in the Pit and exhaled at us by all the dead. Seven billion dead and damned souls crying out, breathing the wind from hell right in our faces."

"No," I said.

"Listen to it. It can't be anything else. The breath of hell blowing hot and hungry in our faces."

"Shut the fuck up."

He chuckled in the dark, and for a moment that sound was louder and more horrible than the moans. "People aren't just throwing words around when they called this an 'apocalypse.' It is. It is the Apocalypse; the absolute end of all things. Wind of hell, man. Wind of hell."

They gave me a bonus next day at mess call. Anyone who finds a zom in camp and puts his lights out gets a bottle of booze. A real bottle, one from a warehouse. I got a bottle of Canadian Club whiskey.

They opened the fence long enough to throw Preach's body into the mud on the other side. No one asked me how he died. As a society, we were kind of past that point. What mattered is that when Preach died unexpectedly in his sleep I was on my pins enough to take a shovel to him and cut his head off.

That night I drank myself to sleep early. I used to think Canadian Club was a short step down from dog piss, but it was the best booze I'd had in six months, and it knocked me right on my ass.

I didn't sleep well, though. I dreamed of Preach. Of the way he thrashed, the way he beat against my arms and tore at my hands, the way he tried to fight, tried to cling to life.

I woke up crying an hour before dawn and was still crying when the bugle screamed.

--2--

My arms ached from the sledgehammer. As I swung at the post I tried to remember a time when they didn't hurt. I couldn't. Not really.

Swinging the hammer was mostly everything that filled my memories.

Six days a week, going on eighteen months now.

The first week I thought I'd die. The second week I wished I would. One of the guys—a shift supervisor who used to work cattle in central Florida—started taking bets on how long I'd last. The first pool gave me ten days. Then it was two weeks. A month. Until Christmas. Each time the pools got smaller because I kept not falling down. I kept not dying. I won't say that I kept alive. It didn't feel like that then and doesn't feel like that now. I didn't die. I lasted longer than the shift supervisor said I might.

On the other hand, outlasting the supervisor's last prediction of, "Four months and you'll be swallowing broken glass to get out of this gig," was not the victory I expected. Each new day felt like a defeat, or at best a confirmation that escape was one klick farther down the road than yesterday.

Some of the guys seemed to thrive on it. Fuck 'em. Some guys in prison thrived on being turned into fish. That wouldn't be me. Not that I ever did anything to warrant it, but when I watched prison flicks or read about it in books, I knew that I couldn't have survived it. Maybe I could take the privations, the beatings and all of that, but I couldn't take being somebody's bitch. And yet, even the worst prison from before would be better, cleaner and less terrifying than my current nine-to-five.

I stood on the soup line, waiting my turn for a quart of hot water with some mystery meat and vegetables that tasted like they've been boiling since before the Fall. I looked over at a guy sitting on the tailgate of an old F-150. The man was holding a piece of meat and staring at it, crying with big silent sobs, snot running into the corners of his mouth. Nobody else was looking at him, so I looked away, too. I was four back from the soup and my soup bowl—a big plastic jug with a handle that had graduated marks on it like it was used to measure something once upon a time—hung from the crook of my right index finger. I looked down at it and saw that some of yesterday's stew was caked onto the side. I didn't know what was in that, either.

I closed my eyes and dragged a forearm across my face. Even doing that hurt. Little firecrackers popped in my biceps and I could feel every single nerve in my lower and mid-back. They were all screaming at me, sending me hate mail.

The line shuffled a step forward and now I was even with the crying guy. I recognized him—one of the schlubs who were too useless even to swing a sledge so they had him working clean-up in the kitchen trucks. I tried to stare at the back of a big Latino kid in the line in front of me, but his eyes kept sneaking over to steal covert looks. The man was still staring at the piece of meat.

Christ, I thought, *what did he think it was?*

Worst case scenario was that they were going to be eating dog, or maybe cat. Cat wasn't too bad. One of the guys I currently shared a tent with had a good recipe for cat. Cat and tomatoes with bay leaves. Cheap stuff, but it tasted okay. Since the Fall I'd had a lot worse. Hell, I'd had worse before that, especially at that sushi place near Washington Square. The stuff they served there tasted like cat shit.

I caught some movement and turned. The guy had dropped the chunk of meat and had climbed up onto the tailgate.

The Latino kid, Ruiz, turned to me. "Bet you a smoke that he's just seen God and wants to tell us about it."

"Sucker's bet," I said. But I had an extra smoke and shook one out of the pack for the kid. The kid nodded and we both looked at the man on the tailgate.

"It's not right!" the crying man shouted in a voice that was phlegmy with snot and tears. "We know it's not right."

"No shit," someone yelled and there was a little ripple of laughter up and down the line.

"This isn't what we're here for!" screamed the man. "This isn't why God put us here—"

"Fucking told you," said Ruiz. "It's always God."

"Sometimes it's the voices in their heads," I suggested.

"Put there by God."

"Yeah," I said. "Okay."

The screaming man ranted. A couple security guards wormed their way through the crowd, moving up quiet so as not to spook him. Last week a screamer went apeshit and knocked over the serving table. Everyone went hungry until quitting time. But this guy wasn't going anywhere. His diatribe wasn't well thought out and it spiraled down into sobs. I didn't get in the way or say shit when the guards pulled him down and dragged him away.

We watched the toes of his shoes cut furrows in the mud. Maybe it was because the guy didn't fight that the chatter and chuckles died down among the men on the food line. We all watched the guards take the guy into the blue trailer at the end of the row. I didn't know what went on in there and I didn't care. The guy wouldn't be seen again, and life here at the fence would go on like it had last week and last month and last year. It was always like that now. You worked, you ate, you slept like the dead, you jerked off in the dark when you thought no one was looking, you tried not to hear the moans, you drank as much as you could, you slept some more, you got up, you worked. And sometimes God shouts through your mouth and they take you to the blue trailer.

And sometimes in the night you listen to the wind from hell blow through the mouths of the dead and nothing—not booze or a pillow wrapped around your head—will keep that sound out.

For eighteen months that had been the pattern of my life and my world.

I was pretty sure that it was the pattern all up and down the fence line, from Kenneth City to Feather Sound, following a crooked length of chain link that we erected between us and the end of the world. Crews like mine, three, four thousand men, working in the no man's land while a line of bulldozers with triple-wide blades held the dead back. Every day was a race. Every day some of the dead got through and you heard shotguns or the soft *thunk* of axes as the safety seams cut them down. We were the lowest of the low, guys who don't have a place in the world anymore. I used to broker corporate real estate. Malls, airports, shit like that. Back then the land was something you could own rather than try to steal back. Closest thing to a blue collar job I ever worked was managing a Taco Bell franchise for an uncle of mine while I was in college. I used to call it honest work.

Some guys still throw the phrase around. Guys standing ankle deep in Florida mud, trying not to get carried away by mosquitoes, swinging a sledge-hammer to build a fence. Honest work.

What the hell does that even mean? Guys like me were about the lowest thing on the food chain. Well…convicts were. Guys who stole food or left gates open. They had to dig latrines and hunt for scraps in the garbage. I heard stories that in some camps food thieves were shoved outside the fence line with their hands tied behind their back. Never saw it happen, but I know guys who said they had.

Not sure how I felt about it, though. If I saw it, I mean. Would I give a flying shit? With my stomach grinding on empty almost all the time, how much compassion could I ladle out for a heartless fuck who stole food so that we'd all have less.

I might actually watch. A lot of the guys would.

It's what we'd have since we don't have TV.

I chewed on that while I stood in line waiting for food.

I watched the real swinging dicks go to work. The construction crews who came in once we had the double rows of chain-link fence in place, using the last of the working cranes to fill the gap between the two fences with cars. A wall of Chevys and Toyotas and Fords and fucking SUVs, six cars high and two cars deep. Maybe a million of them so far, and no shortage of raw materials rusting away waiting for the crews to take them from wherever they stopped. Or crashed.

I wondered where my cars were. The Mercedes-Benz CLS I used to drive back and forth to the train and the gas-sucking Escalade that I bought as a deliberate fuck-you to the oil shortage.

The guy on the soup line grunted at me and I held out my plastic jug and watched dispassionately as the gray meat was sloshed in. "Bread or crackers?"

"Bread," I said. "Got any butter? Any jelly?"

"You making a fucking joke?"

I shrugged. "Hey, there's always hope."

The guy chewed his toothpick for a second. He gave me a funny look and handed over a bread roll that looked like a dog turd and smelled faintly of kerosene. "Get the fuck out of here before I beat the shit out of you."

I sighed.

As I moved on he said, loud enough for people to hear, "You find any hope out here, brother, you come let me know."

A bunch of the guys laughed. Most pretended not to hear. It was too true to be funny, too sad to have to keep in your head while you ate.

I thanked him and moved on. You always thank the food guys because they'll do stuff to your food if you don't. Even the shit they serve can actually get worse.

Ruiz followed me and we found a spot in the shade of a billboard where we could see the valley. On this side of the fence everything was either picked clean or torn down. Every house behind him had been searched and marked with codes like they used after Katrina and Ike. X for checked and a number for how many bodies. Black letters for dead and decaying. Red letters for dead and walking around. Not that we needed to be told. We were in the lines right behind the clean-up teams. We'd hear the shots, we'd see them carrying out the bodies. Anything that came out wrapped in plastic with yellow police tape around it was infected. We'd been seeing this house by house since we started building the fence, and the sound of earthmovers and front-end loaders digging burial pits was 24/7.

I thought about that and wondered if it was true.

"Dude," I said, nudging Ruiz with my elbow.

He was poking at a lump of meat. "Yeah?" he said without looking up.

"When's the last time you heard quiet?"

"What d'you mean? Like no one screaming?"

"No, I mean quiet. No guns, no heavy equipment, no noise at all. Just quiet."

I didn't mention the moans, but he knew what I meant. No one ever had to say it; everybody knew.

Ruiz flicked a glance at me like the question disturbed him. He ate the meat, winced at the taste, forced it down. "I don't know, man. Why worry about that shit? It's cool. We're cool."

"It's not cool. Once we're done with the fence, then what? We sit behind the wall and do what? There won't be any work, and without work why would they feed us?"

"America's a big place," he said. "Fence is a long way from done."

"We're not going to fence the whole place," I said.

Ruiz brightened. "The hell we're not. You got no faith, man. You think we're going to be done when we fence the peninsula?"

"That's what I was told."

He laughed, almost snorting out the greasy broth. "You're a gloomy fuck, Tony, you know that? Is that the kind of shit you think about when you're swinging the sledge? Look around, man. Sure, things are in the shitter now, but we're making a stand. We're taking back our own."

"Taking what back?"

"The world, man."

"Christ on a stick, I never thought you were that naïve, Ruiz. We *lost* the world," I snapped. "We own a piece of shit real estate that we wouldn't even have if it hadn't been for lucky breaks with natural rivers and those wild fires. What 'world' do you think we're going to take back? Yeah, yeah, I know what you're going to say…that there are a couple dozen other teams like ours, and that we're all going to meet somewhere up north when all of the fences intersect and we'll all celebrate with a big old American circle jerk somewhere in, like, Mississippi or some shit."

"It's possible," he said, but his grin was gone.

"No it's not." I ate two more forkfuls. "First off there isn't enough material to build fences like that everywhere. We got one factory turning out fencing material and cinderblock? We have no working oil rigs, no refineries, and pretty soon we're going to run out of gas. When's the last time you saw a helicopter or a tank? They're done, dry, useless. We're always short on food because we haven't had time to replant the lands we've taken back and we got shit for livestock. Half of what the scouts bring in have bites, and you can't breed that stuff and you sure as hell can't eat them." I stabbed a piece of meat and wiggled it at him. "We're eating god knows what, and I don't know about you, man, but I don't know how many more months of this shit I can take. The only thing I got to spark my interest each day is trying to predict whether I'll have constipation or the runs."

He said nothing.

"So, what I'm saying, Ruiz, is we won't last long enough—people, resources, the whole shebang—we won't last long enough to rebuild, even if we could somehow take it back. Why do you think that guy went apeshit on line just now? He got that. He knows. He understood what the wind is saying."

Ruiz cut me a sharp look. "The wind? What are you talking about?"

I hesitated. "Forget it. It's all bullshit."

"No, man, what did you mean?"

"It's nothing, it's… Ah, it's just some shit that guy Preach said once."

"The one you used to bunk with? What'd he say? What about the wind?"

I didn't want to tell him. I was surprised that it was that close to the tip of my tongue that it spilled out like that, but Ruiz kept pushing me. So I told him.

"The moans," I began slowly. "Preach said he knew what they were."

"What?"

"The...um...wind from hell."

Ruiz blinked.

"That's what he said. He told me that people were right about what they said. That when there was no more room in hell..."

"...yeah, the dead would walk the Earth. Fuck. You think that's what this is? Hell itself on the other side of the fence. Is that what you think?"

I didn't answer.

"Do you?"

"Just drop it," I muttered, turning away, but Ruiz caught my arm.

"Is that what you think?" he asked, spacing the words out, slow and heavy with a need to understand.

I licked my lips. "I don't know," I said. "Maybe."

He let me go and leaned back. "Christ, man. What kind of shit is that?"

"I told you, it's just something that Preach told me. I told him to shut up, that I didn't need to hear that kind of stuff."

Ruiz gave me a funny look. "You told him, huh? When'd you tell him?"

I didn't answer. That was a downhill slope covered in moss and loose rocks. No way I was going to let myself get pushed down there.

After a long silence Ruiz said, "Fuck."

We sat in silence, me looking at Ruiz, and Ruiz staring down into his bowl. After a while he closed his eyes.

"God," he said softly.

I turned away. I was sorry I said anything.

--3--

That night even the booze wouldn't put me out.

I lay on my cot, too tired to swat mosquitos. Feeling sick, feeling like shit. After lunch we'd gone back to work, and Ruiz didn't say a single word to me all day. Wouldn't meet my eyes, didn't sit with me at dinner. I felt bad about it, and that surprised me. I didn't think I could feel worse than I did. I didn't think I much cared about anyone else, or about what they felt.

Fucking Ruiz.

But I did feel bad.

Some of the guys sat by the campfire and swapped lies about what they did when the world was the world. Ruiz sat nearby, the firelight painting his face in hellfire shades; but his eyes were dark and distant and he didn't look at me. He stared through the flames into a deep pit of his own thoughts.

I went to my tent, chased the palmetto bugs out from under the blanket and lay down. Someone was playing a guitar on the other side of the camp. Some Cuban song I didn't know. I didn't like the song but I wished it was louder. It wasn't, though. It couldn't be loud enough.

The dead moaned.

The wind from hell breathed out through the mouths of the hungry dead.

Fuck me.

I closed my eyes and tried not to hear it. Tried to sleep. Drifted in and out.

It wasn't Ruiz's whispered voice that woke me. It was the feel of his callused hands closing around my throat.

I woke up thrashing.

I tried to cry out.

I had no voice, the air was trapped in my lungs.

Ruiz was a strong kid. Bigger than men, less wasted by the months on the fence. Made stronger by the sledge than I ever was. His hands closed tight and he leaned in close, his face invisible in the darkness, his breath hot and filled with spit against my ear.

"Say you're wrong," he growled. "Say you're wrong."

I tried to. I wanted to take it back. I wanted to take it all back. What Preach had said. What I'd said. I wanted to unsay it.

I really wanted to.

I could feel the bones in my throat grind and crack. Ruiz was a strong kid. I thrashed around, but he swung a leg over and sat down on my chest, crashing me down, bending the aluminum legs of the cot, pinning me to the ground.

The breath died in my lungs. It used itself up, burned to nothing.

"Say you were fucking lying." His voice was quiet, but loud in my ear.

And, just for a moment, the sound of it blocked out the moans of the dead; for a cracked fragment of a second it silenced the wind from hell.

"Say it," Ruiz begged, and the words disintegrated into tears. He sagged back, his hands going slack as he caved into his own grief.

I tried to say it. With the burned-up air in my lungs I wanted to say it, just take back those last words. But my throat was all wrong. It was junk. The air found only a tiny, convoluted hole in the debris. I could hear the hiss of it. A faint ghost of a sound, a wind from my own hell.

Ruiz was crying openly now, his sobs louder than anything in the world. In my world.

I'm sorry, I said. Or thought I said. *I take it back.*

Ruiz didn't hear me. All he could hear was the moan of the dead.

But me?

I couldn't hear it.

Not anymore.

Faces

A Monk Addison Story

Author's Note

Sometimes a character belongs to a single novel, sometimes to a series of novels, sometimes in both, and sometimes he's most comfortable only in the short form. I have two such characters, Sam Hunter, a werewolf private investigator whose adventures have been collected into a single volume, *Beneath the Skin*, also published by JournalStone; and the other is Monk Addison. Both of those story cycles seem to want to be told as noir mysteries with a supernatural edge.

This is the fourth published Monk story, and at this writing I'm in discussions for both a comic book adaptation and a possible TV series. So…who is Monk? Once upon a time he was a soldier, but he became glutted with the horrors of war and dropped out, went wandering, tried to find himself in the lost temples of ancient religions. What he found was not salvation, but purpose. And a bit of a curse. Monk moved back to 'the city' (could be any city, really), and mostly chases down bail skips except when his true calling requires his attention.

Faces

--1--

I live down the hill, across Boundary Street, deep in the shadows of a part of the city you never go to unless someone steered you wrong.

It's cold down there, except on summer nights when you can feel the day still burning on your skin and there isn't enough air conditioning in the world to chill you out. The rest of the year, though, it's cold. Not icy, but damned cold, like the inside of a cellar where you know bad things took place. Walls are slick with it and when your breath plumes in the air the color of the steam is off. A little gray, sometimes. Or a little yellow. Like that.

Those of us that live down here are okay with it. I mean, we don't *like* it, but we know it's where we're supposed to be. People like us. We're the mushrooms growing in the damned cold shadows. Take a bite out of us and maybe you die, maybe you get visions, maybe you wince and spit us out.

I'm being poetic. Fuck it. I'm drunk and it's Tuesday and you're allowed to get drunk alone on a Tuesday down here.

--2--

For the record, I didn't plan to kill anyone.
Can't always say that. It was true enough tonight, though.
Hence the booze. And maybe the poetry.

--3--

The day started out on the rails, chugging along, making the usual stops.

I had a morning meeting with two of the bail bondsmen I do scut work for. Scarebaby & Twitch. Real names. J. Heron Scarebaby and Iver Twitch. You can't make this shit up. Not sure if their parents hated them or they lost a bet with God, but those are the names they were born with. Scarebaby was a lawyer who'd got disbarred because he got caught sliding it to a lady foreman on a jury for a trial in which his client was facing twenty to life. Understand, Scarebaby is roughly the size of a Thanksgiving Day parade float—overinflated and ponderous. He looks like Charlie Brown, if Charlie Brown was a middle-aged, overweight, hypertensive slimeball. Exactly like that. Four hundred pounds of comprehensive disappointment to himself and, from what I've heard, his four ex-wives.

His partner, Iver Twitch, is a beanpole with narrow shoulders and oddly delicate hands. He claims to be a descendant of Hungarian minor nobility, and I think he maybe is. He didn't inherit any money, but he has that inbred look a lot of the old blueblood families seem to have. Eyes too close together, unhealthy pallor, too much nose and not enough chin. No trace of mercy or compassion for any human being he has ever met. He likes dogs, though, so I cut him some slack there.

No one wonders how Twitch and Scarebaby found each other or why they formed a partnership. You don't have to wonder, the universe loves to orchestrate that kind of thing.

They ran a storefront office on Mercy Street. I asked them if they picked that spot as some kind of statement, but neither of them got the joke. I've been running down bail skips for them ever since I got back to the world. Before that I was a monk—which is how I got the nickname—and before that I was a killer working black ops jobs for Uncle Sam. After a while I could tell the difference between the red on the flag and the red on my hands, which sounds like more poetry, but it's not. So I went looking for answers. Found a few; found more questions, though. Found out some pretty disturbing stuff about myself, and that made me walk out of the temple and come home to Boundary Street.

My friend, the tattoo artist Patty Cakes, says that I'm still a monk. Some kind of warrior monk; but she's high most of the time, so take that with a grain of salt. I'm nothing anywhere near that noble. I'm just a killer who looked inside his own head and found that being a killer was more useful to the world than sitting in a lotus position contemplating my navel or some shit.

The scut work for Scarebaby and Twitch wasn't anything noble. They paid me to find people who've decided running is better than showing up to their court dates. I did that and I was good at it, and made enough bank doing it to drink as much as I wanted. I don't ever get to sleep without some help from Jack Daniels, Jim Beam, Jose Cuervo or the rest of my support group.

The case I was there to get, though, well...

Let me tell it front to back.

Scarebaby was behind his desk and Twitch was standing by the window, looking out to see if there were any good-looking women walking by. There were. There always are. I was in one of the brown leather visitor chairs with a folder open on my lap. The name on the folder was Antoine Hoops: thirty, black male with brown eyes, a shaved head, a threadbare little attempt at a goatee, and prison tattoos running up both sides of his neck. He had spent more than half of his life inside and had served max time on an eight-year bit for molesting a nine-year-old girl.

"He's a charmer," said Twitch without turning.

"Yeah," I agreed. "What was he arrested for this time?"

"Same thing," said Scarebaby. "Attempted rape of a minor."

"And he got *bail*? With his priors?"

Scarebaby spread his hands. "He has a good lawyer."

"How?" I asked. "Who'd represent a turd like him? No public defender got a repeat sex offender out on bail."

Twitch snorted. "It wasn't as hard as you think, Monk, because the victim is an illegal. Conchita Delgado, fourteen. Worked as a room maid at a hotel uptown. No green card, of course. She was picked up the same night as Hoops, and Immigration wants to ship her back to Guadalajara. This is all eleven months ago, and she has some feisty little immigration lawyer working for her, trying to keep her here at least until the trial. That trial was set for yesterday and Hoops was a no-show."

"If she's an illegal," I asked, "how'd she file charges?"

"She didn't," said Twitch. I saw his head turn and nod continuously as a pair of secretarial types walked by, laughing and oblivious to their observer. The girls were pretty and Twitch's thoughts probably weren't. "A nurse saw the vic and Hoops struggling and rushed up to help."

"Brave woman," I said.

"Stupid," said Scarebaby. "Could have gotten herself killed."

Twitch half-turned. "Didn't though," he said with the kind of edge that let me know they'd been arguing about it. He turned all the way and looked at me. "Hoops tried to scare her off, but the nurse works over at Heaven's Gate."

Heaven's Gate was a shelter for battered women and children. Disgruntled husbands and boyfriends sometimes show up to try and force their women to come home and stop making a fuss. Sometimes that gets ugly. Or, maybe I should say "uglier." Not unusual for the staff to get up in their faces, and I know that a lot of the women who work there—staff and volunteers—had first come there seeking refuge.

"Which nurse?" I asked.

"Darlene Crowther," said Scarebaby.

"Darlene?" I laughed. "How bad she hurt him?"

Twitch gave me a nasty little smile. "Hit him blind-side with a taekwondo flying kick," he explained. "Knocked him over and kicked out his front teeth, broke his nose, cracked some ribs and kicked his nutsack halfway into his chest cavity. And then she Tasered him."

"Nice," I said.

Darlene is six hundred pounds of tough crammed into a ninety-pound body. Tough in the way honey badgers, wasps and rattlesnakes are tough. Small, but no sane person would mess with her. I wouldn't.

"Miss Crowther filed charges," said Scarebaby, his lack of sympathy clear in his voice.

"Is the victim going to testify?"

"Her lawyer says so, but it's not certain. She's very scared of Mr. Hoops, and besides, she's being deported."

"Then…"

"A passerby caught some of the attack on his cell phone," said Twitch.

"Was the video clear enough to win a case?" I asked.

"Probably," said Scarebaby, "though frankly I don't give a cold, wet shit. My concern is—"

"*Our* concern," corrected Twitch.

"*Our* concern is the fact that we fronted fifty large for bail and after behaving himself for nearly a year, Mr. Hoops has absconded."

I smiled. He was the only person I'd ever met who wasn't trying to be cute or clever when he said "absconded."

"Not that I'm trying to say no to a bounty," I said, cutting a look at Twitch, "but how come you haven't gone out looking for him?"

Twitch used to be an investigator but lately he hasn't done any active legwork. "I've taken a more managerial position in the firm," he said.

Scarebaby looked down at his folded hands and smiled but made no comment.

"You want the job or not?" asked Twitch, his face and voice stiff.

"Sure," I said. "I'll find him."

They both smiled their approval and relief.

"For the record," said Twitch, "I personally do not care in what condition you 'find' Mr. Hoops. He sticks his dick into kids."

Scarebaby nodded. "All we have to do is produce him to the courts."

"In whatever shape," added Twitch.

Another nod from Scarebaby. "In, as you say, whatever shape."

There wasn't a lot of love in the room for Antoine Hoops. I wasn't feeling a glow in my heart, either.

--4--

The folder had the usual stuff. Last verified address, list of known associates, complete physical description, and all the rest. I spent a couple of hours banging around the places he'd be most likely to hide out. Stores that I knew had back rooms with cots that the owners would rent out to whoever wanted to lie low; the row of shitty hotels on China Street; a motel by the boulevard. Came up dry. The staff don't talk to cops but they'll talk to me, even though they know what I do. Word gets around. People know where I stand. If the guy was just wanted on a drug beef or for burglary they wouldn't be talking to me. This guy was a pedophile, though, so different rules apply. Everyone knows where I stand with stuff like that.

Understand something—I'm a big, mean, tough, violent son of a bitch and no one ever hurt me without me hurting them back. I've never been a victim of sexual or violent abuse. My old man was a drunk and an asshole, but that was between him and his PTSD. He never laid hands on me. My mom died of cancer when I was four. So I don't know abuse firsthand. I've seen it, though. In Iraq and Afghanistan. In Syria and India. Other places. Here in the city, too. I've seen it and I'm not the kind of cat who can look away. I can't pretend not to hear or not to know. Shit like that pushes my buttons even though I don't know why I have those buttons. Moral outrage, as a concept, sounds too grandiose, but that's pretty much what it is.

People know this about me and they don't get in my way or in my face when I'm hunting for a sexual predator. Not that they go out of their way to help me. The street is still the street. They just know how I'll react if someone like Hoops slips away because of them. Very bad things have happened in the past.

I got my first lead just as the sun was starting to slip out of the sky and slide down behind the skyline. I was having a beer at a club on 8th. The Al Skorpion Band was playing and it didn't sound like anyone was in the same key. Al looks like Archie from the comics and sings like Tom Waits, if Tom had spent the afternoon having the shit kicked out of him behind a dumpster. Growly and mean, but I liked his lyrics. Stuff about bad luck and poor choices.

My beer was only halfway gone when a woman slid onto the stool next to me. There were eight empty stools, so I figured this was either a pro hoping to score a quick one or someone looking to make a hundred because I'd been putting that number out there for information. She nodded to the bartender and he put a glass of candy-colored fizz in front of her. He cut me a look and I nodded, and he took a five out of the change I had on the counter.

"Say it," I suggested when I was alone with the woman.

"You're Monk Addison," she said. "I seen you around."

"Okay."

"You're the guy with all the tattoos."

I shrugged. "Everybody's got some ink these days."

"You're the one with the faces," she said. Without asking permission she reached out and pushed up the sleeve of my hoodie. The tats start above the wrist. Small and large faces. Most of them in black and white. Nothing on my hands or face. Nothing on my dick, because that would be weird. The woman leaned in and peered at the faces she could see. I let her turn my wrist so she could see more of them. Then she sat back and drank two thirds of her cocktail.

I looked at our reflections in the mirror behind the bar, but didn't turn towards her. She was mid-forties, kind of nice looking, kind of used up. Maybe I'd seen her around. Hard to tell. She was a type. Aging hooker. Too much make-up because she was terrified of losing her looks. Every wrinkle, every line, every bit of sag means that she gets to charge less for doing more. It's built-in erosion. Of the body as the soul. Getting out of the life means facing up to entering the minimum-wage job market with no experience and a face that tells everyone who has eyes what you've been doing for the past twenty-plus years. It's sad, and I don't judge for two reasons. First, I don't know what put her on the street. There's always a back-story and it is never pretty. Second, when I was young I earned my pay by killing people. Sometimes I still do. I have absolutely no grounds for moral judgment.

Except for shit-eaters like Antoine Hoops.

"People talk about you," said the woman. "They tell stories. Freaky shit about why you have those tattoos."

"Who gives a shit?" I asked. "Look, can we put some top-spin on this?"

She blinked, then smiled. "Sure, honey. Just making small talk."

"Never in the mood for it," I said.

"Okay."

"Okay. What's your name?" I asked.

"Bambi."

"Your real name."

"Honest to god. My folks hung that on me."

"Jesus."

"Kind of started me down a certain road, you know?" she said.

"No shit."

"Life happens," said Bambi. She sipped her drink. "This guy you're looking for...? There's a couple hundred to find him?"

"*One* hundred," I said.

She finished her drink and started to get up. I sighed.

"Okay, two. Whatever," I grumbled. "But only if I put hands on him."

She sat back down, trying not to smile too much. "I know where his sister lives."

"So do I."

"Oh yeah? Which sister?"

I turned to look at her. "He only has one. Rachelle."

The smiled grew. "That's his blood sister and they don't talk at all. She wouldn't piss on him if he was on fire."

"I like her already."

"Hoops' father was a no-show from the jump and his mom crack-whore'd herself into HIV. She died when Antoine and Rachelle were teenagers. They spent time in foster care, but Rachelle was adopted and Antoine never was. He got really tight with another foster kid, a girl who was a couple of years younger."

The file mentioned foster care, but there was nothing about this. Bambi nodded, knowing she'd set the hook. I took out my wallet and peeled off two fifties and laid them flat on the bar between us.

"Hey," she said.

"Half up front, half when I put this asshole in a bag."

"That wasn't the deal."

I studied her. "You said you heard about me. You ever hear anyone say I don't pay my debts?"

"No."

"You ever hear that I fuck around?"

"No…"

"Then take the money and let's cut to the chase. I want to wrap this up tonight. You give me a cell phone number and when I have Hoops I tell you where to meet me. If he's actually *at* the address you give me, then maybe I'll sweeten the pot."

She thought about it for about half a microsecond and then the fifties disappeared.

"Her name is Cheryl Carbone," she said. "She used to work out of the Velvet Motor Lodge, but she got out of the life after she had a kid. A little girl. Works at McDonald's. Lives on this little street off Boundary. The one with the worst-ever name for a street to live on."

"Misery Street," I said.

"Yeah."

Like a lot of people down here she was superstitious about even saying the name. It was a bad luck street that lived up to its name. Not sure who had the comprehensive jackassary to hang a name like that on a residential street, but it lived up to it.

Misery.

You got to be on the poor side of fucking poor to want to live there. No, check that. You have to *need* to live there. No one wants to. I know the guy who mops the floor at Powder Brothers funeral home, and he says that even *they* hate getting gigs over there. And they are frequent flyers. When the guys whose job it is to sell funerals get freaked out by your address, your karma is polluted.

"What makes you think Hoops is there?" I asked.

"I saw him go in the front door."

"When?"

"Couple hours ago. I was doing a house call at the corner. On the Boundary Street side, you know? Not on…"

"Got it."

"Her house is two doors down from the corner, and I saw Hoops get out of an Escalade and go running to the front door."

"Whose car?"

"Don't know, and don't ask if I copied down the plates. I didn't. But who drives Escalades around here?"

I nodded. The upper echelon of the three different drug gangs all drove identical black Escalades. Keeping up with the Joneses.

"How'd you know it was Hoops?" I asked.

She shrugged. "Seen him around a bunch, here and there. Got to know him a little. He was bouncer at *Pornstash* for a few months. Pretending to be gay so he could work there. Then he beat up a kid who was cruising the place. Young kid, maybe fifteen with a fake I.D. Looking for love in all the wrong places."

"*Pornstash* isn't a bad joint."

"Maybe not most of the time, but it wasn't the best place for a little fish like that to be. Fifteen, you know?"

"Point taken."

"Kid tried to come on to Hoops, and that asshole took him out back like maybe he was game for a blowjob, but then he stomped the shit out of the kid. Really hurt him, too. Big Larry came out to take a leak because the bathroom was full and he saw what was going on. He tried to put Hoops down—you know how Big Larry is, he'll pick a fight with anyone and he nearly always wins—but Hoops busted the crap out of him. Only ran off when other guys started coming out of the place. Laid low at Cheryl's. I seen him there before, because I do that gig on the corner about every other week. Sometimes more. When the cops busted him this last time, after he raped that girl he went to prison for, they bagged him at that intersection. Not sure if he was going to Cheryl's or coming from. But he's back there now, bold as brass."

"Not too bright going back there."

She signaled for another drink. "Maybe he figures it was too obvious and the cops wouldn't think he'd go anywhere near there."

"Or maybe he's an idiot," I suggested.

"Or maybe that." Her drink came and I paid for it. "Look, Monk...I know you have this reputation of being a scary S.O.B., and you look big and mean enough to handle yourself...but Hoops took Big Larry apart without breaking a sweat. No one's ever done that, far as I know. And don't get fooled thinking that Hoops lost his edge because that nurse Darlene kicked his ass. She suckered him. And she better watch *her* ass, too. Antoine Hoops is no joke."

I finished my beer. "Don't worry, sister. If I get my ass handed to me I'll make sure you get the rest of your money."

She looked genuinely hurt, and turned away to look at something else. Anything else that wasn't me. She fished a business card out of her purse and slid it across without meeting my eye. It had her name and cell number and nothing else. I sighed, picked it up, left mine on the deck along with my change for the bartender and stood up.

"Cheryl has a five-year-old daughter," said Bambi. "She's in that house with Antoine."

"Thanks," I said, but she didn't even nod. I went out, feeling like a dick for offending her.

--5--

I walked the nine blocks along Boundary Street. I had my earphones in and was listening to the live stream of Oswald Four deejaying from *Unlovely's*. He was in a mood. I was in a different mood.

Sometimes I cut looks up the side streets that ran from Boundary Street up the hill. The lights were so bright up there. That part of the city probably has an official name, but everyone calls it the Fire Zone. I've only been up there a few times, but it's not right for me. Or, maybe it's that I'm not right for it. I always feel unclean up there, like I should be wearing a sign around my neck.

Up there you can hear the Music. That's how everything thinks about it. Music, with a capital M. It's not just tunes and tracks. There's something about the Music up there. I think it's been played so long, so well, with such artistry and passion and insight that maybe it's become alive. Am I being fanciful? Maybe. Or maybe I'm underselling it.

You can't really hear the Music on Boundary Street, but everyone here knows about it. We even talk about it sometimes, but the echoes of the Music don't reach this far down the hill. Or, maybe no one down there in the shadows strains hard enough to hear. If we want to hear it, we have to tune into Uncle Oswald's show. I once heard someone say that Oswald Four *was* the Music. That they were two halves of a whole. Not sure if I believe that, but I can't make a compelling case against it.

So I listen in and imagine what it would be like to be the kind of person who belonged up in the Zone. I think about that as I walk around down here, and it's always on my mind every time I'm on Boundary Street.

You see, down here you don't get to see Oswald Four live. Down here you won't find Snakedancer leading the faithful in complex line dances under the tracking eyes of the watchful laser lights on Gotham Road or along Harlequin Street. Snakedancer's one of the people who belong up the hill. Up in the light.

Down along Boundary Street the clubs play sweaty blues and icy jazz and some soulful R&B that will rip you a new one if you open up to it. On Thursday nights at the Cavern you can catch Elton Leonard and his five piece working over Thelonious Monk tunes like *Straight, No Chaser* and *Bright Mississippi,* and even *Green Chimneys,* and Elton plays it even funkier than Monk did, and he does it with nine fingers. He has all ten, but he never uses his left little finger and won't say why.

Down here you can go into The Stumble Inn for some Irish fight songs, and on any given night you can hear pretty much the entire Wolf Tones songbook, and a rousing version of the Pogues' *Young Ned of the Hill.* And some newer, less violent stuff that Happy O'Hanlon's been writing since he came back from County Tyrone. Get a few drinks in him, though, and he'll be singing *The Belfast Brigade* or *Republican Guns* and cursing like a longshoreman. And if the blues is calling to you, then you can go to Blackbeard's where Crash Gordon and Nine Mile Sutton have been holding court, apparently, since just after the Lincoln-Douglas debates.

But what you won't hear is the Music. Not out loud. Maybe it's just that no one down here can hear it. For us, the darkness is way too loud.

Bad thoughts to have while walking a cold mile to find a child molester.

--6--

Misery Street.

The place had all the inviting charm of a colonoscopy.

I stopped at the corner and leaned for a few moments against the brick wall, chewing gum and watching the street. It was short and crooked, dirty and empty. Eighteen houses on each side, with as many abandoned cars as working hoopties lining one side. No pedestrians, but that didn't mean there was no one looking. Streets like this have a lot of unemployed people, a lot of elderly poor, a lot of shut-ins who have been so comprehensively detached from social contact that the entirety of their engagement is what they see out of the windows; and so they look. All the time.

The sun was gone and the afterglow had faded to a muddy orange, darkening to a muddy nothing at the edges. Shadows owned the street and of the three streetlights on Misery, one was working, trying to combat the gloom with a piss-yellow glow. I pushed off the wall and walked away, went to the end of the next block, turned right along Beale, which paralleled Misery, and then cut into a narrow alley that ran behind the houses. No lights at all there. I debated using my cell-phone light to pick my way through the trash, broken beer bottles and dog shit, but didn't. Couldn't risk being seen. If Hoops was in there with Cheryl, it meant that her kid was probably there, too. Danger, Will Robinson.

The backyard of Cheryl's house was dark except for the muted glow of the kitchen light as seen through drawn curtains. There was no security system, of course, but I saw the faint glint of light on something metal and crouched down to see what it was. Someone—almost certainly Hoops—had strung several lines of hairy twine hung with tin cans filled with pebbles. Smart, if you're in an episode of *The Walking Dead*. Naïve otherwise. At least the way he strung it.

I took my folding knife from my pocket, flicked the blade into place, took a firm hold on one end of the top line and cut the twine. Then I lowered the cans to the crabgrass very carefully. Not a sound. I stepped over the lower two lines.

The back door was typical of this kind of neighborhood. Crap. But the lock was okay. A deadbolt of the kind guys at Ace Hardware insist are pickproof. They aren't.

I leaned close to the door and heard the sound of a TV playing too loud. Canned laughter. A sitcom. Useful. My lockpick set is top of the line and given time I can pick damn near anything up to lower-end industrial locks. There's some noise but the fake sitcom laughter washed it out. The door clicked open.

Bounty hunters going after bail skips don't need warrants. I could have kicked that door in if I wanted to. Odd set of laws we have in this country. If it wasn't for Cheryl and her kid I would have gone in hard and loud. A bit of urban shock and awe. Instead I pushed the door open and slipped into the tiny kitchen, then closed the door to decrease the chance of a sudden draft of cold air whipping through the house. The kitchen light was on and there were pots on the stove. I cut a look at them and started to move deeper into the house, then I stopped. Turned. Looked again at the stove. Two pots. One of pasta and one of sauce.

The pots were cold and maggots wriggled through the sauce.

I turned again to the sound of laughter and all at once the house felt different. Empty. A husk.

I don't like to use a gun but I carry one, an old Navy Colt .45 loaded with hollow-points. The gun was in my hand as I moved out of the kitchen, through the darkened dining room and into the living room. The TV was on, turned to one of those vintage channels. *Friends* was on because *Friends* is always on. Every day, on one channel or another. I stood there, the gun limp in my hand. Chandler was being sarcastic. Joey was saying something stupid. Rachel's hair looked great. The audience was laughing themselves sick.

I felt sick, too.

They lay where he'd left them. Cheryl Carbone was on the floor, wrists and ankles tied with belts. The little girl was on the couch. She wasn't tied. There were flies on them. The maggots would come later.

Their eyes were open. The little girl's eyes were filled with things I can't even name. Even in death there was such an expression of horror that it was almost unbearable to look at her. I had to look, though. Someone has to because the dead deserve to be noticed, to be acknowledged. Even the poor ones. Maybe especially the poor ones. Most of the world ignores them every day.

Now they were going to go into the ground and be forgotten, which was a crime nearly as great as what had been done to them. If I looked away I'd be complicit in that crime. I would be guilty of catering to my own need *not* to see, which is a special kind of sin. A coward's sin that you never get a chance to wash away.

I sucked in a breath and then went upstairs, checking the other rooms, looking for Antoine Hoops even though I knew for sure he wasn't here. Then I came back downstairs and stood looking at the mother and child. Hoops had taken his time with them, and mostly with the little girl. The mother had been made to watch. Her body was covered with bruises in the shape of open-hands and knuckles. He had forced her to keep watching.

Her throat was the wrong shape, so it was clear he'd strangled her.

How the girl died was less obvious and I didn't need to find out. She was dead. At five she was as old as she would ever be. Hoops had stolen all the rest of the years of her life. Maybe the kid would have grown up to be like her mom—a hooker and then someone working at a fast-food joint. Maybe the kid wouldn't have gone to college or made anything of herself. Maybe. But that isn't anyone's call to make, and it didn't mean that she was disposable just because she wouldn't amount to some standard of personal success. She was a whole person. A beautiful little child and she had died badly.

So I stood there and looked at her, and at her mother. I wept for them. Not a lot. Not sobs. Just some cold tears that burned my cheeks. Their faces were turned toward me. As pale as the ghostly faces tattooed on my flesh.

When I heard the scuff of a shoe on the floor behind me I didn't whirl around or raise my gun. I was already sure who I'd see there.

I was right.

They were both there. Cheryl and her daughter. Pale as candle wax, standing in the doorway to the dining room. I could see the shapes of the chairs and tables through them. The little girl stared at what was left of her physical body on the couch, taking it all in with the wide, wise, knowing eyes of the very young. Her mother held her hand. I saw that the marks of violence were not visible on the little girl's ghost. That nearly broke my heart because it showed that her spirit was already rising above what had been done to her.

Every single thing that had been done to Cheryl was still there. The broken teeth, the burst lips, the eyes swollen nearly shut, the cigarette burns. All of it.

Cheryl looked down at her body and then up at me.

I knew what she wanted. Dead people don't linger just to hang out with me. I'm not a place of comfort, if you can dig that. Vengeance isn't comforting. It never is.

Cheryl pointed to my chest. I sighed and unzipped my hoodie and then pulled up the t-shirt I wore underneath. I don't know if the faces on my skin look different when a dead person looks at them, but I suspect they do.

"You don't know what you're asking," I said.

Her finger was steady, pointing. Telling me she *did* know.

The tattoos that had been inked into me must have told her. Or, maybe there's some asshole on the other side of life—Charon or whoever—handing out fucking pamphlets. I don't really know how the dead find out about me. All I did know was that Cheryl Carbone wanted something from me that she thought would set the world back on its wheels. For her and for her daughter. That's what people think revenge will do. It doesn't. At best it stops the bad guy from doing more harm, and for a lot of the dead—for the ones whose faces are inked onto me—that's enough. I think they feel that it balances the scales and maybe gives their deaths some meaning. Maybe it does. The cost, though. That's a motherfucker.

You see, the way it works is messed up. Something I learned about while I was in Southeast Asia. There's a magic in skin art. In certain kinds of skin art. If I take some blood from the crime scene and mix it with tattoo ink, then have that used to ink the face of the victim onto my skin, it creates a bond. Temporary but intense. I relive the last few minutes of the victim's life. I see who killed them and sometimes I learn something that will help me find the killer. If I do that, and if I take the killer off the checkerboard, then, sure, all future potential victims are saved; but the ghost who "hired" me has to pay the fee. And that fee is that they have to haunt me. Haunt my life.

You wonder why I drink myself to sleep every night? You try this shit. Try drifting off to Slumberland with dozens of ghosts standing around your bed. Most of them are quiet, but that's not much comfort. Some weep all the time. A few are screamers.

There's no way out of it for me except death, and I'm not ready to punch out quite yet. So I deal. I accept. And I drink.

But, man, I don't want to add another face. Not one more.

I said, "I'll find him with that."

Cheryl's eyes went wide, filled with tears that were as translucent as crystal. When her tears fell they splatted on the floor and then vanished as if they'd never existed. She jabbed a finger toward her daughter's body on the couch.

"I know how she died," I said. "I know he made you watch."

The finger jabbed and jabbed.

"Don't make me live it," I begged.

Jab. Jab. Jab.

"Listen to me," I cried. "If I do this your daughter moves on and you don't."

The finger stopped, trembling.

"Is that what you want? You want to be separated from her forever?"

The temperature in the room suddenly dropped so fast and so low that I could see my breath puff out as I spoke.

"Cheryl," I said gently, "let me try to find him some other way, okay? Give me a day. One day. And if I can't, then I'll..."

I let it hang because it didn't really need to be said.

The little girl looked up at her mother and then closed her eyes and leaned her forehead against Cheryl's hip. The young woman knelt and gathered her daughter into her arms. I could hear my heart beating. It was the only sound in the world.

The ghosts faded out and left me alone with the empty bodies.

--7--

I didn't call the cops.

The dead couldn't get any deader and I didn't want official eyes finding any leads that would have them dogging my trail.

Instead I creeped the place, going through every closet, every drawer, looking for anything. Found a stash of kiddie porn magazines hidden in the back of the bathroom closet. I burned them in the tub.

There weren't any glaring clues, but there was a story to be read in that place. A new deadbolt lock on the little girl's room and no trace of the key for it. There were scratches on the outside of the door. Fingernails. I think Hoops kept Cheryl in line by holding her daughter hostage in a locked room. And it was clear that he slept in there, too.

I can't imagine what kind of utter hell that was for the mother, and I could imagine her out in the hall, begging, pleading, tearing at the wood with her nails, while inside a big man tore the innocence out of a child. Over and over again.

Why hadn't Cheryl called the cops?

Probably afraid that Hoops would kill the girl. He must have made credible threats, and eventually he used up his options at the Carbone place. One last fling, this time with an audience, and then lights out. What triggered it? The impending court case? Maybe. With the video evidence it was likely Hoops would take another long fall. If he was locked up, then Cheryl could risk going to the cops and child protection services. With that kind of evidence Hoops would never see the outside of a super max prison. Never. So he gave himself a going away party, and then ran.

However, Bambi had said that she'd seen him get out of an Escalade a few hours ago. What did that tell me?

The gang-bangers who ran drugs had their hands in all kinds of crime. Extortion, money laundering, gambling, human trafficking. Their people sometimes had to skip town. That meant each gang had to have a travel agent, which is what they call someone who makes arrangements. Fake I.D.s, passports, all the right papers, as well as transportation and lodging. Full service.

Three gangs with Escalades in this part of town.

Those gangs had a lot of muscle, a lot of soldiers.

I stood in the living room with the dead mother and her little girl. Not the ghosts, just the bodies.

"Trust me," I said to them, hoping the ghost of Cheryl Carbone could hear me.

--8--

You can do a lot of damage if you don't give a shit about what happens to you.

I found Luis Delgado, second in command of *El Spiritos*, the gang on the east side of the neighborhood. He didn't know that I knew where he lived. I do. When he went upstairs to take a shit I was in the shower stall with the curtain down. I waited until he had his pants around his ankles and was squeezing one out then I reached out around the edge of a curtain and put the mouth of my .45 against the corner of his jaw.

Pretty sure it helped him evacuate his bowels.

I stepped out of the shower with the gun rock-steady and my finger over my lips. He did not make a sound. Delgado's eyes went wide with shock, fear, humiliation and outrage in equal measures.

"I'm not here for you, Luis," I said quietly. "You tell me what I want and I'm gone. Lie to me or fuck with me and they find you dead on the crapper. It's your call."

He started to say something but the first syllable came out too loud, so I tapped him with the gun barrel. He stopped, took a steadying breath, and tried again.

"You out of your fucking *mind*?" he snarled.

"Seems to be the general consensus," I said. "You know who I am?"

"You're that freak. Monk."

"Good."

"The fuck you want?"

"Looking for a guy," I said. "Antoine Hoops. You know him?"

"What if I do, you stupid—"

I leaned close. "Don't get mouthy with me, Luis. I'm having a real bad day and I'm okay with spreading the bad mojo around. Like I said, this isn't about you. It's about what I need. It's about me putting Hoops in a bag. Tonight. I'd have gone through channels but you're famous for dicking people around, and I don't have time for that, so I figured this would work. You either have an answer for me or you don't. In either case you don't see me again after this. We go our separate ways and this never happened. Make this complicated and I go ask Esteban."

Esteban Morales was Luis' boss. He was currently out of town or I'd have been in *his* bathroom. Besides, Luis was more middle management, which meant that he was likely involved with matters like travel arrangements.

Luis was in one of those no-win situations. Sitting on the toilet, naked from the waist down, no weapon and a gun barrel cold against his skin. I had all the cards. His best case scenario was posthumous revenge, which wouldn't do much for him.

"All you have to do is the smart thing, Luis," I said.

He turned his head so that the barrel rubbed its way from jaw to upper lip. It was a deliberate act, trying to make a point that he wasn't afraid. And also that he was going to tell me the truth. I moved the barrel back one inch so he wouldn't have to talk funny.

"We got nothing to do with Antoine," he said.

I looked into his eyes for a long five count. Then I nodded.

"Anyone protecting Hoops is going to have a bad night," I said. "You and me have no beef unless you make one."

He said nothing, but he gave the tiniest of nods.

I left his bathroom.

The second name on my list was Nikolai Gorlov, a Romanian who ran guns and heroin and had forty percent of the import on unlicensed pharmaceuticals coming down from Canada. His office was in a double-wide parked at the far corner of a junkyard across the river. Lots of line-of-sight for his guards, and he has dogs, too.

He also likes to go to the movies. One of those new theaters where they have leather La-Z-Boys and the ushers come and take food and drink orders. Insanely bourgeois, with tickets priced at twenty-eight dollars per. I followed him in my beat up old piece of crap car and wasn't seen because I know how to do this stuff. He bought a ticket for a Liam Neeson middle-aged action picture. I bought a ticket for a Pixar thing that started forty minutes later, but slipped into the same house as my target. The place was two-thirds empty. Gorlov had three guys with him. Two of them positioned on aisle seats where they could watch him. The third who sat next to him and accompanied him to the bathroom.

Gorlov downed two beers during the first act and had to take a piss right about the time Neeson was threatening someone on the screen. The guard took up station just inside the washroom and as I entered he shifted to block my way. He was a big son of a bitch. Nearly my size, with a face like an eroded wall.

"Occupied," he said, although it was a four stall men's room.

"Yeah," I said and hit him in the throat. There are ways to do that so you kill someone and ways to do it so you just fuck up their evening. The guard wasn't my target, so I let him thrash around on the floor trying to breathe. I quickly took his Glock and a .32 throwdown from him and dropped them into a toilet stall. Gorlov yelled and tried to pull his own piece. I took that away, too, and pointed it, and my own gun, at him. One barrel pressed beneath each eye.

"Shut. The. Fuck. Up," I said.

He did. It's so much easier when you choreograph this stuff so that there isn't a chance for people to do something stupid.

"Tell your boy there to guard the door," I said. "No one else gets in, and he doesn't make a fuss."

The guard was trying to get back to his feet. His face was as dark and swollen as an eggplant and he was sucking air in small, high-pitched gasps. Gorlov said something to him in Romanian. The man glared hatred at me, but he leaned against the inside of the bathroom door.

"Short and sweet," I said. "I'm looking for Antoine Hoops."

"Why?" asked Gorlov.

"For a bunch of shit you do not want to be part of."

"Is this about the little spic bitch he—?"

I used the guns to run him back against the edge of the sinks. He had to bend backward and his shoulders and the back of his head hit the mirror. He winced and cursed and I pressed the barrels hard.

"Right now I only want him," I said very softly. "One more wrong word out of you and I'm going to add names to my list. Tell me you understand."

"I...yes. Yes, I understand," said Gorlov. "Why do you want

him?"

"He raped and murdered a woman and her five year old daughter. He's going to be trying to get out of town. If your people are finessing that for him you need to tell me right now. And you need to tell me where I can find him. Otherwise you are accessory to a crime that is going to be what everyone will be talking about at your funeral."

"Who in the fuck *are* you?"

"Monk Addison." I smiled. "Maybe you heard of me."

His eyes went wide and his face lost all color. "Like…with the tattoos…?"

"Like that."

When I drove away three minutes later I wondered if Gorlov was enjoying the rest of the movie. I didn't have to tell him not to make a call to warn Antoine Hoops. The look in Gorlov's face told me that he'd heard a lot about my tattoos. Maybe he was superstitious or maybe he just didn't like to tempt fate. In either case he told me what I needed to know.

--9--

This time I kicked the door in.

Motel doors are tough but outrage is tougher. The lock ripped out of the frame in a spray of splinters and it crashed open all the way to the wall. I was through right away, stepping down from the kick into a flat-out run, seeing Hoops on the bed, meeting him as he came up, bending to drive my shoulder into him.

That was the plan.

He was fast, though. And he was good. Maybe Darlene had been able to blindside him, but I wasn't that lucky.

Hoops began turning as he rose so that when I hit him I went over and around his hip and slammed into the wall next to the bathroom door. I fell hard and badly, pulling the lamp from the night table down on top of me. Hoops froze for a moment, caught between his desire to find out who I was and maybe beat the shit out of me, and a wanted man's need to run. If he hadn't wasted that time—however short it was—he'd have had me, because the double impact of wall and floor knocked most of the air out of my lungs.

That's why they call it fatal hesitation, I guess.

He decided to run for it and bolted for the open doorway. Hoops got halfway before the lamp I threw hit him between the shoulder blades. It made him hit the frame rather than run through into the parking lot; he rebounded, hissing in pain. By then I was in the air at the end of a flying tackle. I wrapped my arms around his thighs and bore him down. We fell half in and half out of his room, both of us swinging punches that hit door, carpeted floor, concrete, and occasionally each other. He drove his elbow into my face and I turned to catch most of it on my cheek, which hurt me and hurt him. I short-punched him, trying for his balls and catching his inner thigh instead. He howled and tried to head butt me, but I tucked my chin and his forehead hit mine instead of my nose. He grabbed my hair and slammed my head against the frame, which started a chorus of church bells ringing inside my skull. I stuck my thumb in his eye. He screamed and brought his knee up and used it to push me back to a better punching range and then he hit me with three hard, fast shots. Right, left, right. Hard punches even though he threw them lying on his back. I used my arms to make a cage around my head and let him break his hands on my elbows and forearms. He could hit, though, god damn him.

I twisted and dropped my weight onto him, leading with a pile-driver elbow. He tried to squirm away, but there wasn't enough room in the doorway and I hit him hard in the belly. Air whooshed out of him, and that should have been it.

Antoine Hoops had a stomach like a piece of cast-iron boilerplate. The elbow show hurt him, but it didn't stop him. In fact it galvanized him and he began thrashing around, punching and clawing and biting. The sheer, shocking intensity of it drove me back and suddenly he was climbing on top of me and he did more damage to me in five seconds than anyone's ever done in any fight I've been in. He was fast as lightning and his punches hit like cruise missiles. He wasn't trying to win a fight. He was trying to beat me to death.

He was winning, too.

I don't think I ever faced anyone as tough as him. Ever.

Then suddenly he reared back, falling off of me, flinging his hands up to shield his face. Hoops screamed.

My head felt broken and the darkness was covering me like a layer of ash. Soft but thorough, and I felt myself falling down.

Out of the corner of my eye, though, I saw a shape come walking in through the open doorway. Small, slender, pale. I could see the streetlights outside through her body. Antoine Hoops scuttled back from her like a crab, shrieking louder than any sound in the world. High-pitched screeches that hurt my ears. His eyes were huge, unblinking. Drool sprayed from his mouth as he screamed.

The slender figure moved toward him with slow, inexorable steps. Smiling the worst smile I have ever seen. Filled with madness and malice and a cruel, dark delight that was appalling to witness.

Hoops scrambled to his feet, turned, looked for a way out. The ghost was between him and the door. He jagged right and left, again caught by that fatal hesitation, and then he dodged wide and ran around the specter. I was still sprawled on the floor and he jumped over me.

But I caught his ankle. It was all I could manage.

His body mass kept moving until my grip jerked him up short, then he fell.

He tried to avoid the door frame.

Didn't.

The sound his head made when it struck the frame was like a melon being dropped out of a second story window. Heavy and wet.

Hoops sagged down to the floor in a twisted sprawl. I lay there and watched the light go out of his eyes.

Then the ghost came and stood over me, looking down at me with eyes that were filled with strange, swirling lights. Terrible lights filled with a terrible joy that in any other circumstance I would have labeled as malicious. Not now. Not with this ghost. So what did I call that kind of joy? Are there even words?

I'd seen ghosts before. Sometimes they come and witness the end of the monsters who had killed them. Not sure if they need to see it for closure, or if they enjoy it. Don't know and never want to know.

I looked up into these eyes.

I guess I'd expected Cheryl Carbone to need to see this man die. It would have been appropriate somehow. But Cheryl was nowhere around.

Her little girl stood there watching me.

God. I will never forget the smile that was on her face when she came into the room. I'll never forget the savage joy on her face as Antoine Hoops fell. The gleeful hunger that twisted her mouth when he died. I could have accepted that smile on the face of her mother. I couldn't bear to see it on the face of a child.

I'll never forget.

God almighty.

I'll never forget.

She walked past me and out the door, and I fought my way onto my feet, swaying and damaged and sick at heart. I stumbled after her but she was already at the edge of the motel parking lot. I quickened my past, first to a sloppy loping jog and then to a full run, but no matter how fast I moved I couldn't catch up with her. She rounded a corner and by the time I reached that she was on the far side of Boundary Street, where she paused. I slowed to a limping walk.

The girl looked up the hill toward where the clean lights of the Fire Zone glimmered in the night. A fingernail moon was etched into the night sky and someone had spilled a bag of diamonds across the heavens. She didn't look up at those lights. Then I saw Cheryl Carbone come walking up to her. Even from halfway across the street I could see that Cheryl's bruises were still there and that she was frowning in uncertainty at her daughter. The little girl held out her hand and Cheryl took it and they began walking up the hill.

"Wait," I called, though I don't know why. Maybe it was that I needed to understand what had just happened. Neither of them were clients of mine, they weren't bound to me or trapped with me, but the girl had participated in the killing of Antoine Hoops. This was all new.

My legs were rubbery and my ribs hurt, and there was

something wrong with my head. Concussion or maybe even a skull fracture. I tripped, staggered, dropped to my knees.

"Wait," I said again.

The little girl turned to look back at me. The smile was gone. They kept walking. I think she waved at me. Or maybe she waved me on to follow. I don't know.

The Fire Zone isn't heaven. It's brick and asphalt, flesh and noise. Oswald Four plays the Music up there, and Snakedancer leaps and twists, and there are colors that flash in the air out of nowhere.

I knelt and watched them go. They both turned one last time. They were pretty far away by then so I don't know how much I can trust what I saw. Maybe it was wishful thinking, but were their bruises, cuts and burns gone now? Was the little girl's smile different?

I don't know.

They turned away from me, and the little girl led her mother up the hill, and after a long time they were gone.

I got slowly to my feet and stood on the curb there on Boundary Street. Down in the shadows. Down in the cold.

Where I belong.

JONATHAN MABERRY is a NY Times bestselling suspense novelist, five-time Bram Stoker Award winner, and comic book writer. He writes the Joe Ledger thrillers, the Rot & Ruin series, the Nightsiders series, the Dead of Night series, as well as standalone novels in multiple genres. His YA space travel novel, MARS ONE, is in development for film, as are the Joe Ledger novels, and his V-Wars shared-world vampire apocalypse series. He is the editor of many anthologies including THE X-FILES, SCARY OUT THERE, BAKER STREET IRREGULARS, KINGDOMS FALL, HARDBOILED HORROR, OUT OF TUNE, ALIENS: BUG HUNT, and NIGHTS OF THE LIVING DEAD, co-edited with zombie genre creator, George A. Romero. His comic book works include, among others, *CAPTAIN AMERICA*, the Bram Stoker Award-winning *BAD BLOOD, ROT & RUIN*, the NY Times best-selling *MARVEL ZOMBIES RETURN*, and others. His *ROT & RUIN* novels were included in the Ten Best Horror Novels for Young Adults, was an American Library Association 'Best Books For Young Adults,' an ALA Popular Paperbacks for Young Adults (Top Ten), Lone Star Reading List, winner of the Nutmeg Children's Book Award, and the Pennsylvania Young Reader's Choice Award Nominee. His first novel, *GHOST ROAD BLUES*, won the Bram Stoker Award for Best First Novel and was named one of the 25 Best Horror Novels of the New Millennium. A board game version of V-WARS: A Game of Blood and Betrayal, was released in early 2016. He is the founder of the Writers Coffeehouse, and the co-founder of The Liars Club. Prior to becoming a full-time novelist, Jonathan spent twenty-five years as a magazine feature writer, martial arts instructor and playwright. He was a featured expert on the History Channel documentary, *Zombies: A Living History,* and a regular expert on the TV series *True Monsters.* He is one third of the very popular and mildly weird Three Guys With Beards pop-culture podcast. He was named one of the today's Top Ten Horror Writers and his books have been sold to more than two-dozen countries. Jonathan lives in Del Mar, California with his wife, Sara Jo.

www.jonathanmaberry.com

WHISTLING

PAST THE

GRAVEYARD

AND OTHER STORIES

JONATHAN MABERRY

NEW YORK TIMES BESTSELLING AUTHOR

INTRODUCTION BY *NEW YORK TIMES* BESTSELLER SCOTT SIGLER

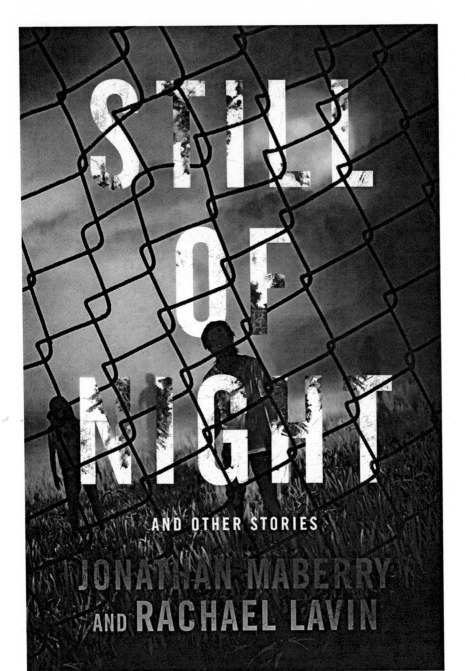

STILL OF NIGHT

AND OTHER STORIES

JONATHAN MABERRY
and RACHAEL LAVIN